AGATHA CHRISTIE'S
POIROT

100
YEARS OF
Agatha Christie
STORIES

ABOUT THE AUTHOR

Dr Mark Aldridge is Associate Professor of Screen Histories at Solent University, Southampton. His previous publications include the definitive book about the film and television adaptations of Agatha Christie's work, *Agatha Christie on Screen*, which was published by Palgrave Macmillan in 2016. Originally from Devon, he now lives in Hampshire with his partner, James, and is currently writing *Agatha Christie's Marple*.

Agatha Christie

POIROT

THE GREATEST DETECTIVE IN THE WORLD

MARK ALDRIDGE

HarperCollins*Publishers*

HarperCollins*Publishers*
1 London Bridge Street
London SE1 9GF
www.harpercollins.co.uk

HarperCollins*Publishers*
1st Floor, Watermarque Building, Ringsend Road
Dublin 4, Ireland

This paperback edition 2022

2

First published by HarperCollins*Publishers* 2020

ISBN 978-0-00-829664-3

Printed and bound in the UK using 100% Renewable Electricity
by CPI Group (UK) Ltd

MIX
Paper from
responsible sources
FSC
www.fsc.org
FSC™ C007454

A NOTE FROM THE AUTHOR

Although arranged chronologically, this book is designed so that you may read it however you choose – whether from cover to cover, or by dipping into sections that you particularly want to find out more about (or, indeed, skip sections that you are less interested in). There are no major spoilers in the main text, although a handful are in the endnotes (and clearly signposted as such).

ACKNOWLEDGEMENTS

Since I began work on this book I have been grateful to receive assistance and support from many people, both formally and informally. I am particularly grateful to James Prichard and all at Agatha Christie Ltd, as well as Mathew Prichard and the Christie Archive Trust, and David Brawn at HarperCollins. By its very nature this project has been a complicated one, and their co-operation and help has been invaluable.

At Solent University my research and writing has been supported on a practical and personal level by my colleagues. Special thanks are due to Paul Marchbank and Darren Kerr, who both helped me to undertake the work for this book, including funding for many trips to archives over the years. I am also grateful to my other colleagues for listening to my updates and grumbles, with particular thanks due to Dr Jacqueline Furby, Dr Stuart Joy, Dr Terence McSweeney, and Dr Donna Peberdy.

Alongside Mathew Prichard at the Christie Archive Trust, I would like to thank archivist Joe Keogh for his keen assistance, and Lucy Prichard for her hospitality and help as a sounding board for many discussions about this project and others.

It now feels like a long time since I began writing up this book, but with me along the way have been the consistently

OPPOSITE: Poirot by Abbey, which would appear on reprints of *Poirot Investigates* and various other editions.

supportive and helpful Dr John Curran and Dr Claire Hines, who read drafts of every chapter and provided invaluable feedback, corrections, and general help. The book is incalculably stronger for their input. And a big thank you to Terence Caven for his design, and David Brawn for sourcing all the pictures and writing the captions.

Several people have taken the time to help me with parts of my research, or simply been happy to talk over the project and offer their input. Specific thanks to Steve Arnold, Rhett Bartlett, Marcelle Bernstein, Catherine Brobeck, the Dankworth estate, Kemper Donovan, Mark Gatiss, Dr Julius Green, Ian Hallard, Sophie Hannah, Haruhiko Imatake, Ralf Kramp, David Morris of CollectingChristie.com, Alexander Orlov, Tim Postins, Dawn Sinclair at the HarperCollins archive, Mark Terry, Maria Weissenberg, and John Williams. Special thanks to Brian Eastman for helping me pin down so many elusive details about the Poirot television series and taking the time to be interviewed. I would also like to acknowledge the important work of Christie biographers Janet Morgan and Laura Thompson, whose books were valuable resources during my research.

For the past few years I have been a regular part of both the International Agatha Christie Festival in Torquay and the Agatha Christie Conference, and I would like to express my thanks to their organisers, including Tony Medawar at the festival, and Dr J.C. Bernthal, Dr Mia Dormer, and Sarah Martin at the conference. The other regular attendees at these events have proven to be an invaluable support group, and many thanks to them all for their interest in my projects, as well as their own work and specialisms that have informed this book.

Finally, I would like to thank my friends and family for their support, particularly my partner James.

CONTENTS

FOREWORD

What is required, of course, is *order*.

Order is paramount. Order is a good and beautiful thing. Order is what the little Belgian prizes above all things. But order is a hard thing to come by when assembling memories. What, you may ask yourself (standing in the metaphorical witness box of one of those tiresome trials which he himself never seemed to attend), was your first encounter with M. Hercule Poirot? A thrilling childhood viewing of *And Then There Were None* and the Margaret Rutherford Miss Marple films had taught me that Christie was very much up my street, but it was on foreign holidays (where Christie still seems to belong) that I first properly engaged with the little man with the egg-shaped head. The Mallorcan apartment we'd rented, you see, had the *lot* – a whole shelf of Christies with those incredibly scary Tom Adams covers and the strange, mustardy coloured pages of the foreign edition. *The ABC Murders. Death on the Nile. Five Little Pigs. Hallowe'en Party.* I can still remember one sultry Spanish evening, breathlessly explaining the plot of *The Murder of Roger Ackroyd* to my slightly bemused parents as we trudged home from the local tapas bar. Indiscriminately, I devoured them (the books, not my parents). There was no order, you see! No way of appreciating the incredible run of copper-bottomed

OPPOSITE: Mark Gatiss's 2008 appointment with David Suchet.

classics that Christie produced in what was a genuine golden age of crime writing. Which is why it's so pleasing to see each novel given a (spoiler-free) synopsis in Mark Aldridge's delightful, detailed and compulsively readable history of the great detective. And also to see the pleasingly gushing reviews from the papers of the time (*The Observer*'s cross-word-compiler 'Torquemada' is a particular delight). It's thus possible to see Agatha Christie grow from a popular but easily dismissed sausage-machine into a national treasure.

But just who *is* Hercule Poirot? Albert Finney's spluttering, sinister pug-in-a-hairnet Poirot? Peter Ustinov's clubbable, delightful, portly Poirot? David Suchet's avuncular, twinkling Poirot, his little grey cells owning many a childhood? John Moffatt on the radio? Austin Trevor? Charles Laughton? Kenneth Branagh? There have, you see, been an awful lot of Poirots, although, as Mark Aldridge demonstrates, few actually met with Dame Agatha's approval. Leading us by an infectiously learned hand, Mark travels all the way from Styles to Styles, from the detective's faltering beginnings right through to his creator's demise – and beyond. To the rich afterlife which has propelled Poirot into the front rank of fictional detectives and into one of the most beloved characters in popular culture. Mark's text is peppered with fascinating fragments from Christie's correspondence and that of her family. Her own sometimes crotchety response to publishers, editors and (most entertainingly) fans, as well as unpublished portions of her autobiography. There are wonderful blind alleys and curious near-misses all along the way. Did you know that Orson Welles played Poirot *and* Dr Sheppard? That there was a 1962 TV pilot in which Martin Gabel's Poirot watches TV in the back of his car? That Ronnie Barker played Poirot (straight) at the Oxford Playhouse? It's a feast for both the dyed-in-the-moustaches fan and the newcomer alike, a testament to a still-thriving industry born of sheer talent, hard work and what we would now call brand management. Mark brings order to a sometimes chaotic narrative, along the way nailing the unique, Sunday-night charm of the Suchet series and the reasons why the Ustinov *Evil under the Sun* is still the best time anyone can have in the cinema.

And though he mysteriously describes *Spice World – The Movie* as a 'classic comedy caper', he rightly dismisses the version of *Appointment with Death* which I myself was in. Some crimes even Papa Poirot cannot forgive.

MARK GATISS
London. 2020

INTRODUCTION

Mes amis, we have cause for celebration. The great Hercule Poirot, the incomparable private detective, has now been entertaining us for a full century. Ever since *The Mysterious Affair at Styles*, written by Agatha Christie during the First World War and first published in 1920, the reading public has keenly followed the Belgian detective's adventures as he investigated mysteries throughout the highs and lows of the following decades.[1] We have seen Poirot solve mysteries on trains, ships, and even a plane, with the results usually delivered to a warm critical and popular reception. He has solved cruel murders, uncovered international conspiracies, and found missing jewels for relieved owners. While doing this, he has sometimes been ably assisted by friends including Captain Hastings, Inspector Japp, his valet George, secretary Miss Lemon, and crime writer Ariadne Oliver – but it is always Poirot's own little grey cells that are needed to solve the crimes.

Some have tried to tell Poirot's life story by weaving together the scraps of information found in dozens of stories written across more than half a century, but any attempt to create a conclusive biography of the detective is a futile task. Many 'facts' are irreconcilable, and there are

OPPOSITE: Investigating the murder of Roger Ackroyd in Collins' Library of Classics edition, illustrated by Mackay (1940).

gaps and contradictions alongside extraordinary anti-ageing abilities. Even Christie often had to double check details of Poirot's life with her agent, and so it's no surprise that there are inconsistencies. Thankfully, this doesn't matter, because to make Poirot real would be to make him mundane and minimise his brilliance as a creation. This creative force, and the woman behind it, is what this book celebrates and explores.

Following the publication of *The Mysterious Affair at Styles*, Agatha Christie's stories only grew in popularity before reaching a productive peak in the 1930s, a decade that saw a dozen novels starring Poirot. The pace then slowed a little, with the detective finally being retired by his creator in 1975's *Curtain: Poirot's Last Case*. Christie had actually prepared Poirot's swan song during the dark days of the Second World War, although she continued to place him in new stories for the next three decades, with this final manuscript designed to be published after her death. In the event, Christie would outlive her creation by a few months, as she died in January 1976. In total, she had created mysteries for Poirot to solve in thirty-three novels, dozens of short stories, and a handful of plays that would variously debut on the stage, radio and television.[2]

However, the story of Poirot does not end there. While Agatha Christie fiercely protected her creation throughout her life, by the 1970s there were signs that Poirot had the potential to become a mainstay of multiple media, with the big budget 1974 film adaptation of *Murder on the Orient Express* kickstarting a franchise of sorts. Later decades also saw a long running television series and one-off screen dramas, as well as faithful radio productions. But Poirot's reach has even moved beyond these traditional outlets for adaptations, as he has also appeared in almost every conceivable artistic form, from graphic novels to computer

Agatha Christie photographed at home with daughter Rosalind for *The Sketch* (1923).

games and animations. Meanwhile, some of his lesser-known adventures have been uncovered and published to new audiences, and 2014 saw the first official original Poirot novel to be written by someone other than Christie. In *The Monogram Murders*, Sophie Hannah took readers back to the golden age of detective fiction for what was to become the first in a series of new Poirot mysteries.[3] In short, Poirot has never really gone away, and is as popular as ever.

Any biography of Agatha Christie will show her to be a determined person. Born Agatha Miller in 1890, her early life is difficult to fathom for many of us in the twenty-first century, especially with its (by modern standards) baffling interplay between wealth and poverty. She was part of a family with the trappings of the upper-middle classes, including servants and a beloved home, but her father's poor management of money made their situation precarious. Even the day-to-day events of Christie's life as a child feel like they are from such a distant age that it seems incredible that anyone experiencing them would still be working and publishing new material as late as the 1970s. Christie would later claim that she had 'a very lazy youth'. She recalled that her father, Frederick Miller, was 'a gentleman of substance who never did a hand's turn in his life – and a most agreeable man. I never went to school. I had nothing much to do but wander around the garden with a hoop, which was in turn a horse or ship, making up stories. It was a very happy and satisfying life; you did a certain amount of work but on the whole it was play all the time. Leisure is a great stimulant of the ideas. Boredom is a better one.'[4]

The creative stimulation provided by this boredom meant that Christie was no stranger to story writing as a child, especially when it was encouraged by her mother while young Agatha was suffering from the flu. 'I suppose I was trying things, like one does,' she later recalled. 'I first tried to write poetry. Then a gloomy play – about incest, I think ... some of the writing wasn't too bad but the whole thing was pretty poor.'⁵ These stories included one called 'The House of Beauty', which she later claimed was 'the first thing I ever wrote that showed any sign of promise'.⁶

In around 1908 Christie completed her first novel, called *Snow Upon the Desert* ('I can't think why,' she claimed dismissively).⁷ Although never published, the typescript still survives and offers an insight into the juvenilia of Christie. She penned a lengthy story (at nearly 400 pages) concerning a group of people who are involved with the 'coming out' into society of young women in Cairo, just as Christie had done in 1907. While certainly overlength (this was likely the book she later referred to as 'a long, involved, morbid novel'), with a winding story of relationships between vaguely connected characters, there are several smaller moments or turns of phrase that indicate Christie's growing talent. These include one character being described as 'as indiscreet as a babbling brook', while young dreamer Melancy Hamilton wishes for more when confronted with the mundanity of day to day life, as she complains about dull discussions of breakfast choices – 'eggs were so painfully prosaic', she thinks, before despairing 'That people could talk of *eggs* when there were blue skies and waters, and picturesque locals to watch'. Like a young Christie, Melancy fantasises about interesting lives and adventures, and we are told that 'to a discerning observer she expressed infinite possibilities'.

In *Snow Upon the Desert*, Melancy Hamilton has come to Cairo in the hope that it will help the deafness affecting her. Initially she is only hard of hearing in a crowd, but with indecent haste she is completely deaf by the end of the first

The portrait of Poirot by W. Smithson Broadhead in *The Sketch* (1923).

The February 1936 *Strand* magazine featured the Poirot story 'Problem at Sea' (retitled, despite no cabin number mentioned in the text) and a cover by Jack M. Faulks.

third of the book. It's probably telling that by the time Christie had finished writing this story she felt encumbered by this heroine of her own making, as she realised that her deafness made dialogue very difficult, and perhaps this character's enforced insularity also explains the book's propensity for rather overwritten meditations on characters' thought processes. In the end the author found a straightforward solution to her woes, as she granted Melancy a miraculous recovery of her hearing upon the character's return to England. We might see some parallels with Hercule Poirot himself here – another character whose traits she would come to dislike and felt restricted by. Could there even be a predecessor of this later difficult creation in *Snow Upon the Desert's* brief description of 'a little foreign looking man' who lunches with some of the characters at one point? Certainly, we see forerunners of some other characters, most significantly in the two young lovers Tommy and Crocus, who decide to elope and then go on to solve a minor mystery in the final act. Their sparring relationship and gung-ho attitudes seem to mark them out as early versions of Tommy and Tuppence, the excitable investigators who meet in Christie's second published novel, *The Secret Adversary*, and then marry.[8]

The typescript of *Snow Upon the Desert* was read by the novelist Eden Philpotts and the literary agency Hughes Massie, and both offered helpful advice, but it was not deemed good enough to publish. Nevertheless, Christie persevered with her writing when time allowed. Eventually, it was a bet with her sister, Madge, that paved the way for Poirot's debut. This bet, made in 1916, concerned the difficulty – or otherwise – of writing a mystery novel. 'At the time my sister and I used to argue a lot whether it was easy to write detective stories,' Christie later recalled. By this point, in the midst of the First World War, her life had inevitably moved on, and she was now working in a hospital dispensary to help the war effort having married Archibald Christie on Christmas Eve 1914, when she was twenty-four. The possibilities of writing her own piece of detective fiction clearly fired her imagination. 'It was never a definite bet,' Agatha Christie clarified in her autobiography. 'We never set out the terms – but the words had been said.' This is where Christie's determination would come to be so valuable. 'I thought perhaps now is the time for writing a detective story: I had a good idea going round about medicine. Then I had a holiday from hospital. Mother said "Why don't you go and stay on Dartmoor if you are going to write that book?" I think I spent three weeks in a hotel by myself, going for walks. I don't think I spoke to anyone and I managed to finish *The Mysterious Affair at Styles*, I got it typed; I can't say I had high hopes. I started sending it to publishers. And it started coming back.'[9]

High hopes or not, the result of this bet would eventually transform Christie's life, and the world of detective fiction.

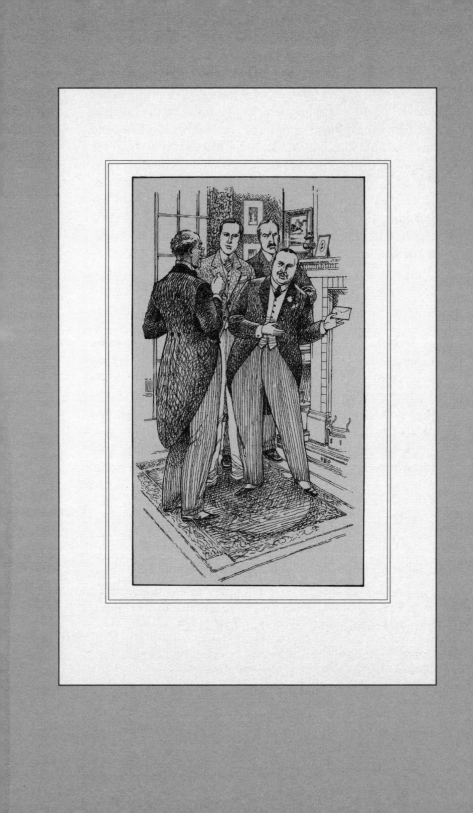

CHAPTER ONE:

THE

1920s

The period between the completion of Agatha Christie's first detective novel, *The Mysterious Affair at Styles*, and its publication in book form was a frustratingly lengthy one for Christie. However, her tenacity in getting the book completed and then published would bode well for the challenges that she'd face during the 1920s. She would soon prove her skills as a writer of mysteries and thrillers time and again, which included a slew of Poirot short stories and five novels featuring the detective before the decade was out. For her first effort she'd written a murder mystery steeped in influences from her own reading of the genre, most particularly Sherlock Holmes, but presented the plot in such a way that it felt fresh and unpredictable, while setting a template that she'd continue to offer twists on for more than half a century.

OPPOSITE: Hercule Poirot 1920s-style, drawn by David Cuzik for the limited edition of *The Mysterious Affair at Styles* for Agatha Christie's centenary in 1990.

The Mysterious Affair at Styles
(Novel, 1921)

Set in 1916, *The Mysterious Affair at Styles* concerns the inhabitants of the eponymous English country house, in which the wealthy matriarch Mrs Emily Inglethorp is murdered. Several family members, including her younger husband Alfred, are obvious suspects, but the accumulated evidence eventually presents a surprisingly complex picture. In the days when typescripts would be sent to prospective publishers in order of desirability (or likelihood of interest), the initial rejections meant slow progress as the companies held on to the story for months at a time. For a while Christie gave up hope, as she explained in an unpublished portion of her autobiography:

ABOVE LEFT: The British first edition published by The Bodley Head in January 1921 with jacket art by Alfred James Dewey. **ABOVE RIGHT:** American paperback edition published by Avon with cover art by David Stone (1957).

I had really forgotten about it. In fact I had by that time written off *The Mysterious Affair at Styles* as being just as much as failure as the first novel I had tried to write [the unpublished *Snow Upon the Desert*]. It was no good, I evidently had not got the knack. Still I might try something else some day for fun if I had the time.[1]

Although she generally didn't lack perseverance, Christie had become busy with family life following the birth of her daughter Rosalind on 5 August 1919. Eventually, it was publishing house The Bodley Head that showed an interest, although by Christie's later recollection more than two years may have passed since she had sent it to them.[2] The Bodley Head's first reader's report had seen *Styles* as a potentially worthwhile commercial venture, despite feeling that it had 'manifest shortcomings'. The report claimed that the book was an 'artificial affair', while the positives of characterisation and atmosphere were undone by a court-based denouement that was considered to be less dramatic and thrilling than it should be. The second reader's report echoed these concerns about the ending, which was felt to be improbable, but decided that publishing the novel was 'quite worth doing'. Christie was asked to change the final chapter for publication, which she did. In doing so she set the template for the lengthy reveal in the company of key characters and suspects by the detective in domestic surroundings that would become famous components of her novels, although this type of scenario actually occurred less often than many may assume.[3] One area that pleased the writers of both reports was the 'exuberant personality' of the 'jolly

Following its eighteen-week serialisation, John Lane advertised that *The Mysterious Affair at Styles* would be published in August 1920. It wasn't.

The 1937 Japanese edition featured a Poirot copied from a 1936 *Strand* magazine.

little man' who operated as the story's Sherlock Holmes and was identified as the novel's most original feature. The identity of this 'welcome variation' on the detective character was, of course, none other than Hercule Poirot.

It's no surprise that The Bodley Head noted similarities between the Poirot of *Styles* and Sherlock Holmes. For one thing, the emphasis on seemingly innocuous details that have a greater significance – such as ash in the fire grate, or the arrangement of apparently ornamental items – echoes the approach to solving mysteries advocated by the original consulting detective. But perhaps more significantly, the relationship between the detective and his less accomplished assistant (and narrator) has particularly close parallels – if Poirot is this story's Holmes, then Hastings is most definitely its Watson. It's through the eyes of Arthur Hastings, our establishment figure as an invalided captain who is recuperating near to Styles, that we first meet one of the Belgian refugees finding refuge away from the war being waged across the Channel:[4]

Poirot was an extraordinary looking little man. He was hardly more than five feet, four inches, but carried himself with great dignity. His head was exactly the shape of an egg, and he always perched it a little on one side. His moustache was very stiff and military. The neatness of his attire was almost incredible. I believe a speck of dust would have caused him more pain than a bullet wound. Yet this quaint dandyfied little man who, I was sorry to see, now limped badly, had been in his time one of the most celebrated members of the Belgian police. As a detective, his flair had been extraordinary, and he had achieved triumphs by unravelling some of the most baffling cases of the day.

This description of the odd-looking little Belgian would be solidified and repeated over the next five decades and more. While events changed around him - characters, locales, even wars - he stayed fixed (mostly, at least - the mysterious limp is soon healed). Christie later felt exasperated when asked to clarify the physical details of Poirot, but recalled that she twice saw people who fitted the description. In a draft discussion of Poirot and his cases penned for a newspaper serialisation in 1938 she pondered:

> Anyway, what is an egg-shaped head? Have I ever seen an egg-shaped head? When people say to me 'Which way up is this egg?' do I really know? I don't because I never do see pictorial images clearly - but nevertheless I know that he has an egg-shaped head - covered with black, singularly black, hair - and I know his eyes occasionally shine with a strange light - and twice in my life I have actually seen him - once on a boat going to the Canary Islands - and once having lunch at the Savoy - and I have said to myself 'Now if you had only the nerve to have snapshotted the man on the boat' and then when people have said 'Yes, but what is he like?' I could have produced the snapshot and said 'This is what he is like' and in the Savoy perhaps I could have gone to the man and explained the matter. But life is full of lost opportunities.[5]

1944 Avon paperback with cover by A. Gonzales.

In her autobiography, Christie remembered Poirot's creation in terms of necessity - she needed a detective for her story, but also needed one unlike those that had gone before. Having dismissed the likes of a schoolboy investigator or a scientist, she found inspiration in the Belgian refugees who had settled near to her home. 'People always think you have a real person starting you off, but it isn't the case,' she said later. 'Some characters are suggested to you by strangers you've never spoken to - you see someone at a picnic and make up stories about them like a child. I was worried about finding a detective for my first book, and we'd had Belgian refugees at the beginning of the war, so I thought that quite a good idea. But I didn't really know any.'[6]

Once the broad background of the detective had been settled, why not make this detective character a retired police officer, she reasoned. 'What a mistake there,' she later conceded, as Poirot must surely have been well over 100 by the time of his later cases.[7] Christie also decided to make him 'very neat - very orderly', before wondering 'Is this because I was a wildly untidy person myself?'[8] Certainly she saw some elements of Poirot's character as a reaction against her own personality. 'If you are doubly damned - first by acute shyness and secondly by only seeing the right thing to do or say twenty-four hours late what can you do? Only write about quick witted men and resourceful girls whose reactions are like greased lightning!'[9]

All that was left was to decide his name. Christie fancied that, like Sherlock Holmes and his brother Mycroft, the name should be a 'grand' one, and so she settled on the amusement of this small man being named Hercules. When a surname of Poirot was decided upon (Christie claimed not to remember how or why), Hercules didn't seem to fit, and so the Belgian sleuth was christened Hercule instead.[10] Just as Holmes had been an outsider due to his egotistical attitude

1954 Pan paperback with art by Roger Hall.

and obsessions, so Poirot can never truly blend into the scenery; he stands out from his English contemporaries while his idiosyncrasies allow much of society to underestimate his powers of deduction. The Bodley Head's request to rework the courtroom setting of the ending to take place elsewhere would unwittingly reinforce this template of Poirot as an outsider. The original ending had the retired detective testifying in court at length, describing his solution to the case, which effectively made him part of the traditional system of law and order, rather than set apart from it as a private individual. Conversely, the final version leaves the likes of

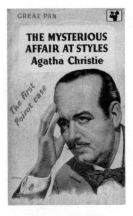

1958 Pan paperback with art by Jack Keay.

Inspector Japp (also introduced in this first novel) with the more mundane tasks of ensuring that the law is upheld and the villain prosecuted; for Poirot, the simple satisfaction of piecing together the puzzle can now be the prize.

The plot of *Styles* balances interesting and plausible elements (the nature of the poisoning, for example, is effectively depicted – unsurprisingly, given Christie's familiarity with poisons from her wartime service in a dispensary) with first class misdirections and a vivid set of characters. Alongside this are some less convincing elements that Christie would soon offer better examples of, such as a less than believable disguise and a highly unlikely disposal of key evidence. If the story sometimes requires an excessive suspension of disbelief then at least it happens infrequently and briefly, and the unconvincing elements soon fade away while the overarching story grips the reader as the puzzle pieces slot into place. Essentially, the novel is an exercise in distraction, as Christie works to keep the reader from looking too closely at some suspects and events. She employs a layer of obfuscation with suspicious characters

An Albert Finney-inspired Poirot on this Italian omnibus of *Styles* with *Lord Edgware Dies*.

and a story with a highly satisfying double bluff at its centre. Compared to her later novels, these distractions are overly complicated, as Christie seems to signify a slight lack of confidence in her technique by throwing in so many clues and red herrings that the reader would have to be very astute indeed to ignore them all and tread the correct path to the solution. The result is a busy mystery that shines because of the overall impression it leaves once the author shows her hand at the end.

As was common during this era, the first appearance of *The Mysterious Affair at Styles* in print was as a newspaper serialisation rather than as a novel. In this case, Christie was paid £25 for the rights for the story to appear in *The Times*'s 'Colonial Edition', also known as *The Weekly Times*, between February and June 1920. By October 1920 the book was finally published as a novel in America, but not yet in Britain, which prompted Christie to write a letter to her publishers that dispensed with niceties and opened with a simple question: 'What about my book? I am beginning to wonder if it is ever coming out'.[11] It's worth bearing in mind that at this point a year had passed since the positive reader reports, and the wartime events of the story were threatening to make it feel like a period piece by the time it was available in bookshops. Meanwhile, Christie had gone into battle with The Bodley Head over a single detail, the spelling of the word 'cocoa'. Christie correctly insisted on the final 'a', but (to use Christie's own description) the 'dragon' at the publisher who oversaw such details insisted that 'coco' was correct. The debate might seem innocuous, but the memory of the incident was strong enough that Christie remembered it for her autobiography decades later. This seems to have been something of a turning point in the relationship between author and publisher – whereas Christie had earlier assumed that The Bodley Head would know best, she now knew that not to be true. 'I was not a good speller, I am still not a good speller, but at any rate I could spell cocoa the proper way,' she explained in her autobiography. 'What I was, though, was a weak character. It was my first book – and I thought they must know better than I did.'[12]

Despite requesting pre-Christmas publication, it wasn't until 21 January 1921 that the novel was made available in Christie's own country, with the requested dedication to her

Yet another anniversary: Tom Adams' painting for HarperCollins' 2016 edition marked 100 years since *The Mysterious Affair at Styles* was first written by Christie.

mother, and a cover depicting characters in candlelight that Christie approved of, calling it 'artistic and "mysterious"!'[13] The novel was well received, with *The Church Times* saying that 'the book held the attention well', while commending the first-time author for offering a surprising solution that the reviewer had not worked out beforehand. 'Looking back, knowing the solution, it is possible to point to a good many faults,' the review also claimed, but 'a book of this type must be judged on the first reading.'[14] *The Times Literary Supplement* received the book even more warmly, with the reviewer writing that 'The only fault in his book is that it is almost too ingenious … In spite of its intricacy, the story is very clearly and brightly told.' Referring to the bet between Christie and her sister regarding the writing of a satisfying mystery, it was judged that 'Every reader must admit that the bet was won.'[15]

Almost five years after it had been written, *The Mysterious Affair at Styles* had finally found an audience, quickly selling out of its initial run of 2,000 copies. Agatha Christie had continued her writing in the meantime – having signed a six-book contract with The Bodley Head, she had 'nearly finished a second one' by the end of 1920. This second novel, *The Secret Adversary*, was published in 1922, but it didn't feature any characters from her first book. However, for her third novel Christie brought the Belgian detective with the egg-shaped head with her, ready to solve an even more complex case, having established a style of mystery writing that her publishers were keen to see repeated. 'So I went on writing detective stories,' she later said. 'I found I couldn't get out.'[16]

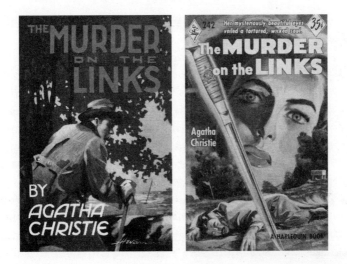

The Murder on the Links
(Novel, 1923)

While Arthur Conan Doyle had been the clearest influence on *The Mysterious Affair at Styles* it was another mystery
writer, Gaston Leroux, who Christie claimed had had the
biggest impact on the second Poirot novel, *The Murder on the
Links*. Alongside the likes of Anna K. Green's *The Leavenworth
Case* (which seems to have influenced *Styles*), Christie cited
Leroux's *The Mystery of the Yellow Room* as a novel that she had
particularly enjoyed. Regarding such influences, Christie
later conceded that 'When one starts writing, one is most
influenced by the last person one has read or enjoyed'.[17]
Her interest in Leroux's style and story was combined with

ABOVE LEFT: The first Bodley Head edition of *Murder on the Links*,
painted by H.T. Warren. **ABOVE RIGHT:** The American Harlequin edition
from 1953.

Poirot non sbaglia mai!

AIUTO, POIROT!

di **AGATHA CHRISTIE**

A 1934 edition from Italy, where Poirot was often depicted on the covers.

a real-life case in France in which the wealthy inhabitants of a house were attacked by an apparently random gang robbery, only for facts to emerge later that turn the story on its head. It may also be that Christie misremembered the influence of *The Mystery of the Yellow Room* on *The Murder on the Links* as, aside from the French setting and the use of rival detectives, Leroux's mystery has rather more in common with *The Mysterious Affair at Styles*.[18] In later years she claimed that Leroux's novel 'reads rather peculiarly now'.[19] In an unpublished portion of her autobiography she ponders on a more straightforward reason for Poirot's new locale: 'I suppose I had been reading a lot of French detective stories lately, and it seemed to be rather fun to have one over there.'[20]

Whatever the origins, Christie had been encouraged to bring Poirot back to help solve this case, and in retrospect felt that she should have started to resist such demands. 'Now I saw what a terrible mistake I had made in starting with Hercule Poirot so old,' she wrote. 'I ought to have abandoned him after the first three or four books, and begun again with someone much younger.'[21] Despite these later sentiments, Christie is perhaps rather clutching at straws here to justify her eventual frustration with the character himself – she had never been much concerned with accurate continuity or a definitive idea of the world of Poirot, and considering that readers have generally been unfazed by Poirot's miraculous lack of ageing it hardly seems to be a good reason to have abandoned him.

Neither Christie nor Poirot had been idle since the publication of *Styles*, with Christie introducing the young investigators Tommy and Tuppence in the novel *The Secret*

Adversary, while keeping Poirot alive in the pages of British magazine *The Sketch*, which had commissioned a series of short stories, published from March 1923 (more of which shortly). Although it would take a few years before Christie felt that she was a full-time professional author, she and Archie hadn't neglected the most important business of being a writer, as they consistently wrote to The Bodley Head in order to ensure that the royalties received were accurate and punctual. Judging by the surviving correspondence, they rarely were. For Poirot's second novel, we are once more told the story through the eyes of Hastings, whose self-aware opening ruminates on the best way to captivate the reader from the off. In this case, a trip on the Calais express train results in a fortuitous meeting that eventually results in marriage for Hastings, but not before some baffling murders are solved. While *Styles* had seen Christie telling a story that,

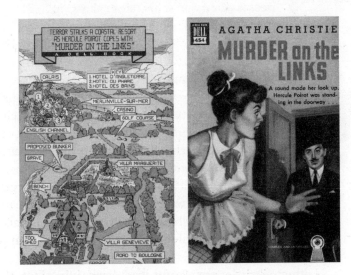

Dell released a series of paperbacks with attractive maps. This 'mapback' edition from 1950 sported a front cover by Al Brulé with an unfortunately positioned logo.

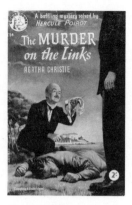

Corgi Books' 1957 edition with cover art by Eastman.

The 1960 Pan paperback with art by David Taylor.

in summary, would eventually be revealed to be rather straightforward (albeit operating between layers of red herrings and misdirection). *The Murder on the Links* has a clever but convoluted tale at its core. Christie herself would later acknowledge that her early books could be 'unnecessarily complicated, with quantities of clues and subplots'.[22] Perhaps there's also the sense of a difficult second Poirot novel for Christie, as the author seems to be working out and developing her style, in this case even more determinedly operating sleights of hand to ensure that she is always one step ahead of the reader. However, the reader may take solace from the fact that they generally feel one step ahead of Hastings, making deductions that he misses, often due to his rather short-sighted attitudes and dismissal of key evidence.

Readers who are familiar with the genial Hastings of most adaptations may be surprised to see his misanthropic side, occasionally apparent in *Styles* but even more evident here. While Hastings may share rooms with Poirot, this is no good-natured and jovial relationship. Instead, Hastings is rather defensive and dismissive, often seeming to be rather irate with Poirot, although it isn't always clear if we should be siding with his more questionable opinions or not: 'A woman, I consider, should be womanly. I have no patience with the modern neurotic girl who jazzes from morning to night, smokes like a chimney, and uses language which would make a Billingsgate fishwoman blush!' By the time we are re-introduced to Poirot we have insight into his methods that start to differentiate him from the evidence-based detective of *Styles*, as we're now told that 'He had a certain disdain for tangible evidence, such as footprints and cigarette ash, and would maintain that, taken by themselves, they would never enable a detective to solve a problem. Then he would tap his egg-shaped head with absurd complacency, and remark with great satisfaction: "The true work, it is done from within. The little grey cells – remember always the little grey cells, mon ami."' However, there's little time for rumination, as the book heads straight into its central mystery, as Hastings and Poirot travel to France, having been summoned by a potential client to discuss an urgent matter in person. On their arrival they discover

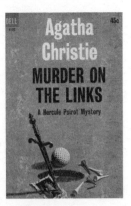

1964 American paperback edition from Dell, illustrated by William Teason.

that he has been found dead on the local golf course that morning, stabbed in the back. Before the mystery is solved another person will meet their demise, while Poirot looks to the past to help solve the case. The cast of characters (and suspects) discuss all manner of evidence while being overheard by others, leading to an overly tangled web of deceit and misunderstandings. However, in 1969 the crime author Michael Gilbert introduced a reissue of the book and found such misdirection to be a positive trait: 'If you have not read the book before, I would be willing to bet that you will still be doubtful of the killer *one page* before it is revealed to you. All the craft of Miss Christie is employed in this book, and when she is in form her bowling is practically unplayable.'[23]

We learn more about our two protagonists throughout the book, as Poirot's presence and somewhat enigmatic questioning and examinations irritates rival local detective Giraud, while Hastings finds love in the form of Dulcie Duveen, whom he nicknames 'Cinderella'. Christie wasn't sentimental about the coupling: 'If I had to have a love interest in the book, I thought I might as well marry off Hastings!', she wrote in her autobiography. 'Truth to tell, I think I was getting a little tired of him. I might be stuck with Poirot, but no need to be stuck with Hastings too.'[24]

The Murder on the Links was initially serialised under the title *The Girl with the Anxious Eyes* in *The Grand* magazine from December 1922 before its British publication as a novel in May 1923. Christie had been dissatisfied with the cover for *The Secret Adversary*, and this time she stipulated her recommended design in a letter to her publisher: 'I suggest for the cover a green patch of grass on the links, the grave and near it the man's body with a dagger sticking out of it.'[25] Once presented with the publisher's chosen design she was annoyed enough that she recalled the disagreement in her autobiography decades later. 'Apart from being in ugly colours, it was badly drawn, and represented, as far as I could make out, a man in pyjamas on golf-links, dying of an epileptic fit.'[26] In the end, a different cover was used for publication, no doubt due to the strength of Christie's feelings regarding the original version. As a result of this sort of dispute, three titles into her six book contract with The Bodley Head Christie's dissatisfaction was starting to solidify into an exit plan, with the aim of finding a better – and more rewarding – outlet for her creative labours.

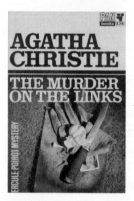

A photographic cover from 1964.

The Times Literary Supplement considered the novel to be 'a most complicated affair, the unravelling of which by the Belgian detective provides the reader with an enthralling mystery story of an unusual kind.'[27] *The Observer* cited Christie as the frontrunner in the competition of new mystery writers, saying that 'she has an unusual gift of mechanical complication'. Its review also carried a note of warning about such a talent, saying that 'it is a mistake to carry the art of bewilderment to the point of making the brain reel' and that 'it is possible to be fatigued with wandering up and down blind alleys'.[28] However, it was a succinct review in the *Daily Express* that most clearly alluded to Christie's elevated status as a mystery writer with only her third novel. '*The Murder on the Links* is one of the best mystery stories I have read,' it said. 'Miss Agatha Christie stands in a class by herself as a writer of detective stories.'[29]

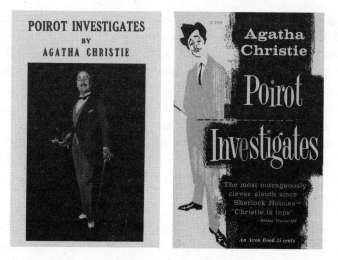

Poirot Investigates
(Short stories, 1924)

By January 1923 Agatha Christie was already making plans that looked beyond The Bodley Head. At the request of Bruce Ingram, the editor of British magazine *The Sketch*, she had compiled a collection of short stories featuring Poirot, which she also sent to an agent in order to find suitable international periodicals for their publication. While The Bodley Head seemed unsure of the short stories' relevance to them, Christie was arranging serialisations of the collection in the United States and India. Simultaneously, she was exploring ways to curtail her contract with her current publisher as soon as possible.[30] Although The Bodley Head had

ABOVE LEFT: The Bodley Head's first edition reused the 1923 study of Poirot by W. Smithson Broadhead from *The Sketch*. ABOVE RIGHT: The American Avon cover from 1956 with another portrait.

accepted her standalone thriller *The Man in the Brown Suit* (1924), they had refused a manuscript called *Vision*, a story that Christie had written around fifteen years earlier. A typescript for an unpublished short story called *Vision* survives, but at fourteen pages it's rather unlikely to be the same one that was sent to her publishers as a potential novel, but it may well have provided the basis for an expanded version. The surviving version opens atmospherically ('As the night mail for Scotland steamed out of St Pancras, Roden West felt a subtle sense of relief steal over him. A sensation as of the loosening of a chain') before exploring our protagonist's feelings for another character, Nina. The story then moves into the realms of science fiction, with a thought transference process that has the potential for dramatic consequences that are not properly explored or explained in a story that feels incomplete. If this tale was indeed expanded and sent to The Bodley Head, then it's obvious why it would have been rejected as it's quite unlike Christie's previous novels.[31]

The Bodley Head's refusal to consider *Vision* led to a dispute over whether Christie could count this as one of the

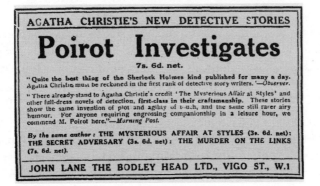

'Quite the best thing of the Sherlock Holmes kind published for many a day,' declared *The Observer*, and was repeated in the publisher's advertisements.

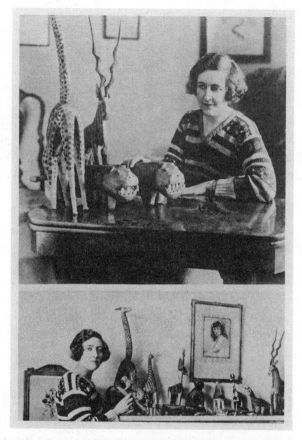

Agatha Christie posed for photographs in 1924 with wooden animals brought back from Rhodesia while accompanying her husband Archibald Christie on the 1922 British Empire Expedition trade junket.

six books stipulated by the contract.[32] In truth, Christie had never expected *Vision* to be published, but was using it as leverage to ensure that the forthcoming collection of Poirot short stories would be accepted as one of the contracted books.[33] She would win that portion of the fight, and *Poirot Investigates* was eventually counted as the fifth book of the six-book deal, although not before some stern words had been exchanged when it came to the nature of the contract: 'I do not want to include cinema, dramatic or foreign rights,' Christie scolded them, disputing their automatic inclusion without consultation or agreeable terms.[34]

In all, twenty-four Poirot short stories were published by *The Sketch* during 1923, in two sequences of twelve. Once more narrated by Hastings, they offer a substantial range of quality and ingenuity. Often they are light confections, and those that are most successful have germs of genius that Christie would later revisit and exploit in more substantial works. It's certainly worth remembering that the

The Bodley Head's second printing from 1928 featuring the new portrait by Abbey.

stories were designed to be read in the context of a magazine that elsewhere deals with the lighter end of society and fashion. There was no expectation for weightier matters to be brought into the publication via these mysteries, and on these terms the stories work extremely well. As a collection they are best enjoyed in small doses. Of the initial run of stories from *The Sketch* only eleven were selected for inclusion in *Poirot Investigates*, and Christie initially suggested only eight.[35] Three of these, 'The Adventure of the Western Star', 'The Million Dollar Bond Robbery' and 'The Jewel Robbery at the Grand Metropolitan', are reasonably straightforward stories of thefts, generally hinging on one important piece of misdirection, which Poirot reveals to the reader without too much effort being expended. There's also 'The Kidnapped Prime Minister', which opens with the unfortunate claim that 'war and the problems of war are a thing of the past', and has the British government rush to Poirot for help. Intriguing deaths are the focus of 'The Tragedy at Marsdon Manor', 'The Mystery of Hunter's Lodge' and 'The

Adventure of the Egyptian Tomb', which result in satisfying cases for Poirot, even if one of them relies on a questionable understanding of psychoanalysis. In 1936 'The Mystery of Hunter's Lodge' was reprinted in several newspapers, this time as part of a series of stories selected by Christie's peer in detective fiction authorship, Dorothy L. Sayers. Sayers introduced the story by discussing Poirot:

> Hercule Poirot, the Belgian detective, has his full complement of little vanities, which are as endearing to his readers as they are irritating to his rather stiff English friend, Captain Hastings. He likes to blow his own trumpet; he is fond of delivering little lectures on detective method; he is as ready as any woman to attract public attention - a trait offensive to the right-minded British male.
>
> He is not a specialist in any particular branch of detection; his tools are logic, and the faculty for disentangling the essential from the inessential. In this tale his personality is a little clouded by influenza and tisane; yet he contrives, characteristically, to find an excessively simple solution to an apparently complicated problem.[36]

Meanwhile, 'The Adventure of the Cheap Flat' operates as rather a mystery in reverse, as Poirot and assorted characters try to ascertain the whole story behind what appears to be a harmless surprise of a couple's good fortune when flat hunting. For this book collection, Christie agreed with her publisher's suggestion also to include both 'The Disappearance of Mr Davenheim' and 'The Adventure of the Italian Nobleman', the latter which she preferred over their other suggestion, 'The Case of the Missing Will', although eventually The Bodley Head got the author to agree to the inclusion of this other story as well ('I hope it will make an immense difference in the sale of the book!' she wrote sarcastically), explaining the rather odd length of the collection as eleven stories.[37, 38] In fact, the stories suggested by the publisher were sensible additions. Both 'The Disappearance of Mr Davenheim' and 'The Adventure of the Italian Nobleman' have satisfying twists (the former is clearly influenced by the Sherlock Holmes story 'The Man with the Twisted Lip'), and while 'The Case of the Missing Will' may be a lesser story in its own right, as a straightforward adventure that has very little in the way of deduction it operates as a neat palate cleanser at the conclusion of this collection. Christie's personal preferences didn't always chime with those of her reviewers and readers, and some have argued that the stories collected herein were actually weaker than those left out. These subsequently appeared in assorted short story collections in the USA and most were finally brought together in *Poirot's Early Cases*, a collection created in order to ensure that an Agatha Christie book was published in time for Christmas some half a century later.[39]

Pan featured Poirot on two paperback editions by Roger Hall (1954, top) and Jack Keay (1958).

Relatively few changes were made to the original stories for book publication, and at Christie's suggestion it sported a portrait of Poirot from *The Sketch* on its dustjacket.[40] The proposed title for the collection alternated between *The Grey Cells of M. Poirot*, which had been the overarching title for the stories as collected in *The Sketch*, and *Poirot Investigates*, with Christie expressing a preference for the latter. The story 'Jewel Robbery at the Grand Metropolitan' retained Christie's original title, having been renamed 'The Curious Disappearance of the Opalsen Pearls' for the magazine. The

Another Avon cover from 1956.

Bodley Head did request that the text of 'The Adventure of the Egyptian Tomb' was elaborated on, but the eventual changes were relatively small, including an extra section that cements Poirot's apparent belief in the power of the supernatural, and a lengthier discussion with the cast of suspects in Egypt. 'The Million Dollar Bond Robbery' added a few more details to Poirot's meeting with his client's fiancé compared to the magazine version, while in 'The Tragedy at Marsdon Manor' the mechanics of the murderous deed are expanded upon. Finally, 'The Disappearance of Mr Davenheim' has a handful of significant changes from *The Sketch*, including the removal of some details regarding Poirot's fussiness when it comes to dust and crumbs. This story also loses some of the crueller character touches in its transition to book publication. In this mystery, Poirot has a bet with Inspector Japp that he will be able to solve the case without visiting the scene of the crime. When Poirot appears to lose, both Hastings and Japp joke at his expense to a greater extent in the original *The Sketch* publication. In the magazine, Hastings originally wrote 'I replied that in this case Poirot had certainly brought his fate upon himself, and that there was no need for Japp to reproach himself', with Japp agreeing:

That's true. He certainly did ask for it! Past his day, of course, but a shrewd old fellow in many ways. But in a case like this he's out of his depth. Fancies himself though, doesn't he? Thinks there's nothing on God's earth like Hercule Poirot!

Perhaps to spare the characters' blushes, this exchange was removed for the book. The stories in *Poirot Investigates* show a still developing set of characteristics for both Poirot and Hastings, who share rooms, sometimes interrupted by their landlady (unnamed at this point but elsewhere revealed to be called Mrs Pearson). In 'The Adventure of the Western Star' it's Poirot rather than Hastings who recognises a film star, whereas the opposite scenario had occurred in *The Murder on the Links*, showing his knowledge of popular culture to be changeable – and we learn that both he and Hastings are readers of *Society Gossip* magazine. The relationship between the two is still strained at times, with Hastings looking 'coldly' at Poirot during 'The Tragedy at Marsdon Manor' after a gentle joke regarding his interest in beautiful women. Hastings' sensitivities often relieve him of his sense of humour, especially when being goaded by Inspector Japp.

A Spanish Poirot investigating in 1960.

The book was well received upon its publication in March 1924, with *The Observer* pointing out that the short story form could be even more difficult for a mystery author, and that Christie had succeeded in her attempts, further proving herself to be a 'first rank' detective story writer. 'All of [the stories] have point and ingenuity,' the review read, 'and if M. Poirot is infallibly and exasperatingly omniscient, well, that is the function of the detective in fiction.'[41]

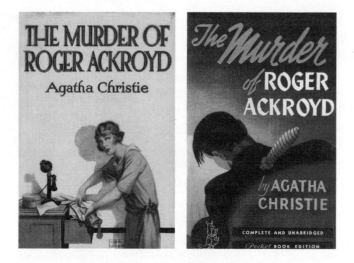

The Murder of Roger Ackroyd
(Novel, 1926)

In what would become a recurring theme with Christie, it was the taxman that motivated some of the decisions she made in the mid-1920s. Now an established author, she entered into a remarkably cordial correspondence with the Inland Revenue which wondered, in a gentle sort of way, exactly where her earnings were going. It transpired that Christie had little idea herself – she occasionally received cheques, which she cashed and spent. While the tax office seemed more amused than annoyed, it suggested she take her financial affairs more seriously. The result was that Christie returned to the literary agency of Hughes Massie (having

ABOVE LEFT: The first Agatha Christie book published by William Collins had a dustwrapper painting by Ellen Edwards (1926).
ABOVE RIGHT: The first American Pocket Books cover was by Isador N. Steinberg (1939).

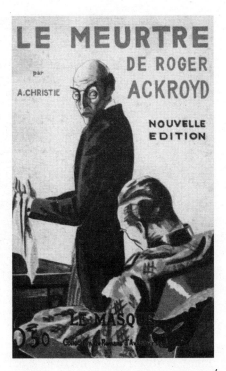

The iconic 1927 French cover for la Librairie des Champs-Élysées imprint reappeared on facsimile editions in 1997.

initially sought advice there before her first book was published) and met with the man who would represent her for the rest of her career, Edmund Cork. 'He seemed suitably horrified at my ignorance,' she later wrote, 'and was willing to guide my footsteps in future.'[42] One of the first of those steps was to move Christie away from The Bodley Head once her six-book contract had been fulfilled following the publication of the adventure-mystery *The Secret of Chimneys* (1925), and settle her with a new publisher that could offer better terms. The chosen company was William Collins, Sons & Co. (now HarperCollins), which has remained her publisher

A contemplative Poirot on the Spanish cover in 1946.

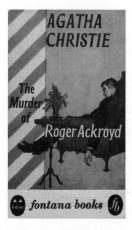

Collins' Fontana paperback cover (1957).

ever since. Surely Collins could scarcely believe their luck when Christie delivered her first manuscript for them, *The Murder of Roger Ackroyd*, a novel that would outshine all that she had written before and become acknowledged as one of the greatest pieces of detective fiction ever written.

Elements of the surprise that is eventually revealed to be central to *The Murder of Roger Ackroyd* were independently suggested to Agatha Christie by two people – her brother-in-law, James Watts, and Lord Mountbatten, (although she had already undertaken similar subterfuge in *The Man in the Brown Suit*). However, while the twist is clever in itself, the fact that Christie finds a way to make it work is what deserves the most acclaim. Initially, the mystery seems straightforward, as a wealthy businessman is found murdered in his study near to the village where Poirot has retired to grow marrows. His retirement is interrupted by the case, and for this investigation he's joined not by Hastings, but by his new neighbour, Dr Sheppard, who lives with his sister Caroline, an unforgettable character who gossips her way through the unravelling of the mystery. Caroline was a favourite creation of Christie's, who described her as 'an acidulated spinster, full of curiosity, knowing everything, hearing everything: the complete detective service in the home'. Christie also cited her as influential in the development of Miss Marple, who would make her print debut in 1927 in the short story 'The Tuesday Night Club'.[43,44] Dr Sheppard's presence as narrator allows us to reacquaint ourselves with the (to British society eyes) odd little Belgian with his curious quirks. When the doctor's peaceful gardening is interrupted by a marrow whizzing its way from the detective's side of the fence, Sheppard describes his neighbour's 'egg-shaped head, partially covered with suspiciously black hair, two immense moustaches, and a pair of watchful eyes', before getting his name wrong ('Mr Porrott') in a sign that Poirot's fame had not reached the heights he may have imagined. Certainly, Sheppard underestimates Poirot's abilities and gives us a first-hand account of his surprise that the detective is able to piece together the ingenious truth of the mystery. The narration allows us new insight to Poirot's methods, and the doctor is presented as more amiable than Hastings, but he is also prone to

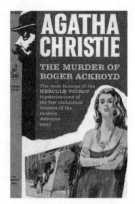

Poirot's face was used as a series logo in a range of Cardinal paperbacks in 1961.

character flaws that mark him out to be someone unsuited to a long-term friendship with the detective.

At the time of its publication as a novel in May 1926 *The Murder of Roger Ackroyd* initiated a great deal of discussion about the 'rules' of crime fiction, and especially the question of whether or not Christie had played fair with the reader.[45] Christie mulled over this argument many years later, but was always satisfied that she had misdirected rather than misled: 'I have a certain amount of rules. No false words may be uttered by me. To write: "Mrs Armstrong walked home wondering who had committed the murder" would be unfair if she had done it herself. But it's not unfair to leave things out.'[46]

The reviews of the book itself were almost universally positive, but generally indicated some unease with the nature of the solution it was often seen as exceptionally clever but potentially problematic, raising questions of whether all readers would be happy with Christie's sleight of hand. However, in the decades since its publication, the reputation of the book has only grown, and in 2013 the Crime Writers' Association named it the greatest crime novel of all time. The solution is generally regarded as masterful and satisfying, perhaps only disappointing those who feel annoyed that Christie has caught them out so absolutely. An astute reader has every chance to work out the murderer's identity if they can bid goodbye to their preconceptions of the genre and its form. The nature of the novel's structure means that it has been widely discussed, and the writer Pierre Bayard devoted an entire book to an analysis of the mystery, called *Who Killed Roger Ackroyd?*, in which he postulates a fascinating alternative theory regarding the culprit, which will not be spoiled here.

In the context of Christie's development as an author, we can see the book as an example of her restlessness with the crime genre. She would describe her writings as 'half way between a crossword puzzle and a hunt in which you can pursue the trail sitting comfortably at home in your armchair', but the puzzles themselves were ever changing, even in this early period.[47] Despite the perceived clichés in her work as she revisits the same broad scenarios and locations in multiple mysteries, she was never happy just to rework the same plot beats and structure by simply swapping out names and motive. She relished challenging the form, which in turn made her more sophisticated as a writer than many have credited her for. Here, a reading of the novel's blurb may indicate a retread of themes explored in her first two Poirot novels, but the reader will eventually discover that this is far from true.

Tom Adams' exquisite 1966 paperback cover for Fontana Books.

The Murder of Roger Ackroyd is now generally referred to as Christie's masterpiece, perhaps because of its combination of traditional Christie mystery elements with the astonishing solution. Christie was pleased by the fact that it was her greatest success to date, but in her autobiography seems slightly bemused that it was still being discussed and read many years later. Although Christie placed it in the top ten of her own books when asked in 1972, in 1975 the writer Julian Symons claimed that the author was not particularly enamoured with the book, as he recounted that 'When *The Murder of Roger Ackroyd* is mentioned she says "oh dear oh dear, surely I've written something better than that?"'.[48]

The Big Four
(Novel/short stories, 1927)

Given that Collins can only have been pleased with the quality and reception of Agatha Christie's first book for them, the publisher would surely have been concerned when the novelist disappeared following the breakdown of her marriage, and then perhaps privately thrilled when she returned accompanied by exceptional levels of attendant publicity. Over the years, the story of Agatha Christie's disappearance in December 1926 has attracted extraordinary levels of attention from writers in all areas of fact and fiction, but the facts are simple. Following the death of her mother earlier in 1926 and then the breakdown of her marriage to

ABOVE LEFT: The first edition of *The Big Four* was unique in that the British and American first editions shared the same jacket design (1927). **ABOVE RIGHT:** The 1950 Avon cover offered thrills, frills and a Poirot police badge.

Archie, Agatha left the family home and retreated to The Swan Hydropathic Hotel in Harrogate, where she stayed under a pseudonym influenced by the name of her husband's mistress. It seems likely that Agatha had had some form of breakdown. 'I married at twenty-four and we were very happy for eleven years,' she later remembered. 'Then my mother died a very painful death and my husband found a young woman. Well, you can't write your own fate. Your fate comes to you.'[49]

Understandably, the very public search for Christie appeared to embarrass her, having never been keen on publicity. 'Being an author is very difficult because it spoils a lot of your private life,' she would tell an interviewer many years later. 'People come up to you and say "How do you do? I did enjoy so-and-so". You thank them and then they want to get away and you want to get away and it is all very embarrassing.'[50] When she was eventually found Christie claimed amnesia and rarely referred to them again.[51] The events would haunt her for the rest of her life – following the abduction of Muriel McKay in December 1969 (in an apparent case of mistaken identity in an attempt to extort money from media mogul Rupert Murdoch, whose wife was the intended target) the press quickly turned to Christie to comment on the mystery. 'BBC rang me up (so did a lot of newspapers!) to suggest I would like to comment on disappearance of Mrs McKay "as disappearing tricks are right up your street, aren't they?",' Christie wrote to Cork in January 1970. 'A very brash and impertinent young man. I refused and was rude to him.'[52]

Although the experience instilled an understandable distrust of the press for capitalising

Collins' Detective Club released a colourful hardback in 1931. A reissue in 2017 reprinted the original *Sketch* version of the text for the very first time.

The Big Four was one of the launch titles in Avon's Pocket-Size Books series in 1941.

on a deeply personal trauma, the crises leading up to Christie's brief disappearance would have little impact in the long term on the mysteries she wrote. In the short term, however, they created something of a bump in the road. Unable to concentrate on writing, Christie was nevertheless in need of money and so reworked two existing ideas for her next two Poirot novels in order to make it as easy as possible to fulfil her contractual obligations. For *The Big Four* the alterations were minimal, as the book would essentially reprint a twelve-part serial already published in *The Sketch* in 1924 under the umbrella title *The Man Who Was Number Four*. These linked short stories outlined the nefarious deeds of a 'big four' of criminals, who were setting out to disrupt world order. It was Christie's brother-in-law, Campbell Christie, who suggested that these stories could be minimally reworked to create a 'new' novel, and there is still some debate regarding his contribution – it's possible that he wrote most (or even all) of the new linking material ready for its publication in January 1927.[53]

However, if anything, stringing the serial together as a novel only weakens the mysteries. They manage to be both inconsistent and repetitive (twice in the first hundred pages Poirot is inspired to make a sudden exit from a train before it reaches its destination), littered with non-sequiturs that are more jarring when read in quick succession. While the reader may detect a mellowing of Hastings, who's happy to indulge in light-hearted laughter about the case with both Japp and Poirot, this perhaps signals another problem with the book – that Poirot simply doesn't fit into *The Big Four*'s world of spies and international politics, which leads to awkward adjustments to his character. It might be better to imagine Tommy and Tuppence, married investigators always looking for a big adventure, in Poirot's place – thrill-seekers who would be happy to run around the world in order to unmask the evil cartel behind a collection of murders and thefts of sensitive material. They would also have imbued the novel with a better sense of fun, whereas Poirot's established grounding in real-life domestic cases makes the image of him battling a group of spies like an action hero feel unconvincing rather than exciting.

Nevertheless, there are still some great ideas on display in *The Big Four*, notably the explanation of the apparently invisible murderer in the chapter 'The Importance of a Leg of Mutton', which has some prime Poirot deduction, and the shocking story behind the death of

The Big Four was one of many Christies to be published as a green Penguin with Jan Tschichold's iconic Penguin logo (1957).

a premier chess player in 'A Chess Problem'. Given the early publication date of the short stories it's no surprise that after *The Murder of Roger Ackroyd* the novel feels like a regression of Christie's style, but the presence of Poirot in this adventure of international conspiracy also shows us a glimpse of a road not travelled.

As far as the author was concerned, she considered *The Big Four* to be 'rotten' and, along with the subsequent Poirot novel *The Mystery of the Blue Train*, the first time that she had to force herself to work to order for financial and contractual reasons. This led to her determination always to have a manuscript 'in hand' wherever possible, to alleviate the pressure of deadlines and allow for the realities of life to interrupt her writing when needed. Nevertheless, upon its publication in January 1927 the novel was a commercial success, no doubt helped by Christie's name having been so prominently featured in the press. It was also reviewed

W. Francis Phillips' cover for the Pan paperback (1961).

positively by many critics, with the *Daily Express* describing it as 'one of the liveliest and most entertaining mystery stories that has been written for some time', while *The Observer* made the point that 'the short interpolated mysteries within the mystery are really much more interesting than the machinations of the "Big Four"', once more revealing where Christie's strengths lay.[54] Although it deserves credit for satisfying so many of its readers when published, one can only imagine the shock of murder mystery aficionados picking up the next Poirot book by the author of *The Murder of Roger Ackroyd* only to find an international thriller with evil masterminds, laser-like energy beams, thefts of radium, and an exploding mountain inhabited by spies.

In April 1927 Collins took out an advert in *The Manchester Guardian* to showcase some of its newer books. *The Big Four* was one of the titles to be mentioned ('a thrilling story'), while it claimed that 'The publishers hope to receive Mrs Christie's manuscript for her next detective novel, *The Mystery of the Blue Train*, very soon,' before giving a somewhat coy update on the author herself: 'Mrs Christie has been recuperating in the Canary Islands after her recent illness.'[55] The dramas of 1926 had been put to one side, and it would soon be business as usual once more.

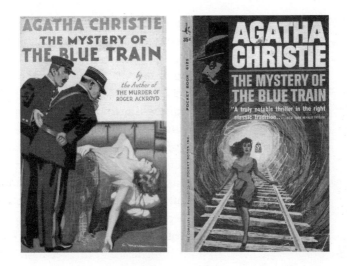

The Mystery of the Blue Train
(Novel, 1928)

Personal insights from Agatha Christie regarding her own stories are relatively rare for an author with such a lengthy and distinguished career. Much of her autobiography covers her childhood and matters away from her writing – but, when she did discuss her own works, there was one recurring opinion. As she said in 1966, 'Easily the worst book I ever wrote was *The Mystery of the Blue Train*. I hate it.'[56] Objectively, it's not difficult to imagine that it was really this period of Christie's life that she was so unhappy with, rather than her writing, but there's no doubt that Christie made this novel the

ABOVE LEFT: The 1928 Collins' first edition hardback painted by C. Morse, a pseudonym of Salomon van Abbé. **ABOVE RIGHT:** American paperback cover from Pocket Books, illustrated by Harry Bennett(1962).

focus of her misery at this time. In an unpublished portion of her autobiography, she elaborated on her feelings further:

> I have always hated *The Mystery of the Blue Train*. Presumably I turned out a fairly decent piece of work, since some people say it is their favourite book (and if they say so they always go down in my estimation). It was terribly full of clichés, the plot was predictable, the people were unreal. It got better towards the end because when you have lived with a thing long enough, and pushed yourself on, you cannot help allying yourself a little with what you are writing about. But it certainly had no zest, no *joie de vivre*, no faintest flash of enjoyment about it.[57]

While *The Mystery of the Blue Train* is not without its flaws, few readers could agree with Christie's complete dismissal of it even though such feelings lingered long in her memory. Perhaps any reader with no knowledge of the context of the writing of the novel could view it as simply a slightly lesser Poirot mystery. However, read with a recuperating Christie in mind, forcing herself to complete a book in the shadow of the death of her beloved mother and the end of her marriage, it's not difficult to see evidence of the laborious hard work and systematic processes that Christie has undertaken to transform a good Poirot short story into a full-length novel. This short story was 'The Mystery of the Plymouth Express', originally published by *The Sketch* in 1923, and much remains unchanged.[58] The basic story concerns a woman who is found murdered in a train carriage (in the novel she is travelling towards the French Riviera, rather than the short story's Devon), having apparently been

Pan paperback cover by John Pollack (1954).

the victim of a plot to steal valuable jewellery that she was travelling with. The book then expands on some obvious potential villains in both the victim's husband and the lover of the dead woman, a mysterious Count. There's also a web of alibis that will take the considerable powers of deduction of Poirot to untangle.

The struggle to expand the original story is all too obvious from the opening, as Christie offers both narrative dead-ends and disorientating shifts of focus in an attempt to lend some atmosphere and mystery early on. While this material may have been added for stylistic reasons, much of it is also evident as padding, especially when re-read with the knowledge of which plot threads remain relevant, and which come to nothing. In fact, the story itself is a relatively rare Christie that is only really satisfying on its first reading as she works to obfuscate and distract from the actually rather simple (if ingenious) plotting of the murderer. The truth is that the neatly plotted short story does not offer enough material for the fully expanded novel, something that Christie was clearly well aware of, and so she provides a plethora of distractions, particularly extraneous characters, to ensure that the bare bones of the mystery are not inspected too closely, lest the reader should work out the case rather quicker than the author would like.

Pocket Books' dramatic cover from 1957 by James Alfred Meese.

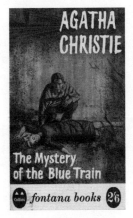

The UK paperback from Fontana Books (1958).

One remarkable element of the novel lies in its coldness – and even viciousness – towards many of the key characters. Our murder victim, the American heiress Ruth Kettering, is disfigured by a blow to the face following her strangulation with a length of cord, a brutal way to

A Collins advertisement for 'Poirot's Greatest Case written down by Agatha Christie'.

kill a young woman (and further evidence that however one might describe Christie 'cosy' is not an apt adjective). Inevitably there are plot reasons for the attack that makes Kettering's face unrecognisable, but it provides a lingering image for the reader to digest over the course of the novel. This harshness is accentuated by the lack of a narrator who would usually filter such brutality through their own squeamishness or respect for the victim, as Hastings remains in the Argentine. Instead, we get a third-person narrative and our first appearance of Poirot's valet George, 'an intensely English, rather wooden-faced individual'. George (or, as Poirot is wont to pronounce, 'Georges') doesn't intrude on the mysteries in which he is present, as he usually functions as a solid sounding-board for Poirot's ruminations. On this occasion Poirot doesn't play a part in the novel for quite some time, and keeping the detective off-stage for so long means that the mystery takes longer to develop than usual. However, Poirot seems sure that he will be able to solve this case whatever his involvement, as this is the novel in which he quietly but confidently introduces himself as 'probably the greatest detective in the world'.

The 1963 Fontana paperback, illustrated by John Baker.

In a typical bout of hyperbole, *The Mystery of the Blue Train* was publicised as 'Poirot's greatest case' by Collins upon its British publication in March 1928, with some adverts even featuring a bizarre introduction to the story by Poirot himself (but surely not penned by Agatha Christie), in which he wrote:

> *Mesdames et Messieurs,*
>
> *Oui, c'est moi, Poirot, back from ze long retiral. I have done something zis time so clevaire with my leetle "grey cells". You will be thrilled and surpris. Mais oui, you will gasp with ze mouth as I spread my net. I am ... what you say? ... swell head, yes? Ah well, but I am not such a top 'ole detective? ... je crois que oui!*
>
> Hercule Poirot, P.O.I.
> *Nice, Le 25 Mars, 1928* (Prince of Investigators)

If divorced from its origins and read simply as a new Poirot murder investigation then there is much to admire in the ingenuity of the murderer's plan and way it is initially presented to the authorities in *The Mystery of the Blue Train*. Certainly *The Times Literary Supplement* received the novel as warmly as ever, although the reviewer seemed to be more in awe of Poirot's detective skills than Christie's construction, which is a perspective that is difficult to untangle. However, it's true that without Belgium's greatest detective on board the police would surely have struggled to make sense of the case, which only adds to his increasingly legendary reputation. In the course of the investigation Poirot allies himself with Katherine Grey, a thirty-three-year-old woman who has worked as an elderly lady's companion and is now resident in St Mary Mead. We can only speculate about how *The Mystery of the Blue Train* would be remembered if one of Katherine's neighbours, Miss Jane Marple, had caught Le Train Bleu in her place...

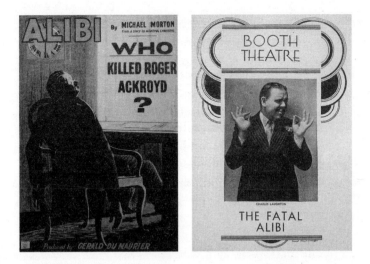

Alibi
(Play by Michael Morton, 1928)

Agatha Christie was highly proprietorial over her works when it came to adaptations. This was particularly true when it came to film and television, but it was also the case regarding the stage. With this in mind, why was it that Christie allowed another person, the dramatist Michael Morton, to write Poirot's first appearance away from the world of magazines and books in the play *Alibi*? Julius Green, in his history of Christie's writing for the stage, suggests that this may have been the result of pressure from her agents who would have felt that Christie should concentrate on writing novels (which were known to be profitable), and certainly it seems to have been a financially judicious move.[59]

ABOVE LEFT: The poster for the first UK production of *Alibi*, with art by Templeton (1928). **ABOVE RIGHT:** The programme for the 1932 Broadway production, with Charles Laughton reprising his West End role.

Agatha Christie made no secret of her general unhappiness with changes made by Morton in order to present her mystery *The Murder of Roger Ackroyd* for the stage. 'I much disliked his first suggestion, which was to take about twenty years off Poirot's age, call him Beau Poirot and have lots of girls in love with him,' she wrote in her autobiography. In an unpublished section she elaborated on the personal impact of this, writing that Morton 'upset me, although I fought as valiantly as I could at that time. I was too nervous and submissive to be a good fighter at that period'.[60] Nevertheless, Christie accepted that her creation was only growing in stature:

> I was by this time so stuck with Poirot that I realised I was going to have him with me for life. I strongly objected to having his personality completely changed. In the end, with Gerald Du Maurier, who was producing, backing me up, we settled on removing that excellent character Caroline, the doctor's sister, and replacing her with a young and attractive girl ... I resented the removal of Caroline a good deal: I liked the part she played in village life: and I liked the idea of village life reflected through the life of the doctor and his masterful sister.[61]

Caroline's replacement was the younger Caryl, and there's something of a romantic frisson in her relationship with Poirot at the play's denouement. After they say their final goodbyes ('Perhaps one day...' says Poirot as she leaves), stage directions inform us that 'Poirot turns back to table, takes rose out of specimen glass which is on table, kisses it, and puts it in his button-hole'. One other crucial amendment not mentioned by Christie is the fact that the Poirot of this play is described as 'the great French detective', rather than Belgian – an identity change that would have horrified him.

If *The Murder of Roger Ackroyd*'s greatest success was in its experimentation with the mystery form, then *Alibi*'s greatest weakness is the way it tries to force the story into a more conventional mould. Its translation to the stage inevitably means that the literary twist so central to the original novel must be lost, leaving only a rather mundane skeleton of a story behind. Although the range of Poirot stories available at the time was relatively small, perhaps *The Mysterious Affair at Styles* would have been a better choice for the theatre because, even if it's a weaker novel, it has greater reliance on simple but important visuals. If well staged, *Styles*'s emphasis on these physical clues could be a satisfying part of the puzzle for the audience, alongside the spoken word and alibis, with the placement of a door bolt and the arrangement of ornaments allowing the most observant audience members to make some important deductions. In fact, one of her notebooks that covers stories written in the early 1950s shows a plan for the first two acts of a potential adaptation of *The Mysterious Affair at Styles*, involving Poirot. The plan is incomplete, and another page that

Charles Laughton in a publicity still from the 1928 production.

may have included more text has been ripped out, but even though the idea doesn't seem to have progressed any further it's intriguing that Christie was even considering this. If time had allowed her to mellow regarding Poirot in the theatre, it certainly didn't last, as she continued to remove the character from stage adaptations of novels that had featured him. In 1956, she justified her dislike of Poirot on stage by saying that 'However impeccably acted, they would never be quite *my* Hercule Poirot'.[62]

When *Alibi* opened at the Prince of Wales Theatre in May 1928 it was the slow plotting of the first few scenes that seems to have grated with several critics. 'In the first act,

Francis L. Sullivan replaced Charles Laughton as Hercule Poirot in the UK's first touring production.

drearily long and annoying, characters kept walking on and off the stage,' wrote the critic for the *Daily Express*, who went on to clarify that 'when the action really started, and the detective got to work, *Alibi* became a most interesting play.'[63] However, the most plaudits were reserved not for Morton or Christie, but Charles Laughton, a rising star of theatre whose performance as Poirot was the highlight of nearly all those who reviewed the play. Laughton was the first person to play Poirot in any dramatic form – before any films, radio plays or television productions – and it's difficult to imagine now how difficult it must have been to set the template. Pictures show a non-ostentatious moustache nestling on the upper lip of the twenty-eight-year-old, dressed in black tie with a flourishing flower in his buttonhole, while he seems to be surprisingly serious in these posed shots. *The Church Times* stated that it was Laughton's portrayal of Poirot 'which more than anything else contributes to the success of *Alibi*', and that the play 'has been received with the greatest cordiality; but calmly considered, the story of a murderer and its carefully concealed denouement is an affair of words rather than action.'[64] The *Daily Express* described Laughton's performance as 'so subtle, and yet so dominating, that it gripped the house. At the end the shout "Laughton! Laughton!", to which we are now becoming accustomed, was heard on every hand. The play was an adaptation by Michael Morton of *Alibi*, a book by Agatha Christie [sic], once famous as the missing woman novelist. She was missing again at the end last night when they shouted "Author!" for she hid in a box.'[65]

When *Alibi* toured Britain Laughton was replaced by Francis L. Sullivan in the role of Poirot. Photographs of Sullivan make him look slightly jauntier than Laughton – how much this is down to the photographer we can't know, although Sullivan's moustache curves upwards at the edges in a rather more impressive way than Laughton's more demure effort. Sullivan received positive, if slightly more muted, reviews, with *The Manchester Guardian* saying that 'Mr Sullivan as Poirot brought a capable finish to the part'.[66] This wasn't the last time that Sullivan would play the role of Poirot, while Laughton would also reprise the part for a brief Broadway run in 1932, which ran for only twenty-four performances under the title *The Fatal Alibi*.[67] Although the play wasn't popular there (unlike in London, where it ran for 250 performances) the overall success of the production demonstrated that, with the right care and attention, Poirot could live and breathe outside of the confines of the written word. In the event, the next time he was to appear on stage Christie would ensure that it was her own words that he was speaking.

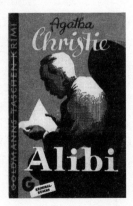

A 1961 cover for *Alibi*, the German title for *The Murder of Roger Ackroyd*.

CHAPTER TWO:

THE

1930s

1930 was a good year for Agatha Christie, and she had every reason to feel that she was deserving of some good fortune at last. Aside from her well-documented difficulties at the end of the 1920s, she'd continued to face personal tragedy as the decade drew to a close with the death of her brother Monty in 1929, and Christie was determined that 1930 would signal a new, more positive, period of her life. Although she'd left her first publisher The Bodley Head for Collins in 1926 she had continued communication with Allen Lane, nephew of The Bodley Head's co-founder John Lane, about both business issues regarding the first six books and personal updates, including postcards from her travels. Allen Lane had become a friend, and in correspondence from July and September 1930 she called it a 'wonderful' and 'marvellous' year.[1] The source of her happiness

OPPOSITE: Hercule Poirot sporting a particularly lavish moustache in *The American Magazine* serial of *13 at Dinner*, aka *Lord Edgware Dies* (1933), illustrated by Weldon Trench.

Hercule Poirot: Master Detective was a three-book omnibus which included an exclusive introduction in which Poirot writes a letter introducing himself to his American publisher (1936).

was no doubt the fact that during a trip to Ur, Iraq, she had met the archaeologist Max Mallowan, and they'd fallen in love. When she wrote the July letter they were engaged; by the time of the September one they were married. They would stay together until Christie's death in 1976, and when contemplating their longevity she later said, rather too modestly, that 'My husband and I get on very successfully considering he is so highbrow and I am so lowbrow.'[2]

It wasn't just Christie's personal life that had positive developments in 1930. Following the appearances of spinster detective Miss Marple in some short stories printed in magazines from 1927, later collected as *The Thirteen Problems* in 1932, Christie had put her new character in a novel of her own, *The Murder at the Vicarage*. Published in October 1930, this was the first of twelve novels to feature the all-seeing resident of St Mary Mead over the next forty-six years. While Miss Marple would never quite eclipse the fame of Poirot in the public eye, she became a real competitor for Christie's affections. In later years the author would express a preference for the character of Miss Marple over the rather more ubiquitous Poirot. However, the 1930s would see a bumper crop of novels featuring the Belgian detective, as Christie entered what many consider to be the golden age of both her works, and detective fiction more generally.

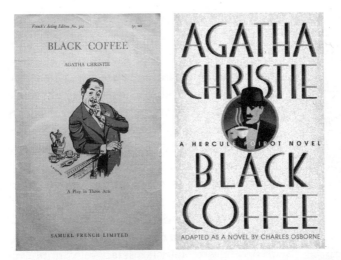

Black Coffee
(Play, 1930)

Largely forgotten for several decades, the play *Black Coffee* has had something of a resurgence since the 1990s, in part due to a novelisation by Charles Osborne, but also because as the only original Christie play to star Poirot it has been ripe for revivals amongst theatre troupes. For many years it was considered to have been written by Agatha Christie as a reaction against *Alibi*, in which Michael Morton had adapted *The Murder of Roger Ackroyd* for the stage to Christie's general dissatisfaction. However, more recently a convincing argument has been put forward by Christie historian John Curran that this tale of hyoscine poisoning in a country house owned by

ABOVE LEFT: The 1952 acting edition of *Black Coffee* published by Samuel French was unique for depicting an illustration of Poirot on the cover by S. Pogorsky. **ABOVE RIGHT:** Charles Osborne's novelisation in 1998 became a major bestseller for St Martin's Press in America.

<image:caption>An Italian playscript omnibus, pairing *Black Coffee* with the *Rule of Three* trio of one-act plays 'The Rats', 'The Patient' and 'Afternoon at the Seaside' (1991).</image:caption>

the wealthy research scientist Sir Claud Amory pre-dates the writing of *Alibi* by several years. In fact, Curran has argued that several elements point to it being written between *The Mysterious Affair at Styles* and *The Murder on the Links*, making this only Christie's second full length mystery to feature the detective.[3] Certainly, the evidence presented is convincing – not least the presence of Hastings without mention of his fiancée, whom he meets in the second Poirot novel, as well as some repeated elements from *Styles*. But perhaps the clearest case for the argument that this is an early piece of writing dusted off several years later is less tangible. Simply put, *Black Coffee* (which Christie had originally called *After Dinner*) is remarkably unsophisticated and falls substantially below the level of quality that she'd been achieving in her original writing since the mid-1920s.

The story itself is a very straightforward murder mystery concerning the death of Sir Claud, involving lengthy debates over the access that various characters have had to a box that may hold the key to the poisoning. The play features a wealth of mystery clichés, from the ominous striking of a clock to the lights going out just before the murder takes place. Audiences unfamiliar with Christie's best work have every chance to find it an enjoyable evening at the theatre that confirms all of their suspicions regarding her handling of the genre. Those who know her work a little better are more likely to be a little disappointed in its straightforward nature, as in an unwelcome departure from her normal writing of mystery plays there's no final twist here that turns the story on its head. The culprit is simply identified and, after a failed attempt to assassinate Poirot, is placed into custody by Inspector Japp's men.

One area of the play that's of particular interest is the softening of Poirot's character. As with *Alibi*, the play ends with a somewhat wistful conversation between Poirot and a female character, although there is no hint of romance between them on this occasion. For the earliest runs of the play Francis L. Sullivan played Poirot once more, having previously portrayed the detective in the touring production of *Alibi*, before appearing for *Black Coffee*'s two-week try-out at London's Embassy Theatre between 8 and 20 December 1930. On 11 December Christie wrote to her husband that 'I like Francis Sullivan better than Charles Laughton as Poirot. He makes him much more lovable – a real dear,' demonstrating that Poirot for the stage wasn't to be the overly fussy character that he was generally written to be for the page.[4]

Elsewhere in this letter it's made clear that Christie was excited by the long-awaited debut of her work on the stage, as she would later express a preference for writing plays over novels. Speaking to the BBC in 1955 she said that 'The real work is done in thinking out the development of your story ... three months seems to me quite a reasonable time to complete a book if one can get right down to it. On the other hand, plays I think are better written quickly. Of course writing plays is much more fun than writing books. You haven't got to bother about long descriptions of places and people or about deciding how to space out your material.'[5] Before *Black Coffee* Christie had written other, unproduced, plays with the pleasingly melodramatic titles of *The Clutching Hand* and *The Lie*, but had been beaten by her sister when it came to West End productions, as Madge's play *The Claimant* had been staged there in 1924, much to Christie's envy. In the thick of the performances of her own debut, Christie was

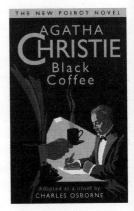

The UK paperback of the novelisation, illustrated by Andrew Davidson (1999).

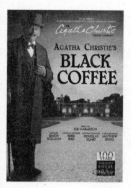

Black Coffee was revived by the Agatha Christie Theatre Company in 2014 with Robert Powell as Poirot.

delighted by the production. 'Oh! It has all been fun – *Black Coffee* I mean,' she wrote. 'It was fun going to rehearsals and everything went splendidly on the night itself except that when the girl said (in great agitation!) "This door won't open!" it immediately did! Something like that always happens on a first night.'[6] Christie went on to say that the repertory company had been thrilled with the reaction to the play, in terms of commercial success as well as the critics, claiming that the reviews were good, and 'not the haughty ones they usually have about a detective play'.

An option to produce a full run of the play was swiftly taken up, and *Black Coffee* opened at St Martin's Theatre (eventual home to *The Mousetrap*) in April 1931, later transferring to two other theatres before closing in June 1931. Some reviews were indeed reasonably kind ('well finished, most intelligent and very pleasing,' said the *Daily Express*) although others were rather begrudging – the critic for *The Manchester Guardian* snarked that 'Miss Christie is not, on this occasion, in pursuit of novelty' before wondering why 'adult people can be found in fairly large numbers to sit undismayed through the execution of such ritual as this'.[7] Meanwhile, *The Observer* wrote that 'Miss Agatha Christie is a competent craftsmen, and her play, which is methodically planned and well carried out and played, agreeably entertains'.[8] This would be a fair summary – but much better mysteries for Poirot were on the horizon.

Austin Trevor as Hercule Poirot
(Films, 1931–34)

Although Christie had often pondered on the question of what an egg-shaped head actually meant in reality, she'd been happy with the physical portrayals of Poirot from both Charles Laughton and Francis L. Sullivan on stage, even if she had misgivings that they were rather too tall for the detective as she saw him. Despite their relatively young age both actors were made up in a manner to suggest an older man, and by all accounts their mannerisms tallied with Poirot as Christie and her readers had come to envisage him. However, the same cannot be said of Poirot's debut appearances on the silver screen, as Austin Trevor performed the part in three films with a physical appearance that had little

ABOVE: Austin Trevor as Poirot (left) confronts John Deverell as Lord Halliford in *Alibi*.

in common with the character as described by Christie in the books. The actor was thirty-three years old when he first assumed the part in the 1931 film version of *Alibi* and offered a rather suave and youthful version of the detective, who is once more described as French, and - *mon Dieu!* - depicted without a moustache.

Although this was Poirot's debut on the cinema screen, it wasn't Christie's first brush with film. In years to come she would become intractably opposed to screen adaptations of her work, largely because of disappointing and upsetting experiences on the occasions she did consent to the appearance of her stories on film and television. However, this wasn't always the case - in 1922 she responded to news of her sister Madge's successful play with the honest statement that 'I shall be furious if she arrives "on film" before I do!'[9] Christie's screen debut would come six years later, with a film called *The Passing of Mr Quinn* [sic], ostensibly based on one of her stories featuring the intriguing detective Harley

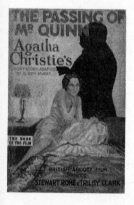

The first Agatha Christie film in 1928 bore little resemblance to her short story, as the novelisation proved.

Quin, but in reality the plot was far removed from Christie's original tale of a revisited tragedy.[10] More successful was a 1929 German film adaptation of the Tommy and Tuppence debut adventure *The Secret Adversary*, which offered a complicated story at a frenetic pace but was never less than entertaining. However, it was the earlier Christie 'adaptation' that set the template for the three Poirot films starring Austin Trevor, as not only did the first two Poirot films share the same director and producer as *The Passing of Mr Quinn*, Leslie S. Hiscott and Julius Hagen respectively, but the rationale behind the production itself was the same. There wasn't any innate desire to bring these particular stories to the screen, but rather a keenness to adhere to a

A two-page advertisement in *The Bioscope* for Twickenham Film Studios' *Black Coffee* (1931).

government-enforced quota that was designed to ensure that British pictures, based on stories by British authors, were still being made alongside more Hollywood-influenced fare. So was born the 'quota quickie', relatively inexpensive British films made quickly in order to follow this regulation, rather than to satisfy any artistic (or even particularly commercial) desire.

Production on the first Poirot film, based on Michael Morton's stage adaptation of *The Murder of Roger Ackroyd*, *Alibi*, began in February 1931. Work on *Black Coffee* followed shortly after, even before the first film had been released. This second film was even announced while the play was still running in the West End, which raises the possibility that the film deal may have encouraged a curtailment of the stage run – in years to come, *The Mousetrap* would famously circumvent such a possibility by the inclusion of a clause that forbade a film production while the show was still running. Both Poirot films would be released later in 1931, but unfortunately we are reliant on contemporary reports and reviews, and only a handful of photographs, to build up a picture of what they were like as no prints are known to survive.

One thing we can gather is that the films appear to have been quite static adaptations of the plays, and don't seem to have made great use of the cinematic medium's increased flexibility when it comes to locations, atmosphere and pacing. The reviews were certainly mixed, with *Variety* saying of *Alibi* that it 'cannot be rated as good, or placed as anything but a second feature for the grinds, merely because it deals with the good old hunt-the-murderer theme in the good old way ... it is well knit along the familiar lines'. It also seemed that Poirot was struggling to escape the shadow of Charles Laughton's stage performance, as the reviewer noted:

Promotional photos in *The Bioscope* for *Black Coffee* starring Austin Trevor and Adrianne Allen, with Richard Cooper, Philip Strange and Elizabeth Allan.

Alibi was a successful stage play here, although it probably would not have achieved the run it did had not Charles Laughton, who starred in it, been the hit of the town at the time. [The film] compares unfavourably with the stage version, lacking the vivid characterisation which made the old Haymarket show so noteworthy. Development is cramped, along stage lines, but while suspense values are occasionally good, comedy values are practically non-existent. Trouping is not too hot. Austin Trevor is the best as the detective ... Women mean nothing. Probably not the players' fault, anyway, as the production doesn't suggest anything more than an attempt to make money with a fast one.'[11]

The critics may have been largely dismissive of the film, but audiences and exhibitors were rather keener. A follow up article in *The Bioscope* mentioned 'extraordinary requests from exhibitors in connection with the Twickenham film *Alibi*. I was not able to see the picture when it was trade shown recently, but I've since had a private view of it, and I feel that provincial exhibitors to whom it is now being presented will agree that this is one of the most gripping of all the mystery yarns which Julius Hagen has produced.' The article also drew attention to Trevor, who was generally marked out as one of the best features of the production. Calling his performance 'singularly fine', the article then revised up the magazine's opinion of the film, writing that 'Cinema audiences seeing *Alibi* will, I feel, be kept in suspense to the last moment. I confess I failed entirely to detect the criminal until the climax was within a few feet. Leslie Hiscott's direction has made *Alibi* the complete mystery film, and the photography and recording are tip-top.'[12] However, the dissimilarity between Trevor's physicality and the character as described by Christie didn't go unnoticed.

In *Picturegoer Weekly*, a magazine for film fans, one columnist wrote:

> A number of readers have written me complaining that although Mr Trevor's acting in the part leaves nothing to be desired, he is emphatically nothing like Poirot as described in Mrs Christie's novels. I am a great Poirot 'fan' and the moment I heard that Trevor was going to impersonate him on the films I realised that it was bad casting. The detective is described by the authoress as an elderly man, with an egg-shaped head and bristling moustache. Austin Trevor is a very good-looking young man and clean shaven into the bargain. By a coincidence I happened to run into him in the street this week, and I put the matter to him. Trevor admitted that he was unlike Mrs Christie's conception of Hercule, but blamed the powers-that-be for giving him the part. He thinks it is because some years ago he happened to play a Frenchman in a picture.[13]

Many years later, in a 1965 interview for *Tatler and Bystander*, Trevor recalled that 'I was playing Captain Lutte in Noël Coward's *Bitter Sweet* at His Majesty's Theatre and they thought I was good at French accents. That seemed sufficient reason for playing Poirot and nobody even bothered to make me up.'

As with the stage production, the *Alibi* film will have suffered from the issue that the story's famous twist was not preserved for this medium. Any distinctiveness of *The Murder of Roger Ackroyd* was completely lost by the time it had been translated first to stage and then to screen. We don't know if Christie ever saw the film, but if she did then it made no lasting impression – in a letter written four decades later Christie mentioned the changes made by Morton for the

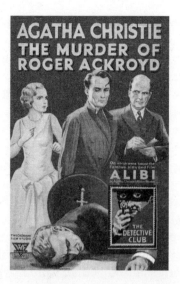

Collins' film tie-in edition for *Alibi*, published in their Detective Club imprint in 1931.

stage production, but also said that she was unaware of any film version.[14]

The appearance of *Black Coffee* on film also resulted in the screen debuts of the characters of Inspector Japp (here played by Melville Cooper) and Hastings (Richard Cooper), but it's curious that the critical reception indicates that some were already fed up with Poirot films. Some critics believed that there had already been a series of Poirot film mysteries, even though this was only the second Poirot picture – perhaps an indication that they felt rather generic. *Variety* was a little warmer in its reception this time, calling it the 'sort of film which is never less than interesting but never much more so … It's not by any means a great film, but it's the sort of stuff which will go quite well here … Sort of quota footage which doesn't let the theatre down. Within its scope quite acceptable.'[15] *Picturegoer Weekly* was more damning, writing

The poster for the French version of *Black Coffee*, *Le Coffret de Laque* (1932).

that 'This picturisation of Agatha Christie's stage success is too slow to grip the attention and is certainly not up to the level of the other Poirot stories we have had.'[16]

A year after the release of *Black Coffee*, the story made another appearance on screen. This time, however, the film was a French production, filmed at the Haik studios in Paris and starring members of the esteemed theatrical troupe Comédie-Française, including René Alexandre who played 'Preval', who may have been this film's version of Poirot. Once again no print of the film is known to survive, but the film's posters were a horror-tinged painting that showed a mysterious disembodied hand reaching for a box in an image that reflects the new name for the mystery, *Le Coffret de Laque* (*The Lacquered Box*). Judging by the contemporary *Variety* review the film featured comedy, including a 'gentlemanly idiot' and a cast with a tendency to overact. While considered to be entertaining, the reviewer also despaired at 'the childish transparency of it all'.[17]

There was a gap of three years between *Black Coffee* and the third and final appearance of Austin Trevor's Poirot on screen, in the first adaptation of a novel rather than stage play, and the only one of these early Poirot films known to survive. The novel in question was 1933's *Lord Edgware Dies* (more of which shortly), a highly visual puzzle that would seem to be both timely and suitable for the medium of film. It's therefore a bit of a shock that a story that so heavily focuses on appearances and related subterfuge should be told in such a bizarrely low-key manner on screen. Crucial events - such as the dinner party where a murder suspect has the seemingly perfect alibi - are discussed in conversation rather than being shown, which makes the film feel like a radio production being played out on screen. It's certainly a story told out of apparent necessity (whether driven by finances or quotas) rather than any passion for the mystery, nor even any particular interest in the clever mechanics of this sophisticated tale. Not unreasonably, Trevor's Poirot seems a little bored by the proceedings, while Richard Cooper's Hastings makes great play of the comedy 'silly ass' role so common in films of the period. Inspector Japp also returns, but is this time played by a blustering John Turnbull. Director Henry Edwards makes no real effort to inject the proceedings with any tension, and although the story is largely unaltered from the novel, it's an unexciting screen treatment. No doubt this was due in part to the low budget, rushed production, and short running time of approximately 75 minutes – all typical elements of the 'quota quickie'. While the *Monthly Film Bulletin* considered it to be 'Quite good entertainment', *Picturegoer Weekly* was more dismissive, describing it as a 'Workmanlike detective yarn ... Too much dialogue and a tendency to slowness rob the picture of a lot of legitimate suspense.'[18,19]

As the popularity of Christie and Poirot grew, so her agent Edmund Cork started to set his sights higher when it came to film adaptations of her work, as he looked to Hollywood for a potential new deal, something foreshadowed by a *Variety* review of *Death in the Clouds*, which informed its readers that 'The Poirot stories have been filmed successfully only once, in England. They should be made here'.[20] However, it would take several years for Christie to really make an international impact on film.

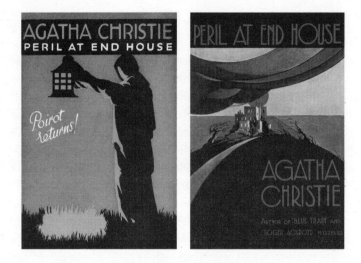

Peril at End House
(Novel, 1932)

Four years had passed since *The Mystery of the Blue Train* by the time Christie published her sixth Poirot novel, *Peril at End House*, and the reader may detect a definite lightening of the mood. While murder and betrayal are never far away in this tale concerning threats to the life of heiress Magdala 'Nick' Buckley, the mystery is played out in the holiday resort of St Loo in Cornwall, a thinly disguised version of Christie's own beloved Torquay in South Devon. Although there's a cruelly plotted death at the hands of our cleverly disguised murderer, there's none of the melancholy atmosphere that had pervaded the previous Poirot novel. With both the attractive setting and a hyperbolic title reminiscent

ABOVE LEFT: 'Poirot returns!' proclaimed Collins' first edition cover in 1932. **ABOVE RIGHT:** The first US jacket from 1932, published in Dodd, Mead's 'Red Badge Mystery' range.

of film serials that Christie had enjoyed, such as *The Perils of Pauline*, Christie almost seems to be overtly setting out the stall of this book as a first-class holiday read with an intricate, but not overcomplicated, puzzle at its core.

Certainly there is a sense that Christie has returned to the world of Poirot after a four-year publication gap both refreshed and happier – and Captain Hastings is back in the fold. Christie later remembered that 'quite early on I banished him to the Argentine, but I think he came back once...'[21] – in fact, Hastings would stay by Poirot's side for three more novels during this decade, with 1937's *Dumb Witness* then being his final appearance until the publication of *Curtain: Poirot's Last Case* in 1975.[22] Perhaps his reappearance also contributes to the sense of pleasant familiarity that the reader may feel from this particularly enjoyable mystery. While Poirot is still teasing his associate, perhaps rather unfairly referring to him as 'my old imbecile' while going on to reaffirm his claims of being the greatest detective that ever lived, there's a little more warmth between the two characters here than readers had previously encountered, although Hastings is suspicious of Poirot's positivity towards his friend's abilities: 'As a result of long habit, I distrust his compliments,' he informs us. It's certainly good to have someone we can trust and is somewhat likable amongst a cast of characters who are otherwise almost uniformly self-centred – from Nick's obnoxious friends to the suspicious Australian couple who have installed themselves near to her familial estate at End House. The embedded sense of entitlement to family riches and estates from certain characters is a recurring theme in Christie's novels, where hereditary windfalls can never be underestimated as motivation for

Poirot as depicted on the Italian edition in 1933.

murder. As inherited wealth is now viewed with more suspicion and certainly less reverence, some characters now read more negatively than Christie probably intended.

Peril at End House also marked the beginning of a period that saw the volume of new works from Christie reaching a peak, with a particular emphasis on Poirot, whose critical and popular success was only growing. The next seven years would see Poirot featuring in twelve novels as well as a collection of shorter stories, a play for radio, and a one-act play that premiered on television. The sheer quantity of work here would be remarkable enough in itself were it not for the fact that these novels also represent some of the very best mysteries ever written by Christie. Alongside these new adventures for Poirot, Christie also managed to present a character-based drama in the form of 1934's *Unfinished Portrait* (her second non-mystery novel to be published under the pseudonym of Mary Westmacott, following 1930's *Giant's Bread*), as well as the standalone mystery adventure novel *Why Didn't They Ask Evans?* (1934), while her publisher collated various short story collections. Just as her readers and critics might have expected the author to start to experience burnout she then topped off an exemplary decade with a masterpiece in the form of the detective-less *And Then There Were None* in 1939. Unlike her experience with *The Mystery of the Blue Train*, Christie now seemed happy to continue writing apace. She later downplayed this achievement, saying 'Oh, I'm an incredible sausage machine, a perfect sausage machine!' before admitting that her success in the mystery genre may have also created barriers: 'You are rather chained to it and nobody wants a book of any other kind from you.'[23]

Collins White Circle Crime Club paperbacks with their distinctive green covers added Agatha Christie's photo to some in the range (1958).

However, the books she was writing were far from formulaic. Although they sometimes expand on ideas Christie has used elsewhere, or would use again, each is presented in an intriguing and exciting way that only helped to cement Christie's growing reputation as the queen of crime.

Peril at End House was published in early 1932 as the first Poirot novel to form part of Collins' newly established imprint the Crime Club.[24] The British cover of the book, which moodily depicted a lantern being held aloft, reflected the still growing celebrity of Poirot - while *The Mystery of the Blue Train* had focused on Christie herself with the splash 'by the author of *The Murder of Roger Ackroyd*' on its cover, now Poirot was the focus: 'Poirot returns!' The emphasis on Poirot continued on the covers of the British first editions for the next few years, with similar claims ranging from 'Poirot solves...' to 'featuring Hercule Poirot' and even 'Agatha Christie's Greatest Poirot Story' for *Death in the Clouds*, which fared better than *Lord Edgware Dies*' slightly exasperated 'Poirot again!'

Critics expressed joy with the return of Poirot in *Peril at End House* and both the quality and entertainment value of the novel itself. *The Times Literary Supplement* wrote that 'The actual solution is quite unusually ingenious, and well up to the level of Mrs Christie's best stories. Everything is perfectly fair, and it is possible to guess the solution of the puzzle fairly early in the book, though it is certainly not easy... the plot is arranged with almost mathematical neatness, and that is all that one wants.'[25] *The Observer* considered it to be an 'uncommonly good story' in its introduction to the novel, before going on to explain that 'the reader will, at the end, wish he had not read it, because it cannot again give him the same fresh enjoyment'.[26] *The Church Times* once more highlighted Christie's particular skills, writing that Poirot is 'at the top of his form in *Peril at End House*; his little

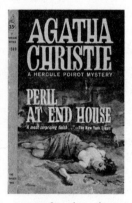

Fontana Books' 1961 paperback by John Rose.

...inspired perhaps by Cardinal's US edition by James Meese (1959).

grey cells are functioning as vigorously as ever, and he welcomes difficulties for the sheer joy of conquering them. Mrs Christie makes the utterly impossible entirely probable, and leaves us wondering how the trick is done'.[27] When a cheap paperback reprint of the novel was published in 1938, *The Observer* fairly described it as 'a particularly happy example of her special gift.'[28]

In a rare move, later in the decade Christie agreed a deal to allow the novel to be adapted for the stage by another writer, still featuring Poirot. Perhaps it was because of the quality of the personnel attached to the project – Arnold Ridley as the adapter (at the time best known for the stage success *The Ghost Train*) and the extensive involvement of Francis L. Sullivan who would play Poirot once more as well as handling many of the producer duties. The play premiered in Richmond on 1 April 1940, with Sullivan joined by Ian Fleming as Hastings, an actor who had also played the part of Dr Watson in a handful of early talkie Sherlock Holmes films alongside Arthur Wontner as the great detective – in fact, *The Manchester Guardian*'s review even called his portrayal of Hastings 'unmistakably our old friend Dr Watson, hardly at all disguised'.[29] Sullivan took charge of the production, even putting some noses out of joint with his advanced plans, including for a New York run that never materialised. The contract had been arranged so that Sullivan would have had one-third rights of any film sale, indicating that he had considerable leverage with Christie.

Ridley's script presented the mystery in a thoughtful

Francis L. Sullivan reprised the role of Poirot again in 1940.

manner, opening at the Majestic Hotel before moving to
End House itself for the remainder of the play. The adaptation makes clever use of a potential case of mistaken identity for the murder, designed for maximum impact on an
unwary audience. Reviews were generally positive, often
focusing on Sullivan, with *The Observer* concluding that
the events on stage 'provide appropriate entertainment on
modest, old fashioned lines.'[30] *The Manchester Guardian* wondered if all audiences would follow what it considered to be
a complicated story, but commended the production on its
own terms, before rather unfairly revealing the identity of
the villain, while *The Times* wondered if the production was
rather too heavily reliant on dialogue. Despite this reasonably warm reception the play was not to have a great future,
and would quietly disappear when it closed after little more
than six weeks.

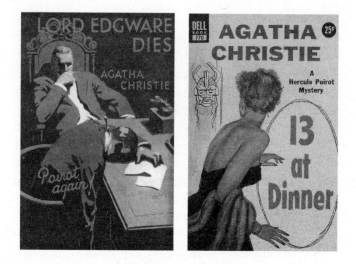

Lord Edgware Dies
(Novel, 1933)

'Lovely weather still. I do enjoy the bathing. I've got on well with work,' Christie wrote to her new husband in October 1930, while she was on holiday in Rhodes. Without skipping a beat, she then turned to more bloodthirsty matters: 'Lord Edgware is dead all right, and a second tragedy has now occurred ... Poirot is being most mysterious and Hastings unbelievably asinine.'[31] So Christie outlined the status of her new Poirot novel, *Lord Edgware Dies*, which would be given the equally prosaic but more evocative title *Thirteen at Dinner* for its American publication (a rare occasion where

ABOVE LEFT: The UK first edition cover for *Lord Edgware Dies*, illustrated by Alfred Lambart (1933). **ABOVE RIGHT:** Rejecting its aristocratic title, the publishers retitled the book *13 at Dinner* for the US market. Griffith Foxley provided the cover for the 1954 Dell paperback.

the name under which her mystery was sold Stateside arguably works rather better than the British one).

Lord Edgware Dies opens with a minor mystery, which Christie cleverly establishes in a nonchalant manner that underplays its later significance. Initially, Poirot is asked by Lady Edgware, a.k.a. the actor Jane Wilkinson, to act as an intermediary on her behalf as she seeks her divorce from Lord Edgware, who is refusing to respond to her request. However, when Poirot speaks to Lord Edgware he learns that the English peer has received his wife's letter and responded in the affirmative, and so a divorce will be no problem. Jane Wilkinson is delighted to hear this, but the missing response troubles Poirot, especially when Lord Edgware is soon found dead, having been stabbed in the neck.

What conclusions are the reader to draw from the situation so far? We later learn that much of the murderer's plotting occurred to the character while the early events of the novel took place, and certainly the reader is presented with enough people, ideas and alibis that they could conceivably plot the murder in the same way. This initial meeting between Poirot and Jane Wilkinson takes place at a performance by the impressionist Carlotta Adams, based on real-life performer Ruth Draper who had showcased similar skills in a successful stage career. Christie even refers to the character with Draper's name in parentheses when Adams is mentioned in further correspondence, and readers of *Lord Edgware Dies* will likely soon realise that the impressionist sparked not only the creation of a character, but also some of the mechanics of the mystery. Where the book really shines is in the way that it makes a reasonably straightforward ruse seem

Poirot as imagined by Weldon Trench from the story's *American Magazine* serialisation (1933).

impossibly difficult to untangle, until some important clues, such as a discussion of the judgement of Paris, catch the eye.

Lord Edgware Dies fizzes with energy, as a reinvigorated Christie wrote the story on her travels while deeply in love. In her correspondence she attaches no stress to its creation, just a workmanlike attitude to churning out the words, but she had clearly been struck by a substantial bolt of inspiration. Writing to Max, she said that she felt the book was turning out to be:

> a very popular mixture, I think. Just a bit cheap, perhaps. No love in this letter, darling. Because, you see, I must keep my mind on what the wicked nephew does next. And when I've written to you I find myself thinking of things I'd say to you and you to me, instead of what the new Lord E. says to Poirot.[32]

There's a lightness of touch to Christie's characterisation in the book, as she weaves the path of the story through

an array of society figures from both sides of the Atlantic, with the inevitable baggage that their different backgrounds bring. When we meet Jane Wilkinson's new beau, the Duke of Merton, it doesn't require a modern eye to crack Christie's character code and wonder why she has taken such an interest in a man who seems to be gay. Hastings guides us through this complicated society view: 'I drew in my breath sharply. The Duke of Merton had so far been the despair of matchmaking mammas. A young man of monkish tendencies, a violent Anglo-Catholic, he was reported to be completely under the thumb of his mother, the redoubtable dowager duchess. His life was austere in the

Coverage for the story in *The Enquirer* (1934).

Dell's 1944 'mapback' edition was illustrated by Gerald Gregg.

extreme. He collected Chinese porcelain and was reputed to be of aesthetic tastes. He was supposed to care nothing for women.' Amusingly, *The Church Times* (always one of the most entertaining reviewers of Christie's work) also noted the description. 'Of course, all Anglo-Catholics, violent or not, are under the thumbs of their mother, their grandmother, or the curate,' wrote the periodical's pithy diarist.[33]

Following the book's publication in September 1933, *The Observer* considered it to be 'one of Hercule's finest efforts ... There are no headaches in *Lord Edgware Dies*. The book is clearness itself, and its remarkable ingenuities leave the reader thrilled, but not jaded.'[34] *The Times Literary Supplement* drew attention to the characters, writing: 'The large number of suspects – some of them actors and one a trained impersonator – adds to his difficulties and our enjoyment.'[35] Similarly, it was the characterisation that caught the eye of *The Yorkshire Post*. 'It is a little heartless of Mrs Christie

Britain's Queen of Crime

LORD EDGWARE DIES

Agatha Christie

fontana books 2'6

This 1958 Fontana paperback reused a painting commissioned for a hardback reprint in 1953.

to let us develop a certain affection for two of the victims, the murderees [sic] of fiction are usually more impersonal,' its reviewer wrote. 'On the other hand, it helps destroy sympathy for the murderer – who in this case has undoubted charm, and is not allowed to commit suicide in the normal manner on being discovered... the super subtle alibi upon which the plot turns seems to be beyond the imaginative powers of the person who designs it. It is certainly too much for the average reader, but he will enjoy himself tremendously making five wrong guesses.'[36]

While much of *Lord Edgware Dies* is ingenious, it lacks the iconography to make it one of the more famous Christie mysteries in the eyes of the general public. For this, Christie would usually need to merge plot and place in a perfect confection (which itself makes these stories ripe for the screen adaptations that help to make her mysteries endure). Her most famous novels achieve this through, for example, a series of murders on a mysterious isolated island, which continue until none remain. Or...

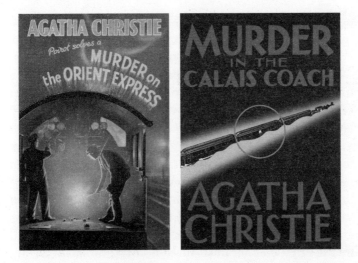

Murder on the Orient Express
(Novel, 1934)

'But everyone knows the solution!' comes the chorus cry among fans whenever *Murder on the Orient Express* finds a new lease of life through the likes of another adaptation or republication. For those who have enjoyed the resolution of probably Christie's most famous mystery and found it to be unforgettable this is an understandable reaction given that the final act of the novel is referenced endlessly in many forms, from books to serious movies to sitcoms. And yet, readers continue to discover (and be surprised by) one of the most famous literary endings of all time. As long as new

ABOVE LEFT: The first edition jacket for *Murder on the Orient Express* by an unknown artist (1934). **ABOVE RIGHT:** Changed to *Murder in the Calais Coach* for the American market, the 1934 Dodd, Mead jacket highlighted the eponymous sleeping car.

people become interested in detective fiction, there will be fresh audiences waiting to discover the genius that lies at the heart of *Murder on the Orient Express*.

There were two particular influences on the novel. The first was the mode of transport itself – 'Trains have always been one of my favourite things,' wrote Christie in her auto-biography.[37] 'All my life I had wanted to go on the Orient Express. When I had travelled to France or Spain or Italy, the Orient Express had often been standing at Calais, and I had longed to climb up into it ... I was bitten.'[38] The first time Christie was able to make a journey on the Orient Express was in 1928, on her debut trip to Ur in Iraq. It was during her second visit (this time travelled mostly by sea) that she first met her husband-to-be, Max, and it seems that

The book had the honour of being the very first in the Collins' White Circle Crime Club paperback range in March 1936, with its generic black and green cover design. The series would eventually run to more than 300 titles.

the romanticism of the train and their meeting merged somewhat in her mind, and she returned to the Orient Express for part of her honeymoon – although her memories of this journey included less than romantic fellow guests in the form of bed bugs.[39] When Christie travelled on the Orient Express again in late 1931, this time alone, she wrote a lengthy letter to her husband outlining the people she had met on board. This cast of characters were often described in less than favourable terms, and it's no great leap to see this as the genesis of serious thought about a novel set on the train. She also used the journeys to ensure the complete accuracy of the story she had plotted. Regarding a later trip she said, 'I was able to check on the way back what I'd been thinking about on the way out. I had to see where all the switches were. One man took the journey especially after he read it.'[40]

The first Pocket Books edition from 1940 by H. Lawrence Hoffman.

The second key influence regards the plot, in which an odious passenger on the Orient Express is murdered during a snowdrift, indicating that the murderer must be one of the staff or passengers. We soon learn that the murdered man, Ratchett, was not all that he seemed, as he appears to have had close links with an infamous abduction and murder of three-year-old Daisy Armstrong from her wealthy family. The reader doesn't need to be particularly

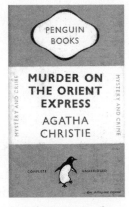

A green Penguin edition was released in 1948 with Edward Young's famous cover design.

well-informed to make the connection between this and 1932's real-life kidnap and murder of the child of wealthy and famous aviator Charles Lindbergh, which had been a sensation for newspapers around the globe. Even unpleasant details such as the resultant suicide of a servant are

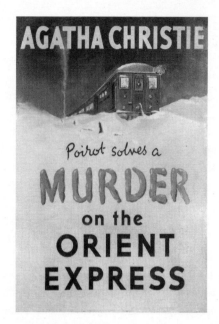

The jacket for Collins 1953 hardcover reissue of *Murder on the Orient Express* was uncredited.

preserved in this barely disguised retelling (a European nursemaid jumps from a window in Christie's reworking, but in reality a housemaid killed herself by drinking silver polish to avoid further heavy-handed questioning from the police). Christie doesn't present her version of these events as the central mystery, but offers it up as the potential motivation for whoever murdered the man responsible. It also provides a shorthand understanding between the author and the reader about the severity of the past crime that is alluded to.

Perhaps the best testament to the quality of *Murder on the Orient Express* is the fact that it spent nearly forty years being celebrated by casual readers and aficionados alike before it was exploited in a form that could introduce the famous

Eileen Walton's striking 1959 artwork for the book was copied for an early Greek edition.

story to an even wider public – in this case, the 1974 film starring Albert Finney. Unlike 1939's *And Then There Were None*, which Christie reworked as a play to great success, despite showing some willing she did not translate *Murder on the Orient Express* to the stage, although even by the late 1940s she was still considering the possibility of writing a play version that would have started with the child's kidnapping in New York and wouldn't have been presented in the conventional whodunnit mould.[41] While the play of *And Then There Were None* was then in turn repeatedly adapted for cinema and television screens, and her 1952 West End play *The Mousetrap* constantly reappeared in the press while an endless parade of anniversaries were celebrated, *Murder on the Orient Express* simply sat quietly on the bookshelves of libraries, shops and homes, drawing in readers through word of mouth and consistent critical acclaim.[42] It may be considered to be the purest example of Christie's popular and critical success, and in a rare filmed interview in the 1960s Christie declared – after some prevarication ('Oh dear

AGATHA CHRISTIE
Murder on the Orient Express

FONTANA BOOKS

The Fontana paperback of 1964 with an early Tom Adams cover.

that's a tall order!') – that it was probably the best Poirot book.

Nevertheless, despite its fame and the adulation that accompanies it, *Murder on the Orient Express* is not a book that can be particularly recommended to new readers of Christie's work. It's a first-rate puzzle, but the novel lacks the fluidity and pace of other mysteries that make for a more accessible first experience of Agatha Christie. This is because the book's structure shows how Christie's dominant interest at this point was in exposing the pure mechanics of the mystery to the reader in order to dare them to work out the solution for themselves – here performed by an episodic interviewing of the key suspects, who provide all the clues and evidence needed to solve the crime. This makes the novel something of a disjointed experience at times, with a cast of characters (and suspects) who seem to be deliberately archetypal in order to make them memorable and distinct from each other, as we follow Poirot questioning them in turn. Christie would soon push this principle of emphasising the puzzle over plot even further in the 1936 Poirot novel *Cards on the Table*.

As a writer of mysteries Christie had found a winning formula early in her career, but was not happy to rest on her laurels – she continued to challenge herself and her readers. A close analysis of the overlapping alibis and various witness statements will lead all involved to the incredible, but only possible, explanation of the murder. While Poirot also suggests a more palatable alternative solution, both he and Christie know that it would not withstand the scrutiny of her readers, even if it may satisfy the police.

Murder on the Orient Express was published in the UK in January 1934, and a month later in the United States under the title *Murder in the Calais Coach* in order to distinguish it from Graham Greene's novel, *Orient Express*. Reviews were positive once more: 'Mrs Christie makes an improbable tale very real, and keeps her readers enthralled and guessing to the end,' said *The Times Literary Supplement*, for example.[43] *The Manchester Guardian* sounded a note of caution, however: 'The "little grey cells" work admirably, and the solution surprised their owner as much as it may well surprise the reader, for the secret is well kept and the manner of the telling is in Mrs Christie's usual admirable manner. But

The 1965 Pocket Books paperback.

at the end of it one feels that M. Poirot was just too easily omniscient.'[44] The line between a detective's apparent omniscience and underlying skill may be a blurred one, but there is no doubt that Christie plays fair here, as anyone who re-reads the book with the solution in mind will know. The author must have struggled to fathom that people would continue to read her books afresh for some time after initial publication, because she gives away the solution to this mystery in a passing conversation in *Cards on the Table* two years later. It seems incredible now to realise that one of the most enduring writers of all time considered their work to be at least ephemeral, if not disposable – when it has proven to be anything but.

Three Act Tragedy
(Novel, 1935)

When the actor Sir Charles Cartwright hosts a dinner party at his Cornish home, Crow's Nest, the guests are shocked when a seemingly senseless fatal poisoning takes place. When most of the guests meet again some time later, it should come as no surprise to the reader that another murder is not far away. So far, this is all as expected in a Christie murder mystery – but, whether wittingly or not, *Three Act Tragedy* is an Agatha Christie novel that actually puts her regular readers at a disadvantage. Those who have followed Christie's mysteries may find that their expectation of wholly methodical and logical approaches by the culprit will not necessarily

ABOVE LEFT: *Three Act Tragedy* was the first Agatha Christie novel to debut in the UK with a photographic jacket. **ABOVE RIGHT:** Dodd, Mead's 1934 jacket by R. B. Haberstock with its US title, *Murder in Three Acts.*

be shared by the villain of this particular story, for whom there may be other motivations. However, Christie herself never loses focus on a rationale for murder that will even shock Poirot at the mystery's conclusion.

As the title indicates, the theatrical world plays a significant part in the structure of this story, a novel that also displays the growing fascination with the significance of characters' psychology. The book is initially laid out like a theatre programme, in which Poirot is credited with 'Illumination', and there's even a different name for each 'act' ('Suspicion', 'Certainty' and 'Discovery'). Christie seems to be having a great time playing with these theatrical devices in literature, while keeping a key secret or two hidden and providing plenty of entertainment in the form of the charming Sir Charles and one of her own favourite characters, Mr Satterthwaite. Satterthwaite had formerly accompanied the enigmatic Mr Quin in a series of short mysteries, most of which were collected as *The Mysterious Mr Quin* in 1930. While Quin was as unknowable as the collection's title suggested, Satterthwaite was more firmly grounded in the real world, and although we are told that he already knows Poirot this is a rare pairing. Much of the book focuses on Satterthwaite and Cartwright, indicating that Christie was happy to let Poirot play second fiddle on this occasion as she appeared to continue to lose interest in him as a character.[45] While he may not be the focus of the story, Poirot gets some good moments as he provides an incredible solution through deduction and investigation. At the very end of the novel Christie allows

Poirot was depicted on a series of early Danish covers, including this one from 1938.

An early American paperback cover from Avon (1951)

Poirot to make the reader laugh, but it isn't clear whether he's in on the egocentric joke himself.

Psychology and structure go hand in hand in *Three Act Tragedy*, which shows exemplary planning on the part of Christie. Asked about her methods later, Christie said:

> Usually you think first of the basic design – you know, 'That would be an awfully good double-cross or trick.' You start with the wish to deceive, and then work backwards. I begin with a fairly complete diagram, though small things may change in the writing, of course. One's always a little self-conscious over the murderer's first appearance. He must never come in too late; that's uninteresting for the reader at the end of the book. And the denouement has to be worked out frightfully carefully. The further it comes towards the end, the better. That's even more important in a play, where an anti-climax ruins everything.[46]

In the earliest planning stages Christie gave the story the title *The Manor House Mystery*, but this wasn't retained beyond her notebooks. When it was published in the United States in 1934 it bore the title *Murder in Three Acts*, and while it wasn't unusual for Christie's novels to be available in America before the UK (where it saw print in January 1935), nor for titles to be amended for a different market, the changes on this occasion were more substantial. Although the identity of the murderer remains the same in both versions of the novel, the character's motivation is substantially different (although with a similar broad basis). This required each version to rework some key moments at points prior to the denouement, and even dispense with (or

Fontana UK's 1957 paperback cover.

add) some sections to shore up the motivation and give the reader a fair chance to work it out. Several decades after publication of the book Christie discussed it in correspondence with her agent, in which she mentioned that she thought the ending as published in the United States was probably the original. In the 1930s Christie wrote her books quite some time ahead of their publication as novels and so the different publication dates of the two editions can give us no real clue to the timing of the (re)writing, but on the balance of probabilities her recollection seems unlikely although not

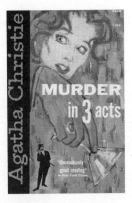

Another Avon cover, this one from 1958.

impossible (bearing in mind that, like most of us, Christie frequently misremembered events, especially later in her life – she would have been over 80 when writing this letter). The American ending hinges on a question of identification as motivation for murder, one which can be universally true. However, the motivation in the British edition is the result of a detail of English law; it's understandable why this could be changed for international markets, but not vice-versa. Nevertheless, we can't be completely sure.

In *The Manchester Guardian*, the reviewer heaped praise on the novel, claiming that 'Mrs Christie's *Three Act Tragedy* is up to her best level ... the mechanics are ingenious and plausible, the characters (as always with Mrs Christie) are life-like and interesting.'[47] *The Times Literary Supplement's* reviewer suggested that 'Very few readers will guess the murderer before M. Hercule Poirot reveals the secret', although they then went on to question the murderer's methodology.[48] Such concerns were also hinted at in the *Daily Mirror*, which concisely informed its readers that 'You may not believe in it all, but you *must* enjoy it.'[49]

Death in the Clouds
(Novel, 1935)

If some Christie novels struggle to claim a position in the top tier of her mysteries because they lack the strong imagery that can cement a story in the reader's memory, then *Death in the Clouds* might be seen to suffer from the opposite problem. The iconography is undeniably striking – for most readers of the time a journey by plane would be an exciting venture, as well as an unusual setting for the murder of a wealthy woman who appears to have been killed by a poison dart from a blowpipe. And yet, how might this crime have been achieved without arousing suspicion, and what's the significance of a wasp in the cabin that seems to

ABOVE LEFT: UK first edition jacket for *Death in the Clouds* (1935).
ABOVE RIGHT: Pocket Books' 1951 paperback, with the US title *Death in the Air*, exaggerated somewhat with the proclamation 'Brutality and murder strike aboard a giant airliner!'

From the author's notebooks, one of numerous sketches showing her meticulously working out the seating plan to make the story work.

have attracted more than its fair share of attention? The aeroplane, blow dart and wasp present some strong visuals for the imagination, which has been taken advantage of by various cover artists over the years. Most notable is Tom Adams' memorable depiction of a giant wasp attacking the aeroplane for the cover of a Fontana paperback reprint, which inspired the 2008 Agatha Christie themed episode of *Doctor Who*, 'The Unicorn and the Wasp'.

It's therefore something of a shame that the promising claustrophobia of the first chapter gives way very quickly to a rather mundane investigation into murder. The intriguing nature of the murder helps to maintain the interest, as does the brief but amusing possibility that Poirot himself may be under suspicion for the crime, but the detection in the bulk of the book is conventional and unexciting, before the novel neatly ties up all of its loose ends with a solution that hinges on a principle that Christie had already used very recently. There are two potential reasons for the decision to frontload the story with the drama of the plane journey which is then passed over so quickly, with the murder occurring at the end of the first chapter – one philosophical, and the other pragmatic. On one hand, it simply may be that Christie wanted the reader to experience the journey in much the same way as Poirot – that is to say, without us being able to spot immediately both the crime and culprit, and so we learn much of the detail of the flight only in retrospect through interviews and discussions. Alternatively, the incomplete correspondence from this era shows a heavy emphasis on discussions of sales of her stories to magazines and newspapers for serialisation. This was no trifling matter as such sales usually were worth much more in financial terms than the advances for her books, generally making them Christie's most substantial revenue stream at this time. Commissioning editors from potential publications would read Christie's new manuscripts with an eye on them being published over the course of several issues (six in this case) prior to their appearance as a novel, and the most common reason for rejection was that Christie's books sometimes took too long to reach the murder or another key dramatic incident. For some periodicals it was essential that this should happen early in order to hook the reader and keep them coming back for the remaining instalments. Understandably, Christie sometimes bristled at the idea that she should write her mysteries with a primary eye on serialisation, but at around

'Hercule Poirot in top form' in this 1957 Fontana artwork.

this time her agent Edmund Cork was working to convince her that it would be economically advantageous to at least keep this in mind when plotting her books. This might be an example of Christie seeing this structure as an easy way to satisfy such demands.

First published as a novel in the United States under the title *Death in the Air* in March 1935, the British publication four months later resulted in some interesting commentary in *The Observer* from 'Torquemada', a pseudonym for the newspaper's cryptic crossword setter and mystery book reviewer, Edward Powys Mathers. The review opened with his positive thoughts on the book overall: 'My admiration for Mrs Christie is such that with each new book of hers I strain every mental nerve to prove that she has failed, at last, to hypnotise me. On finishing *Death in the Clouds* I found that she had succeeded even more triumphantly than usual.' Mathers then highlighted two particular areas of interest, one in terms of structure, the other relating to characters. A keen commentator on her work, Mathers indicated how contemporary readers might notice ongoing developments in the style of Christie, never one to rest on her laurels. 'Agatha Christie has recently developed two further tricks,' he wrote, 'one is, as of the juggler who keeps on almost dropping things, to leave a clue hanging out for several chapters, apparently unremarked by her little detective though seized on by us, and then to tuck it back again as unimportant.' Here, he seems to be referring to actions concerning a broken fingernail that receives nearly a page of attention early in proceedings. More interesting is Mathers' second point, which highlights Christie's growing interest in character psychology as not only motivation, but also a

Another airliner in John Rose's art for the 1961 Fontana cover.

The Pan cover from 1964 by W. Francis Phillips.

clue as she offers the reader 'some, but by no means all, of the hidden thoughts of her characters.' Mathers was not impressed with the development, however, seeming to prefer the more matter-of-fact discovery of clues, as he wrote that 'We readers must guard against these new dexterities.'[50]

Despite these concerns, the basis of the mystery and its solution is strong, and Christie's notebooks show her meticulous planning, which revolved around her plan to disguise the murderous act itself, which echoes her previous Poirot novel and would be seen again later in the decade. Part of this planning meant the design of a seating plan ('I sometimes have diagrams, if things depend on alibis and places,' she explained) that may or may not be relevant to solving the case.[51] It's also interesting that, fifteen years after his debut in *The Mysterious Affair at Styles*, Mathers in *The Observer* started to ask gentle questions about Poirot's age. Perhaps this is a side effect of the detective being placed in surroundings of such modernity as a passenger plane, but Mathers is not too concerned, drawing parallels with Cleopatra, alluding to Shakespeare's description that 'Age cannot wither her, nor custom stale'. Our resident police representative seems to be more problematic, however: 'might not Inspector Japp be allowed to mellow a little, with the years, beyond the moron stage?'[52] The return of Japp with such little development in his character may be due to the interchangeable nature of many of the members of the police force we meet over the years. 'Very often you want to look up a police inspector you have used before to see if he will fit into something you are doing,' Christie later said, 'it is better than creating somebody new and different.'[53]

Agatha Christie
Death in the Clouds

Painted in 1969, Tom Adams' iconic 'giant wasp' artwork with its forced perspective adorned the Fontana paperback throughout the 1970s and left a lasting impression...

At this stage of her career the momentum of Christie's mystery writing was, incredibly, continuing to build from a significant popular base. The striking location, intriguing core mystery and visual details means that *Death in the Clouds* lingers in the memory for longer than its mediocre middle chapters might deserve, but the author was continuing to deliver well-thought-out and highly satisfying murder mysteries at an extraordinary pace. Perhaps the time was right for Poirot's fame to be dealt with more explicitly in the novels, as he next found himself on the trail of a serial killer who is taunting the esteemed Belgian detective.

The ABC Murders
(Novel, 1936)

Few stories can provide a 'hook' that is as strong as *The ABC Murders'* tale of a serial killer working their way through the alphabet to select their victims, who seem to be otherwise unrelated. The inherent appeal is twofold – the impression of a cold-blooded, systematic killer working to their own rules is a chillingly mesmeric one, while many readers might also pause to work out who among their friends and family may have been at risk from an otherwise random attack. An Emily Ellis of Eastbourne, for example, would do well to cross her fingers and hope that the culprit is apprehended before their fifth murder.

ABOVE LEFT: The UK first edition cover showing the ABC Railway Guide. **ABOVE RIGHT:** The first US edition from Dodd, Mead had a more sinister-looking jacket (1936).

The *ABC Murders* doesn't rely on a coincidental appearance of Poirot when a murder happens to be committed – instead, he's directly taunted by an unknown killer who sends him letters signed 'ABC'. These letters, sent to his flat at Whitehaven Mansions, appear to forewarn Poirot about forthcoming murders, which take place in alphabetical order, with the first letter of the town matching the first letter of the victim's name, while the bodies are accompanied by an ABC railway guide.[54] This direct solicitation of Poirot marks him out as a detective of some repute, as his involvement indicates either considerable arrogance on the part of the killer, or that the Belgian sleuth is expected to play a key

The Railway Guide also appeared on the 1944 Pocket Books edition in America.

role in events in a way that will only benefit the person carrying out the attacks. By the time we reach the third victim, Sir Carmichael Clarke of Churston, Poirot is actively working with newly promoted Chief Inspector Japp and his companion Hastings to try to avoid a fourth murder, expected to occur in Doncaster at a popular horse racing event.[55]

Hastings returns to the role of narrator for this book, but several key chapters are written in the third person. In the foreword, Hastings explains that 'In this narrative of mine I have departed from my usual practice of relating only those incidents and scenes at which I myself was present.' Pre-empting objections, Christie had Hastings clarify that 'I wish to assure my readers that I can vouch for the occurrences related in these chapters. If I have taken a certain poetic licence in describing the thoughts and feelings of various persons, it is because I believe I have set them down with a reasonable amount of accuracy.' Despite these assurances, this approach doesn't always convince and shows the constraints that Hastings' presence placed upon Christie.

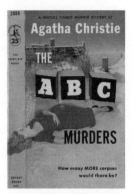

The 1955 Pocket Books cover used a photograph as its main image.

In a narrative masterstroke, these third-person chapters show us the apparent villain of the piece, Alexander Bonaparte Cust (note his initials), as he mulls over his ill health and personal difficulties, always in tandem with the ABC murders. However, if we're to believe that Hastings wrote these sections himself then the artistic licence has been considerable, as he offers insight into Cust's thinking throughout, even to the extent of quotations that come into his head and the specifics of his mannerisms at any given point. Christie is wanting to have her cake and eat it when it comes to Hastings' involvement, and so it's probably for the best that he would soon be sent back to the Argentine.

Nevertheless, the fact that our probable murderer is revealed so early suggests a richly structured tale, as this is only one layer of the story. 'How admirable is Agatha Christie in this,' wrote *The Yorkshire Post*'s reviewer. 'Simpleton that I am, it was not till I was two-thirds of the way through that I began to suspect that there was more in her plot than met the eye.'[56] Certainly there is much more for Poirot to discover, including motivation that echoes one of her most recent novels, and Poirot seems to engage with this particular puzzle with more interest than some of his other cases. Psychology is important once more, but this time our murderer has made even better use of it than Poirot.

Following abridged serialisations, *The ABC Murders* was published as a novel in early 1936 to great commercial success, which would be fortuitous timing as it coincided with the latest renegotiations with her American publishers, Dodd, Mead & Co. An offer of $4,000 per book was made (equivalent to around $75,000 now), but the strong sales for this novel enabled Christie's American agent, Harold

Ober, to ask for a full $1,000 more.[57,58] In May 1936, Christie's British agent Edmund Cork was pushing for her usual £850 advance from Collins in the UK to be increased, as well as an increase of royalties to as high as 25%: he wrote to the author that he thought her works would soon be worth an advance in excess of £1,000 each, the equivalent of nearly £70,000 now.[59] By this time Christie actually had several novels in hand, but a savvy Cork told Collins that Christie didn't like to commit to as much as five books. Eventually Collins agreed to increase her advance over the course of the next few publications, creeping closer to the unprecedented £1,000 per title. However, it wasn't just the commercial success that continued, as critical response was positive once more. *The Manchester Guardian*'s reviewer wrote that

Jack Keay's sinister cover illustration for Pan Books (1958).

'In the smooth and apparently effortless perfection with which she achieves her ends Mrs Christie reminds one of Noël Coward; she might, indeed, in that respect be called the Noël Coward of the detective novel.'[60] *The Yorkshire Post* made the fair point that the mystery's red herrings (especially in terms of its structure) meant that the reader may underestimate the cleverness of the book for most of its length: 'If Mrs. Christie's new novel has a defect it is that only in retrospect can one appreciate all the implications of the course of events and the line of investigation. But one lays the book down with a feeling of satisfaction that is indeed rare.'[61] Meanwhile, *The Times Literary Supplement* sounded a note of caution for detectives everywhere – 'If Mrs Christie ever deserts fiction for crime, she will be very dangerous; no-one but Poirot will catch her.'[62]

The dramatic potential of the mystery was immediately recognised, but the story struggled to be successfully adapted in any meaningful way until the Poirot television series starring David Suchet over half a century later. In 1943 it was the basis of an American radio play as part of the well-known *Suspense* series, although it removed Poirot in favour of an emphasis on Cust, who was played by ex-stage Poirot Charles Laughton. The production is a suspenseful and fast-paced half hour that happily translates Christie's core idea to a new medium. There was the potential for the story to make a greater impact on the big screen, however. After about a year of negotiations regarding film adaptations of Christie's works, January 1936 saw a flurry of correspondence about a potential movie of *The ABC Murders* as all was in place for MGM to sign up for an adaptation of the novel for a fee of $7,500, accompanied by options to make screen

Fontana's 1962 cover by John L. Baker also focused on the victim.

versions of *Murder on the Orient Express*, Miss Marple's novel debut *The Murder at the Vicarage*, and the standalone *The Sittaford Mystery* for the same price.[63] Edmund Cork acknowledged the difficulty of finding an actor to play Poirot, and that a single great success on film was needed to negotiate for more money, but confidence was high as the film was even mentioned in the pages of *Variety* as a forthcoming attraction.[64]

The ABC Murders was one of the first titles in HarperCollins' 1995 paperback relaunch.

There were two sticking points in the negotiations – the first was that MGM wished to be able to place Poirot in original stories of its own, and the second was that the film company wanted the freedom to introduce love interests for the detective. In an uncharacteristic move it seems that Christie relented somewhat on the first point, on the proviso that any original story could not be put into print (no doubt she was remembering the novelisation of the 1928 film *The Passing of Mr Quinn*, which featured Christie's name on the cover alongside the possibly pseudonymous G. Roy McRae, despite only being very loosely based on her original short story). However, she wouldn't agree with the possibility of Poirot having a love affair, and the deal stalled, with it being completely cancelled by May 1936. There was also a separate offer from British studio Oxford Films in October 1936, which went nowhere. In the end it would be more than two decades before MGM and Agatha Christie finally brokered a deal, which brought Margaret Rutherford's Miss Marple to the screen in the early 1960s. Poirot did not return to cinema screens until *The Alphabet Murders* (1965), an MGM comedy thriller very loosely based on *The ABC Murders*.

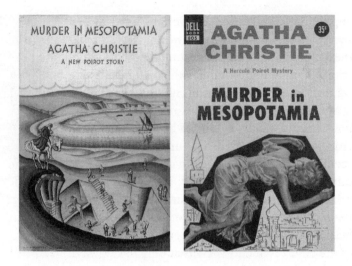

Murder in Mesopotamia
(Novel, 1936)

To what extent should the reader of a mystery novel be expected to suspend their disbelief? In particular, how important is it that the reader truly believes in the plausibility of the events and motives that lead to murder, and then the solving of the case? Without some suspension of disbelief we would find most fiction impossible – including the question of whether we may consider the character of Poirot to be wholly credible as a real person. This doesn't trouble most readers; we understand him, his character is reasonably consistent, we enjoy following his investigations, and that's quite enough for most. But when does a novel stop being credible

ABOVE LEFT: The UK first edition with an illustration by Robin Macartney (1936). **ABOVE RIGHT:** The 1954 American paperback cover by Griffith Foxley.

enough to be enjoyed? Most would probably agree that if we were abruptly told that, in the world of these characters from the 1930s, an anachronistic piece of technology has been invented that can provide the solution to the mystery, this would feel like a stretch too far for an Agatha Christie novel, even if it might be fair game for science fiction. By contrast, less problematic but undeniably far fetched is the recurring principle in Christie's mysteries that characters are seemingly too short sighted to notice amateur disguises and other visual tricks that would surely not convince outside of fiction. The reader, then, accepts some flawed elements of the narrative while rejecting others, because the reader has learned to trust the author through a mutual understanding of the rules of the universe that they have created. So, when Agatha Christie introduces a revelation at the end of *Murder*

The first of two 'mapback' designs for this title from Dell was this 1947 edition, with the front cover by George A. Frederiksen and the map art by Ruth Belew.

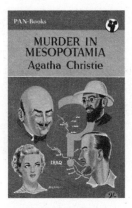

There were two Pan covers that feature Poirot himself, this one by Philip Wilding (1952).

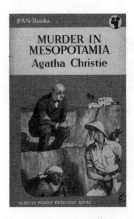

In 1953, Pan issued a second design by 'Sax'.

in Mesopotamia that's so outlandish that few readers can possibly believe it could happen in reality, does it undo all of the good groundwork that she has laid up to this point? Probably not, but it might present itself as a rare example of Christie eschewing logic to the extent that the reader will be left unhappy when the last page is turned.

Nevertheless, there's a welcome freshness to *Murder in Mesopotamia* that harks back to the early era of Christie's works. Poirot has returned to an archaeological dig, following his earlier trip in 'The Adventure of the Egyptian Tomb', as Christie was influenced and reinvigorated by her travels and work with her archaeologist husband. But more influential than this is our narrator, the thirty-two-year-old nurse Amy Leatheran, who in some respects feels like a more mature version of the type of heroine Christie had used in the likes of 1924's *The Man in the Brown Suit* and her other adventure novels that decade. By Leatheran's own admission she isn't an experienced writer, and the casual tone that Christie allows her to use in her writings make the novel feel modern and personal in a way that a third-person narrative – or one supplied by the likes of Captain Hastings, absent here – would struggle to deliver. Within the narrative, the nurse is writing a record of events in order to answer queries that have arisen since details of the case were made public – the case in question being the murder of Louise Leidner, wife to Dr Erich Leidner who is leading an archaeological dig in Mesopotamia. In a surprisingly rare instance of Christie adopting the 'impossible crime' form of mystery, Mrs Leidner has been found dead in a room that was under observation, having been struck with a blunt instrument. There are no cheats when it comes to the solution to this part of the story – Christie presents us with a perfectly fair and yet surprising explanation, even if it's almost inevitably somewhat reliant on good fortune on the part of the murderer.

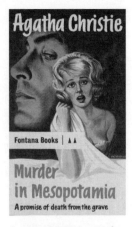

Fontana's 1962 cover by Jack Keay.

Not only did Christie draw on her general experiences for this novel, but she also created fictional characters based on real people, reflected in this book's dedication to her 'many archaeological friends in Iraq and Syria'. The most notable instance of this concerns the victim, who was clearly based on a woman with whom Christie had been friendly at the dig where she met Max, Katharine Woolley. Those who knew Woolley have painted her as a person who normally cared little for the company of women, preferring to surround herself with men who found her attractive and somewhat irresistible in terms of her demands. Her own marriage was a matter of convenience in order to allow her to remain on the dig when some funders were unhappy with her presence as a single woman, despite her archaeological skills. This marriage to Leonard Woolley, who was leading the excavation, solved the issue. There is no doubt that some of the subtleties of the relationship were excluded from the novel in order to make it suitable for more conservative readers of the time, as well as to avoid making too many explicit links between Katharine Woolley and Mrs Leidner. However, these real-life details would have helped to at least go some way towards explaining the novel's unsatisfactory denouement, as they would have helped to justify some of the crucial backstory that fails to convince.

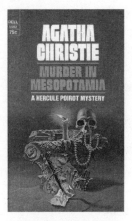

William Teason's 1973 cover for Dell.

Sherlock Holmes in Mesopotamia? Peter Cushing and André Morell intruding on to a 1979 German paperback.

There's enough incident and interest in the early portion of the novel that readers would be forgiven for forgetting that it has been sold to them as a Poirot mystery, but he's a welcome addition when he finally makes an appearance more than a third of the way through events. His absence didn't seem to worry readers or critics, with the book being even more commercially successful than its predecessor in some areas. Nevertheless, Christie was dismayed when she discovered that the British serialisation in the magazine *Woman's Pictorial* featured several changes, including the alteration of many character names and a change of title to the insipid *No Other Love*. The changes were spotted by her agent but only at a point where it was too late to demand they were reverted – knowing the likelihood of an angry reaction, he hoped that Christie would not find out what had happened. However, she did, and he was correct in his second guessing of her response.[65]

Published in the UK in July 1936, the critical reception reflected that there was much to enjoy in the novel, but that one key revelation left a trail of dissatisfaction in its wake. In its otherwise generous appraisal *The Times Literary Supplement* wondered how one character 'could have been so forgetful and unobservant as to render the principal preliminary condition of the story possible'.[66] *Action* magazine pointed out that 'Few will guess the solution, as Mrs Christie has drawn the red herrings very cleverly across the trail, but the final clearing up wants a lot of swallowing. This is definitely not up to the high standard Mrs Christie has set herself as queen of the British detective-story writers.'[67] The usually positive *Yorkshire Post* complained about 'one staggering improbability' but was otherwise warm towards the mystery.[68] On the whole, Christie should have considered herself lucky that this 'staggering improbability' did not leave such a sour taste that readers would abandon her, but it's astonishing that no intervention was made by either agent or publishers before the unsatisfactory ending saw print. 'Torquemada' resumed his critical discussion of Christie's works in his latest *Observer* review, under the headline 'Poirot Perplexes':

> I for one cannot understand why he [Poirot] has allowed Agatha Christie to make him party to a crime whose integrity stands or fails by a central situation which, though most ingenious, is next door to impossible ... Of course, the queen of detective story writers is, as a married woman, entitled to her own opinion; but even a pseudonymous and therefore sexless reviewer need not subscribe to the theory that the queen can do no wrong.[69]

While there's much to enjoy in *Murder in Mesopotamia*, its final revelations cast a shadow that's difficult to escape, and the story marks a contrast to the usual – but not uninterrupted – brilliance of Agatha Christie's Poirot mysteries.

Cards on the Table
(Novel, 1936)

In 1938 Agatha Christie wrote of Poirot and his many criminal cases that: 'He has his favourites. *Cards on the Table* was the murder which won his carefully technical approval.' If Poirot particularly admired the ingenuity of this case, then it may have been due to the way it was presented to him, and the way that the reader of the mystery as written is forewarned by the author that no tricks will be employed. The basic premise of *Cards on the Table* is that four characters play bridge while their host sits out the game – but at the end of play it's discovered that the host has been murdered at some point in the evening. In her foreword Christie is entirely upfront about the fact that these players are the only

ABOVE LEFT: The UK first edition of *Cards on the Table* dealing out the inevitable Ace of Spades. **ABOVE RIGHT:** Dodd, Mead's first US cover in 1937.

four suspects, one of whom must have committed the crime. However, there's no usual trail of physical clues to uncover: 'The deduction must, therefore, be entirely psychological,' she wrote, 'but it is none the less interesting for that, because when all is said and done it is the mind of the murderer that is of supreme interest.' In this respect, Christie seems to have created this novel to entertain herself as much as any of her readers, as she sets out to create a different type of puzzle for the reader to attempt to solve, likely without success. The result is a leisurely paced but intelligent book that emphasises logic and motive above action.

Perhaps inevitably, Poirot is also present on the evening of *Cards on the Table*'s murder, although his game of bridge takes place in a separate room, where he's accompanied by three people who the reader may have encountered elsewhere. The first, Colonel Race, had previously appeared in Christie's 1924 thriller *The Man in the Brown Suit*, while the

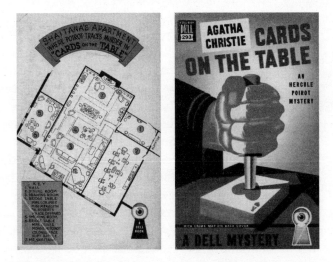

Dell's first 'mapback' design for *Cards on the Table*, with the front cover by Gerald Gregg (1949).

CARDS ON THE
TABLE
Agatha Christie

The 1951 Pan cover by
Carl Wilton.

Agatha
Christie
Cards on the Table

fontana books

The 1958 Fontana cover
– not necessarily a
scene from the book!

second member of the party, Superintendent Battle, had been introduced in 1925's adventure mystery *The Secret of Chimneys*. The final player in this game is mystery writer Ariadne Oliver, who had earlier assisted Christie's 'detective of the heart' Parker Pyne. Over the years many have tried to work out exactly how much of Christie herself we can see in Mrs Oliver, but on the whole it's only really her asides about life as an author of mysteries that give the sense of autobiography at this stage. Elsewhere, the sometimes rather manic figure doesn't closely correlate to what we know of Christie herself. Her description of Ariadne Oliver as 'a hot-headed feminist' is a loaded statement, as is the eye-roll we may detect when Christie writes that 'when any murder of importance was occupying space in the Press there was sure to be an interview with Mrs. Oliver, and it was mentioned that Mrs. Oliver had said, "Now if a woman were the head of Scotland Yard!"'. Christie didn't seem to agree with her creation here, as she would later say that 'Very few people really stimulate you with the things they say. And those are usually men. Men have much better brains than women, don't you think? So much more originality'.[70]

Ariadne Oliver's principal function in the novel is the way that she operates as a welcome dose of sharp-edged comedy due to her refusal to kowtow to society's expectations for women. After a lengthy description of Oliver's trials and tribulations when it came to maintaining her 'rebellious' hair style, Christie tells us that 'One day her appearance would be highly intellectual - a brow with the hair scraped back from it and coiled in a large bun in the neck – on another Mrs Oliver would suddenly appear with Madonna loops, or large masses of slightly untidy curls,' before drily stating that on 'this particular evening Mrs. Oliver was trying out a fringe', with the wording suggesting that the trial could not be considered a success.

For Christie, as well as Poirot, *Cards on the Table* seems to have been a mystery that was particularly satisfying, although she didn't include it in her 1972 list of her ten favourite books that she had written, with *Murder on the Orient Express* and *The Murder of Roger Ackroyd* as the only two Poirot stories to make the cut. In 1966 she recalled both the novel and the crossword setter who had so frequently positively reviewed her books:

> Quite good, the bridge one, an interesting technique … I like crossword puzzles and sometimes do *The Times* – but I'm not up to the advanced Torquemada-type. And I'm sort of fascinated by the elimination sort of puzzle: Mr A gives Mr B a lift in Mr C's car, and you have to work it out. But I can't do visual puzzles at all. You know, you're given four things and you have to spot the odd man out; I can never see what's wrong with the fourth thing. I'm very unobservant, which rather wrecks things – never notice anything different in a room, or if someone has had a haircut, until I really have to look. Perhaps that's why I'm drawn to detection; I suppose you often admire the things that aren't your strong point.[71]

Published as a novel in late 1936, the book was an immediate commercial success, with Christie's agent writing that each of her novels appeared to be outpacing the previous one.[72] Less than two weeks later, he wrote again to say that it looked to be a bigger success than anticipated, while earlier

A clever Italian cover from 1987.

in the year Christie's American agents had even received a letter from mystery writer Mary Hastings Bradley to say that she noticed that commuters immediately turned to the story's serialisation in the *Saturday Evening Post*, which no doubt justified the $14,000 that the magazine had paid for it.[73,74]

Several reviewers took the opportunity to eulogise about Christie in general terms with the publication of this novel. Christie was 'a model to writers of detective tales' according to *The Manchester Guardian*, while *The Times Literary Supplement* judged that the author's 'great merit is that her plots are just complex enough to interest the reader, and not complex enough to muddle him.'[75,76] In *The Observer*, 'Torquemada' himself reflected that:

> I was not the only one who thought that Poirot or his creator had gone a little off the rails in *Murder in Mesopotamia*, which means that others beside myself will rejoice at Mrs Christie's brilliant come-back in *Cards on the Table*. This author, unlike many who have achieved fame and success for qualities quite other than literary ones, has studied to improve in every branch of writing in each of her detective stories. The result is that, in her latest book, we notice qualities of humour, composition and subtlety which we would have thought beyond the reach of the writer of *The Mysterious Affair at Styles*. Of course, the gift of bamboozlement, with which Agatha Christie was born, remains, and has never been seen to better advantage than in this close, diverting and largely analytical problem. *Cards on the Table* is perhaps the most perfect of the little grey sells.[77]

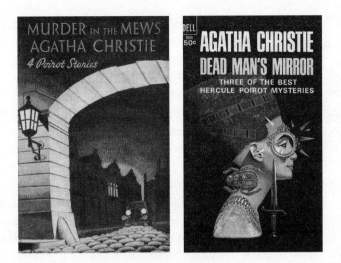

Murder in the Mews
(Short stories, 1937)

Murder in the Mews is something of an anomaly at this point
in Agatha Christie's career. Most of her Poirot short stories
had been written in the early 1920s, and although many had
been collected in various books by this point (including
some exclusively for the American market and book clubs)
they weren't a priority, as the detective was now firmly established as the star of a regular series of more lucrative novels.
However, this book is also anomalous for other reasons, as
rather than being the usual collection of a dozen or so short
stories, here we have three longer than normal short stories

ABOVE LEFT: Robin Macartney's painting for the first edition, a book
published exclusively in the UK (1937). **ABOVE RIGHT:** *Dead Man's
Mirror* was a shorter collection in the USA, shown here in its 1966
paperback with art by William Teason.

An illustration from the original serial in *Perth Daily News* (1937).

with a fourth conventional length mini mystery to finish: 'Murder in the Mews', 'The Incredible Theft' and 'Dead Man's Mirror', followed by the shorter 'Triangle at Rhodes'.

Christie's notebooks indicate that work was undertaken on these new stories during 1935, and so she seems to have written them with a new collection in mind. The three longer stories are reworkings of mysteries that had been published in magazines during 1923, so it seems that bundling together these stories was seen as an efficient way to add an extra book to Collins' schedule, which at this point was publishing three Christie titles a year. The fact that these mysteries were freshly reworked rather than presented as per the original publications may also tell us that Christie had started to realise how her writing had increased in sophistication over the years.[78]

The first case is a new take on an idea first presented in 'The Market Basing Mystery'. 'Murder in the Mews' offers an exploration of a mysterious death that seems to have occurred during the fireworks for Guy Fawkes Night, and is a cleverly conceived and entertaining tale. We follow the well-plotted aftermath of an apparent suicide that seems more likely to be murder, given that the dead woman appears to have held the gun in her right hand, even though the wound was on the left side of her head. The reader would do well not to feel too smug as they wander along what seems to be a well-trodden path of deduction, as Christie will be one step ahead of most by the end.

'The Incredible Theft' is an expanded version of *The Sketch*'s 'The Submarine Plans'.[79] In the original story we can see the Sherlock Holmes influences that were often strong in the early Poirot cases, as the detective is asked to investigate missing plans of vital importance for the government. This is reminiscent of 'The Adventure of the Bruce-Partington Plans', which also concerned missing blueprints for a submarine, and similar cases such as 'The Adventure of the Naval Treaty'. Christie's take on this type of adventure is at least as good as Conan Doyle's, although the missing documents sub-genre is not the most exciting form of mystery. For this extended version she also updates the plans in question so that they are now for a new type of fighter plane.

'Dead Man's Mirror' feels like firmer ground for Poirot, although it's this collection's second story to hinge on the question of whether a death can be judged suicide or murder. Poirot is abruptly requested to visit the wealthy and titled Gervase Chevenix-Gore, a man keen on wagers and adventure. As part of the story's expansion from the original story 'The Second Gong' Christie has Poirot discuss his annoyance with the summons with Mr Satterthwaite, who no doubt flatters him by saying he felt 'privileged' to see Poirot's deductions when they had met during *Three Act Tragedy*. It will surprise no one that Poirot's host dies before the detective reaches him, while for all of Poirot's recent ruminations on the importance of psychology, it's the physical clues that will lead to the solution of this mystery.

Hercule Poirot again on the Pan paperback (1954), with art by Roger Hall.

It's in the final short story, 'Triangle at Rhodes', that psychology really moves to the fore. Initially, this story about the tangled relationships between three people who Poirot encounters while on holiday is more reminiscent of Christie's character study novels published under the pseudonym Mary Westmacott than her usual mysteries, before a particularly dastardly crime takes place. In her notebooks, Christie toyed with the idea of making this story

Penguin Crime   2/6

Murder in the mews
and other stories

Agatha Christie

Penguin's 1963 reprint of the collection sported a particularly striking photographic cover.

a full novel, and she wasn't the only person to do so. In his review of the collection, 'Torquemada' of *The Observer* argued that '"Triangle at Rhodes" is just the one which should have been made the longest ... This plot would, I think, have furnished forth a whole novel' – perhaps Christie was reading, and this provided the nudge needed to write the 1941 Poirot novel *Evil Under the Sun*, which mirrors some of the key plotting and character motivation from this clever short story.[80] However, even before that an echo of this sort of relationship will also be seen in *Death on the Nile* later in 1937.

Overall, *Murder in the Mews* is a somewhat unusual but welcome collection of pleasantly diverting mysteries. Plans for the collection took some time to firm up, and as late as October 1936, just five months prior to publication, a rather different set of stories was envisaged. Along with 'Murder in the Mews' and 'Triangle at Rhodes' there were plans to include 'Problem at Sea', 'How Does Your Garden Grow?', 'The Regatta Mystery' and another short story yet to be chosen.[81] These had all debuted in *The Strand Magazine*, but for reasons unknown a different direction was chosen.[82]

AGATHA CHRISTIE
Murder in the Mews

FONTANA BOOKS

Tom Adams' cover for Fontana (1964)

Murder in the Mews was published in March 1937, although when it appeared in the United States three months later it was missing the story 'The Incredible Theft' and was renamed *Dead Man's Mirror*. Reviewers in the UK complained that shorter mysteries tended to be less satisfactory than full novels, both generally and specifically when it came to Christie. 'There is sufficient in the latest exploits of the little Belgian to remind us that his creator is our queen of detective writers,' wrote 'Torquemada', 'but by no means enough to win her that title if she had not already won it.'[83] *The Times Literary Supplement* felt that: 'It would seem that nowadays – it was not true of Sherlock Holmes, when the rules were less rigid – the shorter the detective story the less good it will be ... All are of quite a high standard as long-short stories, but none is as good as any of Mrs Christie's full-length detective novels.'[84]

Poirot's First Appearances on Television and Radio
(1937–39)

The 1930s was the decade that cemented Poirot's position in the public consciousness, something that hadn't gone unnoticed by those that might wish to capitalise on any literary success. In the late 1920s and early 1930s this is exactly what theatre and film had done, but towards the end of the decade it was the turn of radio and the new medium of television to bring Poirot to the masses. Unfortunately, none of the British radio and television productions from this decade survive, but scripts and other paperwork give us a good flavour of what was seen and heard by audiences.

It might be a surprise to learn that Poirot appeared on

ABOVE: Agatha Christie with actor Anthony Holles recording Poirot for BBC radio in 1937.

'Behind the Screen'—II

By AGATHA CHRISTIE

The following is the second instalment of the Serial Thriller, which will be continued in our next four issues, by Dorothy Sayers,
Anthony Berkeley, E. C. Bentley and Ronald Knox. See page 1109 for our competition in connection with this feature

WITH Mrs. Ellis's shriek, Wilfred regained possession of his faculties. The numbing feeling of paralysis passed away. He was himself once more, cool, efficient, able to take command of the situation.

Crossing the room, he knelt by Dudden's body. He was vaguely aware of the others; of Mr. Ellis, half risen from the card table, his mouth open, his eyes staring; of Amy, of Robert, of Mrs. Ellis. They were all there behind him, waiting, peering, listening for the authoritative words he would soon speak.

He was careful not in any way to disturb the position of the body—a queer huddled position—he noted it automatically. The most cursory examination was all that was needed. Dudden was dead. The blood had welled from a wound in the neck, near the angle of the jawbone.

There was a curious expression on Wilfred's face as he bent over the dead man. Those eyes—those dead staring eyes—why surely . . . No, this wasn't h i s business. He mustn't i m a g i n e things. But it was odd—distinctly odd.

He rose to his feet. . . .

'He's dead', he said briefly.

'Oh!' It was a low moaning cry that broke from Amy's lips. She turned deathly pale, swayed, and clutched at her mother.

'Come, my dear, come'. The stout woman was compelling. 'Come, Amy love. . . .'

Putting her arm round the girl, she led her gently from the room. Her supporting arm kept the girl from falling.

Wilfred drew a sigh of relief as the women left the room. His eyes met those of Mr. Ellis. The latter seemed to be recovering from the shock.

'This is terrible—terrible', he ejaculated. 'What is it, my boy? Suicide, I suppose. A terrible thing to happen in one's house'.

'It's not suicide', said Wilfred.

'Not suicide—eh?'

'I'm not saying the wound couldn't have been self-inflicted. It could, though it's very unlikely. But in that case the weapon would have been still in the wound'.

'The weapon?'

'Yes. He's been stabbed—stabbed with a sharp, narrow blade and there's no sign of such a thing anywhere near him. This is a case for the police, Mr. Ellis.'

'You mean——'

'This is murder!' He repeated the word: '*Murder*. . . .'

'Murder? You can't mean it?'

'There's no doubt of it. You must ring up the police at once'.

'I—I——'

Mr. Ellis hesitated, swallowed nervously, then went shakily from the room.

Really, Wilfred supposed, he ought to have offered to telephone for him. The old man was so upset that he hardly knew what he was doing, whereas he, Wilfred, was perfectly calm and collected. Nevertheless, he had felt the strongest objection to leaving the room. His place was here.

His attention was suddenly drawn to Robert. The young man was standing by the edge of the screen. He was staring downwards with fascinated eyes. Wilfred could see the Adam's apple in his throat jerking up and down, while his long pale fingers twisted and untwisted themselves nervously. A thoroughly neurotic type, Wilfred thought rather disgustedly.

How strangely the boy was staring at Dudden. No—that was odd—he was not looking at Dudden at all. His fascinated gaze was elsewhere—on the tiny rivulet of blood. It seemed to fascinate him. He looked almost hypnotised. Suddenly, with a convulsive shudder, R o b e r t seemed to come to himself. He turned abruptly and almost ran from the room.

Wilfred felt a sense of relief. He was alone. Once more, he bent over the body, examining it carefully. Curious attitude—the man might have been asleep, but for that tell - tale stream of scarlet. And his eyes—most peculiar! An unpleasant man, given to all the same Wilfred had never noticed before — Oh! well, why think of it?

He raised a hand to brush the hair from his forehead and then started nervously.

There was blood on his fingers!

How did it come there? He had been most careful in his handling of Dudden. He had not touched the wound. He bent lower. There were dark smears on the cloth of Dudden's coat near its lower edge. He touched them—yes, they were faintly damp.

'You're wanted in the parlour'

They were smears of blood. How had they got there?

A slight sound made him turn his head. For a moment he saw nothing. The room was the same as usual—almost indecently peaceful. The patience cards still laid out on the table, Mrs. Ellis's book, a paper cutter between its pages, lying on her chair, a silk scarf of Amy's lying on the arm of the sofa. It was all as usual, as he had seen it a hundred times before.

The sound was repeated and now Wilfred recognised it for what it was. Someone was pushing the door very cautiously open. He waited. Suddenly the rubicund face of Mrs. Hulk came peering round the door, an expression of mingled fear and excitement animated her countenance. She seemed taken aback at the sight of Wilfred. Then she pushed the door a little further and came in. Her hands fingered her apron.

'E's dead, is 'e?', she asked, in a hoarse voice.

Wilfred nodded. He had just time to note that an expression of distinct satisfaction passed over her face when the doorbell rang. Mrs. Hulk went to answer it. There was a murmur of voices and Wilfred heard her say: 'E's in th re. The young gentleman's there, too'. Two men entered the room. The first wore the uniform of a police inspector, the second Wilfred put down correctly as the police surgeon.

'Evening', said the Inspector. 'Are you Mr. Ellis?'.

The script for 1930's *Behind the Screen* was printed in *The Listener*, including Agatha Christie's chapter.

the fledgling medium of television before he turned up on the more firmly established radio broadcasts that the BBC had commenced in 1922. Christie had a busy ongoing relationship with the Corporation during the 1930s, sometimes fending off occasionally impertinent demands for original stories, but also occasionally complying with requests for material for radio broadcast. This included her participation in the serials *The Scoop* and *Behind the Screen*, which were written by various members of the Detection Club of which Christie was a member along with her most respected contemporaries. While the BBC made repeated overtures to Christie, in private its employees were often rather dismissive of her work, and in 1934 they even rejected a story that she had specially written for them after not inconsiderable pressure, 'In a Glass Darkly'. The author had no problem selling this story to a publication and quickly replaced it with the prosaically titled 'Miss Marple Tells a Story', after she was asked for a story that did just that. This sort of incident can hardly have helped the relationship, which would deteriorate over time.

The first television appearance of Poirot took place on 18 June 1937, at which point the BBC had been broadcasting the world's first regular 'high definition' broadcasts for just eight months. While technically a permanent service, the small audiences (made up of wealthy people in the London region only) and lack of experience lent it the air of ongoing experimentation. So it was that schedules were made up of diverse programming, with drama generally restricted to extracts from existing plays and shorter pieces. This meant that a one-act Poirot play written by Christie featuring only four characters was ideal for the live medium with its small studios at Alexandra Palace. This play, *The Wasp's Nest*, seems to have been originally written for a 1932 charity performance that was cancelled.[85] The script is based on Christie's short story of the same title that had first been published in the *Daily Mail* in 1928, and this television production would be its debut performance.

Francis L. Sullivan, who apparently felt that he had some ownership over the play, played the part of Poirot once more following his successful appearances in the role on stage. Joining him in the studio were Wallace Douglas as Claude Langdon, Antoinette Cellier as Nina Bellamy, and D.A. Clarke-Smith as Charles Harborough for this neat tale of the potentially deadly consequences of love rivalry. The twenty-five minute production followed such televisual delights as a ten minute *Fashion Forecast*, fifteen minutes with *Friends from the Zoo*, and a ten-minute newsreel from Gaumont. The

Francis L. Sullivan as Poirot, with Douglas A. Clarke-Smith, Antoinette Cellier and Wallace Douglas in the 1937 television performance of *The Wasp's Nest*.

cast performed the play twice, at 3.35pm and 9.40pm, and were given a lengthy write-up in the television version of the *Radio Times* listings magazine. 'Televiewers will be the first to see this Agatha Christie play, which has never previously been performed anywhere,' it said, before giving potted biographies of both Sullivan and Christie. All seems to have gone well, with a short review in *The Observer* remarking that 'the first performance of Agatha Christie's *The Wasp's Nest* on Friday was excellently done'.[86]

Poirot only had to wait another five months before he would make his debut on radio, with a play written specially for the medium, *The Yellow Iris*, on 2 November 1937. Christie always seemed more interested in radio when she was presented with a particular challenge, and here she wove the story of a poisoning between various musical numbers being performed as part of the cabaret where the murder takes place. It isn't clear if this unusual structure was Christie's suggestion, but it seems more likely to have been at the (rather misguided) request of the BBC, which was experimenting with different types of radio drama at this point. Although often called an adaptation of the short story of the same name, the history of *The Yellow Iris* is difficult to untangle. Christie was asked to write something for BBC radio in January 1937, and it seems likely that *The Yellow Iris* was the eventual outcome, but in the meantime a short story version of the mystery was published in *The Strand* in July, some four months before its radio appearance. It seems likely that both radio and print versions were written more or less concurrently.

Although Poirot's brush with television had elicited little more than a faint murmur of interest, the appearance of his new case on the mass medium of radio was much more keenly anticipated, with mentions of the forthcoming attraction in a handful of newspapers as well as the normal listings. Christie came along to the rehearsals for the play, which starred Anthony Holles as Poirot. Holles had worked extensively on stage and screen, including the 1932 Sherlock Holmes film *The Missing Rembrandt*, which also starred fellow Poirot performer Francis L. Sullivan. The music was written by Michael Sayer, with lyrics by Christopher Hassall, who had often collaborated with Ivor Novello. Acting as compére for the cabaret side of events was Cyril Fletcher, an entertainer who would perhaps become most famous for his 'odd odes', as relayed on the BBC's consumer affairs and light entertainment television show *That's Life!*

This drawing accompanied the *Radio Times* listing for *The Yellow Iris* in the 29 October 1937 edition.

'I had hoped to say such nice things about Agatha Christie's *Yellow Iris*,' wrote Joyce Grenfell in *The Observer* the week of the play's transmission. 'Hercule Poirot was played, as I imagined him, by Anthony Holles. But that was the only happy thing in the broadcast. The play itself turned out to be a ten minute sketch padded with cabaret and dance music, and made to spread over forty minutes. When the sketch was playing my interest was sustained. But the sequences were so brief and the intervening music – though good in its proper place – so prolonged that my attention wandered. Much better [to] have treated the piece as the short sketch it really was.'[87] Such a complaint could have been anticipated, as even reading the script is a frustratingly fragmented experience. Grenfell was not the only one to take issue with the intrusion of the cabaret into the mystery. 'Fervid Christie fans – followers of that suave, garrulous French sleuth [sic], Hercule Poirot – must be feeling a little sore this morning,' wrote Jonah Barrington of the *Daily Express* before agreeing with his *Observer* colleague on the intrusion of the cabaret performances. *The Manchester Guardian* similarly concluded that, in competition with the

E.M. Stephan as Hercule Poirot in 'The Incredible Theft', from the 6 May 1938 edition of *Radio Times*.

cabaret, 'there was not much detective thrill left ... Let the drama department as a general rule keep crime and cabaret apart; the mixture is apt to curdle.'[88]

The next time the BBC presented Poirot on the radio, on 10 May 1938, it was a more traditional affair. E.M. Stephan, the broadcaster's French instructor (as part of its educational offerings), was chosen to play the Belgian detective in an adaptation of 'The Incredible Theft' as the second part of a series called *Detectives in Fiction*, following the appearance of Sherlock Holmes the previous month. Stephan had never appeared in a play before – but, as the *Radio Times* put it, 'the part should suit him to perfection'. No doubt he, and the listening audience, were relieved that on this occasion Poirot did not need to compete with cabaret singers. Meanwhile, in South Africa actor Harcourt Elliott played Poirot in a 1939 radio adaptation of *Peril at End House*.

In an early sign that American broadcasters would find it easier to gain permission for full adaptations of Christie's works than those in Britain, 12 November 1939 saw Orson Welles star in an hour-long adaptation of *The Murder of Roger Ackroyd* for CBS radio as part of *The Campbell Playhouse* series, which had adapted a range of literary classics. Twenty-four-year-old Welles played the parts of both Poirot and the narrator Dr Sheppard, although it's unlikely that any listeners would detect that they were both played by the same man as each excellent performance feels completely different. The broadcast, a recording of which survives, opened with Welles telling the listeners that: 'Tonight we broadcast our version of what is generally regarded as one of the greatest of the modern mystery murder novels,' before launching into a defence of the genre as a 'moral form of entertainment'. Welles was accompanied by a strong cast, including Alan Napier as Ackroyd, who would later play Bruce Wayne's butler Alfred in the 1960s *Batman* television show.

From the very beginning, with Poirot interrupting the announcer's plug for Campbell's soup, the whole production is lively and entertaining, as well as faithful to the novel in both spirit and detail. Welles' Poirot even uses Christie's specific descriptions of the detective early on to conjure up an image of him for those listening. The appearance of this story in the series alongside the likes of *Rebecca*, *Les Misérables* and *A Christmas Carol* was a strong indication that not only was Poirot reaching ever higher levels of fame, but that Christie's works were increasingly gaining recognition as classic pieces of literature in their own right. However, it's not clear how much Christie herself actually knew about the production – when her agent sent on the £150 fee for the use of her material, he described it to her as 'excerpts'. It may have been best for all involved that Christie was unaware that the production had been a full-blown adaptation of the type that she typically disapproved of.

Dumb Witness
(Novel, 1937)

'Mrs Agatha Christie inscribes her new book *Dumb Witness* to her favourite dog, a fact that in this dog-worshipping country is enough of itself to ensure success,' said *The Manchester Guardian* when reviewing Christie's latest Poirot mystery following its publication in July 1937.[89] The canine star of this novel was duly given great prominence, as the first edition (and many subsequent versions) gave the cover over to the story's terrier dog, Bob, who would be the 'dumb witness' of the title. Bob was based on Christie's own dog, Peter, whom she had adopted in the mid-1920s, and appears on the first edition cover. 'Peter, of course, became the life

ABOVE LEFT: Agatha Christie's own dog, Peter, was immortalised on the front of the UK first edition (1937). **ABOVE RIGHT:** In America, the book was published as *Poirot Loses a Client*, as seen on Dodd, Mead's first jacket design.

and soul of the family,' she remembered in her autobiography, where she described how he slept on her secretary's bed and 'ate his way through a variety of slippers and so-called indestructible balls for terriers'.[90] Peter was an important enough part of the family that when Christie raised the prospect of her marriage to Max with a young Rosalind, it was the dog's approval that sealed the deal for her daughter.

Perhaps similarly, a reader's approval of this novel often seems to hinge on their disposition towards dogs. The crime that Bob has witnessed appears to be the attempted murder of his mistress, the wealthy spinster Emily Arundell. Initially the dog's ball is blamed for the fall that incapacitates her, but Poirot's appearance after a plea from yet another soon-to-be-murdered victim ensures that no one will get away with foul play, with Bob's innocence to be proven. Some elements of the story had been sketched out by Christie in an earlier short story, 'The Incident of the Dog's Ball', which remained

The UK Book Club edition included four unique black-and-white plates (1937). Claims that the photos feature Agatha Christie and her dog posing for the shots themselves are sadly unfounded.

Avon's glamorous paperback cover from 1951.

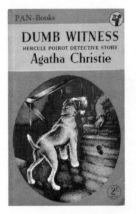

Bob again, here on the 1952 Pan paperback.

unpublished until 2009, likely because she quickly realised that the story could stretch to a novel. There's a sentimentality in Christie's writing of Bob that's reminiscent of some of her lighter and less nuanced short stories, and this can be enough to put off some readers, although his role in the proceedings is not as great as might be expected.

Another unusual ingredient for a Poirot mystery is the apparently supernatural event witnessed by several of *Dumb Witness*'s key characters, in which an 'aura' is seen leaving Miss Arundell's body during a séance. Not for the final time this decade, readers of *The Hound of the Baskervilles* have an advantage in trying to solve this aspect of the mystery. Although Poirot mysteries do not present the supernatural as 'real', Christie did write such stories elsewhere, and even in the 1930s spiritualism remained popular. This included the famous 'medium' Helen Duncan, who apparently produced ectoplasm, which was repeatedly investigated and discovered to be cheesecloth – not that this was enough to save her from being the final person to be convicted of witchcraft in Britain in 1944. This sort of context may have allowed some readers to wonder if the amateur spiritualist sisters who witnessed the event should be taken at face value. The more logically minded may see the 'aura' as evidence of a different kind.

After the oddness of *The ABC Murders*' switching between first and third person narrative, always penned by Captain Hastings, here we see another example of changing perspectives. Hastings joins us as narrator in the fifth chapter after using the earlier chapters to set the scene in the third person – 'The events which I have just narrated were not, of course, known to me until a long time afterwards,' he writes, in his final narration until *Curtain: Poirot's Last Case*. This time we can't blame Christie, as it seems that this Hastings-less opening, which outlines the events in Market Basing that occur prior to Poirot being called in, was a request of the *Saturday Evening Post*, the magazine that most frequently serialised Christie's mystery novels in the United States at this point. Correspondence between Christie and Edmund Cork, her agent,

Poirot and friend on this 1952 Spanish cover.

in May and June 1936 reveal that the magazine had asked for more substantial changes than normal to the story, which at the time was called *The Murder at Littlegreen House*.[91] The magazine was an important stream of income for Christie, and it was felt that making such alterations would be good for the long-term relationship and might even lead to a valuable exclusive deal. The required changes covered the early portion of the book, which presumably encompassed the wholesale addition of these third-person chapters. These were seen to be such a success by Cork that, following his recommendation, they were incorporated into the novel when published later. Less attention was paid to a second request, which seems to have been to make the middle-aged Miss Lawson, the victim's companion and beneficiary, a younger and more attractive character.[92] The *Saturday Evening Post* published the amended story in late 1936 under the title *Poirot Loses a Client*, which was also adopted for the novel's publication in the United States the following year.

Dumb Witness itself is a novel that is probably considered more positively by those who read it quickly, as there are several clues and events that strain credulity if given

Avon's gruesome 1957 paperback, complete with bloody footprints.

more than a passing thought. Whereas an eye-catching kimono in *Murder on the Orient Express* was utilised as a clever piece of misdirection, here a brooch on a dressing gown (odd enough in itself) is a clue that, in contrast with the story's characters, can be quickly and correctly interpreted by even the slowest of readers. This clue was one of the aspects of the novel that *The Times Literary Supplement* took issue with in its review in July 1937, as well as the apparent use of a hammer and nails at night along from an open door: 'These are small but tantalising points which it would not be worth raising in the work of a less distinguished writer than Mrs Christie,' it conceded.[93] Meanwhile, 'Torquemada' in *The Observer* considered it to be 'the least of all the Poirot books', and that it had a 'baldness of plot and crudeness of characterisation'.[94]

The light diversion of *Dumb Witness* makes it difficult to be too mean-spirited towards it, and normally it's simply passed over quickly in the pantheon of Poirot mysteries. Perhaps this particular novel isn't critiqued too heavily because the stories that surround it are generally so strong and cleverly plotted – none more so than the Poirot mystery that immediately followed it, which is one of the most ingenious cases that he would ever investigate.

Death on the Nile
(Novel, 1937)

While *Murder on the Orient Express* is undoubtedly Poirot's most famous case, it's no surprise that on the two occasions that a big budget film of that particular novel has been produced it was *Death on the Nile* that followed it into production. One of Christie's most clever and intriguing novels, it arguably makes for a better introduction to the author, as well as a story more suited for the screen than its more famous predecessor. When asked about the appeal of her books decades later, Christie said that 'Murder stories are mainly done for entertainment with a dash of the old morality play behind them; you defend the innocent and pin down the guilty.'[95]

ABOVE LEFT: *Death on the Nile* had a jacket by Robin Macartney in its first UK edition. **ABOVE RIGHT:** The Sphinx appeared on the first American edition from Dodd, Mead in 1938.

Christie had already used the title 'Death on the Nile' for a story featuring her 'detective of the heart' Parker Pyne a few years earlier, but other than the setting and the presence of an interesting cast of characters, there's nothing to connect the two. In this Poirot novel, we witness the detective observing the toxic relationship between three people holidaying in Egypt. Two, Simon and Linnet Doyle, are recently married; the third, Jacqueline de Bellefort, was set to marry Simon before he broke the engagement in order to wed her friend Linnet instead. Jacqueline's stalking of the newlywed couple includes their trip on the steamer that also has Poirot on board. Several of the other passengers also seem to have a connection with Linnet and her wealth, and when she's found murdered in her cabin it transpires that those who knew her best have excellent alibis – so what's the truth behind the crime?

Perhaps *Death on the Nile* pushes its luck a little when presenting the array of characters on this tour along the Nile: all seem to have some sort of secret that may be motive for murder, but this is the sort of suspension of disbelief that readers have to accept with even the best closed-circle murder mysteries. The list of suspects may also be a little overpopulated, but they also provide entertaining window dressing around the central mystery. The most memorable occupants of the steamer include the elderly Mrs Van Schuyler, who fellow passenger Mrs Allerton describes as 'The very ugly old American lady who is clearly going to be very exclusive and speak to nobody who doesn't come up to the most exacting standards! She's rather marvellous, isn't she, really? A kind of period piece.' There is also Salome Otterbourne, a romance novelist who sports a turban, speaks in a 'high

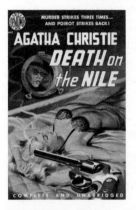

Poirot Strikes Back on the 1951 Avon paperback.

complaining voice' and struggles to get her sea legs – a spoof of certain genre writers, who Christie clearly enjoyed depicting. Christie also jokes about the cliché of a murderer killing themselves before becoming victim to traditional justice, which was sometimes a favoured outcome for Poirot stories.[96] Alongside Poirot and a reappearance from Colonel Race, also on board are a solicitor, a doctor, the trustee of Linnet's estate, Linnet's maid, and several other characters with good reason to seem suspicious.

Pan Books' 1949 paperback with cover art by Stein.

Christie's notebooks show that the mystery was initially sketched out with Miss Marple in mind, who at this point had appeared in only one novel and several short stories. However, she seems to have quickly decided on Poirot as detective; perhaps this was for commercial reasons, or because Miss Marple was not yet a figure who ventured far from her own village of St Mary Mead. 'Papa Poirot', as he is sometimes referred to, often found some sentimental interest in the relationships of younger people, including the relationship-focused 'Triangle at Rhodes' in *Murder in the Mews*, and it follows that Christie later said that the murder of Linnet on the Nile saddened him.

In a foreword written for the Penguin paperback edition of the novel, Christie remembered that:

Death on the Nile was written after coming back from a winter in Egypt. When I read it now I feel myself back again on the steamer from Assuan to Wadi Halfa. There were quite a number of passengers on board, but the ones in this book travelled in my mind and became increasingly real to me – in the setting of a Nile steamer. The book has a lot of characters and a very elaborately worked out plot.

I think the central situation is intriguing and has dramatic possibilities, and the three characters, Simon, Linnet, and Jacqueline, seem to me to be real and alive.

The novel is an excellent example of Christie using location as character alongside her suspects and victims. While the mechanics of the mystery might take place just as well on a pleasure cruise working its way up the Thames, here the reader is given ample opportunity to get to grips with Egypt as a location, at least as seen through the eyes of Agatha Christie. These location-focused mysteries are an ongoing sub-genre for Poirot, and Christie herself thought that the book was 'one of the best of my "foreign travel" ones, and if detective stories are "escape literature" (and why shouldn't they be!) the reader can escape to sunny skies and blue water as well as to crime in the confines of an armchair.'[97] This is a marked contrast to novels such as *Cards on the Table*, which had turned its back on the atmosphere of location in favour of an emphasis on psychology and the practicalities of murder, again demonstrating that there can be no such thing as a 'typical' Agatha Christie book. Nevertheless, the mechanics of the mystery are once more important here, hence Christie's provision of a plan of the cabins – essential for the reader who wishes to double check the alibis of those involved.

It didn't take long for *Death on the Nile* to be recognised as a particularly strong mystery. Edmund Cork wrote to the author that 'If I may do so without impertinence, I should like to say that it seems to us that *Death on the Nile* is one of the very best. I enjoyed it tremendously, and I am confident it is going to be your most successful novel.'[98] Although the murder takes quite some time to arrive (40,000 words at Cork's estimate), her agent pointed out that there was plenty of incident and tension to grip the reader. Certainly the

Saturday Evening Post liked it very much, and its editors may have been flattered that the publication garnered a mention in the story, before offering a substantial $18,000 for the serial rights, although the UK's *The Strand* and the Amalgamated Press publishing company passed on it because the crime occurred so late.

Critics generally saw the novel as a return to Christie's very best form following its November 1937 publication, with *The Observer*'s 'Torquemada' writing that 'she is back on the very centre of the bull' and that when Poirot reveals the truth 'we are very angry with ourselves indeed,' but 'anger is swallowed up in admiration.'[99] *The Times Literary Supplement* agreed that 'Hercule Poirot, as usual, digs out a truth so unforeseen that it would be unfair for a reviewer to hint at it', while *The Manchester Guardian* wrote that 'M. Poirot's little grey cells had indeed been obliged to work at full pressure to unravel a mystery which includes one of those carefully worked out alibis that seem alike to fascinate Mrs Christie and to provide her with the best opportunities for developing her own skill.'[100, 101] *The Yorkshire Post* wondered if the opening was a little banal, but conceded that the novel 'is good Agatha Christie, almost from beginning to end; and, anyway, to invent something like a new alibi is a remarkable feat for any detective story-writer nowadays.'[102]

The dramatic potential for the story was noted by seasoned Poirot performer Francis L. Sullivan, as well as others, but Christie wasn't keen on bringing the detective back to the stage. Nevertheless, after mulling over the possibility of an adaptation of 'Triangle at Rhodes' or *Three Act Tragedy*, *Death on the Nile* was decided upon by Christie. Sullivan needed a little convincing

Fontana's glamorous paperback from 1960, illustrated by Eileen Walton.

AGATHA CHRISTIE
Death on the Nile

FONTANA BOOKS

Tom Adams went full Tutankhamun for his 1968 Fontana cover.

when he heard that Poirot was to be removed for the stage version (an especially important decision in light of the ongoing film negotiations, which could have made the character unavailable), but after Christie offered him a list of suitable protagonists including a retired barrister or an ex-diplomat, he embraced the suggestion of a clergyman. The actor was particularly excited by the possibilities of the costume – 'Oh yes,' he's reported to have said, 'purple silk front and a large cross.' 'He saw it, you see,' Christie wrote to Max. 'Not the speaking part – the appearance! – I bet you whoever played Hamlet argued a good deal as to whether to play it in a hat or not.'[103] And so, Canon Pennefather took the place of Poirot in the 1944 play *Murder on the Nile*. This adaptation worked its way through several permutations both in draft form and on stage, with titles including *Moon on the Nile* and *Hidden Horizon*, while Christie also toyed with different endings, none of which altered the surprising and memorable identity of the murderer.

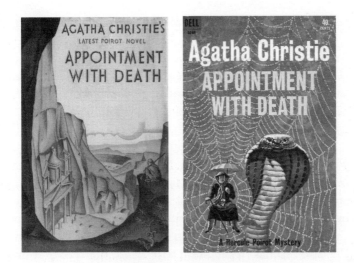

Appointment with Death
(Novel, 1938)

Since her earliest writings, strong matriarchal figures had often been important elements in Christie's stories. Christie's own family had been composed predominately of independently minded women, and she'd encountered many more on her travels. In her first (unpublished) novel *Snow Upon the Desert* we are introduced to Miss King, the guardian of her increasingly deaf niece who is 'coming out' in Cairo, where Christie herself had 'come out' not long prior to her penning this novel around 1908. Miss King is an entertainingly brusque figure ('I don't believe in London,' she snaps at one point, 'too many microbes') whose membership of the

ABOVE LEFT: *Appointment with Death* featured Robin Macartney's fourth and final cover (1938). **ABOVE RIGHT:** In the US, William Teason painted this evocative cover for Dell paperbacks (1963).

Society for the Suppression of Bad Language provides the younger characters with a great deal of amusement. In fact, it's the characterisation that provides the most interesting elements of the book. Christie's skills in creating characters would sometimes be dismissed in reviews, but rarely fairly, as even this early work shows she had a skill for conjuring up memorable figures.

Christie's first published novel, *The Mysterious Affair at Styles*, would cast a matriarch, Mrs Emily Inglethorp, as the murder victim, with her position of power within the family (and her wealth) being judged sufficient motive for murder by at least one person. It's this position, rather than her character, that's important for this puzzle, but by the time Christie reaches *Appointment with Death* the reader is provided with plenty of opportunity to learn about the latest female head of the family to be disposed of: Mrs Boynton.

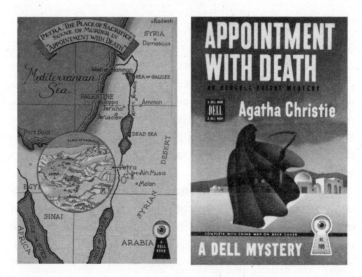

Ruth Belew's cartography accompanied a cover design by Gerald Gregg on the 1946 cover for the Dell 'mapback' edition.

A former prison warden, Mrs Boynton's tyrannical disposition towards her family results in the novel's chilling opening line, as overheard by Poirot – 'You do see, don't you, that she's got to be killed?'

While modern readers may struggle to feel fully sympathetic towards family members with such extraordinary senses of entitlement as witnessed here (as they seem to view inherited wealth as their absolute right and Mrs Boynton as a sadistic barrier between them and it) we are still given plenty of reasons to dislike the victim and her 'malevolent eye'. Cruel heads of family are a recurring trope in Christie, but when they're women they receive a particularly rough ride. 'To have too much power is bad for women,' Christie has one observer say, unchallenged: 'It is difficult for a woman not to abuse power.' Mrs Boynton was based on a real woman who Christie encountered when taking a trip up the Nile with Max and Rosalind in 1933, after which a similarly domineering character was pencilled in to take part in *Death on the Nile*, before becoming the star of her own murder mystery as the unwilling victim instead. 'Sometimes when you're writing you get involved with some character and you can't see how to manage him or her; you throw them out and start again,' Christie said later. 'It's like auditioning actors.'[104]

Appointment with Death features another Middle Eastern setting, this time in Petra, Jordan – another indication of how much Christie loved her travels in this part of the world, and was perhaps pining for another return visit. While there we're soon introduced to the whole Boynton family, controlled by the mother as if by invisible string. The excellent opening chapters put the reader right into the

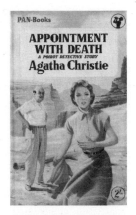

A casual Poirot on the first Pan Books cover in 1957.

Poirot appearing again on a Spanish cover in 1959.

midst of this family drama, with a good dose of mystery from the very beginning. By the time Mrs Boynton is found dead while sitting in the open air, with the precise time of death difficult to identify, we've been given plenty of reason to suspect anyone related to her. When the case is solved by Poirot, questions of psychology have been raised once more, and will be revealed to have been a crucial part of the mechanics of the mystery, perfectly dovetailing with the puzzle of alibis and locations.

When the novel was serialised in Britain's *Daily Mail* it was prefaced a few days earlier by an introduction from Christie in which she discussed the character of Poirot and some of the cases he had solved. In this piece she writes candidly about her frustrations with the character, with some of her oft-quoted criticisms of him originating here:

> And now what of relations between us – between the creator and the created? Well – let me confess it – there has been at times a coolness between us. There are moments when I have felt – why – why – why did I ever invent this detestable, bombastic, tiresome little creature? Eternally straightening things, forever boasting, always thinking in contrasts and tilting his egg-shaped head.

By the end of the article Christie concedes a new-found warmth towards Poirot, however, in which she is mindful of his crucial popular appeal:

> Yes, there have been moments when I have disliked Hercule Poirot very much indeed – when I have rebelled bitterly against being yoked to him for life (usually it is

only at these moments that I receive a fan letter saying 'I know you must love your little detective by the way you write about him'.) But now, I must confess it, Hercule Poirot has won. A reluctant affection has sprung up for him. He has become more human, less irritating. I admire certain things about him – his passion for the truth – his understanding of human frailty and his kindness. And he has taught me something – to take more interest in my other characters – to see them more as real people and less as pawns in a game.

By this point some reviewers were noticing a softening in the character and mannerisms of Poirot, perhaps as Christie worked to make him more personable and less obtrusive as a character in novels rich with suspects and subterfuge that

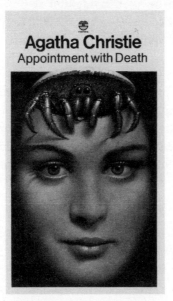

A nightmarish painting by Tom Adams for the 1980 paperback, when the Fontana covers were becoming more horrific.

needed to command the attention of the reader. *The Times Literary Supplement* claimed that Poirot 'has lost none of his skill' in its May 1938 review, but that 'the solution appears a trifle tame and disappointing.'[105] *The Manchester Guardian* particularly commended the novel's use of psychology: 'One reason for the leading position won by Mrs Agatha Christie is that she deals not merely with the mechanics of crime but treats also psychological problems of universal interest,' the review read. 'For ingenuity of plot and construction, unexpectedness of denouement, subtlety of characterisation, and picturesqueness of background *Appointment with Death* may take rank among the best of Mrs Christie's tales.'[106] *The Observer* reviewer also enjoyed the novel: 'I have to confess that I have just been beaten again by Agatha Christie. There is no excuse, I was feeling in particularly good form,' wrote 'Torquemada', who then compared it positively with the similarly well-received *Death on the Nile*, saying that it 'must be counted mathematically nearly twice as brilliant, since the number of suspects is reduced by nearly half.'[107]

When Christie transferred the story to the stage for a 1945 production she predictably removed Poirot, but also supplied an extra twist in proceedings that managed to extend Mrs Boynton's villainy, which results in an ending that's arguably superior to the novel. In the stage version, the victim was too much of a scheming manipulator to allow any of her family to have the final word, even after her death.[108]

Hercule Poirot's Christmas
(Novel, 1938)

If looked at superficially, *Hercule Poirot's Christmas* could feel like something of a regression of style for Agatha Christie. Its country house murder harks back to her earliest Poirot stories, but following on from more exotically located murders there may be something comforting about the Belgian sleuth's return to more familiar surroundings. However, if this is how the reader approaches the novel then they've been lulled in to a false sense of security. The book's dedication to Christie's brother-in-law should serve as a warning for the faint of heart:

ABOVE LEFT: Collins' first edition cover for the UK (1938). **ABOVE RIGHT:** Initially released as *Murder for Christmas* in the USA, it was quickly retitled *A Holiday for Murder* for subsequent editions.

> *My dear James,*
>
> *You have always been one of the most faithful and kindly*
> *of my readers, and I was therefore seriously perturbed when*
> *I received from you a word of criticism. You complained*
> *that my murders were getting too refined – anaemic, in fact.*
> *You yearned for a 'good violent murder with lots of blood.'*
> *A murder where there was no doubt about its being murder!*
>
> *So this is your special story – written for you. I hope it may*
> *please.*

Christie certainly delivers on this promise, despite the fact that she later conceded that 'I don't like messy deaths. I'm more interested in peaceful people who die in their beds and no-one knows why.'[109] In *Hercule Poirot's Christmas* we meet the wealthy but unpopular Simeon Lee, who in an uncharacteristic move has invited his entire family for Christmas, despite their loathing of him and often each other. Also present is the son of Lee's former business partner, with whom he mined diamonds, who alludes to a dark past. The novel counts the days as we move towards Christmas and the surely inevitable murder, which occurs on Christmas Eve. An inhuman scream and great clattering of falling furniture alludes to a struggle, and by the time the family reach Simeon Lee he is dead, inside his locked room. 'Heavy furniture was overturned,' Christie describes. 'China vases lay splintered on the floor. In the middle of the hearthrug in front of the blazing fire lay Simeon Lee in a great pool of blood ... Blood was splashed all round.' The victim's daughter-in-law is then moved to quote from *Macbeth*: 'Who would have thought the old man to have had so much blood in him?' Poirot accompanies the Chief Constable Colonel Johnson to the

An early Spanish edition from 1943 with Poirot dominating the cover.

scene in order to assist the local detective, Superintendent Sugden, who Johnson rather unfairly describes as a man with little imagination. There will need to be some exercising of the little grey cells before a solution is arrived at, but many readers will correctly work out the significance of the physical clues, even if the name and actions of the culprit eludes them. Once more, those familiar with *The Hound of the Baskervilles* may have an advantage – this time in working out why Poirot becomes so interested in a portrait of Simeon as a young man.

In making the victim of this book a cruel and unsentimental head of the family, surrounded by those who would be better off if he were dead, Christie is reusing some of the basic premise of *Appointment with Death*, but this time with a male focus. Perhaps due to the rate of her writing during this period, it's common for threads from one book to be picked up again shortly afterwards and reused in a slightly different manner. Certainly, there are notable examples this decade of both motivation and method of murder being revisited, albeit in different contexts and in a way that means that the reader is unlikely to notice any similarities until all is revealed. However, although *Hercule Poirot's Christmas* has quite explicit similarities with its Poirot predecessor early on, the story that results from it is really very different. It's almost as if Christie is playing with the reader, showing them that she is perfectly capable of telling very different stories that may appear to have a similar basis. In *Appointment with Death*, it was the psychological tricks of the murderer that became key to solving the case, but here it's the practicalities of the crime, including physical clues and the location of suspects, that need untangling in order to provide a solution.

Party frocks featured on the 1952 Avon paperback.

Poirot appeared on this Spanish edition in 1958.

The Fontana paperback of 1959.

Hercule Poirot's Christmas was published in Britain in December 1938, although its publication in the United States, under the title *Murder for Christmas*, was the rather less festive February 1939.[110] *The Times Literary Supplement* enjoyed the appearance of 'a good violent murder', but was concerned that 'M. Poirot in his retirement is becoming too much of a colourless expert. One feels a nostalgic longing for the days when he baited his "good friend" and butt, Hastings, when he spoke malaprop English and astonished strangers by his intellectual arrogance.'[111] Such thoughts on Poirot's character echoed some criticism of his more recent cases, and *The Church Times*'s reviewer agreed in part: 'Poirot has mellowed with the years, but his faculties are unimpaired; though a more serious being, he is no less wise or intelligent,' the review stated, going on to say that Christie offers a 'legitimate and convincing twist at the end of the story'.[112] 'Torquemada' considered the novel to be 'a major Christie', despite some flaws, because the author 'once more abandonedly dangles the murderer before our eyes and successfully defies us to see him. I am sure that some purists will reverse my decision on the ground that the author, to get her effect, has broken what they consider to be one of the major rules of modern detective writing; but I hold that in a Poirot tale it should be a case of *caveat lector*, and that rules were not made for Agatha Christie.'[113] *The Manchester Guardian* wondered if the novel overused manufactured effect, such as the question of an open window, 'but how small are such blemishes compared with the brilliance of the whole conception!' For this genre of novel, the reviewer judged that 'Mrs Christie reigns supreme'.[114]

The 1930s saw Christie publish no fewer than twenty novels in total (including those under the name Mary Westmacott), as well as short story collections and plays for both stage and radio. The 1940s would see a gradual easing off from this prolific pace, and in turn a further movement away from Poirot, who would star in only six of the fifteen novels Christie published – indeed, there would be only two new Poirot novels between 1943 and 1951. Christie's interests increasingly lay elsewhere, especially the theatre, but she could not resist the commercial and critical interest in her little Belgian sleuth

Pan Books' photographic cover from 1967.

entirely. When we first met Poirot, the Great War was still ongoing. We followed him through the wealthy 1920s and the more troubled 1930s, but the coming of the new World War would change the world that he inhabited, not just politically, but in terms of society. The Second World War saw the disappearance of the country houses filled with servants where he had cut his teeth as a private detective, while the higher classes of society readjusted to a world that had, for once, moved on without consideration for them. Things would never be quite the same again.

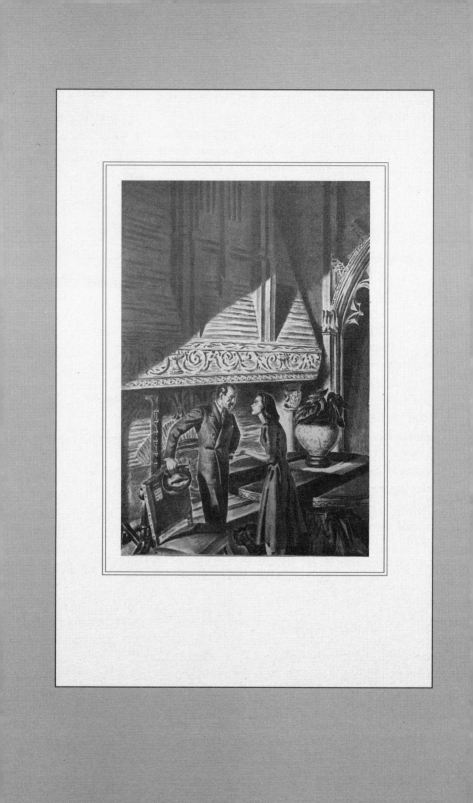

CHAPTER THREE:

THE

1940s

The Second World War was slow to arrive in the world of Hercule Poirot. That's not to say that the characters and events in Christie's stories were uniformly designed to exist in their own bubble, as the author had always been happy to acknowledge the changing world. Generally, this took the form of asides uttered by key characters, who discussed issues ranging from the economic impact of the First World War to the resultant difficulty in hiring servants; from the slow but definite rise of feminism to the building of new housing estates – and, most frequently, characters railing against the taxman and his ever-changing terms. Christie occasionally made politics the focus of her stories, but it was in her analysis of the smaller resultant events, such as the impact on characters, that her strength really lay.

OPPOSITE: The magazine *Collier's: An Illustrated Weekly* serialised *One, Two, Buckle My Shoe* in August 1940 as *The Patriotic Murders*, ilustrated by prolific Christie artist Mario Cooper.

Even aside from Christie's preferred focus away from politics, there were practical considerations that explain why Poirot was not much of an active participant in the war. If we take Christie's novel *Evil Under the Sun* as an example, her agent acknowledged delivery of the manuscript of this novel on 17 February 1939. On the same day, Adolf Hitler unveiled the Volkswagen to the German public, while later that month the Jewish population of Berlin was ordered to hand over any valuables to the state and a hundred Jewish people a day were given notice to leave Germany within two weeks. By September 1939, Europe was at war. In the end, this pre-war novel was not published until June 1941 in a country that had by then endured the Battle of Britain, and so conditions were markedly different from those during which Christie had originally penned a bright (but ruthless) story about Poirot on holiday. It's obvious that any contemporary references to war or other global events would have been long out of date by the time any book was actually published, and therefore understandable that the war was largely referred to in general terms only – and, in fact, acknowledged more heavily once peace returned.

For Poirot, the 1940s began in much the same manner as the previous decade. Four novels starring the detective were published between 1940 and 1943, approximately mirroring the pace of his appearances in the 1930s. However, Christie's attention was wandering elsewhere, as the 1940s saw her publish two non-crime novels under the pseudonym Mary Westmacott, as well as some excellent standalone mysteries, including 1949's *Crooked House* and two new cases for Miss Marple. New Poirot novels did appear in 1946 and 1948, as well as a connected short story collection, but the regularity of his appearances was slowing just as his celebrity elsewhere was growing. One result of this was a range of radio appearances on both sides of the Atlantic.

Sad Cypress
(Novel, 1940)

Sad Cypress concerns the poisoning of two people in unclear circumstances. The first victim is a wealthy woman whose estate now passes to her niece, Elinor Carlisle. Elinor's involvement in later events, including her preparation of an apparently poisoned sandwich for the second victim, results in her being tried for murder. When Poirot is invited to investigate the case by Dr Peter Lord, who's in love with Elinor, he warns his client that he may uncover more evidence that could condemn her to the gallows.[1] What follows is an underrated novel that is frustratingly good. It's good because it's an excellent mystery populated by intriguing

ABOVE LEFT: The first UK edition cover for *Sad Cypress* (1940). **ABOVE RIGHT:** Poirot himself made a rare US cover appearance on this 1951 Dell edition.

characters with a strong puzzle at its core. The frustration lies in one significant plot hole that – unlike the fundamentally unconvincing denouement of *Murder in Mesopotamia* – could have been fixed with ease. As it stands, the reader is expected to believe that the meticulous plan of the villain relies on a chance choice made by a victim – something that could have been easily solved had Christie allowed said victim to utter four words at an earlier opportunity.[2] This wasn't the last time that Christie was let down by her editors and agent, who should have spotted such inconsistencies and problematic leaps of logic, as many readers were quick to point out the flaw for themselves.

There are several layers of characterisation in *Sad Cypress*, with some of the participants doing little more than provide a function in the mechanics of the plot. However, others have secrets that will reveal a great deal about the machinations of

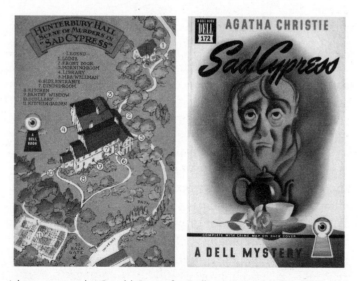

A bizarre cover by Gerald Gregg for Dell's 1947 'mapback' edition, with map by Ruth Belew.

the murderer, while the reader is also afforded insight into the internal thoughts of several key figures. Poirot makes a late entrance to the novel, and this tardiness would become even more of a habit in later years, but in this instance it is to the benefit of the story.[3] Several of Christie's novels deal with a crime in retrospect, and these need to be perfectly structured in order to command the attention throughout, as the selection of suspects and witnesses discussing the same incidents from different perspectives threatens to be tedious if handled poorly. Here, Christie manages to keep the reader intrigued and interested throughout, even during repeated discussions about sandwich paste that would seem mundane in other hands,

The tree and Hercule Poirot appeared on the 1954 Pan cover, art by M.G.

but form part of an excellent puzzle here. Elements of this puzzle and the story's premise had previously been presented in 'The House of Lurking Death', one of the best short stories in 1929's *Partners in Crime* collection. This mystery featured Tommy and Tuppence, who investigate a series of poisonings that may be linked to a wealthy heiress, with a series of pinpricks on a character's arm providing the clue that will lead them to the killer.

Many years later Christie bemoaned Poirot's inclusion in this novel, claiming that '*Sad Cypress* could have been good, but it was quite ruined by having Poirot in it. I always thought something was wrong with it, but didn't discover what till I read it some time after.'[4] Some may disagree, as Poirot's presence as an authority figure gives the reader confidence that more nuanced elements of the mystery will be given the proper level of attention. This includes details relating to roses that grow nearby, the significance of which is twofold as they become a key component in a clever and memorable piece of deduction. Once Poirot has solved the mystery, the courtroom finale rather underplays his role as it allows other characters to take centre stage, signalling Christie's declining interest in him.

When Christie submitted the typescript for *Sad Cypress* in 1938 her agent initially found that it was difficult to place it for serialisation, but in the end the popular American magazine *Collier's Weekly* was happy to pay $27,500 to publish a story that it considered to be one of Christie's very best.[5] From Christie's perspective, the drama was to come later, when she saw the dustjacket for the novel in early 1940, just a couple of months before it arrived in British book shops. It depicted a dark cypress tree in front of a teal background, with bold yellow text for the novel's title and author. Christie's response was forthright. 'AWFUL - so *common!*'[6] She later explained that 'My idea was that a black and white jacket would be very artistic and striking ... the cypress itself is all right but the effect of it is obliterated by the lettering ... yellow is particularly ugly with the blue *and* black'.

Christie's sketch showing her original idea for the cover.

Christie seems to have sketched her own idea for the cover in one of her notebooks, showing a similar cypress tree alongside what appears to be a coffin.[7] This may allude to the original source for the title, the song *Come Away, Come Away, Death* from Shakespeare's *Twelfth Night*, which refers to both the tree ('Come away, come away, death / And in sad cypress let me be laid') and 'my black coffin'. Christie didn't let the matter rest when told it was probably too late to change the cover, pleading with her agent Edmund Cork, 'Can you use all your influence? Do! Can't *bear* the Cypress obliterated by the lettering'.[8] Cork soon confirmed that Collins believed that, in time, a change to the cover would be possible but it seemed unpatriotic to destroy 15,000 copies at a time of paper shortage. In a response that says something about the sometimes curious relationship between author and agent, Cork wrote to Christie say that he felt he'd failed her in this matter.[9] As a result, Collins was given instructions that Christie was to see all jackets before printing, in an echo of her displeasure with the cover of the second Poirot novel, *The Murder on the Links*.

Agatha Christie

Sad Cypress

The 1968 Fontana cover had a painting by Ian Robinson, whose Christie covers were uncredited and regularly confused with those by Tom Adams.

The Collins Crime Club advertised *Sad Cypress* by writing that 'The incomparable Agatha Christie brings all her great talents to bear on this grimly fascinating poison drama.' *The Times Literary Supplement* agreed that the book demonstrated some of her greatest skills:

> Like all Mrs Christie's work, it is economically written, the clues are placed before the reader with impeccable fairness, the red herrings are deftly laid and the solution will cause many readers to kick themselves. Some

occasional readers of detective stories are wont to criticize Mrs Christie on the ground that her stories are insufficiently embroidered, that she includes, for instance, no epigrams over the college port. But is it not time to state that in the realm of detective fiction proper, where problems are fairly posed and fairly solved, there is no one to touch her?[10]

The Manchester Guardian pointed out that 'Mrs Christie has been neglecting Poirot of late, and many readers will be glad to welcome him back in *Sad Cypress*, as successful and perky as ever'.[11] In summary, *The Observer* simply remarked that 'Characterisation [is as] brilliantly intense as ever. In fact, Agatha Christie has done it again, which is all you need to know.'[12]

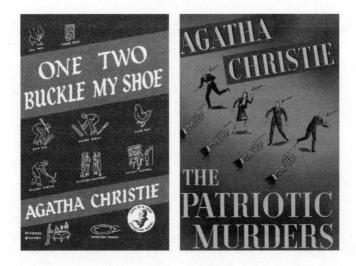

One, Two, Buckle My Shoe
(Novel, 1940)

'Are you having an awful time in London? I suspect so,' Christie wrote to Billy Collins, of the eponymous publishers, in September 1940. 'What a hellish nightmare this war is.'[13] Christie wrote this letter from her holiday home Greenway, in south Devon, as she watched training exercises taking place in the River Dart below – preparations for a possible German invasion. She had bought the house in 1938 but in 1942 she was forced to vacate it to allow the Admiralty to make use of it, something that she willingly did, but with more than a little sadness.[14] When the war was over she returned and found a beautiful frieze painted by one of the

ABOVE LEFT: The UK first edition with drawings referencing the nursery rhyme on which the title was based (1940). **ABOVE RIGHT:** Four suspects appeared on the first US edition with the US title *The Patriotic Murders*.

Hercule Poirot from the *Collier's* magazine serial *The Patriotic Murders*, illustrated by Mario Cooper (1940).

American inhabitants, which ran the length of the library walls and survives to this day.[15] She went on to have many happy memories of staying there with her family each summer, most particularly in later years when her grandson Mathew joined her during the break from school. Mathew, Christie's only grandchild, was born in 1943 following the 1940 marriage of her daughter Rosalind to Hubert Prichard. Despite her relative wealth and privilege, Christie and her family were no casual bystanders when it came to the devastation caused by the war. They endured more significant losses than mere property, as sadly Hubert Prichard was killed in 1944 while on active service.

This changing world underpinned Christie's next novel, which leapfrogged *Evil Under the Sun* in the release schedule despite the other book having been delivered many months earlier. It's likely that this was due to the timeliness of *One, Two, Buckle My Shoe*, which opens with perhaps the least captivating premise of any of Christie's novels, as Poirot makes a visit to the dentist – might it be that the author enjoyed the idea of torturing her sleuth? While Poirot has his fillings attended to, he's subjected to his dentist's ruminations on the status of the prominent banker Alistair Blunt, another of his patients, who we later learn is an essential component in the stable running of the country in tumultuous times. 'Always comes to his appointments absolutely on time,' Mr Morley, the dentist, tells Poirot, 'You'd never dream he could buy up half Europe! Just like you and me.' This claimed equivalence irritates Poirot ('Mr. Morley was

The 1943 Pocket Books cover by H. Lawrence Hoffman.

a good dentist, yes, but there were other good dentists in London. There was only one Hercule Poirot') but he cannot interject while the dentist continues his monologue as he performs work on Poirot's cavity:

'It's the answer, you know, to their Hitlers and Mussolinis and all the rest of them,' went on Mr. Morley, as he proceeded to tooth number two. 'We don't make a fuss over here. Look how democratic our King and Queen are. Of course, a Frenchman like you, accustomed to the Republican idea – '

This is the last straw, and Poirot cannot stop himself from speaking out, mid-operation or not – 'I ah nah a Frahah – I ah – ah a Benyon'!

By the end of *One, Two, Buckle My Shoe* three people have been murdered, including the dentist who had so irritated Poirot, and a woman whose shoe buckle provides an important clue for the detective. Political factions are alluded to (potential enemies of Blunt are stated to be 'The Reds, to

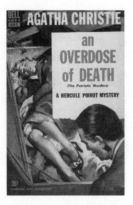

Dell reissued the book as *An Overdose of Death*, with this cover by Carl Bobertz in 1953.

begin with – and our Black-shirted friends, too') but communism is just a red-herring. The basic components of the mystery, including the locations of suspects and timing of the murder, are predominately a technical puzzle, albeit one that doesn't have the high quality trail of clues leading to the killer that the reader will have come to expect. The most interesting piece of psychology comes at the end for Poirot's own consideration, as he must once more decide if justice should always be carried out. The presence of the war was the subject of contradictory correspondence for Christie's agents, as several publications stated that they did not want a war-focused story for their readers, while *Collier's Weekly* requested precisely the opposite. In the end, Christie acquiesced to *Collier's* demands. 'Have spent some miserable days tinkering at this. I think it is all right now,' she wrote to Cork, 'have dragged the war in neck and crop all over the place … I hope they're satisfied as I want the money!'[16] Perhaps the casual mentions of political leaders and factions in the novel are indications of a compromise when it comes to the inclusion of the war – certainly Cork suggested that at least some of these late changes could be kept for the novel, which they were.[17]

When Christie sent her typescript of the story to her agent it was not exactly met with a rapturous response, as Cork wrote to her that he had enjoyed the novel less than some of her others, and Christie agreed with his sentiment – 'not one of my best'.[18] This conclusion was fair, but there are certainly ingenious elements, including a clever method and motive for murder. However, the novel lacks the array of colourful characters that make for the best Christie mysteries, and it doesn't help that the mixture of a dentist, a banker and simmering political tensions will fail to excite many casual readers. The novel is also an example of Christie's propensity for awkwardly fitting nursery rhymes into her stories, and with each chapter named after a portion of the rhyme, whether appropriate or not, it becomes a somewhat irritating link. In America the mystery's title was changed completely, but renaming it *The Patriotic Murders* was no doubt felt to be timely given the contemporary role of nationalism, even if it doesn't make much sense in terms of the actual story.[19]

Nevertheless, the novel offers some good characterisation, and humour, including a grotesque but darkly amusing moment when a porter vomits upon seeing the body that he has to identify. It's also good to see Poirot back to his difficult self from the first chapter, as he takes his place as an active participant in the story, while he later rails against

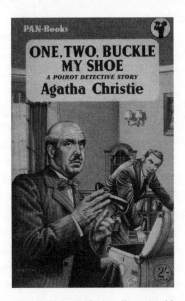

Monsieur Poirot on the 1956 Pan edition, illustrated by Derek A. Stowe.

Agatha Christie

ONE, TWO,
BUCKLE
MY SHOE

fontana books

Collins' Fontana cover
by an unknown artist
from 1959.

sentimentality – 'It is not I who am sentimental! That is an English failing! It is in England that they weep over young sweethearts and dying mothers and devoted children. Me, I am logical.' Some of Poirot's idiosyncrasies, such as his neatness, become crucial to his solving of the mystery, not that Chief Inspector Japp gives him much credit to begin with. This is the final appearance of Japp in a novel, and he's as brusque as ever, but his cynicism and arrogance serve a function for the reader who follows the untangling of the mystery from multiple perspectives.

This time, Christie's opinions on the cover were actively solicited by Billy Collins, but unusually the author had no idea – 'My brain is a blank about *Buckle My Shoe*! ... How about just having a vague patent leather shoe and gleaming buckle – above big black [question mark]?'[20] In the end, the British first edition cover included small line drawings re-enacting the nursery rhyme. Christie saw a draft and declared that 'I think it is very ingenious', which no doubt led to a sigh of relief from her agent.[21]

In its review of the book following its publication in November 1940, *The Times Literary Supplement* drew attention to what it perceived to be a 'dry' and 'joyless' Christie novel, in which 'the atmosphere is not that of places but of a police report. There is no questioning the cleverness of *One, Two, Buckle My Shoe*. Its mystery will not be easily solved. But it is as cold and cheerless as a diagram.'[22] Such an opinion was not shared elsewhere, however, with *The Manchester Guardian*'s reviewer writing that 'it may be said of Mrs Agatha Christie that she is "easy to read" and to be "easy to read", if not the greatest of qualities a writer may possess, is one of the most valuable.'[23] Meanwhile, *The Observer* continued to compliment Christie's writing skills: 'The Queen of Crime's scheming ingenuity has been so much praised that one is sometimes inclined to overlook the lightness of her touch. If Mrs Christie were to write about the murder of a telephone directory by a timetable the story would still be eminently readable.'[24]

Christie herself received something of a forthright complaint, as a reader wrote to her to say that Poirot had become 'wearisome' and 'insufferable'. The author replied with good humour and honesty, acknowledging that 'Poirot is rather insufferable. Most public men are who have lived too long. But none of them like retiring! So I'm afraid Poirot won't either – certainly not while he is my chief source of income!'.[25]

Evil Under the Sun
(Novel, 1941)

More than twenty years after he had first solved a mystery in the pages of an Agatha Christie story, it seems only fair that Poirot is permitted to take a holiday in one of Agatha's favourite places, south Devon, in *Evil Under the Sun*. The place in question is undeniably based on Burgh Island, with its 1930s luxury hotel that has appeared in two Agatha Christie adaptations, including the ITV version of this novel in 2001.[26] Here, Poirot's rest is interrupted by the rather ostentatious behaviour of some of the guests, including the glamorous Arlena Marshall, whose relationships with her husband, step-daughter and potential lover mark her out to be a likely

ABOVE LEFT: The first edition of *Evil Under the Sun* from Collins' Crime Club. **ABOVE RIGHT:** In the US, the 1941 first edition was illustrated by Paul Galdone.

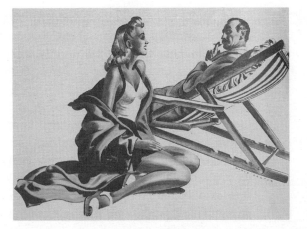

Artwork by Mario Cooper from *Collier's Weekly* magazine serial of *Evil Under the Sun* showed Poirot determined to enjoy his summer holiday (1940).

target for murder. This proves to be the case when she's discovered dead by Patrick Redfern, who had been arranging to meet her for a secret rendezvous away from the prying eyes of his downtrodden wife.

We can only imagine how differently this story must have read to those who eagerly purchased it upon its initial book publication in summer 1941. Written before the war, few can know how this story's range of colourful characters, sundrenched beaches and hefty doses of witchcraft, drug smuggling and betrayal may have been read by a weary reader while bombs fell from the sky and loved ones risked their lives for their country. Like *Peril at End House*, the novel has a sunny veneer while hiding a cruel core. Christie was never afraid to pull the rug from underneath the reader just as we felt we could be confident in our sympathies, and she does so particularly well here. However, while the earlier short story 'Triangle at Rhodes' (collected in 1937's *Murder in the Mews*) offered elements that were an obvious choice for expansion,

A bearded Poirot in the background of the 1957 Fontana cover.

This 1958 Spanish edition featured a new angle on Poirot.

when done so for this full-length mystery Christie supplied a surplus of extraneous characters. The result is that the novel sometimes runs the risk of distracting and frustrating the reader rather than embellishing the story.

A modern reading of the book may suffer from the fact that the frequently seen 1982 film of the novel, starring Peter Ustinov, actually fixes various weaker issues in the novel through its condensing of characters and subplots. The film also imbues the story with tremendous energy thanks to its all-star cast, which also means that the atmosphere of it somewhat dominates Christie's own writing at times. But, as ever, the murder is the thing, and this perfectly constructed puzzle will require the reader to rethink their understanding of not only time and place, but also relationships, before they can even start to reach the solution arrived at by Poirot.

When Christie's agent took delivery of the typescript in February 1939 he keenly announced that he had particularly enjoyed it. Christie was a little more on the ball when it came to ideas for the cover this time, as she sent Billy Collins a sketch for the jacket that had been designed by a friend – 'I do hope you won't hate it! I think it looks marvellously evil myself!'[27]

Unfortunately, no copy of this picture is known to survive, and from the description it's unlikely to be the rather serene picture of a beach that adorned the first edition.

'To maintain a place at the head of detective-writers would be difficult enough without the ever increasing rivalry,' read *The Times Literary Supplement*'s review of the book:

Unbiased opinion may have given the verdict against her last season when new arrivals set a very hot pace; but *Evil Under the Sun* will take a lot of beating now ... Everybody is well aware that any character most strongly indicated is not a likely criminal; yet this guiding principle is forgotten when Miss Christie persuades you that you are more discerning than you really are. Then she springs her secret like a land mine.[28]

The Observer considered the book to be Christie's best since *And Then There Were None* – 'Smashing solution, after clouds of dust thrown in your eyes, ought to catch you right out. Light as a soufflé'.[29] *The Yorkshire Post*'s reviewer enjoyed the book but questioned the credulity of the solution, which was also raised in a lengthy discussion of Christie's works generally in *The Manchester Guardian*:[30]

Is it going too far to call Mrs Agatha Christie one of the most remarkable writers of the day? Consider how many and how various are the tribute that may be paid to her work: well-written – her English is always good, even if she seldom produces a striking phrase; equipped with well-observed characters – her people are always recognisable human beings, even if she seldom creates a memorable character; ingenious – to use an Americanism, ingenuity is Mrs Christie's middle name; humorous – she has a marked sense of fun; dramatic – she has always a surprise in story for the reader; finally, there is that gift for narrative whereby a reader's attention is held throughout. One can, of course, find fault. She has occasionally a somewhat lordly way with probability, though perhaps it may be said that her chief fault is an absence of fault, for a success so unbroken is apt to mean an avoidance of the greater heights.[31]

I CLASSICI DEL GIALLO
MONDADORI

Agatha Christie
CORPI
AL SOLE
TUTTO IN UNA EDIZIONE

Hercule Poirot by artist Carlo Jacono on the 1988 Italian paperback.

Such critical and commercial success were valuable commodities for any publisher, and so when Christie's American agent and publisher had discussions regarding her new contract (*Evil Under the Sun* being the final title for the then-current deal) there was already a request on the table to reduce the advances paid. This wasn't the right direction for earnings to take for a writer of Christie's stature, but her American agent, Harold Ober, was used to listening to such tales of woe. As he relayed this information to Edmund Cork, Christie's British agent, Ober reassured his colleague that he was very aware that now was not the time to send bad news to England.[32] Christie's tax affairs were under scrutiny, causing the author a great deal of stress, and things were only going to get worse.

Five Little Pigs
(Novel, 1943)

For *Five Little Pigs* Agatha Christie revisits a theme that she recently deployed for *Sad Cypress*, which was given away by this new novel's alternative title, *Murder in Retrospect*. The premise of a revisited crime reappeared many times in her stories, including the final Poirot novel that she wrote, 1972's *Elephants Can Remember*. This latter book sadly exposed the potential weaknesses of this approach (most particularly in its use of repetition) – but, unwittingly, it also demonstrated how masterful these earlier attempts were. However the author set herself a particularly difficult task with *Five Little Pigs*.

ABOVE LEFT: The five little piggies from the nursery rhyme adorned Collins' bright yellow cover (1943). **ABOVE RIGHT:** Another title change – to *Murder in Retrospect* – for the US, published the year before the British edition.

In this story, Poirot is approached by young Carla Crale, who wishes to find out the truth about her parents in order to secure a happy relationship for herself. We learn that sixteen years earlier her mother, Caroline, was convicted of murdering the painter Amyas Crale, who was Caroline's husband and Carla's father. The prosecution argued that she had poisoned her husband due to his philandering ways, and Caroline offered little in the way of defence, but while in prison wrote to her daughter to assert her innocence. Caroline later died while still incarcerated, leaving Poirot to try to uncover the truth about a murder that not only took place quite some time previously, but one where there seem to be only five credible suspects – the five little pigs of the title (which enables Christie to echo another nursery rhyme, a trope that she is perhaps starting to overuse). It's to Christie's great credit that these restrictions lead to such a fascinating character study, in which the reader will learn

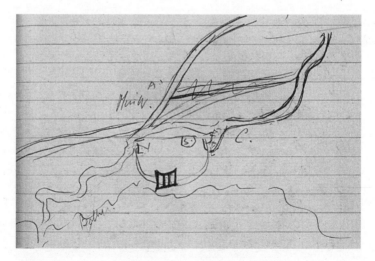

Agatha Christie sketched out the riverside battery at Greenway to help work out the characters' movements in the book.

not only about the suspects in the present day but also try to work out what their current situations and recollections tells us about the murder that took place many years earlier. The actual method and motive of the crime is not necessarily a complex one, but the way in which these retrospective thoughts must be untangled in order to discover the solution means that attention must be paid to evidence, and not just assertions and assumptions made by those suspected of the crime.

Some readers have found the story to be a little slow and lacking in dynamism, especially in its earlier stages, but this may be because the puzzle here relies on the reader gradually working out the true motivations of these well-drawn characters. Meanwhile, Christie supplies one of her very best plain sight clues in a piece of dialogue that will only be appreciated by most when Poirot highlights its significance towards the end of the novel. By now regular readers

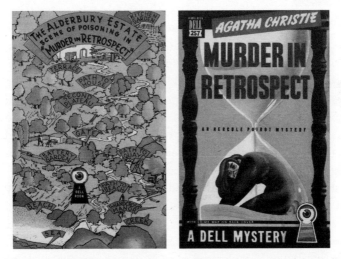

The map of the Alderbury Estate, as featured on the back of the Dell 'mapback' edition. The front cover was by Gerald Gregg (1948).

of Agatha Christie will have been aware that working out and understanding the psychological truth of the cast of characters is just as important as identifying and deciphering verbal and physical clues when it comes to solving the mystery. Just as in *Murder on the Orient Express*, it is important to pay attention to the apparently minor details shared by the suspects when they are interviewed by Poirot.

Five Little Pigs was the first time that Christie's new holiday home of Greenway featured in one of her mysteries, with the Battery overlooking the River Dart providing the location for the murder. Christie even sketched out the area in her notebooks alongside her plans for the story, in a demonstration of her methodical nature when it came to plotting mysteries. *Five Little Pigs* was completed in 1940, the year that really saw the beginning of Christie's substantial problems with tax in the United States, leading to a dispute with the authorities that would take many years to resolve. Any researcher of Christie will have been struck by the sheer quantity of discussions in her correspondence regarding tax, even before the affairs of those working for her, such as her agent, are taken into account. The formation of Agatha Christie Ltd in 1955 essentially made Christie an employee and solved many of these tax problems, but the author would spend many years worrying about her income even while becoming the world's most widely read novelist.

Hercule Poirot in a rare appearance on a Finnish edition cover in 1948.

Five Little Pigs was published in Great Britain in January 1943, sporting a bright yellow jacket design that featured drawings of the nursery rhyme, echoing of the cover of *One, Two, Buckle My Shoe*. Although Cork had written to Christie to say that it would look good as a Christmas present, perhaps it was the difficulties of wartime that led to its official publication being delayed until the new year.[33] Readers in the United States were able to pick the novel up several months earlier, when it was published there under the title *Murder in Retrospect*, the same name given to the story when it was serialised in *Collier's Weekly* in late 1941. When Christie saw the British edition of the book she was forced to compile a list of corrections, with errors appearing even before the story itself started, as *Death on the Nile* was mangled as *Death on the Hill* in the list of Christie's other works, while the third sentence of the novel managed to refer to 'a more request' rather than 'a mere request', setting the standard of typesetting to come.[34]

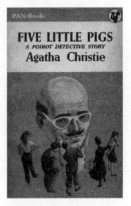

A slew of familiar bouquets were on offer for Christie from the critics, with *The Observer's* review stating that 'Despite only five suspects, Mrs Christie, as usual, puts a ring through the reader's nose and leads him to one of her smashing last-minute showdowns. This is well up to the standard of her middle Poirot period. No more need be said.'[35] *The Times Literary Supplement* stated that 'No crime enthusiast will object that the story of how the painter died has to be told many times, for this, even if it creates an interest which is more problem than plot, demonstrates the author's uncanny skill. The answer to the riddle is brilliant.'[36] Meanwhile, *The Manchester Guardian* simply reminded its readers that 'Miss Agatha Christie never fails us, and her *Five Little Pigs* presents a very pretty problem for the ingenious reader'.[37] Christie considered the story strong enough that in 1960 she adapted it as a stage play, under the title *Go Back For Murder*, with Poirot removed from proceedings.

A bespectacled Poirot on the 1953 Pan paperback, painted by F.V.M.

By the early 1940s Christie was starting to have something of a backlog of book typescripts, just as she was wondering how worthwhile her efforts were when she was receiving very

Agatha Christie
Five Little Pigs

Tom Adams' intricate painting on the 1977 Fontana paperback.

little money while her tax problems rumbled on. This resulted in Christie slowing down her writing, eventually settling on one book a year. It also explains why this surplus, plus the troubles of the war (and the desire to provide for her family after her death, whatever her tax situation), meant that now was the perfect time to pen Poirot's finale. *Curtain: Poirot's Last Case* was sent to her agents by early 1941, with strict instructions that it was not to be published – indeed, its very existence was designated top secret by those involved.[38] Its contents would be unknown to the wider world until its eventual publication in late 1975. At this point, Cork also assured his client that there was no particular need for the next novel to feature Poirot, and that she was free to write as she wished.[39] However, Poirot refused to stay silent.

MYSTERY...INTRIGUE...
ADVENTURE...WITH

hercule poirot

CBS MONDAY THROUGH FRIDAY
OVER YOUR CBS STATION

Poirot Returns to the Radio

The 1940s were still a boom time for American radio and crime fiction, and so it should be no surprise that their paths crossed on occasion, with several series adapting mysteries for the airwaves. One of these programmes was *Murder Clinic*, which ran during 1942 and 1943 and adapted stories from a selection of well-known authors, including Edgar Wallace, Eden Philpotts, Dorothy L. Sayers, E.C. Bentley, Carter Dickson, G.K. Chesterton, Ngaio Marsh, and – of course – Agatha Christie.[40]

Five Christie stories are known to have been adapted, two of which were not Poirot mysteries – 'The Blue Geranium' featured Vivian Ogden as Miss Marple, while an unknown actor played Parker Pyne in 'Death on the Nile', the short

ABOVE: Harold Huber as Poirot in CBS's 1945 radio series, featuring original stories not by Agatha Christie.

The American short story collection *The Regatta Mystery*, with an 1958 Avon cover by David Stone.

story that is not the same as the Poirot novel of the same name. Poirot made his series debut on 6 October 1942 in an adaptation of 'The Tragedy at Marsdon Manor', which opened with the narrator meeting Poirot and mentioning his magnificent moustaches, establishing an important visual element of the character.[41] Like the rest of the series, the breezy half-hour adaptation was written by Lee Wright and John A. Blanton, doing excellent work with this very good short story from 1924's *Poirot Investigates*. The cast is uniformly strong, with an array of original and convincing British accents preserving the story's original location, while widely-used voice actor Maurice Tarplin creates an engaging and convincing portrayal of Hercule Poirot, although Hastings (played by an uncredited actor) gets less chance to shine. Excellent use is made of sound effects and music to maintain the pace and suspense of the entertaining production, and it's a great shame that it's the only Christie adaptation from the series known to survive.

The next Poirot story in the series was 'Triangle at Rhodes' from 1937's *Murder in the Mews*, but little more is known about the adaptation. We can't even be sure who played Poirot, although it's possible that Tarplin reprised his role as he was a regular contributor to the programme, or it could have been Ted de Corsia, who played the part in an adaptation of 'Yellow Iris' on 25 July 1943. This latter production was almost certainly an original adaptation of the short story of the same title, which had appeared in the American collection *The Regatta Mystery* in 1939, rather than a reworking of Christie's radio play version of the tale, which had been performed on the BBC in 1937.[42]

Poirot had not entirely abandoned his creator's home

country in order to bask in the American spotlight, however, as 17 June 1944 saw the BBC Home Service broadcast an adaptation of *Alibi*, the Michael Morton play based on *The Murder of Roger Ackroyd*. While an adaptation of an already adapted play might seem a curious choice, the plays were always easier to license than the novels. The production ran for an hour and a quarter in the *Saturday Night Theatre* slot and starred Basil Sydney as Poirot alongside Arthur Ridley as Dr Sheppard, performing a script adapted by Muriel Pratt. The mystery doesn't seem to have created much interest, perhaps because *Alibi* had been widely seen since its debut more than fifteen years early, but at least it showed that Poirot was still welcome on British radio. The play also appeared on Canadian radio later the same year, adopting a title used by Morton's play in North America, *The Fatal Alibi*.[43] Four years later, Austin Trevor reprised the role of Poirot in a Home Service broadcast of Arnold Ridley's stage adaptation of *Peril at End House*, broadcast on 29 May 1948. This showed that he was still remembered as Poirot fourteen years after he last played the character on film, and he would return to the role again in the next decade.

Across the Atlantic, 1944 saw plans to bring Poirot to American radio on a more permanent basis, as American actor Harold Huber aggressively pursued the possibility of an ongoing radio series starring himself as the detective. Huber and Christie had connected a few years earlier, probably unbeknownst to either party, as *Sad Cypress* included a fleeting reference to the film *The Good Earth* (1937), a drama about Chinese farmers that featured Huber in a minor role. Huber told Christie's American agent that a Poirot series would earn her at least $250 a week, and possibly as much as $750, even though the tax situation would make it difficult to extract any money from the United States. Despite the fact that the series would be nearly entirely made up of original stories rather than Christie's own mysteries – something that would usually horrify her – she agreed.[44] It may be that it was easier for Christie to agree to projects that she wouldn't encounter personally, while her American agents advised that it would be valuable publicity for her books. The trade press confirmed the deal with Huber in March 1944, but it didn't make its debut on air until 22 February 1945, when Poirot was introduced as being 'complete with bowler hat and brave moustache' before his 'first American adventure'.[45] A recorded message from Christie herself then prefaced the story:[46]

> I feel that this is an occasion that would have appealed to Hercule Poirot. He would have done justice to the inauguration of this radio programme, and he might even have made it seem something of an international event. However, as he's heavily engaged on an investigation, about which you will hear in due course, I must, as one of his oldest friends, deputise for him. The great man has his little foibles, but really, I have the greatest affection for him. And it is a source of continuing satisfaction to me that there has been such a generous response to his appearance on my books, and I hope that his new career on the radio will make many new friends for him among a wider public.

In this first episode, 'The Case of the Careless Victim', Poirot establishes himself in New York and introduces the listeners to his friend Inspector Stevens as well as the no-nonsense Miss Abigail Fletcher, who becomes Poirot's secretary. Details about the series are sparse, with only around a dozen episodes known to survive out of more than three hundred, including 'Murder Wears a Mask', in which Peter Donald steps in to play Poirot without explanation.[47] Even episode titles are difficult to uncover due to the lack of details in most listings, although we do know that the format of the programme changed from self-contained half-hour episodes to multi-part stories from August 1946.[48] There was at least one adaptation, 'Rendezvous with Death', which was a much reduced retelling of *Death on the Nile*, and it seems likely that there were more.

RADIO SLEUTH—Harold Huber, well known to movie fans for his character roles portrays Hercule Poirot, the famous fictional belgium detective in "Hercules Poirot, Detective Extraordinary" now being heard on WCLO-MBS Sundays at 8 p. m.

Harold Huber promoting 'Hercules Poirot, Detective Extraordinary' in a US newspaper.

The existing episodes show that this was a fast-paced series that heavily relied on characters describing intricate details, such that it can be difficult to follow at times, although the cast (and so list of suspects) usually remains small. Huber is a very good Poirot, imbuing the detective with the right sense of pomposity and likeability to make him a success on the airwaves. The show was seen as a premium product by its producers, but a *Variety* report nine months into its broadcasts claimed that the programme didn't rate particularly well.[49] The trade paper's review of the episode 'The Case of the Roaming Corpse' in March 1945 claimed that the show to that point had run 'hot and cold, one week a good show, next a bad one.' Huber was received positively, although for some reason the reviewer seemed to believe that Poirot's first name was 'Arnold'. However, the production was warned that stronger scripts were needed if longevity was to be achieved. When reviewed again in August 1946, *Variety* complimented the show's 'tight and fast-paced' script, which indicates that the move to serialised adventures had been a success.[50] Less happily for Huber, January 1946 saw a successful lawsuit filed against him by writer Martin Stern for $16,000 following use of his audition script for the series without the agreed remuneration.[51]

Despite Christie's initial co-operation, the series' existence seems to have rankled with the author. She requested that her agents declined any attempt for the series to be broadcast closer to home or near to large expat communities, whether in continental Europe or South Africa. In 1947 she wrote to Edmund Cork to say 'Perish the thought that I should ever have a synthetic Poirot on the wireless in this country. It's not easy to bear the thought of it in America.'[52] It's worth considering what Christie meant by 'synthetic' here, as from the context is seems likely that her concerns were about the words he was speaking (and, perhaps, the mysteries he was solving) rather than an actor's performance. In other words, in Christie's eyes it seemed that a Poirot who didn't speak her own words was no Poirot at all.

The conditions attached to the series by Christie and her agents increasingly frustrated Harold Huber, who felt that he was excessively hindered by their resistance to selling the series to lucrative international markets. However, some of the scripts were eventually recycled for an Australian series in the 1950s, which starred Alan White as Poirot.[53] In 1948 Huber hit on a new idea, and decided to bring his Poirot to television. Harold Ober wasn't convinced that television was sufficiently well established as a medium to allow Poirot to take a regular spot (he was similarly cautious about a request to broadcast *The Wasp's Nest* on American television in 1949), while Edmund Cork correctly anticipated that the proposal would be firmly declined by Christie in any case. Huber was incredulous, becoming the latest actor to feel he had some ownership over the character given his success in the role. Despite predictions that

Listen Tonight!

Hercule Poirot

master detective, solves your entertainment problems in

MYSTERY of the WEEK

Monday through Friday **6:00** P.M.
CBS Station for Oelwein

A 1946 newspaper ad for the Harold Huber series.

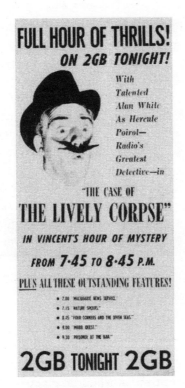

Alan White starred as Poirot on radio in Australia.

a series would lead to between $200 and $500 per episode for Christie, the author stood firm. Her agent specified that the rationale for her declining to agree was emotionally driven, which she rationalised in part by saying that she feared that the goodwill towards the character as imagined by reader could be destroyed by a version on screen that may be quite different. Huber called Ober's office daily to check the progress of his proposal, and then to demand a full explanation for why it was declined. The reason was straightforward; Poirot was Christie's creation, and she could do what she liked with him. Others could not.

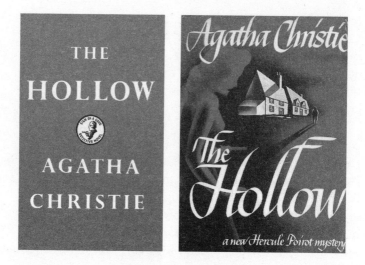

The Hollow
(Novel, 1946)

One of Hercule Poirot's greatest weaknesses must surely be his excessive optimism when he plans his holidays and eventual retirement. Every holiday he undertakes seems to lead to a mystery that needs solving, and usually a murderer to unmask, while even his retirement to the English countryside to grow marrows lasted only a short time before his little grey cells were called upon. When the detective finally arrives in the eleventh chapter of *The Hollow* we learn of his new weekend cottage, and we know that this will not be

ABOVE LEFT: The UK dustwrapper for *The Hollow* reflected post-war austerity with its two-colour printing and complete lack of illustration (1946). **ABOVE RIGHT:** Published in America by Dodd, Mead in 1946, *The Hollow* is a rare example of a Christie book that would change title after its initial publication.

the place for relaxation that he has purchased his piece of the countryside for. Not that Poirot is particularly relaxed anyway, troubled as he is by the asymmetrical landscape that surrounds him. This cottage keeps Poirot on the periphery of this mystery, both figuratively and literally, as a short walk away is the rather grander country house called The Hollow, owned by Sir Henry and Lady (Lucy) Angkatell. It's at The Hollow that family friend Dr John Christow is murdered, with Poirot arriving on the scene just in time to see Gerda, Christow's wife, standing over him with a gun in her hand. Christow's final word, 'Henrietta', refers to his lover, but such an obvious act of murderous revenge would surely be too easy a case for the great Hercule Poirot.

A WHITE CIRCLE POCKET EDITION

'Look for the woman' – a 1948 Collins White Circle paperback for the export market.

Christie was once again inspired by real life for the location of the murder, but this time it was the house and pool owned by Poirot performer Francis L. Sullivan that provided the template for the setting. As a thank you Christie dedicated the book to Sullivan (known as Larry) and his wife Danae, 'with apologies for using their swimming pool as the scene of a murder.' The return to a country house for this novel raises the possibility that Christie's mysteries could start to feel like a pastiche of her earlier work, but the author was unapologetic about revisiting this type of location throughout her career:

> The one thing that infuriates me is when people complain that I always set my books in country houses. You have to be concerned with a house: with where people live. You can make it an hotel, or a train, or a pub – but it's got to be where people are brought together. And I think it must be a background that readers will recognise, because

The Hollow became Murder After Hours for its US paperback outings, including this Griffith Foxley cover from 1954.

explanations are so boring. If you set a detective story in, say, a laboratory, I don't think people would enjoy it so much. No, a country house is obviously the best.[54]

Christie made this observation in 1966, and reflecting on the changes that the new era had brought she noted that 'It's rather dull nowadays, you are always in a cement factory or office. There seems to be less general play of drama in surroundings.'[55] Nevertheless, *The Hollow* marked the beginning of the final era for the traditional country house setting that Christie had previously made much use of.

Christie completed the novel in September 1944, with her notebooks showing that she initially gave it the title *Echo*, inspired by the Tennyson quote that Poirot mutters at one point, which would also inspire the book's eventual title:

> I hate the dreadful hollow behind the little wood
> Its lips in the field above are dabbled with blood-red heath
> The red-ribb'd ledges drip with a silent horror of blood
> And Echo there, whatever is ask'd her, answers 'Death.'

Poirot has his work cut out for him when it comes to trying to solve this case, as the mystery's apparent neatness is enough to make the detective (and reader) wonder if more is at play here, and he will need to work out which of his witnesses he can really trust. This suspicion is obvious, but the motivations behind any apparently misleading evidence will be more difficult to decipher. By the end of the novel Poirot is placed in a situation reminiscent of an earlier case, although the outcome will be quite different.

Harold Ober particularly enjoyed the story, although he had difficulties in securing an outlet for the lucrative serialisation. This concerned Edmund Cork, who considered Christie to be a little downbeat and wished to pass on good news that would provide welcome 'psychological stimulus' as, Cork claimed, people seemed more weary since the VE Day celebrations the previous month.[56]

In the end, *Collier's Weekly* agreed to pay $25,000 for the rights but only on the condition that it was substantially shortened – the main requirement being that the murder should occur much earlier in proceedings. The magazine then serialised the story in May 1946, under the title *The Outraged Heart*.[57] When published as a novel later in 1946 it sold very well, proving that Christie and Poirot were as popular as ever.[58]

Hercule Poirot contemplates blood in the pool on the cover of the 1957 Spanish edition.

'*The Hollow* displays Mrs. Christie at the top of her form,' wrote *The Church Times*' reviewer. 'A mellowed and almost Anglicized Poirot is in charge of enquiries, but the Angkatells and their ill-assorted guests steal all the thunder from him ... It may be disputed whether, in the development of her plot, Mrs. Christie does not put over a bigger bluff than her amiable characters. At any rate, the final explanation is convincing in its simplicity, and yet is clever enough to deceive the very elect.'[59] This bluff (and the way that Poirot is introduced to it) is probably one of Christie's most underrated solutions, but to say more would be to spoil the story. *The Hollow* is also blessed with a cast of characters whose inscrutability will become key to solving the

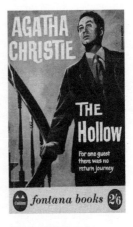

Barbara Walton's dramatic cover from 1961 for *The Hollow*.

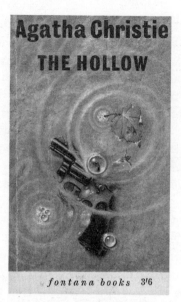

Agatha Christie
THE HOLLOW

fontana books 3'6

An early Tom Adams cover for Fontana Books from 1961 before they introduced the more recognisable white border.

murder. 'From the gossipy and irresistible Lady Angkatell to the dry and depressing wife of the doctor they are all real figures, unlike the pasteboard that serves in too many thrillers,' praised *The Daily Worker*.[60] *The Hollow* certainly demonstrated that Christie could take familiar situations in exciting new directions, but it's telling that when she turned the story into a play in 1951 Poirot was removed once more. Despite his absence, certain sequences in the book have the potential to lend themselves well to the stage, and so it's no surprise that Christie felt she had more to offer when it came to this particular story.

The Labours of Hercules
(Short stories, 1947)

In some respects *The Labours of Hercules* is a decidedly odd book, and some readers may struggle to shake off the feeling that it's something of a private joke that they aren't fully attuned to, but whatever one's classical education there is a lot to enjoy in this varied and highly entertaining collection of mini mysteries.[61] Through the title and introduction Christie clearly establishes the context of these short stories, as she has Poirot emulate his classical near-namesake as the detective decides that his 'final' dozen cases will only be those that mirror the trials of the mythical Hercules.[62] Poirot reaches this decision following a conversation with

ABOVE LEFT: The UK first edition for *The Labours of Hercules* in 1947 came eight years after the stories first appeared in *The Strand*. **ABOVE RIGHT:** A pyjama-clad Poirot appeared on the 1951 'mapbacks' cover from Dell, painted by Robert Stanley.

a friend, Dr Burton, whose appreciation of the classics has not been shared by the detective. Sometimes Poirot's investigations are motivated by an overriding sense of justice; at other times it's due to pressure being placed on him. Here, there seems to be something of an existential explanation and exploration, as Poirot ponders the cases that could serve as his final contribution to the world of crime solving:

> Yet there was between this Hercule Poirot and the Hercules of Classical lore one point of resemblance. Both of them, undoubtedly, had been instrumental in ridding the world of certain pests ... Each of them could be described as a benefactor to the Society he lived in ... There should be, once again, the Labours of Hercules - a modern Hercules. An ingenious and amusing conceit! In the period before his final retirement he would accept twelve cases, no more, no less. And those twelve cases should be selected with special reference to the twelve Labours of ancient Hercules. Yes, that would not only be amusing, it would be artistic, it would be *spiritual*.

The Poirot of *The Labours of Hercules* is particularly self-aware. His fussiness seems a little reduced, while in compensation his amiability is increased as he takes on a range of cases encompassing murders (attempted and actual), thefts, ransoms and blackmail with a wry smile on his face as he enjoys this game of crime solving for his own amusement. In the third case, 'The Arcadian Deer', a chambermaid informs Poirot that a man has arrived to see him. 'Let him mount,' Poirot requests in idiosyncratic English. 'The girl giggled and retired,' Christie writes. 'Poirot reflected kindly that her account of him to her friends would provide entertainment for many winter days to come.' This is not the irritable Poirot who we occasionally glimpse elsewhere, as he

International serialisation of the stories included this Poirot pose for 'The Arcadian Deer' in Australia's *Women's Weekly* in 1945

ingratiates himself into British society enough that he eats steak and kidney, drinks beer, and has a working knowledge of Woolworths.

Readers of this collection will likely be happy to allow Christie the indulgence of these parallels between the Herculean tasks and Hercule's cases. In the first place, these links are not awkwardly inserted passing references, but well-thought-out metaphors and allegories. But perhaps more importantly, the cases themselves are of a very high quality and work with or without the knowledge of Hercules' tasks. However, Hercules is not the only fictional character to play a part in the self-reflexivity of *The Labours of Hercules*, as Dr Burton amuses himself by imagining a conversation between the mothers of Poirot and Sherlock Holmes. We are told that Dr Burton 'began to wheeze gently – his small fat face crinkled up', and when Poirot enquires as to the source of his amusement Dr Burton replies that he is 'Thinking of

A distinctively playful Poirot from Sweden, with art by Olle Eksell (1949).

an imaginary conversation. Your mother and the late Mrs. Holmes, sitting sewing little garments or knitting: "Achille, Hercule, Sherlock, Mycroft...".' Poirot does not find this amusing, but no doubt Christie did, as the ostentatiousness of the name Sherlock had influenced the creation of Poirot's own forename.

The collection's first story, 'The Nemean Lion', is probably its most memorable, and is also the reason that the British first edition used a cover that appeared to imply that Poirot was a Pekingese dog. Poirot is visited by the wealthy businessman Sir Joseph Hoggin, who wants the detective to investigate the disappearance of his wife's beloved canine companion, Shan-Tung. Poirot agrees to the case, believing that the breed's description as lion dogs in some cultures allows this to qualify as the first of the labours. The detective is then surprised to learn that the dog has been returned alive and well, after a ransom has been paid (well within the limits of affordability for such a rich man) and wonders why his client is so keen to find the culprit now that all is well. Superficially the case seems to be a light mystery to kick off Poirot's labours, but by the end of the story the astute reader will have a key suspicion confirmed regarding the darker side of relationships in the client's household. Not only this, but the mystery also has something to say about society and gender. In fact, it's one of Christie's most political stories in some ways, and the argument that it makes regarding women, class and society will be picked up again in a later Poirot novel.[63]

The Labours of Hercules features Miss Lemon, previously secretary to another Christie detective, Parker Pyne, and here she is described as 'a woman without imagination, but she had an instinct.'[64] Although her secretarial skills and accuracy are commended, she is later described rather unpleasantly as 'unbelievably ugly and incredibly efficient'. Viewers of the *Agatha Christie's Poirot* television series may expect Miss Lemon to have a greater role than she actually has in Christie's books, where she simply serves a narrative function and is not depicted as a friend of Poirot nor seen particularly frequently. Chief Inspector Japp also makes an appearance in order to pick Poirot's brains about a missing girl in 'The Girdle of Hippolyta', a clever tale that would have tolerated expansion, although not if the result had been as weak as the not dissimilar *The Mystery of the Blue Train*.[65] Japp is also involved in 'The Flock of Geryon', an unusual tale of an apparent religious sect and criminal conspiracy, in which a culprit from an earlier story reappears on friendly terms.

Other stories in the collection include 'The Lernean Hydra', which feels like classic Christie (in the sense of both archetypes and quality) as Poirot must uncover the truth

The map on Dell's 1951 'mapback' edition emphasised the international scenario of the stories, as did the later 1964 cover by William Teason.

behind the gossip concerning the death of a village doctor's wife. 'The Arcadian Deer' sees Poirot helping a lovesick young man trying to trace a woman he has fallen in love with, a case that takes him to Switzerland, where he stays for 'The Erymanthian Boar', in which he appears to intrude on a criminal rendezvous atop a mountain. 'The Augean Stables' has the British Prime Minister in need of Poirot's assistance again, this time in order to stifle a scandal, while 'The Stymphalean Birds' is a clever tale of blackmail in the fictional country of Herzoslovakia. 'The Cretan Bull' has Poirot investigate a possible case of insanity in a wealthy family, although some of the reasoning and explanations do not bear much modern scrutiny, and 'The Horses of Diomedes' shows him investigating the cocaine-led lives of excess in a particular young and wealthy set.

When first published in *Strand Magazine* during 1939 and 1940 *The Labours of Hercules* then finished with the eleventh story in the collection, 'The Apples of Hesperides', which concerns a mystery relating to a rich art collector and the church. The planned final story, 'The Capture of Cerberus', was turned down by the magazine, almost certainly because the original version of this story was heavily political in nature and featured a thinly disguised depiction of Adolf Hitler. This was not the sort of light diversion that *Strand Magazine* was looking for, and it declined to print it.[66] Christie wasn't particularly perturbed by the turn of events – the magazine had already paid the £1200 fee for the dozen stories, and it was their prerogative to not print any that had been paid for. She discussed the situation with her agent in a matter-of-fact manner, asking for the return of the manuscript so that she could write a new twelfth

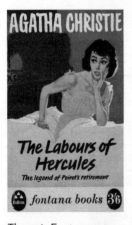

The 1961 Fontana cover, probably by one of the sisters Eileen or Barbara Walton.

story for any eventual book collection.[67] In the end, the original version of the story remained unpublished until March 2009, while the new version didn't appear until 1947, when it was first published in the American magazine *This Week* (under the title 'Meet Me in Hell'), prior to the book collection, which was published in Britain in September the same year.[68] This new version was an entirely new story, albeit with a few reused elements, and it concerns Poirot in the modern life of London, as he travels by tube and visits the neon-signed nightclub 'Hell'. The story also features the reappearance of Countess Vera Rossakoff, a criminal whose charm had always had a strong effect on Poirot when they had previously met.[69] The nightclub appears to have criminal connections, and Japp is on the case, but he would be right to be suspicious of Poirot's motives.

The first Dodd, Mead cover had featured a tiny portrait of Poirot (1947).

The original intention had been for *The Labours of Hercules* to be published in spring 1947, although it isn't clear why it took so long to come out as a collected volume (perhaps the war was a factor), nor why the book was eventually delayed until later in the year. The original draft cover provoked much discussion amongst Christie's family, who felt that it seemed to depict Poirot running naked to the bath. Christie described their responses as 'ribald and obscene ... all I can say is – try again!'[70] The final dog-starring cover was unusual enough in itself, while the earlier American edition broke Christie's domestic rule of not depicting the detective himself, as he featured in one corner.

The Church Times argued that the collection was 'fitted by neat workmanship, and without a jar of artificial constraint, into a highly elaborate pattern ... The detective "short" does not give scope for the finer shades of criminal investigation

Hercule or Hercules? A 1981 cover from Italian publisher Mondadori.

or the closer pursuit of inductive method. But this collection adds to our admiration for Mrs. Christie's fertility of resource and ingenuity. Her cleverness in contriving a dramatic situation, and her agility in extricating her readers, her hero and perhaps herself from an apparently impenetrable enigma, are incomparable; and she maintains her sympathetic touch of human insight.'[71] The Observer's review claimed that detective short stories were 'difficult' and 'unrewarding' by nature, and that The Labours of Hercules was 'neatly constructed but inevitably lacking the criss-cross of red-herring trails that make our arteries pulse over the full distance,' before asking the crucial question, 'will Agatha Christie allow the little egg-headed egomaniac to carry out his frightful threat of retirement?'[72] The answer was no.

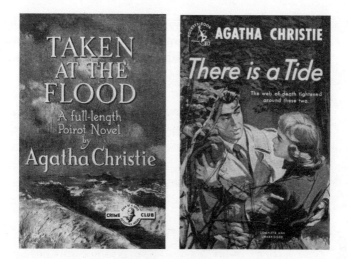

Taken at the Flood
(Novel, 1948)

The Second World War may have been over by the time *Taken at the Flood* was published in 1948, but the suspicion and danger that the war brought casts a shadow over the events that Christie outlines in this Poirot novel. Key to the story's mystery is Gordon Cloade, a wealthy businessman who's killed when his house is bombed at the height of the war. Although Cloade had no children his wider family have long relied upon his wealth, including expectations of inclusion in his will, in order to support them in the long term. The fact that his new wife, a young woman called Rosaleen, survives the attack and so now controls the money perturbs

ABOVE LEFT: The British cover for *Taken at the Flood* – traditional art for a classical title. **ABOVE RIGHT:** Retitled *There is a Tide* for America, the book has a few dramatic covers, including this one by Harvey Kidder (1949).

In 1950 Collins released a paperback in Canada using the US title.

many, but while Rosaleen initially seems sympathetic to the family's demands and requests, her brother, David Hunter, is not, and orders his sister not to give any of her fortune away. The reader may wonder who the villain is here, because while David Hunter is certainly abrasive and impolite, the expectations of Cloade's family is a pathetic spectacle. In fact, this time we may feel that Christie is more firmly against the sense of entitlement from family members that she had implicitly accepted as natural in earlier books such as *Appointment with Death*.

The question of the identity of the villain in *Taken at the Flood* is important not only because Poirot must ensure that justice is delivered ('I am a good Catholic,' he reminds us here) and the puzzle is solved, but also because their identity will be crucial to deciphering the chain of events, in which something seems amiss, but it's difficult to identify any particular criminality. Events unravel in a way that only complicates matters, with a later apparent murder that is then called into question when forensically assessed, and then an apparent suicide that attracts suspicion almost immediately. By the end of the story all is made clear, and the reader learns that chance opportunities can be just as rewarding to the criminal as the meticulous planning we often see in Christie's mysteries. Christie felt that the characterisation of a villain was particularly important to her books, as she explained in a later interview:

> Whoever my villain is, it has to be someone I feel could do the murder. A murderer must have the kind of nature which doesn't have any brakes on it. I suppose vanity is very important. You couldn't have a doubtful murderer

– all brakes are removed and he's certain of what he's doing. But this needn't be obvious to others. Especially as one gathers it is very rarely in real life, when there's a murder, everyone seems so astonished. People always say about the murderer: 'He was such a charming man. So kind, so good to children.' Perhaps one day I shall meet a real one. I never have, so far as I know.[73]

Taken at the Flood endured a variety of alternative titles during the preparation stages for its eventual publication. The title is taken from Shakespeare's *Julius Caesar* ('There is a tide in the affairs of men / Which, taken at the flood, leads on to fortune …') but identifying the precise portion of the quote to be used was surprisingly complicated. It was initially referred to by Collins as *There was a Tide*, but this is probably a small error, with *There is a Tide* the genuine original name for the story. The latter was the title under which the novel was published in the United States, but Christie's British publishers already had a book called *There was a Time* by Taylor Caldwell and they felt that the titles were too similar. Christie wanted to keep the 'tide' motif and so a range of alternatives were suggested and discussed, from *The Ebbing Tide* to *The Incoming Tide*, then *Flood Tide*, before finally settling on *Taken at the Flood*. This time Christie's suggestions for the cover were straightforward – 'Do *NOT* put *any* representation of poor Hercule on the jacket,' she implored, suggesting a stormy sea or ship instead.[74] Both British and American editions featured depictions of crashing waves, although Christie was most aggrieved with a photo of the author that featured on the dustjacket of the American edition.[75] Christie particularly hated

Full throttle suspense in 1955 by artist William Rose.

The US first edition from Dodd, Mead featured crashing waves and a photo of Christie on the back.

photos of herself as she aged, which led to her finally approving of one photograph in 1950 because, she claimed, 'he has taken out the wrinkles!'[76]

'This is a Hercule Poirot story and I think it is for the most part good average Christie storytelling, with a particularly good solution,' read Collins' own reader report. 'Where other authors are content with a nice twist to their tale, Mrs Christie believes in a series of unexpected twists. The only criticism I have to make is that it dragged a little between Poirot's brief first appearance and the point where he begins to take an active part in the story.'[77] Upon publication *The Church Times* was a little more enthusiastic. 'It is something of a relief to turn to a particularly good "Poirot," by Miss Agatha Christie,' read the review. 'There is nothing deep or subtle about the book; yet the author has a real gift for writing a straightforward, honest-to-goodness thriller with the neatest of twists.'[78] *The Daily Worker* felt that Poirot was 'at the top of his form' in this particular book, but *The Observer* disagreed – 'The quintessential zest, the sense of well-being which goes to make up that Christie feeling, is missing.'[79]

In April 1947, more than a year prior to the book's publication in Britain, Edmund Cork had written to Christie about several matters, including the difficulties that Harold Ober was having in selling the American serial rights for *Taken at the Flood*. In a remarkable change of events from the preceding two decades, the usual outlets for Christie's work were no longer interested in 'mystery stories solved by one of the stock detectives', as one described it, and they felt that Poirot's presence detracted from the reality of the story. Two magazines, including the *Saturday Evening Post*, expressed an interest in a rewritten version – but only if it omitted the famous Belgian. Christie agreed to this and made the required changes, but by October the deal had fallen through, with the *Post* declining the reworked version of the story.[80] 'Very annoyed about *There is a Tide*!!' Christie wrote to Cork, 'Really it was a beast to alter!!'[81] For an author who had been quite open about her reason for retaining the services of Poirot – the money he earned her – it's likely that this news contributed to Christie's continued slowing of the frequency of Poirot's appearances. This was all the easier to do now that she was settling into an average of just one book a year, which were becoming the increasingly well anticipated Christie for Christmas. More Miss Marple stories were on the horizon, while the success of her standalone novel *And Then There Were None* in 1939 had threatened to eclipse even the greatest Poirot mysteries. By October 1948 Edmund Cork reported that Christie had 'not written a word all year', a stark contrast to the rapid completion of stories a few years earlier.[82] The mutual dependency that had evolved between creator and character was now weakened, and Christie could afford to return to her fussy Belgian sleuth on her own terms from now on.

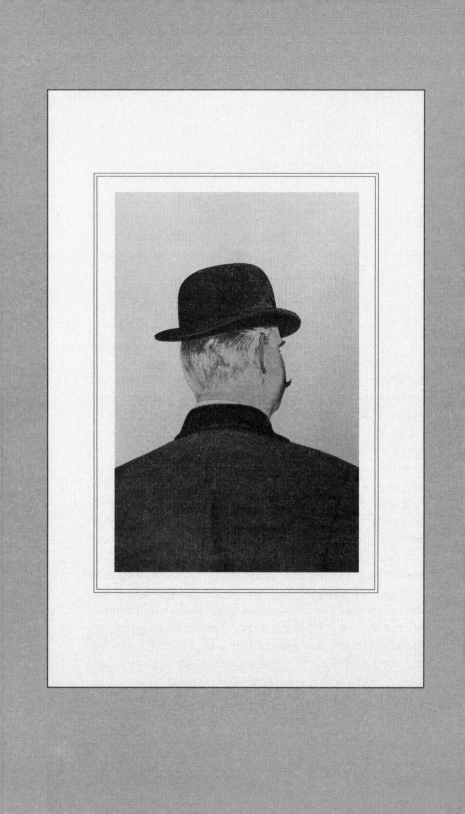

CHAPTER FOUR:

THE
1950s

In September 1950 Agatha Christie turned sixty, and thirty years had passed since her first novel had seen print. However, there was no sign of the author retiring from professional writing, not least because of the income it generated, even when accounting for her tax difficulties. Christie was still writing for pleasure, but increasingly her real interests were in both the theatre and more standalone and distinctive novels, even though she continued to develop Poirot and Miss Marple mysteries that still sold astronomically well. Nevertheless, there was no avoiding the fact that Christie was not going to live forever, and she needed to make decisions about the future, a prospect that she approached with pragmatism. Christie had two issues of particular importance to consider – her tax status, and her desire to provide for her daughter Rosalind, grandson Mathew, and younger

OPPOSITE: Poirot's back! The serial for *Mrs McGinty's Dead* at the end of 1951 in *Woman's Journal* was illustrated by Tanat Jones.

husband Max following her death, whenever that may be. In part, she tackled these issues by gifting the copyright to some of her titles to others, which gave the beneficiary the author's share of profits while also removing a portion of Christie's taxable income. Most famously, Christie gifted the play *The Mousetrap* to Mathew, which time has shown to be an act of generosity that far exceeded expectations, as it has run continuously since its 1952 debut.

Such gestures provided a solution of sorts, but were unsustainable in the long term. As a result, the 1950s saw plans drawn up to create a company, Agatha Christie Ltd, which would effectively make Christie a salaried member of staff rather than an independent writer. With worrying phrasing, this would require Christie herself to be declared 'dead' as a writer, with the company effectively taking her place. While plans were formed Christie repeatedly asked if the new company was ethical, as she had become increasingly risk averse. 'When one has no money or very little, then you're prepared to endure a lot of worry,' she wrote to her agent, Edmund Cork. 'If the money position is not urgent then you've got to decide if the money is worth the worry!'.[1] Christie was not sentimental about the fact that plans needed to be drawn up to address what would happen after her death, but equally tried to detach herself from the process as much as possible, pointing out that it was her daughter as well as new son-in-law Anthony Hicks (Rosalind had married again in 1949) and grandson who would have to address any problems that occurred further down the line. 'If we go into this scheme and it all goes wrong – litigation, decisions against us, etc. – looking definitely on the worst side, full pessimism – how much worse off shall I be, than if I'd left it all alone?' she asked in February 1955. 'I think I'm entitled to know just where I stand about that.'[2] Mindful of the fact that the formation of the company required Christie to live a further five years in order to be used as planned, she reassured Cork that she would make it to seventy – 'the Doll will do her best to live another five years. In order to do so, she must not worry.' Her final declaration on the matter says something of how she viewed the attitudes of both her daughter and son-in-law: 'I leave all complications to you, and to Anthony who, I suspect, may even enjoy them. Rosalind will be counted upon as a brake lever, oiled with persistent pessimism.'[3]

There can be little doubt that the formation of the company was good for the Christie family and, after her death, the Christie 'brand'. It says something of the strength of the family commitment to Agatha Christie's works that Rosalind remained a strong influence on its exploitation until her death in 2004, while Mathew was chairman of Agatha Christie Ltd's board until 2016, with his son James taking over the role following his father's retirement.[4] However, while on the one hand the formation of the company gave Christie stability, on the other it tied her to a more formalised schedule. The author now worked under the expectation that she would write one book a year, which may well have been a great reduction in the output of the 1930s, but became an increasing burden as Christie reached her seventies and then eighties in the following decades.

In terms of Poirot, Christie remained highly protective of the character, and dusted him off for five new novels in the 1950s. In her discussions of him she also seems to become less resentful of the character, probably because her work in the theatre, as well as her Miss Marple and Mary Westmacott novels, were all doing so well that she could demonstrate consistent success beyond her Poirot stories. Their relationship was no longer one of mutual dependence – Christie could survive without Poirot, as she had proven so often in the past, but now had a collection of recent ventures to demonstrate it more tangibly. She also remained disarmingly honest about both her motivations for writing and her general outlook. In September 1951 the *Sunday Express* contacted Christie with three questions for a new article series it was running, called 'How Did They Begin?' – 'How did you begin to write?' she was asked; 'Idleness is the old chestnut,' Christie responded. 'What do you dislike most about your career?' was a dangerous question to ask a woman burned by the press in the past, as she responded 'Publicity.' As for what she liked best about her career – 'Money!'[5]

In 1950 Christie's publishers undertook some highly questionable arithmetic in order to calculate that the new Miss Marple novel *A Murder is Announced* was, apparently, the author's fiftieth book.[6] Christie was coaxed into 'hosting' a party of the precise type that she disliked in order to celebrate the occasion, and *The Daily Mirror*'s London Correspondent was present, ready to report his findings to the newspaper's readers:

> Miss Agatha Christie gave a party to-night to celebrate her fiftieth detective novel [sic] and 'thirty years of undetected crime' that was a really gay affair, with a birthday cake, a hum of publishers' and authors' gossip, and much congratulation from fellow detective writers. Miss Christie is a matronly figure who wears black and looks as though murder would be the last thought on her mind. She never mentioned her income tax and she looks forward to a party some time before very long to celebrate her seventy-fifth novel. She assured her guests that she is not likely to run out of plots or to run into any emotional entanglement with Hercule Poirot.
>
> A French journalist who claims knowledge of the roman policier asserted that the popularity of Poirot in France was traceable to his being a Belgian and therefore not to be taken too seriously.[7]

Mrs McGinty's Dead
(Novel, 1952)

In *Mrs McGinty's Dead* Poirot somewhat reluctantly travels to the country village of Broadhinny in order to investigate the murder of the titular widowed cleaner, who was apparently killed by her lodger for £30 that she kept hidden. Despite the violent murder that lies at its heart, *Mrs McGinty's Dead* is a novel that brings comedy into the world of Poirot at a level that had rarely been seen before. It may well be that this is partially due to two other elements of the book – its unusual emphasis on the working classes, which could be seen as somewhat deprecating, and the

ABOVE LEFT: Poirot was back in the first edition of *Mrs McGinty's Dead* from Collins Crime Club (1952). **ABOVE RIGHT:** The American first edition from Dodd, Mead was published a few days earlier with eye-catching artwork.

reappearance of crime writer Ariadne Oliver, whose presence is most certainly *self*-deprecating for Christie. When she arrives in the tenth chapter, Oliver explains that she is in the village to work with a stage dramatist who is adapting one of her stories starring the Finnish detective Sven Hjerson. Oliver's following diatribe could come straight from the mouth of Christie regarding the changes made to Poirot for the 1928 play *Alibi*, which adapted *The Murder of Roger Ackroyd*:

> So far it's pure agony. Why I ever let myself in for it I don't know. My books bring me in quite enough money – that is to say the bloodsuckers take most of it, and if I made more, they'd take more, so I don't overstrain myself. But you've no idea of the agony of having your characters taken and made to say things that they never would have said and do things that they never would have done. And if you protest, all they say is that it's 'good theatre' … If he's so clever I don't see why he doesn't write a play of his own and leave my poor unfortunate Finn alone. He's not even a Finn any longer. He's become a member of the Norwegian Resistance Movement.

The rawness of Christie's feelings is evident, and it provides some reinforcement for her antagonism towards most adaptations for stage and screen. Poirot himself is little changed for this appearance, although his revulsion towards the guesthouse where he's forced to stay makes him a particularly good focus for humour, and his increasing age is acknowledged ('at my age, one takes no risks'), but the world around him has continued to change. The detective's age becomes increasingly vague as time moves on, and this was a deliberate choice. In the run up to this novel's publication a reader sent Christie and her agent Edmund Cork a sketch of

Poirot as he envisaged him, but it was not published because Cork felt that the accurate depiction of the detective as a centenarian would come as rather a shock to readers.[8]

At the beginning of the novel Poirot ruminates on the modern world, and we learn how his perfect day is dictated by food for the most part. His disdain for modern popular entertainment was clear, and seems to have echoed Christie's own thoughts:

Interestingly Collins adopted the American art for some of its advertising.

> The cinema, more often than not, enraged him by the looseness of its plots – the lack of logical continuity in the argument – even the photography which, raved over by some, to Hercule Poirot seemed often no more than the portrayal of scenes and objects so as to make them appear totally different from what they were in reality. Everything, Hercule Poirot decided, was too artistic nowadays. Nowhere was there the love of order and method that he himself prized so highly. And seldom was there any appreciation of subtlety. Scenes of violence and crude brutality were the fashion, and as a former police officer, Poirot was bored by brutality. In his early days, he had seen plenty of crude brutality. It had been more the rule than the exception. He found it fatiguing, and unintelligent. 'The truth is,' Poirot reflected as he turned his steps homeward, 'I am not in tune with the modern world.'

Another aspect of the modern world that is negatively appraised in the book, and by Christie herself, is the press, key here to solving the mystery of a murder that seems to have its origins set in a crime of the past. This appears to have been influenced by Dr Crippen's mistress, Ethel Le Neve,

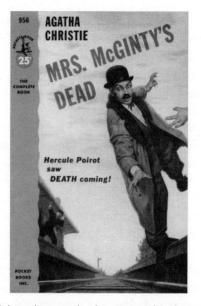

Pocket Books debuted a paperback in 1953 with a dramatic cover by Robert Schultz.

who was exonerated of being complicit in the murder of her lover's wife and went on to try and live a normal life even though there had been huge media interest at the time of the trial. Despite this dark undercurrent the book is amusing and enjoyable throughout, proving to be a rather underrated Poirot mystery that skirts into Miss Marple territory with its village setting. Characters are well drawn, with the accused man, James Bentley, proving to be an entertainingly exasperating witness for Poirot despite his need for assistance in order to prove his innocence. Mrs McGinty herself is also a fully rounded presence despite the fact that we never meet her first hand, so overwhelming is the selection of information about her personality and life.

Perhaps it may also be that in this book Christie's relationship with the reader mirrors that of Poirot and Captain

Hastings, as the detective describes it. 'I remember only his incredulous wonder, his openmouthed appreciation of my talents,' she has Poirot reminisce, 'the ease with which I misled him without uttering an untrue word, his bafflement, his stupendous astonishment when he at last perceived the truth that had been clear to me all along.' Poirot certainly does a commendable amount of research informed deduction in pursuit of this truth, although his actions arguably place some characters in significant danger.

When Christie sent the typescript for *Mrs McGinty's Dead* to her agent in spring 1951 he forwarded it to Harold Ober, who represented Christie in America, with a note saying that Christie liked her new novel very much. Ober liked it too, although he expressed his reservations when it came to selling it as a serial, and he was right to do so as its slightly complicated nature made it a less attractive prospect for Christie's frequent homes of *Collier's Weekly* and the *Saturday Evening Post*. In the end, the *Chicago Tribune* paid a much reduced $7,000 in order to secure the serialisation rights under the title *Blood Will Tell*, which was also adopted for the first American paperback. The original title refers to a rather obscure children's game, but taken at face value it was also judged to be perfectly adequate even without this knowledge, and so the American first edition in hardback was titled *Mrs McGinty's Dead* despite understandable domestic ignorance of its source.

In Britain, *Woman's Journal* expressed interest in publishing the mystery but irritated Christie by requesting reorganisation of the story so it flowed better for a three part publication, including the removal of characters, which Christie did not approve of.[9] Rather more bizarrely, the magazine also wanted to rename

The Tom Adams cover from Fontana in 1964.

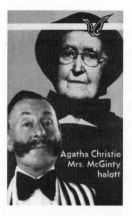

Some notable
moustache
magnificence on this
Hungarian edition
from 1978.

the story *Just Like Mrs McGinty* as it did not like
to use the words 'murder' or 'death' in their story
titles, which Christie felt was a patently ridicu-
lous approach if the magazine was happy to
print murder stories even while being coy about
publicising them as such. Reluctantly, Christie
suggested *A Condemned Man* or *The Paying Guest*
as better alternatives, although in the end the
magazine stuck with *Mrs McGinty's Dead*.[10]

'Poirot is back!' read the strapline on the
British cover of the novel, which at the end
included tributes to Christie following the
celebrations linked to her 'fiftieth' book. These
included Clement Attlee, who had recently
been ousted as Prime Minister in the elec-
tion of October 1951. While in the post he had
written: 'I admire and delight in the ingenuity of Agatha
Christie's mind and in her capacity to keep a secret until
she is ready to divulge it.' Anthony Eden, who would become
Prime Minister in 1955, added that 'Miss Christie weaves a
fresh plot which does not fail to enthral us,' referring to *A
Murder is Announced*. For *Mrs McGinty's Dead*, the review in
The Observer claimed that Poirot was 'slightly subdued' but
that the novel offered the 'usual plethora of suspects and
more murder. Not one of A.C.'s best-constructed jobs, yet far
more readable than most other people's.'[11] Christie received
a letter from Lucy Beatrice Malleson, who wrote crime
fiction under the pseudonym Anthony Gilbert, to commend
her on the book and discuss a play she had written for the
BBC. 'So glad you liked *McGinty*,' Christie responded, writing
from Nimrud in Iraq. 'I always think the last book I have
written is lousy and am much cheered up when one of the
gang like it!'[12]

After the Funeral
(Novel, 1953)

By 1953 Christie was receiving £2,000 on delivery of a manuscript to Collins, with a 20% royalty on sales. These were generous terms, but her publisher suspected that Edmund Cork wanted to improve them even further when it came to paperback rights in particular. Any increase in Christie's favour would have been extraordinary but, Collins conceded, Christie was a special case who deserved special terms.[13] This was true in several ways, including the extent to which she relied on Cork to arrange mundane matters such as the purchase of books, as well as tickets for Wimbledon and other events. Christie's personal and professional lives

ABOVE LEFT: From the 1950s onwards, Christie's UK covers were predominantly typographic, just letting her name do all the work (1953). **ABOVE RIGHT:** The first Dodd, Mead cover with its American title *Funerals are Fatal.*

were interwoven to such an extent that they were generally difficult to untangle – one example of this was the purchase of a car for Christie by Collins, seemingly as a way to reduce tax liability. Tax decisions rarely ran smoothly for Christie, and the maintenance and actual ownership of the vehicle was the cause of much head scratching, especially when something went wrong, such as when the passenger window spontaneously exploded one day. 'You nearly lost an author!' Christie wrote to Billy Collins. 'I thought I was shot!'[14]

Christie had always loved cars and the independence they brought. When discussing her trips to Wallingford in Oxfordshire, where she lived from 1934 until her death, she said that 'Driving a car's a good place for thinking; walking is too. According to Robert Graves washing-up is the best time for thinking and I'm not sure he's not right; anything that involves physical action of some sort is a very good thing for a part of the mind to concentrate on something quite different.'[15]

The first UK paperback was published by Fontana in 1957.

It may be that it was during these journeys that Christie ruminated on the changed landscape and houses that she encountered as she drove through the countryside. The country house of the traditional type had been impossible to maintain in the old-fashioned ways since even before the Second World War, and one of these ageing mansions makes an early appearance in this next Poirot novel, *After the Funeral*. Times were moving on, and while Christie always accepted change she showed a degree of sympathy for characters who missed the old ways, just as she did. Christie later explained that while she enjoyed some elements of hosting at her home (she frequently invited friends to visit her at Greenway in particular), she missed the hubbub and structure of the traditional country house with its staff: 'It's a pleasure to cook for friends who enjoy food. Of course, one wouldn't want to do it all the time – you rather miss servants. They always had an interesting part to play in books and could be really important characters; you just can't get the effect with daily helpers.'[16]

In *After the Funeral*, we meet a cast of characters (and, surely, suspects) following the death of the Abernethie family's patriarch. Those gathered have no reason to suspect foul play and are simply waiting to see precisely how Richard Abernethie's estate will be carved out between them. Events are then put in turmoil when the quirky and little seen Aunt Cora, who was well known for blurting out unpleasant truths, blithely asks, 'But he was murdered, wasn't he?' Few take Cora seriously, but the question packs a punch, and when she's later found dead the characters – and reader – will inevitably wonder how much Cora really knew. Of all the characters in the story, it's Cora's companion Miss Gilchrist who's particularly well drawn, especially when it comes to her awkward placement in society, not only due to her lower class than the Abernethie family (with the subsequent almost innate subservience) and lack of wealth, but arguably also because of her relationship with Cora that seems likely to have been more than platonic. In Miss Gilchrist we see an example of a new type of character who has felt left behind as society moves on, indicating that Christie saw such changes as affecting more than just the landed gentry. Christie also makes part of this modern world a figure of fun in her discussions of modern art, and she's clever enough to make such knee-jerk dismissiveness a part of the story.

The rest of the Abernethie family are helpfully identified through not only some strong personalities, but also a useful family tree supplied by Christie, which is the sort of device that she could arguably have made more frequent use of. However, given the extent to which relationships and identities are kept secret, ready to be revealed, in Christie's mysteries, perhaps the usual absence of a formalised record is understandable. Christie herself seemed to have some disdain for official records anyway, as exhibited by one character's annoyance with – of all things – the national Census, which had occurred most recently in 1951. 'Asking your age at that Census – downright impertinent and she hadn't told them, either!' Janet the kitchen maid recalls. 'Cut off five years she had. Why not? If she only felt fifty-four, she'd call herself fifty-four'. Given this outburst it should be no surprise that Christie herself was no fan of giving accurate information when a white lie was preferable, for whatever reason. Her passports consistently show her to be born a year later than she actually was, while when she married Max Mallowan in 1930 she reduced her age, and he increased his, in order to condense the fourteen-year age gap between them to just six years on paper.

Poirot conducts some of his investigations in this novel using the alias of 'Pontarlier' in the latest vague notion of the detective's apparent fame, which ebbs and flows as stories demand. Poirot uses his powers of deduction to great effect, and the novel itself is a shining example of a multi-layered mystery driven by characters with complex and convincingly drawn motives that we are skilfully diverted away from. *After the Funeral* is a particularly satisfying Christie novel, as she takes the reader by the hand, gently guides them in the wrong direction, and then manages to make the diversion seem obvious by the time the truth is revealed.

The story's first publication as a novel was under the title *Funerals Are Fatal* in the United States in March 1953, with it appearing as *After the Funeral* in the UK two months later. In 1963 a version of the story was filmed as *Murder at the Gallop*, with Margaret Rutherford's Miss Marple replacing Poirot, much to Christie's annoyance – a tie-in paperback bearing

Flora Robson, Robert Morley
and Margaret Rutherford star in

Murder at the Gallop

M.G.M.'s hilarious new thriller based on

AGATHA CHRISTIE'S

AFTER THE FUNERAL

fontana books

Not to be confused with a Miss Marple story... The film tie-in paperback of *After the Funeral* (1963).

photographs from the film and its title was issued, which only irritated her further. This substitution was repeated in the 1964 film *Murder Most Foul*, which placed Rutherford's Miss Marple in a story approximating *Mrs McGinty's Dead*. This helped to secure Christie's distrust of the film industry, although it was the 1965 Poirot film *The Alphabet Murders* that would be the last straw.[17]

'It begins like one of those stock family inheritance murders, but *of course* she is fooling you,' read *The Observer*'s review of the book. 'Never mind whether the [method] would have worked, roll over on your back like a wasp immobilised by a spider bite in the thoracic ganglion, and enjoy the unfair, paralysing, stab of surprise. Construction may be a bit ragged but the familiar smooth, almost edible, scone-like readability is there. Also Poirot, who has thought up a new messy trick to annoy you with: he drinks crème de cacao after dinner.'[18]

By November 1953 Collins was aware that 'there will not be an Agatha Christie for some considerable time. It may be we shall have one more publication in the late autumn of next year, but even that may not be probable.'[19] Christie usually wrote quickly, aiming to finish a book within three months and generally writing during winter. 'There are always moments when you get bored with the people and the plot,' she said. 'Then you go back and sit around for a few days before you get back into it.'[20] However, Christie's success in the theatrical world was making demands on her time. On the back of *The Mousetrap*'s ongoing popularity a new play, *Witness for the Prosecution*, had opened in the West End in October 1953 and was on course to be another success. When her next production *Spider's Web* opened in autumn 1954 Christie became the only female playwright in history to have three of her plays running in the West End at the same time, and so it's understandable that her works for the stage commanded much of her attention at this point. However, the writing of *Spider's Web* meant that Collins needed to be prepared for the possibility of a year without a Christie novel in 1954 – a rare event.[21] In order to avoid a missed year, the possibility of a new volume of short stories was raised once more, having previously been discussed and dismissed just two years earlier. There was an expectation that the lead story could be either 'Three Blind Mice' or 'The Witness for the Prosecution', given the success of the plays derived from them. To this point there had been no great willingness to create new short story collections in the UK with the frequency seen in the United States because of a feeling that they would only interfere with the market for the full novels.[22]

In December 1953 Christie gave tacit approval for a short story collection, while she still hoped to have a novel in time for February 1954, but Cork insisted that Collins mustn't count on it for autumn publication. However, Christie also made clear that the collection should not include 'The Witness for the Prosecution' as the short story was so different to the play that it might disappoint, having already insisted that 'Three Blind Mice' was not to be published in the UK at this time. Collins then looked at the American collections *The Under Dog* and *Three Blind Mice* to see if any of their contents would be usable – but by January 1954 there was a general feeling at the publisher that the standard of the stories was below that which Christie had achieved more recently. Alongside problems of chronology (such as Poirot's relative youthfulness and the inclusion of Hastings) this meant that plans for a collection were quietly dropped while Collins waited for *The Mousetrap* to end so it could print 'Three Blind Mice', potentially in a 1955 collection.[23] It is still waiting. These decisions would cast a long shadow, as they opened the door for the rather odd short story collections that followed later. These included 1960's *The Adventure of the Christmas Pudding*, an unusual mix of Poirot stories with a solitary Miss Marple tale, as well as various unfocused collections that appeared once Christie stopped writing novels.

AGATHA CHRISTIE
After the Funeral

The 1970 paperback with art by Tom Adams.

In the end, Collins did receive a new novel for 1954 in the nick of time, as the standalone thriller *Destination Unknown* was delivered in July 1954, which was rush released for November the same year. Christie was able to reassure her publishers that she was already progressing on her next title, and that a novel called *Hickory Dickory Dock* would be the Christie for Christmas in 1955. For this novel Poirot would return to solve a crime once more.[24]

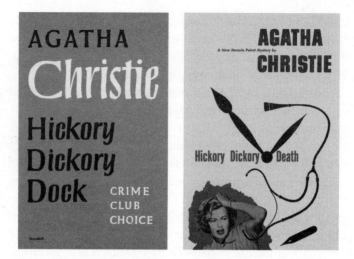

Hickory Dickory Dock
(Novel, 1955)

The mid-1950s saw Christie sketch out several distinctive approaches to the murder mystery story, and one of the most intriguing was her idea to put Poirot into the world of the board game Cluedo. In one of her notebooks she outlined the idea that Poirot's valet George would ask the detective's advice about a domestic position that his sister in law has been offered in Ireland, which they presumably had some reason to feel suspicious of. This is a premise that has echoes of both the Sherlock Holmes story 'The Adventure of the Copper Beeches' and, with its familial link, the opening of *Hickory Dickory Dock*. The rest of Christie's plan outlined the

ABOVE LEFT: A classic nursery rhyme title on the UK first edition of *Hickory Dickory Dock*. **ABOVE RIGHT:** The original American hardback edition with its slightly different title *Hickory Dickory Death* (1955).

movements of Professor Plum (with a candlestick) et al, with the idea being that the mystery would hinge on questions of misdirected timings and locations. Unfortunately, these ideas do not seem to have gone any further.

In *Hickory Dickory Dock* it's the location that's new ground for the author, as Christie looked for a new place to house multiple suspects and victims for her latest Poirot novel. She hadn't yet entirely abandoned country houses, but exotic ships and luxury trains would have felt out of place in Britain's austere post-war years. As a result, Christie tries to introduce a greater sense of the 'real world' into this story, which unfolds at student lodgings that house a selection of young people from around the world, as well as the landlady Mrs Nicoletis and the warden Mrs Hubbard, who's also the sister of Poirot's 'hideous and efficient'(!) secretary Miss Lemon. Poirot is initially asked to solve a minor mystery, an outbreak of small-scale thefts that has upset and distracted both Mrs Hubbard and Miss Lemon, which he pledges to

Robert Fawcett's art from the *Hickory Dickory Death* serial in *Collier's Weekly* (1955).

resolve at the Hickory Road hostel. While the apparent truth behind the stolen items is uncovered by Poirot with his usual efficiency, almost inevitably someone will be driven to murder before the end of the book.

The novel is certainly an attempt by Christie to keep pace with a changing world, but her outlook doesn't seem to be positive. We're told that young people think of 'nothing but politics and psychology', while by the end of the fifth chapter even Papa Poirot, usually a keen matchmaker, declares that he's fed up with love. There are a few characters and situations that we might imagine are based on Christie's real experiences, such as the workings of a dispensary and an archaeology student who is not close to her parents, but there's an inevitable sense of this being a second-hand account of the lives of young people in the mid-1950s, which is unsurprising given the author's age and background. On the whole, her account of the inhabitants of the house, who are from many different countries and cultures, is somewhat patronising and problematic. In a rather bizarre turn of events, after publication a complaint was made from one reader who seemed to believe that the horrid Mrs Nicoletis, the Cypriot proprietor of the hostel, was based on their own mother, who was apparently a most disagreeable woman of the same name who had run a hostel in France. Christie was exasperated by this, responding: 'I invented the character of Nicoletis! And I'm sure it's all nonsense that I ever stayed in a pension run by a Mrs Nicoletis. If this is supposed to have happened in France, I've certainly never stayed in a hostel for students of any kind ... It's terrible that if you invent a character it should come out so true to life. Positively uncanny! Well, I can't help you further.'[25]

The 1958 paperback from Fontana.

Hickory Dickory Dock became 1955's 'Christie for Christmas', a phrase that would become increasingly well-worn over the years, but the slogan had an apparently 'hypnotic effect' on the book trade in the UK.[26] As a result, the novel's publication was perfectly timed for the end of October, ready to be purchased as a present, with the American edition following shortly afterwards, using the pleasingly melodramatic title *Hickory Dickory Death*. The novel cannot be judged to be a particularly good example of Christie's work, as the mystery's mechanics, its atmosphere and the characters fail to strike particular interest, but Billy Collins assured Christie that he had 'enjoyed it immensely, and think it is quite one of your best. It really is marvellous of you to get it done in the time with all you had on your hands. It is absolutely thrilling that we are going to have another Christie for Christmas.'[27]

'The mouse ran up the clock' – although not until Tom Adams featured one on a cover in 1972.

'Mrs. Christie rapidly establishes her favourite atmosphere by her skilful mixture of cheerfulness and suspense,' read *The Times Literary Supplement*'s review. 'The amount of mischief going on in the hostel imposes some strain on the reader's patience as well as on Poirot's ingenuity; the author has been a little too liberal with the red herrings. Yet the thumb-nail sketches of the characters are as good as ever and in spite of the over-elaborate nature of the puzzle there is plenty of entertainment.'[28] *The Observer* felt that 'Construction a trifle ragged, especially towards the end, when drug-smuggling dressmakers appear, but there is plenty of cosy euphoria.'[29]

Considering that *Hickory Dickory Dock* isn't a mystery that is particularly fondly remembered, it might be surprising that in the early 1960s there were plans to put together

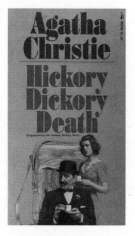

A later Pocket paperback with art by Mara McAfee (1975).

a musical called *Death Beat* which would have been based on the story. Christie was enthusiastic about the plans, and it would have been a collaboration between *Private Eye* contributor and actor John Wells, pianist Alexis Weissenberg, and possibly with orchestration by jazz musician John Dankworth.[30] A full script was written (which excised Poirot), as well as the songs and some design drawings, which show that it would have been a very modern story of relationships and distrust, brimming with atmosphere and set to a light jazz score, but it came to nothing.

1955 saw the formation of Agatha Christie Ltd, and with it a guaranteed four-figure salary for the author. This was no more than she had previously earned (she had recently paid £25,000 tax on £30,000 of earnings – 'Did I really make £30,000 in one year? Where *is* it all?!!' she asked her agent), but it gave her long-term security for her family, while the remainder of the money could go towards the business as well as the taxman.[31] This also marked the point at which her daughter and son-in-law, Rosalind and Anthony, increasingly started to take charge, with Rosalind often discussing her mother's writing and earnings with Cork, and not necessarily in a way that was transparent to the author, even if with the best of intentions.

Poirot Returns to
the Airwaves

Whatever Christie's objections to a 'synthetic Poirot', there was no doubting the fact that the character was a popular choice for those wishing to present detective fiction in a variety of media. One unusual example of this took place in *The Church Times*, which ran a competition in which readers were asked to write preliminary investigations into Prince Charming's 'glass slipper mystery'. For their detective they could choose from Sherlock Holmes, Lord Peter Wimsey, Father Brown, Jonathan Mansel or – of course – Hercule Poirot. Holmes proved to be the biggest draw, but Poirot made an appearance in the summary of readers' entries:[32]

ABOVE: A moustache-twirling Poirot, as depicted by Mario Cooper in *Collier's Weekly* (1940).

Miss Barbara Harris introduced the note sinister when she made Poirot remark:

'So I say to you that here we have not two persons, but one young girl running away, because, my friends, she was afraid.'

And the Rev. A.P. Kirkpatrick also knew his Christie:

'A glass slipper,' said Poirot, '*une mule de verre*. But that is incredible! As an ornament, yes, or for the drinking of champagne by the young ladies of the chorus, perhaps: but for the wear, for the dancing, I ask you!'

Judging by the difficulties the reader was likely to have in deciphering the presented extracts, participation in the competition was probably more fun than the eventual results.

More familiar territory for discussion by the author and her agents was the ever-expanding world of television. Even after Christie declined Harold Huber's proposals for a television Poirot following his successful American radio series, producers continued to try to get the Belgian sleuth on to the increasingly well-established medium. In 1951 frequent television sponsors William Morris made a generous offer regarding a commercial American television series that would have earned Christie and her agents $500 per episode, perhaps even more with repeat fees, as well as not only approval of the scripts but also the casting of Poirot. This was as good as an offer could be – and yet it was once more declined. Appearances on television by characters other than Poirot were looked on more favourably by Christie and her agent, including several one-off plays such as *Murder on the Nile* on NBC in 1950, which is the earliest surviving television production of Christie's works, but like the stage play it removed Poirot from the proceedings of *Death on the Nile*.

Even Christie's friend and erstwhile Poirot Francis L. Sullivan (a.k.a. Larry Sullivan) failed to get the author onside for such a television venture, as he wrote to her about the possibility, presumably suggesting himself for the role. 'I enclose a letter from Larry Sullivan to which I replied rather precipitately saying I was still a mule about television,' Christie wrote to Edmund Cork. 'Afterwards I thought I ought to have consulted you first! But I do dislike poor Hercule being thrown to the dogs. Anyone can have Mr Parker Pyne at any time and it doesn't really matter what he looks like.'[33] Certainly the occasional requests for non-Poirot television series were generally considered more sympathetically, but in the end no ongoing series of Christie adaptations would materialise

MacKill's Mystery Magazine declared 'Murder in the Mews' a complete mystery novel in 1954. The uncredited cover may be by Hans Kresse.

until *The Agatha Christie Hour* in 1982, with 1983's *Partners in Crime* the first to star regular characters on an ongoing basis (Tommy and Tuppence in that case).[34] In the end, the only confirmed appearance of Poirot on television in this decade took place in Germany, where he starred in the final episode of the series *The Gallery of Great Detectives,* which featured seven episodes over the course of nine months, each dealing with a different detective. Sherlock Holmes had been the first, with an adaptation of 'The Dying Detective' in November 1954, and for Poirot it was his most famous case that appeared on screen, as he investigated *Murder on the Orient Express* in the West German broadcast on 24 August 1955, with Heini Gobel starring as Poirot.

On the radio, things were looking up for Poirot. Relations between the BBC and Christie had often been strained, but were thawing somewhat in the mid-1950s, as she wrote another original non-Poirot play for the Corporation, 1954's *Personal Call.* She also allowed it to adapt the Poirot short story 'The Third Floor Flat' the same year, starring French actor Jacques Brunius.[35] After some cajoling she even agreed to take part in a documentary about her work in the *Close Up* strand; broadcast on 13 February 1955 the adulatory programme featured friends and admirers including Richard Attenborough, Margaret Lockwood, and Francis L. Sullivan. Privately, the BBC had not always fallen at her feet, however. For example, in the same month that *Personal Call* was broadcast the possibility of a radio adaptation of *Black Coffee* was dismissed as the BBC's reader's report claimed that it was overly contrived and reliant on strong performances when performed on stage, with apparently insurmountable difficulties if brought to air.[36] The reader was probably right.

Nevertheless, Christie was seen as a draw and worthy of critical attention as well as popular appeal. Poirot had reappeared in a new dramatisation, this time an adaptation of 'Murder in the Mews' starring Richard Williams as Poirot on 20 March 1955, while *The Murder of Roger Ackroyd* had been read in abridged form as the *Woman's Hour* serial in February. By May 1955 plans were in motion to have a series of programmes featuring Christie's work in a 'festival', with an agreement drawn up with her agent on 5 August 1955 for three novels and two short stories (although *And Then There Were None* was unavailable to license at this point, much to the BBC's disappointment). In January 1956 Christie was invited to a luncheon with the Controller of the Light Programme (the BBC radio station broadcasting the 'festival'), but she may have found it fortuitous that she was in Mesopotamia at the time.

ITV's *The Agatha Christie Hour* was accompanied by a hardcover tie-in from Collins featuring the ten short stories in the series.

The Light Programme's Christie season began on Sunday 19 February 1956 with the first of these short stories, 'Death by Drowning', starring Betty Hardy as Miss Marple and Milton Rosmer as Sir Henry Clithering. A ninety-minute adaptation of *The Mysterious Affair at Styles* followed three days later, in which Austin Trevor reprised the role of Poirot once more, with Gordon Davies as Hastings. Trevor may well have been a familiar name for the part for those who recalled his appearance in the role in three films more than twenty years earlier (and another radio production the previous decade), but the season didn't allow any one person to be the dominant depiction, as Poirot was played by a different actor in each adaptation. In 'The Adventure of the Clapham Cook' on 26 February it was Kenneth Kent playing the sleuth, with Peter Neil as Hastings, while *The ABC Murders* on 29 February starred John Gabriel as Poirot with Richard Williams demoted to the role of Hastings, following his

'Murder in the Mews' with Richard Williams is one of the few surviving Christie radio plays from this era, and was released on CD in 2015.

appearance as Poirot in 'Murder in the Mews'. On 4 March there was a rare instance of an adventure from *The Labours of Hercules* appearing independently (Christie didn't like to separate this collection of intertwined short stories), as 'The Nemean Lion' was given the new name 'The Case of the Kidnapped Dog', with Cyril Shaps as Poirot. Jacques Brunius then returned to play the detective in 7 March's *Murder in Mesopotamia*. The season was then rounded off by a rebroadcast of Christie's original radio play from 1948, *Butter in a Lordly Dish* – only the second programme in the season to not feature Poirot, which shows the extent to which his creator was still linked with the detective in the public consciousness.

The 'festival' was well received by at least one reviewer, who wrote in *The Observer*:

The Agatha Christie season is in full swing, and lines like 'What's the great Poirot doing here?' are heard almost nightly. The quality of Poirots varies; John Gabriel (in *The ABC Murders*) has made far and away the best one so far, giving an authentic glitter to the improbabilities of the plot. These plots, so ingenious when uncovered in the books, can show up very bare and contorted in radio adaptations. Instead of reading and anticipating, you listen and observe; it's the bane of adaptation, that the working-out of the plot must be condensed more than the plot itself, which consequently receives undue emphasis. On the whole, though, give me more people being murderous before people being funny.[37]

The repeated appearances of Christie's work (and occasional words from the author herself) were considered to be a success for both her and the BBC. Edmund Cork reported to his client that following the *Close Up* documentary he had received a mass of fan mail and an increase of £500 a week in takings at her West End shows. Christie may have disliked both publicity and the appearance of her works in other media, but there was no denying the fact that such adaptations and transitions were popular with the public and were starting to become an increasingly valuable part of remaining visible and popular to the book-buying and theatre-going public.

Dead Man's Folly
(Novel, 1956)

In late January 1956 Edmund Cork was able to assure Collins that there would be a Christie for Christmas that year. Cork was able to be particularly confident on this occasion because the book in question, *Dead Man's Folly*, had a complex genesis which meant that much of the material for the novel had already been sketched out and written. The tale originated in late 1954, when Christie had decided that her next charitable donation (in the form of assignation of rights to one of her stories) would aid a church in Churston Ferrers, Devon, near to her holiday home of Greenway - specifically, to enable the installation of a new stained-glass window. The story to be gifted would be called 'The Greenshore Folly', starring Poirot,

ABOVE LEFT: So good, they named her twice - on the first *Dead Man's Folly* hardback. **ABOVE RIGHT:** The US 1961 Cardinal paperback.

and perhaps in order to cement the local link the mystery was clearly set in a location based on Greenway itself. However, once Christie completed the story, she encountered an unusual problem – her new novella-length murder mystery was an awkward fit for the magazines that would be expected to buy it for publication, and it proved impossible to sell. With her charitable donation already committed to the church, Christie ended up writing a brand new, and shorter, Miss Marple story to replace it, which used the similar title 'Greenshaw's Folly' for legal reasons but was otherwise completely different. By February 1956 the author was asking for updates on the potential sale of this story, as she wished to see the window in place 'before I die!'[38] In the end, the Miss Marple mystery was sold successfully, while Christie kept hold of the original ideas for her Poirot mystery so that they could be reworked for 1956's Poirot novel, *Dead Man's Folly*; her original version was finally published in 2014.

Dead Man's Folly has an excellent premise, in which a murder-themed treasure hunt at a fête in the grounds of

Hercule Poirot considers his fête in the Australian *Women's Weekly* serial of the story in December 1956.

a Greenway-esque country house has a tragic consequence, as the girl playing the victim is found to have been murdered for real. Luckily, Poirot is on the scene, thanks to the creator of the 'murder hunt', Ariadne Oliver, who sensed that there was something wrong and, as a result, invited the detective, giving him little opportunity to refuse. The opening section in which Oliver implores Poirot to make the journey offers a strong hook and plenty of character and entertainment. Christie is still having a great time with Oliver, as the contrast with Poirot is subtly underlined, including the fact that she seems incapable of even having a watch that runs on time. Christie also seems to enjoy turning Greenway into a place for murder, and we can imagine that the genesis of the story came from her mulling over ideas at her Devon home.

It's undoubtedly the detectives (both official and unofficial) who are the stars in *Dead Man's Folly*. There's an extra spark to the prose when the focus is on them, which it frequently is – whether it's Ariadne Oliver's new haircut or Poirot's annoyance with a jigsaw puzzle. Through Christie's

AGATHA CHRISTIE

DEAD MAN'S FOLLY
A HERCULE POIROT MYSTERY

The 1966 Pan paperback with blue poison bottle.

fictional crime writer we also get another insight into the author's own thinking about her stories and their reception, including a discussion of what she calls 'the fatal flaw' in mystery stories. As Oliver explains: 'There always is one. Sometimes one doesn't realise it until a book's actually in print. And then it's agony!' before clarifying that 'The curious thing is that most people never notice it'. Unfortunately, beyond our two sleuths the characterisation is somewhat weaker, including the owner of the house, the young Sir George Stubbs, and his wife, as well as assorted locals who vaguely allude to hidden secrets that will need to be unearthed. It's also a little odd that, surely unwittingly, Christie has crafted the second Poirot novel in a row that features young people from other countries staying at a hostel, whose rucksacks serve an important plot point.

When the book was discussed by her agent in January 1955 it was decided to make an effort to capitalise on a new Poirot novel (even though he had not really been absent from the shelves of booksellers) by moving to a larger page count for the book. Despite the fact that the novel had almost precisely the same number of words as *Hickory Dickory Dock*, the illusion of a bumper volume meant that a further two shillings could be added to the sale price. It was also time for the near annual discussion of whether a new short stories volume was viable. On this occasion it was decided that while a collection would be profitable, this needed to be balanced alongside the fact that short stories were not judged to be Christie's strong suit, and the plans were mothballed again.

Dead Man's Folly was published in Britain on 5 November 1956, a few weeks after its American publication, and it wasn't particularly well received, with initial sales figures being unexpectedly low (although good for any other author) and the critical reception being somewhat underwhelming. 'Miss Agatha Christie's new Poirot story comes first in this review because of its author's reputation and not on its own merits, which are disappointingly slight,' read the review in *The Times Literary Supplement*:

> They consist almost wholly in the appearance yet more of certainly profoundly familiar persons, scenes and devices ... the little grey cells are rather subdued ... The solution is of the colossal ingenuity we have been conditioned to expect but a number of the necessary red herrings are either unexplained or a little too grossly ad hoc. People are never candid about their vices so there is no need to take seriously the protestations of detection addicts about their

AGATHA CHRISTIE
Dead Man's Folly

Tom Adams' cover from 1970.

concern with the sheer logic of their favourite reading. What should be the real appeal of *Dead Man's Folly*, however, is not much better than its logic. The scene is really excessively commonplace, there are too many characters, and they are very, very flat.[39]

The Observer felt that the book provided a 'Stunning but not unguessable solution,' and that it was 'Nowhere near a vintage Christie but quite a pleasing table-read.'[40] Francis Iles in *The Manchester Guardian* was sympathetic to the book not being one of the author's best, calling it 'a minor Christie ... and of course it is just as easy to pull a minor Christie to pieces as anything else, if one feels one must. But it should be remembered that Mrs Christie's seconds would be most other writers' tops; and as for those who find Poirot boring, stylised figure though he now is ... well, one can only feel that they must be simply determined not to enjoy themselves.'[41] Similarly, *The Times* declared that the book was 'not Miss Agatha Christie at her best. The murder and the solution of it are ingenious, but then, with Miss Christie they always are, and it is pleasant to watch M. Hercule Poirot at work again. The character-drawing is flat and facile, however, and the dialogue, always Miss Christie's weak point, disastrous.'[42]

Elsewhere, the book inspired something of an argument in one of the tabloid newspapers, as Nancy Spain in the *Daily Express* revealed the identity of the murderer in her review, which resulted in one reader understandably writing in to complain. 'Write out 200 times "I promise not to do it again" or accept a challenge to a duel,' wrote Mrs E.O.D. Stalker of Uxbridge. The newspaper responded 'Nancy Spain accepts. And chooses a pistol.'[43]

Cat Among the Pigeons
(Novel, 1959)

In December 1957 Agatha Christie's friend and contemporary, the highly esteemed crime fiction writer Dorothy L. Sayers, died suddenly. Sayers was a few years younger than Christie but hadn't written detective fiction for nearly two decades, despite the acclaim that her stories received. Nevertheless, so close was their association that Christie was inevitably asked for comment following the news. 'She was the best of us all,' she told the *Daily Express*. 'We were good friends, though I had not often seen her recently. She was a fine writer - such good English and so witty. There aren't many detective story writers who are as witty. Could I "solve" her mysteries? Oh yes, most of them. After all, I'm in the trade.'[44]

ABOVE LEFT: The UK first edition cover from Collins. **ABOVE RIGHT:** US first edition jacket from Dodd, Mead (1960).

Pocket's first paperback from 1961, with art by J. Poluno.

The news of Sayers' death must have reinforced the sense that the peak of detective fiction of her type had passed, although Christie continued to enjoy exceptional (and generally growing) sales up to her death in 1976. For her next Poirot novel, *Cat Among the Pigeons*, Christie offered the latest example of a new location suitable for a closed-circle mystery. Perhaps it was seeing her grandson Mathew attend Eton that led to her choice of a boarding school, although in this case it's one for girls, called Meadowbank. The novel's title may have been the result of a more direct suggestion, as Collins' reader report for Christie's 1958 standalone mystery that bore the working title *The Innocent* suggested it was renamed – with *Cat Among the Pigeons* one title on offer. In the end it was called *Ordeal by Innocence* on publication, with the reader's suggestion saved for this novel the following year.[45]

The main crime in *Cat Among the Pigeons* is the murder of gym teacher Miss Springer, who hasn't been particularly popular with staff or pupils. The motive for murder isn't obvious, and it will take some working out to see how a mysterious prince and an unbalanced tennis racquet fit in to proceedings, especially when a second murder takes place that only complicates things further. The boarding school setting of *Cat Among the Pigeons* also allows Christie to superficially seem rooted in the established and traditional, while in practice reworking the environment in order to make the novel feel more modern. This isn't Enid Blyton's Malory Towers; instead we have references to 'oversexed teenagers' and even discussions of push-up bras that become an important plot point, while there is a gay undertone to some descriptions and reactions, not least characters' incredulous responses to suggestions that Miss Springer might have been meeting a man on the night she was shot. Less convincing is the way that some characters are used in order to serve a particular function for much of the book, such as the member of Special Branch who goes undercover as a gardener at the school, thanks to his extraordinarily fortuitous background – 'I ran a column on *Your Garden* in the *Sunday Mail* for a year in my younger days,' he cheerfully assures his superior. There are also story threads that threaten to become unwelcome distractions, such as the early goings on with the Prince of Ramat and the revolution in his country. This plot thread feels old fashioned and unconvincing, offering unwelcome echoes of the confused direction of novels such as *The Mystery of the Blue Train*.

Cat Among the Pigeons is highly readable and captures the interest, but never quite finds its groove. When more than two thirds of the novel has passed without mention of Poirot it could be fair to see his late appearance as an attempt to simply parachute in an established character who might be able to make sense of two murders and an international incident. This feels like a loss of confidence in the book from Christie, who had already established characters that should, by rights, have been able to solve the case, but have not demonstrated strong enough thought processes that any solution from them would seem convincing. Christie originally considered Miss Marple for the story, and she would probably have been able to reside at the school for its duration, although this might have been too similar to her function in 1952's *They Do It with Mirrors*, in which she stays with a friend who's running a centre for delinquent boys. However, Poirot's methodical approach was probably needed here, even if Miss Marple's insight into human nature would

Fontana's cover from 1962 by John Baker.

have allowed her to solve the second murder with efficiency. At least Poirot may be pleased that he's called in by a young person who has heard of him, which means that he fares better in public schools than he did in *Dead Man's Folly*, in which younger characters apparently had no clue who he was. In the end, it may well be that keeping Poirot away from the crime allows him to maintain his dignity as he is likely to have worked out most of the elements of the case with little fuss. The story doesn't really function as a puzzle, except for one important piece of misdirection when it comes to the motive(s) for the two murders.

Collins' reader report for the novel was generally positive, if not exactly adulatory, stating that:

> The new Christie is not a dazzling performance as a piece of classic detective story writing, but personally I found it highly entertaining and there is enough of the cross-word element towards the end to satisfy the purists even though the solution shows the plot to be rather far-fetched. Hercule Poirot does not play a very large part in the action and his fans might complain that he is used as a mere device for unscrambling the devious plots which Mrs Christie has spun. However, I do not think that there can be any doubt that we have in this book an extremely saleable new Christie, somewhat reminiscent of *They Came to Baghdad*, and that the girls' school is a novel and entertaining setting for this author which she handles very well indeed. I think that in many respects this is a more saleable book than *Ordeal by Innocence*.[46]

Following the book's publication in November 1959, *The Times Literary Supplement* suggested that 'Mrs Christie comes out strong again with *Cat Among the Pigeons*' and that 'It has sometimes been held against the author that she is too liberal with her red herrings. *Cat Among the Pigeons* may be called in support of this view. But Mrs Christie's public will not be alienated by any such trifle; their customary gratitude will be called forth by the easy, tonic quality of the style and the general ingenuity and resource-fulness of the story-telling.'[47] The *Daily Express* expressed gratitude towards the author's con-sistency even while in her seventieth year, as it wrote that 'It is splendid to find the Grande Dame of Crime in such fettle.'[48]

Cat Among The Pigeons

A Pocket Books cover from 1973 depicted a slender Poirot surrounded by bathing beauties – art by Robert Emil Schultz.

The 1950s had seen Agatha Christie the writer slowly morph in to 'Agatha Christie', the brand. This showed how Christie had come to domi-nate the crime fiction market so absolutely, while she had quietly continued to write her stories with the minimum of fuss. But the for-mation of Agatha Christie Ltd necessitated new thinking, as her writings became assets to be exploited as well as legacy items to be protected. These two foundations of the company have not always been complementary, and the 1960s would show that Christie could sometimes feel caught in the cross-fire between them, as the company's commercial interests cranked into action.

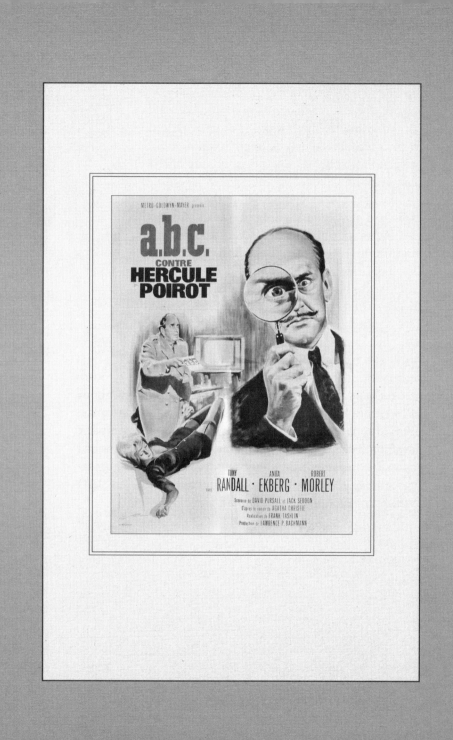

CHAPTER FIVE:

THE
1960s

Agatha Christie was almost untouchable as an author by the 1960s, and even on the occasions when a book wasn't quite at her highest standard the responses from both critics and the public was usually generous and kind. Christie had earned the trust and admiration of a generation of readers, who knew that even if one year's Agatha Christie wasn't quite to their taste, there was still a wealth of novels, short stories and plays that were.

For Christie the actual process of writing was little changed, although she moved over to dictating her novels on to tape rather than writing them out herself. It was a practice that she had dabbled in for many years, and it might explain why her later novels can have under-explored loose ends. Meanwhile her international reputation was still growing. Christie wasn't comfortable with most elements of what we

OPPOSITE: International publicity for Tony Randall as Poirot on the big screen (1965).

would now call fandom, but she co-operated with an official book on her work by G.C. Ramsey and ensured that a Czechoslovakian fan whom she considered to be 'sweet' was gifted copies of her books as they were so difficult to find in her home country. Other experiences were less pleasant for the author. 'In Persia a girl wanted me to autograph a book which had my name on it,' she told an interviewer:

> I couldn't understand a word, of course, so I asked a friend to translate a bit of it. It turned out to be by somebody quite different – all about a yacht club in New York! A terrible lot of girls write fan letters from America. They're always so earnest! ... I'm afraid the fans are sometimes disappointed in my photographs – they write 'I had no idea you were so old.' I get a good many asking curious questions: 'What emotions do you experience when you write?' All a great deal too insincere. What I'm writing is meant to be entertainment. I got one rather upsetting letter from a West African: 'I'm filled with enthusiasm for you and want you to be my mother. I'm arriving in England next month...' I had to write back that I was going abroad indefinitely.[1]

Some commentators have claimed that the 1960s saw a notable decline in the quality of Christie's work, but this isn't true. Apart from the mostly exemplary 1930s, her work had always been variable – something that can be no surprise due to the enormous quantity of her stories. The books in the 1960s were no more mixed than the 1920s or 1950s had been, and over the course of six weeks in 1966 a seventy-six-year-old Agatha Christie sat down and wrote the stand-alone mystery-thriller *Endless Night*, which many consider to be one of her very best novels. The Duchess of Death still had plenty of life left in her.

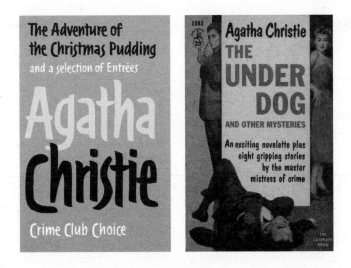

The Adventure of
the Christmas Pudding
and a selection of Entrées

Agatha
Christie

Crime Club Choice

Agatha Christie
THE
UNDER
DOG
AND OTHER MYSTERIES

An exciting novelette plus
eight gripping stories
by the master
mistress of crime

The Adventure of the Christmas Pudding
(Short stories, 1960)

By early 1960 it had been clear for some time that Agatha Christie's various commitments (particularly to the stage) meant that she would not be able to provide a new novel for that year. Consequently, a great degree of effort was dedicated to discussing what could be published for the lucrative Christmas market instead. Various ideas were contemplated, with one early suggestion being a collection of plays that would have included *Go Back for Murder*, her new Poirotless adaptation of the novel *Five Little Pigs*, which had made its stage debut early in 1960.[2] However, Christie's publisher Collins also understood that, while publications of plays

ABOVE: *The Adventure of the Christmas Pudding* was unique to the UK, with stories appearing in different collections in the USA, such as Pocket Books' *The Under Dog*, cover by James Meese (1955).

were increasingly popular, they couldn't compete with prose and so other possibilities were considered.

By March 1960 the short story 'Three Blind Mice', a fore-runner to *The Mousetrap*, was once more pencilled in to lead a British collection, no doubt by people who had little under-standing of how violently Christie opposed its publication while the play was running.[3] In April, Christie declared that she had the idea for a new novel, but it was clear that this was too late for it to be ready for Christmas and so alterna-tive plans continued. Christie's agent Edmund Cork sent her a list of short stories that hadn't been published by Collins (although most had been seen in American collections) from which she could pick a suitable selection for a new volume. Cork also suggested that a new preface would be enough to enable the book to hang together, as such a disparate selec-tion would be impossible to link in the manner of *The Labours of Hercules*. However, Cork made the fundamental error of suggesting *The Mousetrap and Other Stories* as a title, thus betraying his ignorance of Christie's feelings towards 'Three Blind Mice', as he argued that the play's producers could not realistically object to the revealing of the solution to fifty-thousand readers at this 'late stage' of the play's success.[4] His client immediately objected. 'No - not *The Mousetrap and Other Stories* - in fact I don't want the "Blind Mice" story included,' she responded. 'It will spoil somebody's pleasure in the play, and masses of people haven't seen it yet!'[5]

Instead, Christie turned to a mystery that had not been featured in a British collection to this point, as she argued that a Poirot story that had been published in *The Strand* in 1932 would be a good choice to lead a new collection. 'I would support *The Mystery of the Baghdad Chest and Other Stories* and I could do a little enlarging of that particular story as it has a lot of meat in it,' she offered. In addition, Christie suggested that she could also increase the length of 'The Third Floor Flat', a short story that had first been published in 1929 in *Hutchinson's Adventure & Mystery Story Magazine* alongside 'Four and Twenty Blackbirds' (first seen in *Collier's Weekly* in 1940), 'The Under Dog' (*The Mystery Magazine*, 1926), 'The Dream' (*Saturday Evening Post*, 1937), 'How Does Your Garden Grow?' (*Ladies' Home Journal*, 1935), 'The Adventure of the Clapham Cook' (*The Sketch*, 1923), 'The Perfect Maid' (*The Strand*, 1942), and 'The Cornish Mystery' (*The Sketch*, 1923).[6] This would have made for a perfectly decent selection of unconnected but good quality stories, but Christie also offered a different approach. 'Another idea – how about having just four good length stories?' she asked, suggesting 'Greenshaw's Folly' (*Daily Mail*, 1956) and 'The Under Dog' as the main two mysteries, supplemented by either 'The Dream' and an expanded 'Baghdad Chest', or longer versions of 'How Does Your Garden Grow?' and 'The Third Floor Flat'. In this proposed collection of four longer stories each would be expected to run to 20,000 words, and Christie also welcomed the opportunity to update the language, feeling that this would make for a more attractive proposition overall that would not be too much work for her.[7] Cork disagreed, pointing out that the author would actually need to find a further 40,000 words, which would be a lot of effort, hence the decision to have more than four stories in the collection.[8] A decision had also been made to change the provenance of the title story's chest when the story was rewritten, with Christie mulling over and then dismissing Persia as an alternative point of origin, before 'abandoning the Near East' and settling on Spain as more romantic and 'less difficult'.[9]

By May 1960 the title for that year's Agatha Christie book

The stories 'The Mystery of the Baghdad Chest' and 'Christmas Adventure' had appeared in Polybooks' *Poirot Knows the Murderer* collection in 1946.

Agatha Christie

THE ADVENTURE OF THE CHRISTMAS PUDDING

fontana books

Fontana's paperback edition in 1963 bore an early cover by Tom Adams.

was agreed to be *The Mystery of the Spanish Chest and Other Stories*, but this didn't last long due to the rediscovery of a suitably festive short story that had been little seen since a 1923 appearance in *The Sketch*, 'The Adventure of the Christmas Pudding'. By June this new discovery had been added to the collection that would then bear its name as a title, having been expanded by Christie to make it a more substantial offering.[10, 11] The final book would also include the Poirot stories 'The Mystery of the Spanish Chest', 'The Under Dog', 'Four and Twenty Blackbirds', 'The Dream', and the Miss Marple mystery 'Greenshaw's Folly' – although Christie was probably horrified to see her spinster detective referred to as 'Miss Marples' in the first edition of the book. In fact, the way in which the book treats its two detectives is decidedly odd – nothing is made of their first co-appearance in a British edition, and the first edition doesn't mention either of them on the front or rear covers. In her foreword, Christie wrote that 'This book of Christmas fare may be described as "The Chef's Selection." I am the Chef!', describing the first two stories as the main courses, 'Four and Twenty-Blackbirds' as a sorbet, and the remaining stories as entrées. She then reminisces about her own Christmases, especially when she was young, and explains that these memories fed into her writing of the first story, 'The Adventure of the Christmas Pudding', which is sometimes published under the title 'The Theft of the Royal Ruby'.

In this first story Poirot reacquaints himself not only with great matters of state, this time in his pledge to help a foreign prince recover said ruby, but also his love of central heating. Both factors lead him to a country house, where he hopes to recover the jewel – a plan that results in him playing a part in a murder scene. Poirot breaks down the traditional British ideal of Christmas, offering a contrast with the book's foreword in this literal 'Christie for Christmas'. It also seems to show the author starting to side with older characters and their reminiscences more explicitly, in contrast with her earlier general embracement of younger characters and even their idealised views. Unfortunately, Christie's expansion and apparent updating of the story was probably to its detriment, as it feels rather overstretched and unexciting. An early typescript shows that she trimmed several new elements before publication in order to tighten the story a little, including Poirot's farewell and a lengthier discussion of the mechanics surrounding a body that is found. Nevertheless, despite its shortcomings, the story is a pleasant read, perhaps best consumed after a hefty Christmas dinner.

'The Mystery of the Spanish Chest' is a particularly grisly and memorable case for Poirot, in which a dead body is found in the titular piece of furniture following a party. None of the characters seem to be able to work out how the dead man was stabbed and left in the chest without anyone noticing, but the story's emphasis on Poirot's thought processes allows us to see how he can work out the solution. However, it's unlikely to stump too many readers. Miss Lemon makes an appearance, and on this occasion the unpleasant description of her is that she is 'a human machine ... fortunate enough to have no imagination whatever' who is apparently composed 'entirely of angles'. Originally, this point was made as a reflection of Christie's description of Poirot's flat, but this was removed from the published version. In the unpublished portion Christie described that:

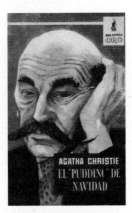

Poirot contemplates Christmas on a 1961 Spanish edition.

The flat of Poirot's choosing was one of the most modern of its kind. It was clean, hygienic, and severely functional. The cushions in the armchairs were square, not round. The right angle, rather than the curve, was the keynote of the furnishing and decoration. Over the mantlepiece was an abstract painting, mainly composed of interlaced cubes. Poirot admired it very much. At first sight Miss Lemon herself seemed to have been selected on the same principle.

The collection's third story, 'The Under Dog', feels like a particularly old-fashioned Poirot mystery to publish at this point, but it seems that Christie thought that it was a good example of a minor Poirot investigation. In this tale Sir Reuben Astwell has been murdered at his country house, and his son is the prime suspect, but another witness claims that the murdered man's secretary is to blame – although her only explanation for this accusation is pure intuition. It's difficult to care very much about the cast of characters presented here, and even Poirot's methodical discussion of events feels a little lifeless, as we have seen this all before, although at least psychology plays a role alongside practical reconstruction in this overlong mystery. Poirot does his best to let the characters show their true sides, including a muted acceptance of the ill-considered claim that 'We all know that Frenchmen are interested in ladies' dresses' when he looks at one piece of evidence. Poirot really comes alive when in close proximity to achieving justice, as he gets excited about the prospect of hanging a criminal, who is eventually captured despite a motive that isn't particularly convincing.

'Four and Twenty Blackbirds' is a snappy mystery that Christie had originally sketched out with Parker Pyne in mind. It zips through several interesting points before it arrives at a clever (although not entirely unguessable) solution. The story concerns a man of routine who suddenly seems to break with his usual order, which may be linked to his twin brother and an inheritance. Readers will quickly work out that they should be suspicious of portions of the story as described to them, but understanding the precise nature of how the different elements come together will take a little more effort. This short and clever puzzle story feels rather out of place in this collection, perhaps explaining why it's singled out as a 'sorbet' in Christie's foreword. The next story, 'The Dream', follows its lead in relying upon a single important piece of misdirection, which the reader may work out sooner than they should, but thankfully isn't the complete story. There is much to like in this tale of a rich man who dreams of killing himself, only to be found dead having apparently followed the method that he had described. Poirot is immediately suspicious, and identifies his misgivings with relative ease, although one particular element of the villain's plot will fail to convince feline friendly readers in particular.

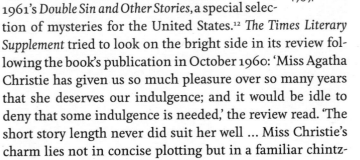

Pan Books released a photographic cover in 1969.

This collection wasn't published in America due to the fact that most of the stories had appeared in other volumes, or would feature in 1961's *Double Sin and Other Stories*, a special selection of mysteries for the United States.[12] *The Times Literary Supplement* tried to look on the bright side in its review following the book's publication in October 1960: 'Miss Agatha Christie has given us so much pleasure over so many years that she deserves our indulgence; and it would be idle to deny that some indulgence is needed,' the review read. 'The short story length never did suit her well ... Miss Christie's charm lies not in concise plotting but in a familiar chintz-and-chine cosiness: and short stories are too constricting.

Only the title story itself comes close to being an exception ... Poirot's little grey cells may not be unduly exercised but there is the irresistible simplicity and buoyancy of a Christmas treat about it all.' Christie's publishers might have been grateful that the reviewer ended by expressing the feeling that 'To attack Miss Christie would be like blocking the chimney against Santa Claus'.[13]

Hercule Poirot
(Television pilot, 1962)

Throughout 1959 and 1960 one particular venture domi-
nated the dealings of Agatha Christie Ltd – a potentially
lucrative deal with MGM that would cover the film and
television rights for most of Christie's stories, with the
exception of some 'reserved' titles, such as *Murder on
the Orient Express* and her plays. The film trade press followed the deal closely, such was its apparent value, which
they claimed could earn the author's company as much as
a million pounds, although in reality it could only have
achieved that large sum if multiple films and programmes
were made each year over the course of a decade. Christie
understood the value of the deal but was hardly excited by

ABOVE: Martin Gabel in CBS's 1962 television pilot, based on the short
story '*The Disappearance of Mr Davenheim*'.

the prospect. When a new problem threatened the arrangement in January 1960 a not exactly despondent Christie simply wrote: 'What will be - will be!'[14] By April 1960, *The Stage and Television Today* was reporting that a contract had been signed, with José Ferrer lined up to play Poirot in a new one-hour television series called simply *Hercule Poirot*. The Puerto Rican actor had won an Academy Award for his performance in 1950's *Cyrano de Bergerac*: given this Gallic past he was perhaps a natural choice for American producers, and his name would remain in the frame for some time. However, when cornered by the press, Christie rightly denied that a deal had been finalised. 'Nothing has been put on the dotted line yet,' she said. 'This has been blowing up for some time. Discuss it with my agent.'[15] MGM producer Lawrence Bachmann was a little more open, saying: 'We hope to get several TV series from them. We are counting on her to help with the preparation of the material, since she has a wonderful power of analysis, but we have made no agreement about future work.'[16]

A prospective deal with MGM had been proposed, drafted, and then cancelled at the last minute in the mid-1930s, when talks collapsed over the studio's desire to rework the character of Poirot as it wished. It's therefore unsurprising that Christie was cautious about this new proposal, and it would be unfortunate for her that her misgivings about the studio's likely treatment of her characters would largely be realised for the big-screen productions. Privately, MGM signalled its intention to make extensive use of Poirot short stories on television, and although Ferrer was the preferred star, he had his own tax complications that had the potential to preclude his involvement; besides, Agatha Christie wasn't excited by the casting of the actor, even if MGM was.[17] Prior to these plans, it had actually been a Miss Marple series that was expected to launch first.[18] Two Miss Marple scripts were completed in April 1960, with production expected for June, but the project never came to fruition.[19] However, it isn't necessarily the case that the plans for this Miss Marple television series then morphed into the Margaret Rutherford films, as the programme ideas were still being sketched out even after the first of those movies were made in 1961. Indeed, the general discussions around the MGM deal focused on television rather than film, with projects for the cinema treated as exceptional. In the end, the deal was finally struck in mid-1960, following extensive involvement of Christie's daughter Rosalind Hicks, and upon exchange of contracts Agatha Christie Ltd was in line for a first payment of $75,000.

By mid-1961 plans for this new Poirot television series had started to solidify, with Los Angeles-based British writer Barré Lyndon sketching out plans for the series, including

Martin Gabel as Poirot and Nina Foch as Mrs Davenham.

publicity material.[20] Lyndon planned that the series would feature international settings, possibly with Poirot utilising a *pied à terre* as a base, while always focusing on the 'uncommon man' and 'unique personality' of the detective himself. In this version of the character, Poirot had resigned from the Belgian police force in search of more interesting crimes to detect, and it's this quest for mysteries with unusual aspects that the series outline stated that writers should keep in mind – bank robberies were to be eschewed in favour of the likes of a shocking crime at a masquerade ball. Lyndon also sketched out that Poirot should be interested in psychology above all else (the 'why' rather than the 'how'), that he should be sophisticated but warm, and have a high regard for women. This Poirot was designed to be mischievous and moral, using his 'little grey cells' with electrifying results – this emphasis would have been aided by a title sequence that superimposed him on to an image of a pulsating brain. Given the expected changes for a general audience watching American network television, Lyndon had sketched out a highly likable version of Poirot and a potentially interesting series. Lyndon even wrote a trailer for the programme, in which Poirot would address the audience, discuss his creator, and go over some of the crimes that he had solved, including 'The Under Dog', 'The Veiled Lady' and *Peril at End House*. The trailer was written to emphasise the programme's unusual lack of action and violence but inclusion of 'intriguing' crimes, while it was also designed to showcase one of the series' most bizarre elements – Poirot's chauffeur-driven car that features all manner of gadgets including a television, telephone, drinks bar and even a bed, perhaps making him out to be something of a playboy figure.

Lyndon outlined a selection of the crimes that Poirot was expected to solve, most of which were clearly based on aspects of some Christie stories, such as *Hercule Poirot's*

Christmas, *The ABC Murders, Dead Man's Folly* and 'The Girdle of Hippolyta'. They included Poirot's own skills being used to aid jewellery thieves in Rome, a young woman's involvement with a crime at a masked costume ball, the disappearance of a French schoolgirl on a train alongside a valuable piece of art, Poirot's suspicion of the police during the festive period, a serial killer working his way through the villages of England led by names in a guidebook, and a 'murder hunt' in California that becomes all too real.

By early 1962 plans for the Poirot series had been finalised and somewhat slimmed down. The programme launched with a thirty-minute pilot, rather than the envisaged hour, and was broadcast as part of CBS's *General Electric Theater* strand on 1 April 1962. The actor playing Poirot had also changed, with Martin Gabel cast in place of Ferrer; Gabel was probably most well-known to the network's audience as an occasional panellist on its popular entertainment programme *What's My Line?* It was decided that 'The Disappearance of Mr Davenheim' would be the story adapted for this pilot programme, which was made on 35mm film just like cinema movies, and so finally released Agatha Christie television adaptations from the restrictions of live studio performances. In the finished production, simply called *Hercule Poirot*, jaunty music heralds the arrival of the detective as he reads about the 'vanished moneyman' Carl Davenham (as he is renamed), as well as watching a report on television in the back seat of his car. Poirot has history with the bank for which Davenham works, and so is a natural choice for Mrs Davenham to call in to help solve the case. Mrs Davenham rents a suite for Poirot to use, and he somewhat callously states that he will solve the crime without leaving the hotel in order to prove a point to the police with whom he has a $20 wager. This is a decent wheeze on the page, and a version of it is present in the original story, but it seems cruel on screen in front of a pleading wife, as is Poirot's claim that 'When I take you to your husband, as in the end I'm sure I shall, he may be dead – but if he's not you'll wish that he were'. The wager also restricts Poirot's actions, which is an odd decision for a pilot that is designed to showcase him, but the episode does have some nice pieces of direction that prevent it from feeling too static, including the use of Poirot's monocle as part of a dissolve into a flashback. Poirot uncovers the truth in a similar manner to the short story, and due to the brief use of some key characters it seems unlikely that many viewers will solve the mystery before him. At the end, Poirot takes a call from Palm Beach regarding three murders that would no doubt have led to a glamorous next episode had the programme been picked up for a series, which it wasn't.

The *Hercule Poirot* pilot has a competent and perfectly entertaining script, but it also feels rushed and a little cheap (as demonstrated by the fact that the actor playing Carl Davenham receives neither a line of dialogue nor even a credit, despite featuring in several scenes), while Martin Gabel as Poirot offers an amiable depiction of the character. It's also a little surprising that, given the emphasis on Agatha Christie in the original plans, the author's name isn't present in the opening titles – instead she must wait until the closing credits for an acknowledgement. However, the pilot demonstrated potential, and it seems likely that it would have been an interesting series if it had continued.

The Clocks
(Novel, 1963)

The Clocks opens with the sort of high-concept premise that Christie had made particularly good use of early in her career, as a dead body is found in a room that has also been populated with several clocks, for reasons unknown. A similar principle had appeared in her 1929 novel *The Seven Dials Mystery*, in which a collection of alarm clocks were part of a murder scene, while *The Clocks'* refinement of the idea had its origins in plans for a short story opening that Christie had outlined for a competition in 1949.[21] This was called 'The Clock Stops' and, like this 1963 novel, the character who discovered the body was an apparently unconnected typist from a local agency. In fact, the greatest mystery that

ABOVE LEFT: The first UK edition cover. **ABOVE RIGHT:** The 1963 Dodd, Mead jacket.

the reader faces when reading *The Clocks* is in trying to work out how so many apparently unconnected elements can possibly work together – from the typing agency characters, to the blind owner of the house where the body was discovered, and then her characterful neighbours. The novel also features two major plot strands, as the murder mystery element is interwoven with the tale of secret service agent Colin Lamb, which might have been Christie's latest attempt to update her stories for readers in the 1960s. 'Modern taste has changed very largely from detective stories to crime stories,' she said a few years later, although most of these crime stories were not to her taste, as she described them as 'just a series of violent episodes succeeding each other. I find those very boring.'[22]

Christie no longer operated with a manuscript 'in hand', so as not to feel rushed as the publisher deadlines loomed, but she worked with efficiency in order to have a new novel ready for the end of the year. In January 1963 she wrote to Cork to say that she had received her salary cheque from

UK hardback Book Club edition with cover by George Chrichard (1963).

Agatha Christie Ltd (which by now was £6,000 a year, plus £3,000 in expenses) and joked that 'it has so stimulated me that I've written my first chapter of AC's next masterpiece entitled (at the moment) *The Clocks*'.[23] Christie wrote this letter while battling snow and broken pipes, although she sat snugly in the cocoon of her strong central heating, working on this new mystery. Christie preferred to write in the dark and cold winter: 'It's a very good plan: you can write during the unattractive winter months and stoke up with energy while the flowers are out.'[24] In the warmer months Christie had only to correct proofs that were sent her way, which were finished in July for *The Clocks*.

Poirot from the 1964 serialisation in *The Australian Women's Weekly*, illustrated by Jake Mills.

Collins was very pleased to learn that Christie's next novel was to be a Poirot mystery, as it had been four years since the last, *Cat Among the Pigeons*, in which he had played only a very small role, meaning that it had been seven years since he made a full appearance, in 1956's *Dead Man's Folly*. However, while Poirot plays a slightly more prominent part in *The Clocks* compared to its predecessor, he doesn't appear until nearly halfway through the novel, and he is quite removed from events once again. Christie was clearly enjoying the other elements of the story rather more than resurrecting Poirot, but the sidelining of him is starting to feel unwarranted and even unfair on the reader, as he solves this case from a distance in a similar manner to the short story 'The Disappearance of Mr Davenheim'.

This regression to an old plot device is just one example of the book harking back to earlier times, as Christie leaned towards nostalgia more heavily as she aged. This is most noticeable during her lengthy, and rather bizarre, description of Poirot's opinions about various mystery writers over the years. We are treated to his – and probably Christie's

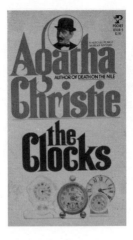

The 1965 American Pocket Books cover.

Tom Adams' cover for *The Clocks* (1966).

– feelings about a range of titles, including the novel that particularly influenced the author half a century earlier, Gaston Leroux's *The Mystery of the Yellow Room*. Poirot also finds time to discuss Ariadne Oliver's stories, which certainly mirror Christie's reflections on her own work: 'Being young at the time, she was foolish enough to make her detective a Finn, and it is clear that she knows nothing about Finns or Finland except possibly the works of Sibelius,' the Belgian detective says. 'Still, she has an original habit of mind, she makes an occasional shrewd deduction, and of later years she has learnt a good deal about things which she did not know before.'

The Clocks benefits from a bustling and inventive opening, with the circumstances of the murder being enough to intrigue any reader, although they should prepare themselves for disappointment when the solution is revealed as there are some significant red herrings at play. The novel's use of different perspectives as the two main storylines develop is also fresh and to its benefit, although we might not be completely convinced by the ways that characters' lives interact and overlap. The plotting isn't helped by the unconvincing nature of the espionage elements, while one important visual clue is likely to be worked out by the reader almost instantly. It's worth noting that one key to the solution is in the form of a child who has been observing events through her window, as she's trapped in her bedroom due to a broken leg, making it likely that Christie had seen and enjoyed Alfred Hitchcock's *Rear Window* (1954). By the time a solution has been arrived at the reader might be surprised by the extent to which Poirot is relying on speculation – perhaps he should have made the effort to play a more prominent part in the investigation.

'*The Clocks* is a decent little Poirot-Christie, up to snuff but not outstanding,' said *The Times Literary Supplement*, 'the trails are so thoroughly muddied, in fact, that only by guesswork can Poirot arrive at the solution and we readers couldn't possibly do so.'[25] *The Observer* described Poirot as 'rather doddery and forlorn now', and argued that the book was 'Not as zestful as usual. Plenty of ingenuity about the timing, though.'[26] Christie was probably not surprised by this reaction, although in fact the reviewers were being quite generous. In a discussion between Cork and publisher Billy Collins shortly after the novel saw print in November 1963 her agent said that Christie 'would like to have improved' *The Clocks*, and that her next novel, *A Caribbean Mystery* with Miss Marple, would be better.[27]

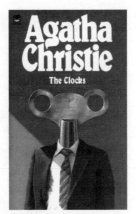

A strikingly surreal design from 1981 for the Fontana paperback.

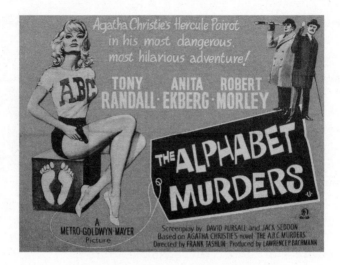

The Alphabet Murders
(Film, 1965)

By early 1963 relations between Agatha Christie and MGM were beginning to break down. The 1962 *Hercule Poirot* pilot had passed by with barely a murmur (it's probable that the author didn't even see it), while Christie had initially held her tongue when she saw Margaret Rutherford as Miss Marple in *Murder She Said*, the 1961 film adaptation of *4.50 from Paddington*. In private she revealed that she didn't care for it, and felt that it looked like a television production (prompting negative comparisons with Billy Wilder's *Witness for the Prosecution* from 1957, which Christie had liked a great deal), while she also felt that Rutherford

ABOVE: 'Agatha Christie's Hercule Poirot in his most dangerous, most hilarious adventure!' The MGM poster setting the scene for the new film (1965).

was quite unsuitable to play Miss Marple, even though she became friendly with the actress. However, Christie wasn't surprised that she didn't care for the adaptations, and so initially restricted her complaints to her usual grumbles about her work being reinterpreted (or, perhaps, misinterpreted), while maintaining an occasional correspondence with the film's producer Lawrence Bachmann. In part this was in order to discuss Christie's script for a proposed (but never made) film of Charles Dickens' *Bleak House*, which she completed in 1962. Although her finished draft was hugely over-length there was still the expectation that the project would happen, with Collins even preparing to publish the script following its release.

This largely cordial relationship would change when Christie learned that the second Miss Marple film would be called *Murder at the Gallop* and was to be based on *After the Funeral*, a novel that had featured Poirot as the detective. She was furious about the change of characters, as well as the sight of Rutherford's Miss Marple atop a horse in a film that concentrated more on farce than mystery. 'They always spoil them,' Christie said of film producers. 'To say one's stories would make such marvellous films and then to murder all one's favourite characters – it's too much!'[28] Such incidents hardened her resolve against any film adaptations, despite the contract that had been signed. In April 1963 Christie was asked who she would choose to play Poirot on screen, and in a typical response she wrote simply: 'I would prefer Hercule Poirot not to appear on screen or stage.'[29]

In the spring of 1963 MGM's plans were continuing to exasperate and upset Christie. Although the studio had signed a deal for the rights to adapt *The ABC Murders* and the short story 'How Does Your Garden Grow?' in March, it was turning to one of Christie's crown jewels for a forthcoming Rutherford project, which again stepped on Poirot's toes.

Margaret Rutherford's Miss Marple would make a brief cameo appearance in *The Alphabet Murders*.

MGM requested the rights to base its new film on *Murder on the Orient Express*, a property that was not part of the main MGM deal. This was difficult enough, even aside from the fact that they wanted to use it for a Miss Marple caper. 'No,' responded Christie, 'I really can't agree to the transfer of *Murder on the Orient Express* from the "reserved" subjects. MGM must do without it – they have plenty of other material. *Orient Express* took a lot of careful planning and technique,' she wrote, before arguing that to have it transferred to a 'farce with Miss Marple projected into it and possibly acting as the engine driver – though great fun, no doubt, would be somewhat harmful to <u>my</u> reputation!'[30]

In July 1963 Bachmann wrote to Christie to say that he was excited about plans for a Poirot film based on *The ABC Murders*, and even claimed that he was especially happy with the characterisation of Poirot – something that would prove to be a disastrous error of judgement. At the same time Bachmann reassured Christie that *The ABC Murders* was expected to retain its original title for the film, unlike the Miss Marple adaptations.[31] In the same letter he revealed that the third Miss Marple film, which was once more based on a Poirot novel (*Mrs McGinty's Dead*), would be renamed *Murder Most Foul* for the screen. 'Can you imagine a triter title?' she asked her agent.[32] Titles were to be the least of her worries, however, as the plans for Poirot came into focus, with the comic actor Zero Mostel joining the project to both play Poirot and work on the script. Confidence was not high in the Christie camp. 'I am sure [Bachmann] feels he will do the same for Poirot with Zero Mostel as he has done for Miss Marple with Margaret Rutherford,' Christie's daughter Rosalind Hicks wrote:

JUSTICE
will be seen to be done at the boxoffice
with
NIGHT MUST FALL
starring Albert Finney as Danny
MURDER MOST FOUL
starring Margaret Rutherford as Miss Marple
THE ABC MURDERS
starring Zero Mostel as Hercule Poirot
MURDER AHOY
starring Margaret Rutherford as Miss Marple
from
M-G-M's BRITISH STUDIOS
ON THE MOVE IN EUROPE TOO!

In April 1964 MGM announced its slate of forthcoming films would include *The ABC Murders* starring Zero Mostel as Hercule Poirot.

> I fear it may be worse … we have really let my mother down very badly over this whole deal. I now realise providing the films are based on a property they can make Poirot into as comic a figure as Miss Marple, if not more so. It is a dreadful thought and we have no legal grounds now of ever breaking their contract. I know my mother is upset but I doubt if I am any less so![33]

This discussion was taking place in the midst of much upset over the fourth (and final) Miss Marple film with Rutherford, called *Murder Ahoy*, which was based on a completely original script.[34] Rosalind pushed for Agatha Christie Ltd to have right of veto even in the event of her mother's death, but this would have been an extraordinary and probably unworkable clause, which MGM's lawyers resisted fiercely.[35] Christie had been upset by the events of *Murder Ahoy*, and even wrote her own disclaimer for the screenwriting credit in the opening titles: 'Based on their interpretation of Agatha Christie's Miss Marple'. She was further distressed when reports reached her that Zero Mostel had told the press that his Poirot would be 'shabby' and 'girl-chasing'. In an April 1964 interview Mostel acted out all the characters from his imagined story for the entertainment of his interviewer Peter Duvall Smith, from 'county ladies and colonels and bright young things' to Poirot himself. 'This is called exploring the characters, though inventing is really the word,' observed Smith. 'Mostel gave me the names of half-a-dozen, but none of them even appears in the book.' As for Poirot, Mostel was looking to reinvent the character to suit his needs:

> I've done a few films, with Bogie and Kazan and so on, but I'm always somebody's relative ... Now, with Poirot, I'm more central. I reckon I can do something with him. I don't think those little grey cells of his are all that remarkable. Sure, he solves his cases but there are usually seven or eight corpses lying around before the end. I reckon I'll give him an eye for the girls, sort of bring out his sex angle. And maybe – just a minute, here's an idea – maybe we'll turn him into a Scotsman, change him from a Gaul into a Gael.[36]

Bachmann tried to allay Christie's concerns, to little effect.[37] Christie later said:

> I kept off films for years because I thought they'd give me too many heart-aches. Then I sold the rights to MGM, hoping they'd use them for television, but they chose films.

It was too awful! They did things like taking a Poirot book and putting Miss Marple in it! And all the climaxes were so poor you could see them coming! I get an unregenerate pleasure when I think they're not being a success. They wrote their own script for the last one – nothing to do with me at all. *Murder Ahoy*, one of the silliest things you ever saw! It got very bad reviews, I'm delighted to say.[38]

The actual script for *The ABC Murders* is unlikely to have supported Bachmann's defence. The censor notes for the United States from April 1964 list the elements of the original screenplay that would have been unacceptable for the cinema screen, and they were extensive. The script was rejected on the grounds that it featured scenarios that were excessively sexually suggestive, with such situations repeating themselves throughout the proposed film, apparently due to fantasy sequences that reflected the smutty mind of Mostel's Poirot. The censor's main issues with the film were:

- An opening scene in which Poirot is engaging in a sexual act with a woman, suggested by sound-effects

- Unacceptably erotic dance movements, which feature Poirot being buffeted between women's bottoms

- A 'midget' being called to bed by an 'amazon', with the line 'I gotta fix a leak' having an erotic significance

- Poirot examining a woman called Beatrice, apparently looking for a concealed weapon, with clear sexual inferences from the dialogue and her reaction to visible evidence of Poirot's sexual excitement when the characters are pressed together in an elevator

- Beatrice removing her negligee and so being in the nude

- A scene in which Poirot and Beatrice gain masochistic pleasure from slapping each other (including deletion of the line 'More! More! More!')

- A near repeat of the 'midget' and 'amazon' scene, with a larger 'amazon'

- A dream sequence in which three women lose their negligees

It's not surprising that Christie was so upset.

On 4 May 1964 there was finally some good news, as Edmund Cork wrote to Anthony Hicks to confirm that MGM had cancelled its contract with Mostel, with the screenplay to be completely rewritten, cutting out fantasies that Mostel had included and maintaining the Poirot character.[39] This was a late change, as Mostel had featured in quite a bit of pre-publicity, and so demonstrates the extent to which this was considered to be an emergency situation.

Although good news, Anthony's response to the news of Mostel's removal was not exactly jubilant, as he wrote to Cork that their best bet was to move slowly, as MGM was keener to move quickly than they were.[40] In the end, a new agreement was designed in order to clarify points of dispute between Christie (as well as her family and company) and MGM, especially regarding original screenplays and their insistence that Poirot should be depicted in line with Christie's characterisation. Rosalind was still not happy, and urged more stringent conditions in the new contract:

I still feel that they have no right to make original screen plays for films and do not like any suggestion that they have ever had this right. My mother also said she would not sign anything which suggested this. It is obviously a very good thing that they have got rid of Mostel, but I feel from

'Tony Randall, as Hercule Poirot, discusses sleuthing strategy with a movie Poirot of three decades ago (Austin Trevor), now playing a cameo role,' declared a lobby card from the film.

his interviews to the press that we were not the only ones who were thankful! ... I feel they will certainly try much harder after the fiasco with Mostel to get a Poirot who will play it straight or at any rate straighter - I honestly do not think my mother wishes to read the film scripts herself after all this trouble.[41]

MGM's lawyers wrote to Christie's own legal team to say that the film studio recognised the importance of maintaining Christie's conception of Poirot, while pointing out that a revised version of the screenplay had been written as a result, which they argued was a demonstration of goodwill towards the author.[42] However, they once more rejected the request for script approval, pointing out that films have many authors and so a shooting script is not necessarily what appears on screen anyway.[43] Before filming could start, MGM's lawyers had pounced on the author Elizabeth Linington, whose 1964 novel *Greenmask!* dealt with a murderer explicitly copying *The ABC Murders*, leading to characters discussing of the book and the wider Christie and detective mystery oeuvres. MGM ensured that Linington was aware that she could not sell the motion picture rights to her book without leaving herself open to legal action. Seemingly written as a response to 'outdated' detective novels of the golden age, *Greenmask!* itself made little impression and is no longer in print.

In the end, *The ABC Murders* went into production in December 1964, with American comic actor Tony Randall cast as Poirot. The project was first renamed *Amanda* after a mysterious character in the film (this title also erroneously appears on the back cover of the tie-in paperback) and then finally *The Alphabet Murders*, to avoid releasing a film that shared a name with the ABC cinema chain. The new script was still a farce, but now it was Hastings (played by Robert Morley) who was the source of many of the attempts at comedy. The film focused on some bizarre elements, such as a murdered clown diving into a swimming pool, as well as beautiful women, and a lot of good actors running about under instruction from an inconsistent script by David Pursall and Jack Seddon, who had also written three of the Miss Marple films. A trade magazine's report from the set quoted director Frank Tashlin saying that Robert Morley had ignored the scripted dialogue 'thank God!', which provoked an irate reaction from the writers. Pursall and Seddon responded in a letter to *Film and Filming*, stating that 'Tashlin's intemperance may well arise from the fact that he had to be continually restrained from making arbitrary and insensitive changes in [sic] the comedy style of the film'.[44] The cast is exceptionally strong, and such strengths make it all the

Tony Randall as Poirot and Robert Morley as Captain Hastings.

worse that the film itself is so confused, as it struggles to work out precisely where it wants to situate itself in the mystery/thriller/comedy/action genres. Joining Randall and Morley for filming were the likes of Maurice Denham, Sheila Allen, Julian Glover, James Villiers, Clive Morton, Cyril Luckham, Sheila Reid, Patrick Newell and Windsor Davies. Also in the cast is Austin Trevor, who had played Poirot in three films in the 1930s. In an interview Trevor stated that 'I would be better casting now than I was then!', as he rubbed his balding head.[45] Meanwhile, two more figures from the wider Christie screen world also pop up, with Margaret Rutherford making a cameo appearance alongside her real-life husband Stringer Davis, in character as Miss Marple and Mr Stringer.

In an attempt to get Christie on side with the project, and clearly demonstrate that it was consulting with her, MGM asked the author to approve Poirot's physical appearance in the film. 'I can't really see any difference,' she protested of the three options she saw. 'Of course the appearance is much younger than H.P. was – even when I first knew him – in fact he looks much more like Hastings! But I think what is lacking is H.P.'s distinctive moustache – that is the first essential for Poirot. He talks about it himself in every book, is undeniably proud of it and it ought to be flamboyant, black, tilts upward

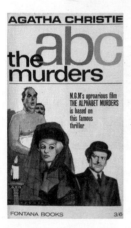

[with] tweaked ends.' Christie argued that the moustache should be black, 'owing to reliance on the dye pot'.[46]

Fontana released an edition of *The ABC Murders* with specially commissioned artwork (1965).

The Alphabet Murders cannot be judged to be a success as either a comedy or mystery, as the muddled movie moves between non-sequiturs that do little to advance whatever plot there is. For example, when Poirot and Hastings seem to be about to fall victim to the hands of the murderer at a sauna, it only leads to comedy of the most obvious kind as Hastings, wearing only a towel, chases after a suspect into a busy street hosting a parade. There's no finesse or wit here, and it's clear that the names of both Poirot and Agatha Christie are attached for purely financial reasons, and not because of any desire to bring their essence to the screen. However, Tony Randall seemed to enjoy the production, judging by his interviews with the press, and his performance is a highlight, especially given the difficulties of acting in a film with such an inconsistent tone. On set he told one reporter that he found Poirot to be impossible to believe in, but didn't consider this to be a negative. He said:

> The success of Agatha Christie is not that her books are possible, but that they are perfect puzzles which the reader

can solve. The only two possible fiction detectives are Dashiell Hammett's Sam Spade, who is fat and makes mistakes, and Raymond Chandler's Philip Marlowe. No one could be quite as cerebral as Poirot. Most of my films have been comedies but I would rather be thought of as an actor than a comedian. I would rather know that I've played a part well than get a big laugh. I am not a clever man. The only thing I'm always right about is that I'm always wrong. Now, someone like Robert Morley, who is in this film with me ... He is really clever. We made this off-the-cuff recording in which we pretended I was interviewing William Shakespeare, and he just answered fluently in blank verse. Isn't that brilliant? So why do I succeed? I hope because I am a good actor.[47]

One difficult issue with these adaptations was that they had a life beyond the cinema, as paperback publishers wished to capitalise on the attendant publicity from films even if they had little in common with the novels on which they were ostensibly based – including them sporting different titles. In the end an agreement was reached whereby film tie-ins could be published in limited runs as long as careful wording was deployed in order to make it clear that the Christie tale within was not closely aligned with the film, and certainly not a novelisation. This was an awkward compromise, but it followed Christie's unhappiness with these films, which also led to her taking a back seat in business discussions generally. With the formation of the company and Christie's advancing age, Rosalind and Anthony Hicks were taking charge and became the main point of contact for discussions about adaptations and new publications.

It took until 1966 for *The Alphabet Murders* to be released in most countries, and although some reviews were more positive than the film's reputation might suggest, many were

In some markets, the film's comedic tone would be ignored in subsequent marketing, such as this German video release.

dire. 'Depressingly unfunny comedy-thriller,' said the *Monthly Film Bulletin*, 'virtually none of the misadventures encountered by Poirot during the course of the case raise even the slightest smile. Even the tangled mystery, solved by a typical Agatha Christie "surprise", is unusually dreary.'[48] Meanwhile, *Variety* argued that the film's 'broad comedy treatment' was 'not always for the best. There is, however, enough diverting action to keep spectator mildly engaged and the name of Christie may help chances in the general market ... Much of the suspense of Agatha Christie writing is lost in converting to comedy, and the result is no more than a parody of the original, insufficiently clever to be outstanding. Tony Randall seems a strange choice for the Poirot role, which he clowns throughout ... But he delivers a very definite characterization, even though it's not the original character.'[49]

Elsewhere, Poirot's general absence from most screens was being noticed, with the *Daily Mirror* asking why 'two famous fictional sleuths have escaped from the TV screen – Agatha Christie's Hercule Poirot and Dorothy Sayers's Lord Peter Wimsey,' in an article about the new BBC series *Detective* in 1964. 'We tried to get them,' the BBC responded, 'but we couldn't obtain the TV rights.'[50] Given the faithful depictions of other characters in this series, perhaps Poirot on television wouldn't have been such a bad idea after all.

Third Girl
(Novel, 1966)

Poirot's first appearance in a new Collins publication during 1966 was not *Third Girl*, which was the year's Christie for Christmas, but in a special collection of Christie short stories called *13 for Luck!* The volume was aimed at younger readers and featured a variety of stories, mostly of good quality and including 'The Market Basing Mystery', a 1923 Poirot adventure that was making its debut in a British book collection.[51] Despite its apparent innocuousness, Christie was very unhappy that the book was released without proper consultation and objected to its advertised focus on non-adult readers, as well as the presence of stories from *The Labours of Hercules*, which she did not like to see published

ABOVE LEFT: The UK first edition cover (1966). **ABOVE RIGHT:** The American first edition designed by Salem Tamer (1966).

independently. 'I also *hate* this silly teenagers business,' she protested to Edmund Cork:

> ... several people came up to me in the States and said 'I believe you are writing specially for teenagers now'. It is *not* true – I say so to everyone. My books are written for adults and always have been. I don't believe you realise in the least how much I mind having things slipped over on me – I *hate* the publishing of *Thirteen for Luck* – just when *Third Girl* ought to have had the field to itself. *Thirteen for Luck* is a very bad title to choose ... And the stories in *Thirteen for Luck* I never would have agreed to ... You've got to keep a beady, firm eye on Collins – I don't trust them.

A self-aware Christie then asked herself: 'Now then – any other complaints Agatha? Yes – ' before outlining another problem for Cork's collection.[52]

Christie's new novel for 1966, *Third Girl*, is an interesting documentation of how she saw the clashes between the old and the new – as well as the old and the young. Nostalgia and memories are once more significant discussion points between several characters, including Hercule Poirot. The 'third girl' of the title is a description of a young woman, Norma Restarick, who takes the third room in a flat share and believes that she may have committed murder – but her muddled thoughts make it difficult to be sure.[53] When she seeks assistance from Poirot, his valet George demonstrates that his own take on women (or 'ladies'), as well as perhaps his very existence, is now very old fashioned. Norma is no happier with the situation, as she flees when she realises that Poirot is so much older than she had expected. Although Christie

The Collins library edition of *Thirteen for Luck* from 1987.

allows plenty of characters to complain about young people, she did have some sympathy with the new generation:

I don't think I should like to be young now. We used to live such a splendid, idle, lazy life. I never went to school and I had all the time I liked to imagine and think things. We used to walk everywhere, to picnics, even to dinner parties. Today everyone seems to work and I suppose you'd feel left out if you didn't. I dare say it's much nobler, but we had much more fun. I feel all the young people are a bit worried – so many of them seem to take tranquilisers. I sometimes think I must be the only woman in England who has *never* had a tranquiliser. Young women come to my house and ask for them and I say 'Will an aspirin do?'[54]

Poirot hasn't been very active in the world of detection since we last saw him, as he has been busy writing his magnum opus about detectives and writers, another character trait that betrays Christie's own interests. As time moved on so Poirot's creator was openly sympathetic about complaints regarding his age:

If I'd known it was for life, I'd have chosen some rather younger detectives. God knows how old they must be by now! I'm afraid Poirot gets more and more unreal as time goes by. A private detective who takes cases just doesn't exist these days, so it becomes more difficult to involve him and make him convincing in so doing. The problem doesn't arise with Miss Marple: there are still plenty of them drifting about.[55]

Poirot wasn't the only person to mirror Christie, as Ariadne Oliver reappears, now looking to have Poirot speak at the annual dinner of the Detective Authors Club, a

Agatha Christie
Third Girl

Tom Adams' *Third Girl* painting first appeared in Fontana in 1968.

fictional version of the Detection Club of which Christie was president. When Oliver and Poirot have the chance for a discussion they practically segue into a comedy double act, albeit one in which they mostly enjoy complaining about whatever comes their way. This includes Oliver's dislike of her new novel (was Christie just having a joke here, or cheekily revealing her true feelings?), but it is young people's tastes that receive the most complaints. Christie had little time for women's fashions in the 1960s ('Those mini-dresses look so cold in winter, very unsexy, like gym tunics. All the girls seem to want to look like orphans') but appreciated men's appearances better, perhaps explaining her references to their tight trousers in both this novel and *The Clocks*. She felt that men 'strutting along in their finery, like Vandyk portraits with their curled hair and their velvets and silks' looked much better than fashionable women of the age.[56] Even the Beatles receive a passing mention in the book, although the context is dismissive ('Long-haired young fellows, beatniks, Beatles...'). Christie was once asked what Poirot would say if he met them; she responded that he would 'Congratulate them warmly on their success and popularity; shudder inwardly at the general untidiness of their appearance; possibly ask if any of them had considered growing a very *fine* moustache.'[57] Previously, Christie had embraced the spirit of young adults and teenagers, but here she is of an age and in a time where she is starting to despair, which also might explain the novel's awkward accounts of drug taking amongst young people. Luckily for Collins' lawyers a further complaint about the tastes of the youth was removed before publication, in which the author described Coca-Cola as an 'abomination'.[58]

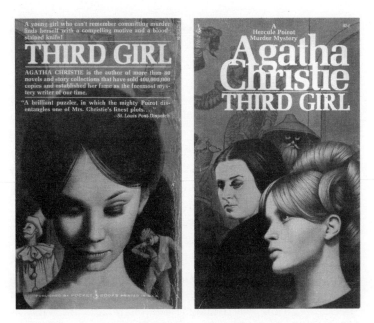

Tom Adams painted *Third Girl* again as one of a series of wraparound paintings for Pocket Books in 1972.

When it comes to clue finding, Poirot is assisted in part by not only Ariadne Oliver, but also Mr Goby, his fact-finding friend who had first appeared as far back as *The Mystery of the Blue Train* in 1928. Here he demonstrates extraordinary abilities in order to give a fantastically detailed account of events at which he wasn't present, marking him out as more plot device than man. As the investigation requires the discovery of not only the culprit but also the crime itself there are many confusing events to sort out, not helped by Ariadne Oliver managing to give a particularly enigmatic clue at one point, when she points the finger at a 'peacock', an illustration of which features on the first edition cover. Elsewhere, Poirot is back to noting the types of physical clues that he has often protested about, such as the presence of damp mud, but at least we should be pleased that his penchant for thinking about nursery rhymes has not been reflected in the book's title for once, as he mulls over 'rub-a-dub-dub, three men in a tub'.

When the finished novel was read at Collins several loose ends were questioned, and although most were fixed prior to publication in November 1966 the finished novel is not entirely plausible and is a victim of the frequent tangents that characters encounter or discuss.[59] Christie was happy with the published book's appearance ('really rather handsome and expensive looking'), while reviews were kind.[60] The plaudits were often vague, however, with *The Times Literary Supplement*'s review stating that 'it's still a pleasure to see *cher maître* at work', while *The Observer* described the book's 'usual double-take surprise solution centring round a perhaps rather artificial identity problem; but the suspense holds up all the way. Dialogue and characters are lively as flies. After this, I shan't be surprised to see A.C. wearing a mini-skirt.'[61,62] Perhaps even more bizarrely, the *Daily Express* summarised the new novel's attempts to untangle the lives of young people and their behaviours as 'Miss Christie goes all Mod.'[63]

Hallowe'en Party
(Novel, 1969)

1969 saw a welcome return to the macabre for Agatha Christie with the new Poirot mystery *Hallowe'en Party*. 1967 had seen the publication of her thriller *Endless Night*, which may have surprised some readers with its cynicism, but it was indicative of her feelings that society was becoming harsher. Christie even studied daily papers for three weeks in order to learn about contemporary crimes, which no doubt influenced her decision to make this novel's murder victim a thirteen-year-old girl who is drowned in a bucket filled for apple-bobbing during the Hallowe'en celebrations. In her examination of the newspapers Christie recalled that:

ABOVE LEFT: The UK first edition featured the first of many pumpkin designs, although this one was yellow. **ABOVE RIGHT:** An orange pumpkin appeared on the first American paperback (1970).

Every day there was somebody murdered, some girl killed, some child missing and strangled. I think it's a sign of the times; there's more violence as a means of passing the time. You read about these boys saying 'We had nothing to do so we thought we'd roll so-and-so', and some boy just sitting quietly is killed. Girls are very silly, if I may say so. They go out with men they've only known a few hours. When I was a girl you used to be told 'Be careful. Don't get into trains alone with a strange man.'[64]

It seems likely that highly publicised and shocking real-life murder cases such as the Moors Murders and Mary Bell had affected Christie's outlook on society in the late 1960s. *Hallowe'en Party* presents a selection of possible villains, but the search for them is complicated by the fact that, just as in the previous Poirot book, half of the work of the detective is discovering if a previous crime ever really happened – and if it did, what the circumstances were. In this case

Hercule Poirot appeared on this 1973 Pocket Books paperback.

it's the girl's claim that she once saw a murder that seems likely to have led to her death. One influence may have been Christie's viewing of the film *Rosemary's Baby*, which was released in Britain in January 1969, as it also mixes contemporary relationship dramas with visions of the supernatural (albeit as more 'real' than the window dressing of this novel), with a child at the centre of events, and the sense that respectable members of society may be hiding dark truths. The American influence extended even further elsewhere, as Hallowe'en parties were not as popular in Britain as they were in the United States, as alluded to by Ariadne Oliver's discussion of her experiences of them when abroad, although she somehow manages to confuse pumpkins with vegetable marrows. Thankfully, the correct vegetable appeared on the cover, albeit with an odd yellow hue. Oliver also recalls the events of *Dead Man's Folly*, which highlights the fact that she seems to have an unenviable habit of turning up at celebrations that will see the murder of an innocent girl in order to hide a secret.

First time in paperback!

Agatha Christie

Hallowe'en Party

The first UK paperback from Fontana (1970).

This new mystery isn't exactly full of high-jinks, but it's a highly memorable and intriguing novel that makes a lasting impression on the reader. This is accentuated by its wholly unsympathetic attitude towards many characters, including children, not least in the violent crime at its core. Christie herself was no fan of hard-boiled dramas, saying that sadistic thrillers were 'like being forced to go into an operating theatre to watch an operation. I don't like to see people hurting other people or animals. In fact it makes me want to have a go at them.' Christie felt that these types of stories were a reflection of the changing wider world: 'Sometimes I'm almost afraid to live in this country because I feel there is a tendency here to enjoy cruelty for its own sake.'[65] Poirot is also surprised by the pace at which society is changing when he questions two teenage boys about some of the suspects in the crime. 'Lesbian?' ponders one boy, in what Christie describes as 'a man of the world voice'. His friend nonchalantly responds, 'I shouldn't wonder.' A seemingly shocked Poirot leaves the boys at the end of the exchange with the assurance that 'you've certainly given me something to think about.'

Perhaps the rather downbeat perspective on society informed the corrupt practices that reappear with particular frequency in Christie's novels at this point, with the betrayal of loved ones or, in this case, the decision that murdering an innocent child was a better solution than facing the truth of the murderer's prior actions. It's as selfish an act as one could conceive. Although the relationships are rather under-developed, this is because several are kept hidden to extend the mystery, and the novel feels mature and measured. It's also made clear that a desire for money and love is nothing compared to the decision to murder in order to maintain or reclaim it. Some of the threads of the story aren't resolved to the complete satisfaction of the close reader, however, with characters sketched out lightly, including an unusually underwritten murderer. The novel features an energetic and exciting opening, one excellent clue hiding in plain sight, and a tone of grim fascination towards the murder throughout.

Tom Adams' horror-themed paperback cover from 1972.

Overall, *Hallowe'en Party* is a somewhat underrated and interesting novel that is a considerable achievement for a woman of Christie's age – the final proofs were approved a month before her seventy-ninth birthday. It cultivates a distinctive atmosphere that shows how Christie was still able to create new stories, albeit with increasingly cruel streaks. Even Poirot refers to this case as an 'ugly murder', and perhaps the reader should be grateful that the discovery of the crime is only relayed to us second-hand, through the descriptions of Ariadne Oliver. *The Observer*'s review drew attention to a 'rather weary Poirot' in a novel featuring 'more atrocities with the usual distribution of suspicion, but it's not really one of her best, lacks that eupeptic zest.'[66]

The lack of 'zest' might be something of a vague criticism, but it's exactly the type of complaint that had been levelled against Christie since almost the beginning of her writing career, and might be interpreted as the reviewer simply not enjoying the novel as much as usual. This is to be expected with an author as prolific as Christie, but there's no doubt that by this stage her novels and detectives were starting to look backwards rather than forwards. Christie wrote only four more novels, and of these it's only 1971's Miss Marple mystery *Nemesis* that compares favourably with what had come before. Age was catching up with the author, but of course this was no surprise to her, and she accepted the inevitable decline with good humour. 'I always think it must end soon,' she said, 'then I'm so glad when the next one comes along and it's not so difficult to think of something new after all. And, of course, as you get older you change, you see things from another angle.' She then mischievously suggested that 'probably I could write the same book again and again and nobody would notice. Perhaps I'd better keep that up my sleeve in case I ever run completely out of ideas!'[67]

CHAPTER SIX:

THE

1970s

Perhaps it is inevitable when a well-loved author continues to publish new material as they move into old age that the anticipation for their next title will only grow, and so it should be no surprise that when Agatha Christie turned eighty in 1970 there were several celebrations to coincide with a new book. Christie herself was still keen to stay out of the limelight as much as possible – in a later, but typical, response to a request for a telephone interview she told her agent's secretary to 'say I'm too deaf or anything you like'.[1] Nevertheless, the publication of her new thriller *Passenger to Frankfurt* in September 1970 was greeted with a wave of publicity, as well as positive sales and reviews that cannot be said to be linked to the quality of the muddled novel itself.[2] Such was the concern of her publishers regarding the book that it not only gained an

OPPOSITE: Albert Finney finally defined the role of Hercule Poirot on film with his portrayal in *Murder on the Orient Express* in 1974.

Agatha Christie

TESTA D'UOVO

cinque avventure di Ercole Poirot

Mondadori

An Italian omnibus
edition from 1974
played up a famous
Poirot characteristic –
the volume was entitled
'Egg Head'.

awkward subtitle ('*An Extravaganza*', indeed) but also an epigraph from Christie that partially explained the reasoning behind the unusual nature of the story, which concerns international politics and espionage. The following year saw something of a return to form with the Miss Marple mystery *Nemesis*, but this was Christie's last gasp of greatness on the page. In 1971 she became Dame Agatha in the New Year Honours list, and even became immortalised in wax at Madame Tussaud's, but her health suffered a blow when she broke her hip, an event that prefaced a slow decline in her overall wellbeing until her death in January 1976.[3] However, thanks to Christie's foresight in 1940, she had pre-prepared her farewell for the Belgian detective which in the end was published a few months before her death. This novel provided Poirot fans with one final masterpiece, but it followed a Poirot mystery that was far from her best.

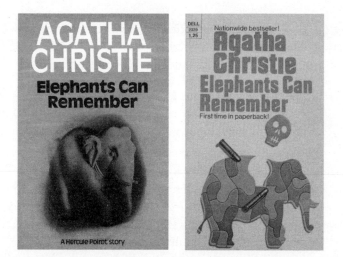

Elephants Can Remember
(Novel, 1972)

Agatha Christie had always been a firm and no-nonsense correspondent with both her agent, Edmund Cork, and her publisher, Billy Collins. Formalities had long since been abandoned, as she had been friendly with both men for more than four decades, but although Christie was usually kind and generous, she increasingly created difficulties for them. A recurring theme in her letters was her irritation when matters that she perceived to be trivial were sent to her for comment or approval when she felt that she had better use for her time, while on the other hand she also insisted on being kept in the loop regarding just about everything to do with her books. This meant that both Collins and

ABOVE LEFT: A photograph was the basis for the UK first edition in 1972. **ABOVE RIGHT:** The Dell paperback revamped the American hardback cover depicting an elephant jigsaw (1972).

AGATHA CHRISTIE

ELEPHANTS CAN REMEMBER

An American library edition published by G.K. Hall.

(especially) Cork found themselves treading an impossibly fine line, as they faced a dismissive reply if Christie considered that her input was not needed, or an angrier response if Christie learned of any decisions that she had not been consulted about, (especially regarding the likes of blurbs and book covers). In general, the tone of Christie's letters turned more negative in her final few years, perhaps in part due to her own irritation regarding her declining health. Although she was often happy, Christie was also easily annoyed, picking letters to respond to almost at random. 'I am sorry to say I have not got much enthusiasm for your project,' she wrote to one harmless correspondent who wished to create stamps featuring great detectives, including Poirot and Miss Marple. 'Frankly I cannot see why one should want stamps representing detectives ... I suppose that people have got to enjoy themselves in their own way.'[4] Explaining her response to Cork, Christie wrote that 'I do not think Hercule Poirot matters much. He has been so terribly represented all over the world already ... Really, the things people suggest to authors are beyond belief in general idiocy!'[5]

In terms of her novels, it was Poirot's turn to solve a mystery in 1972's *Elephants Can Remember*, which revisited ideas that Christie had already established or mulled over elsewhere. The book concerns a potential crime from the past – the deaths of the parents of one of Ariadne Oliver's godchildren, Celia Ravenscroft. Years earlier, the two bodies were found atop a cliff close to their house; both had been shot, but police found it impossible to discover if it had been a suicide pact or a murder-suicide. Just as in *Five Little Pigs*, Poirot is asked to investigate in order to clear the air before impending nuptials, although in this case it's the mother of Celia's fiancé who initially buttonholes Ariadne Oliver. The crime writer is eventually persuaded to look into the case with Poirot, following her questionable belief that predisposition to murder may in some way be hereditary, while the book also allows Christie to make use of one idea that turned up repeatedly in her notebooks: that of twins. Christie had used twins before, and while their presence in detective fiction tends to be unsatisfyingly neat and obvious (and often something of a cheat), at least here it isn't clear to what extent we should consider the mention of the sibling to be a red herring.

By now Christie was operating far below the height of her powers, despite support from both her husband Max Mallowan and daughter Rosalind Hicks. *Elephants Can Remember* has often been disparaged by critics and readers because of its slow pace and repetitive nature, although it's also a perfectly pleasant read for the most part and features one or two clever ideas. However, the scenarios and investigation are simply too woolly to function as a traditional mystery puzzle that Christie had usually excelled at. This is true of not only the prose – the book opens with an extraordinarily indulgent three pages discussing Ariadne Oliver's hats and hairstyles – but also the facts of the case, or rather the absence of them. Evidence is almost non-existent, with even key information left vague; the statements that the deaths occurred anywhere from ten to fifteen years earlier are surely not deliberately contradictory, and even if they are it's not credible that neither Poirot nor Mrs Oliver attempt to pin down such an important detail. The investigation simply meanders along, with Mrs Oliver helming much of it in an especially irritable manner – perhaps another reflection of Christie. The fictional crime writer's bluntness does lead

Poirot and Ariadne Oliver from the 1972 *Australian Women's Weekly* serial.

to some amusing moments, however, including one that reflects Christie's own feelings about meeting strangers – 'I don't feel you are a stranger, dear Mrs Oliver,' says one character; 'I wish you did,' thinks Mrs Oliver in response.

Memory is a particularly important element of several of Christie's later books, and this is never more the case than here. Characters' recollections are the only way to piece together the full story, albeit with a little help from Poirot's investigator friend Mr Goby, who manages to conveniently produce key information once more. The nature of memory itself is often revisited in the book, including Poirot's forgetfulness and Ariadne Oliver misplacing things. Then there are these telling thoughts from Mrs Oliver:

> She'd gone to Celia's christening and had found a very nice Queen Anne silver strainer as a christening present. Very nice. Do nicely for straining milk and would also be the sort of thing a goddaughter could always sell for a nice little sum if she wanted ready money at any time. Yes, she remembered the strainer very well indeed. Queen Anne – Seventeen-eleven it had been. Britannia mark. How much easier it was to remember silver coffeepots or strainers or christening mugs than it was the actual child.

Perhaps Christie herself was finding it easier to remember relatively inconsequential things from the past rather than newer information. Both her correspondence and fiction writing from this late period shows some evidence of occasional confusion or misremembrances, while a 2009 study from the University of Toronto examined the language used in *Elephants Can Remember* and argued that there was evidence that the author may have had Alzheimer's disease.[6] We should be very cautious of any retrospective diagnosis, but there's no denying the fact that Christie's books from the 1970s are more muddled in their plotting and less sophisticated in their language than had been the case only a few years earlier. For example, the opening of the above extract uses the word 'nice' (or 'nicely') four times in three sentences. At the very least, it would be kind for a reader to bear in mind Christie's age and health when reading her later works.

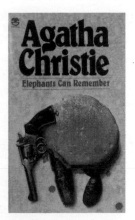

A new-look by Martin Baker for Fontana paperbacks (1981).

Elephants Can Remember is probably Christie's least exciting mystery novel, as it stretches a good idea for a short story beyond breaking point, suffering from the absence of any significant subplot to maintain the interest. Very similar conversations are had again and again, although some of this repetition was removed from the final typescript before publication, including even more of Ariadne Oliver's musings about elephants.[7] This dialogue-heavy and excessively anecdotal novel is not a great finale for Poirot, and thankfully *Curtain* was waiting in the wings.

Nevertheless, *Elephants Can Remember* was another commercial success when published in November in 1972, and Christie was even able to rely on highbrow fans to wave the flag for her. 'I only ever read poetry and Agatha Christie,' claimed Poet Laureate John Betjeman in the *Daily Express* on the day of its publication, although he wasn't going to get around to this new novel any time soon – 'I always wait for the paperback'.[8] Perhaps aware that Christie was now critic-proof, *The Times Literary Supplement* offered a brief summary in lieu of a proper review of the book, while *The Observer* generously summarised it as 'A quiet but consistently interesting whodunnit with ingenious monozygotic solution. Any young elephant would be proud to have written it.'[9] More realistically, *The Guardian* reviewer wrote that 'The mystery is thin. The pleasure lies in renewing acquaintance with old friends.'[10]

Poirot on Radio and Television

By 1970 the deal between Agatha Christie Ltd and MGM had expired, much to the relief of Christie herself, but this had the consequence that other companies now saw an opportunity to bring Poirot to the small screen. In July 1970 the BBC once more explored the possibility of gaining the rights to adapt either Poirot in particular, or some Christie novels and stories more generally, into a television series. The Corporation was abruptly informed that this wouldn't be possible, and this refusal may explain why two years later it was Dorothy L. Sayers' Lord Peter Wimsey who starred in his own BBC detective series – possibly as a replacement for Christie's Belgian sleuth. The absence of Poirot, especially in the light of Wimsey's appearance, was noted by some

ABOVE: Jochen Sostmann as Hastings (left) and Horst Bollmann as Poirot in German television's 1973 adaptation of *Black Coffee*.

commentators. 'Adamant Agatha' was the headline of a *Daily Mirror* article following the announcement of the Wimsey series, which asked:

> What are the chances of Agatha Christie's famed Hercule Poirot coming to the TV screen now that Dorothy L. Sayers's Lord Peter Wimsey is joining the BBC? Slim, indeed. Some years ago Miss Christie did a deal with Hollywood, but as she didn't like the way her stories were transferred to the screen the contract was cancelled from TV producers. There's a wealth of Agatha Christie material in novels, stories and plays. Every week her agents receive inquiries from TV producers. But Mrs. Christie – like Dorothy L. Sayers in her lifetime – remains firmly entrenched against both TV and the cinema.[11]

Christie's antipathy towards the BBC went beyond the question of screen versions of her stories, which she opposed by default – 'Books are written as books and I do not relish the idea of adapting them to television,' she said.[12] In a letter to her agent complaining about the screening of the Margaret Rutherford films on television, Christie added 'BBC say *No*', probably a response to the BBC's attempts to interview the author for her eightieth birthday. Alternatively this may have been a follow-up to a September 1970 request from the Corporation to allow Hercule Poirot to appear on the television programme *Review*, in which the actor Leslie French would have performed some of the detective's dialogue from *Murder on the Orient Express* in character. This request was declined, and when Christie's birthday was featured on the 18 September edition French read a Christie extract as himself instead.[13] Such differentiation may seem minor and even petty, but clearly Christie was keen to make a strong distinction between readings of her novels and dramatisation.

This carried over to radio, with her agent insisting that even if a book were available for a reading it should only be performed by one actor – multiple voices were not permitted. This explains why Poirot featured in no new radio play adaptations this decade, although several stories were read out, including three taken from *Poirot's Early Cases* – 'The Adventure of the Clapham Cook', 'The Veiled Lady' and 'The Adventure of Johnnie Waverly' – all read by Nigel Stock.[14]

One place where Poirot did appear on television was in West Germany, as part of a long-running format that brought stage plays to television. The channel ZDF had already broadcast small-scale performances of *And Then There Were None* and *The Murder at the Vicarage* before it turned to Poirot for *Black Coffee* in 1973. This time the ambition was rather higher, with the production made on colour film and using high quality sets, which are presided over by a painting of Christie herself. While the script is faithful to Christie's original, it also made use of some intelligent and interesting embellishments, such as evidence of some of Lord Amery's inventions.[15] Horst Bollmann as Poirot gives the best screen performance of the detective to this point (of the productions that are known to survive, at least), as he presents the character with a mischievous and charming edge that complements his great intelligence.[16] He is ably assisted by Gert Haucke as Inspector Japp and a moustachioed Jochen Sostmann as Hastings, who even gets a screen kiss during the closing credits.

James Coco as 'Milo Perrier' in *Murder by Death* (1976).

Poirot's increased celebrity also resulted in some affectionate spoofs of the character, perhaps most notably in the form of the fussy, moustache-wearing Belgian detective Milo Perrier (played by James Coco), one of the sleuths hoping to solve Neil Simon's *Murder by*

Death on cinema screens in 1976. A rare appearance of Poirot on British television came about because of a spoof Sherlock Holmes comedy put together by and starring John Cleese, who appeared as Holmes with Arthur Lowe as his Watson in 1977's *The Strange Case of the End of Civilisation as We Know It* for London Weekend Television.[17] Several detectives make unlicensed cameo appearances, and Poirot's lack of height is the butt of a very brief gag in which he is played by Dudley Jones. Elsewhere, TV companies had no luck when trying to forge a more formal route to bring the detective to television. German producers tried, and failed, to get Christie to allow

Dudley Jones in 1977's *The Strange Case of the End of Civilisation as We Know It.*

them to make a documentary film about *The Mysterious Affair at Styles*, but her agent refused to budge.[18] In June 1973 Allen Roberts of New York asked if his production company could purchase short-term rights in the exploitation of Poirot in order to make a television pilot for American network television: 'Please deal with this by a firm rebuff!!' noted Christie when sending the letter on to Cork, 'and pass on same injunction to [American publisher] Dodd Mead, or whoever deals with such demands in New York.'[19] Her agent complied with the request, but only two months later another proposal was received, and this time the idea was so unusual that he felt that the author should be informed before refusal. Michaelangelo Presentations Ltd of London requested the rights to create a modern ballet for television, to feature Hercule Poirot, masterminded by Wayne Sleep and Gillian Lynne, with plans for it to then become part of the repertoire of The Royal Ballet School and the Royal Winnipeg Ballet.[20] 'Definitely no!' Christie replied, 'Definitely Hercule P is NOT to be a television special. Be firm.'[21]

Poirot's Early Cases
(Short stories, 1974)

In 1973 Collins published the final novel that Agatha Christie wrote, *Postern of Fate*, in which she revisited Tommy and Tuppence, who readers had first met as bright young investigators in 1922's *The Secret Adversary*. Her daughter Rosalind Hicks was desperately unhappy with the events surrounding the writing of the new book, as well as its final quality. She saw it as a watershed moment for her mother's future as a writer, which in turn sealed the fate of Poirot. 'I can't say that I enjoyed the book,' she wrote candidly to Billy Collins. 'My mother is very frail now and not at all well and I do hope she

ABOVE LEFT: The UK first edition had a photographic cover design (1974). **ABOVE RIGHT:** Although the stories had been released previously in assorted American editions, Dodd, Mead published the new collection in hardcover.

is not going to sap her remaining strength by starting another book. She is determined to do all she can and I know nothing except her health would deter her. I know we all want to do the best we can for my mother.' Rosalind was troubled by not only her mother's health, but also the quality of work that her name was attached to. 'I really do mind about the kind of book she writes and I honestly feel guilty to think of people paying £2 for such a pathetic effort,' she went on to say. 'I am also quite worried that this might happen again next year.'[22]

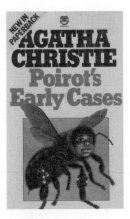

A different Fontana cover style accommodated Tom Adams' cover painting in 1979.

Billy Collins reassured Rosalind that he would not push Christie for another book unless she was well enough, but Rosalind felt that the decision needed to be taken out of her mother's hands: 'Max said in all seriousness that writing the last book nearly killed her and I quite believe it. She finds it hard to recover strength after any extra effort and I feel the kindest thing to do would be to discourage her as much as possible and strictly between you and me if she did write one like the last one I doubt very much if we would publish it ... Please don't think I'm being unkind, I am desperately worried about her health.'[23] Christie had been unwell for some time, particularly with heart problems that made her increasingly frail. Somewhat optimistically Collins mused that 'maybe it is a help for her to be thinking out a plot,' but a new story wouldn't happen.[24] Instead, it was time to turn to Collins' reserve idea for 1974's Christie for Christmas – a new collection of short stories.

By the time plans were drawn up for the contents of this new volume Christie's health had a further hurdle to overcome when she slipped and put her head through a pane of glass in late 1973. 'I had to have over a dozen stitches in my

AGATHA CHRISTIE | PRIMEROS CASOS DE POIROT

A new face for Poirot adorned the Spanish edition in 1975.

forehead and chin down in the local hospital,' she wrote to Cork in January 1974. 'The doctor tells me I must rest in bed as much as I can. I think I am getting better slowly after this shock.'[25] This was the right time to reassure Christie that there was no pressure for her to return to writing, and Cork suggested to the author that a collection called *Poirot's Early Cases* could be published.[26] Christie readily agreed, 'provided of course that it comes out as the usual Christmas book and not at any earlier time of the year, for this will have to take the place of my Christmas novel.'[27] All seemed to be settled, and Cork and Collins collected the names of Poirot short stories that had not been published in any of the core British collections. However, two months later Christie put the plans into disarray.

'When we spoke on the telephone the other day [you] explained that in your projected Christmas book for this year every story was going to be a Hercule Poirot,' Christie wrote to Billy Collins in March 1974. 'I hope to persuade you that the book could also include what you might describe as Agatha Christie's own favourites of her own early stories.' What followed was a surprising list that would make little sense as a collection, including as it did two novels and mentions of a third, alongside a raft of short stories that didn't feature Poirot.[28] Collins was confused. 'Edmund told me that he had spoken to you about this collection, that he had also sent you a list of suggested contents and that you had agreed to this list and would write an introduction,' he wrote to the author, outlining what had indeed been done. Collins rowed back from the expectation of Christie writing a special introduction, but this was not enough for the author who claimed that 'When I saw the proposals for *Poirot's Early Cases* I did not, after reflection, like them ... I did not expect Collins to jump the gun in this way.'[29] A great deal of work had already been undertaken for the new collection, and although Christie felt somewhat railroaded she eventually consented to it, following the suggestion that a 'favourites' collection could also be published in due course, although in the end this didn't happen.

Billy Collins was right to stick to his guns, as overall *Poirot's Early Cases* is a very good selection of short stories that most British readers wouldn't have had the opportunity to read for decades, if at all, although they had all been collected in various American volumes over the years. Nevertheless, Dodd, Mead in the United States also published the new book with the slightly amended title of *Hercule Poirot's Early Cases*, having initially considered a collection of plays instead. 'These stories are vintage Agatha Christie. There is no need to say any more,' read the collection's description, and although any selection is inevitably variable in quality, there are several memorable cases in this bumper volume of eighteen mysteries.[30]

The book opens with 'The Affair at the Victory Ball', a tale of murder and drugs, and the first Agatha Christie short story to be published when it opened the series of Poirot mysteries in *The Sketch* back in 1923. The story features iconography that will become familiar in later Christie stories, including characters such as Harlequin and his compatriots from the Italian Commedia dell'arte. Some parts of the version of the story published in *The Sketch* differ from the typescript that was retained by Christie, which indicates that its editor undertook several minor revisions for the latter section in particular. The general plotting and meaning is identical, but the phrasing is often rewritten between typescript and magazine, while the sequence of events is slightly different. This is the only one of the stories in *The Sketch* that we know to have been so heavily rewritten, and so it's likely that either Christie objected to an over-eager editor, or the magazine was particularly keen to make the first story in the run as strong as possible, in their eyes.[31] The original typescript included an instruction that 'The following sign: ----------? has been placed at a point in each story where the reader may, if he chooses, pause and endeavour to solve the riddle for himself before proceeding to read the solution.'[32] Christie had also originally penned a slightly more detailed introduction to Poirot:

FOREWORD
by Captain Arthur Hastings O.B.E.

Hercule Poirot, formerly chief of the Belgian Detective Force, came to England as a refugee in the early days of the war. Much broken in health, he decided to remain in this country and devote himself to the solving of problems in crime. I myself, after being wounded on the Somme, and invalided out of the army, took up my quarters with him in London. His successes were marvellous. He attributed them all to the system on which he worked: Method, order, and logical reasoning. Observation, he would say, was a good servant. "The hands, the ears, the eyes. They all have their part, but the brain, the little cells of grey, they must be master! A man should be able to solve any problem, if need be, without moving from his chair!" My friend had his peculiarities, an ornament set crooked, a speck of dust; these things roused him to fury! He himself was the most exquisitely neat person I have ever known. Intensely Gallic in appearance, he was, in every sense of the word, a "character".

The second story, 'The Adventure of the Clapham Cook', offers an excellent selection of ideas. Although the premise of a missing domestic servant may seem unexciting initially, Christie has twists in reserve for this good mystery, and these developments offer a nice expansion of scale as the story develops. Characterisation is particularly good, especially when Poirot is berated by a prospective client for not being interested in smaller mysteries. Missing from the book version is an extra coda from *The Sketch*, probably added to emphasise Poirot's deductive power: 'But for Poirot and his amazing powers of reasoning, a particularly cold-blooded murderer would have escaped scot-free.' Following this is 'The Cornish Mystery', a downbeat tale of poisoning that offers a rather vague resolution that seems to rely on a bluff and the questionable skills of Scotland Yard away from the page in order to capture the culprit. 'The Adventure of Johnnie Waverly', which had originally been published as 'The Kidnapping of Johnnie Waverly', is next and is a fairly weak story that strains the credulity of the reader in its tale of a boy being kidnapped from under the noses of a raft of characters attempting to protect him. It has an unfortunate reliance on the stupidity (or at least naïvety) of said characters – including the type of policing skills that Poirot depended upon at the resolution of the previous case.

'The Double Clue' is one of two stories in this collection that would have been sensible inclusions in *Poirot Investigates*, as they tell the reader more about Poirot than most of his shorter mysteries. In this case his relationship with Countess Vera Rossakoff following a jewel robbery makes the rather straightforward story a character study in part, especially regarding Poirot's attitude towards such a strong woman. Following this, 'The King of Clubs' is a case that relies on one very good clue in order to be solved, although the manner in which the dramatic clairvoyant

Zara offers a very specific hint from the psychic realm is odd, especially when it proves to be accurate before being dismissed as coincidence by Poirot.[33] Nothing is quite as odd as the whole of 'The Lemesurier Inheritance', however, which is the only Poirot short story collected during Christie's lifetime that was not adapted for the ITV series *Agatha Christie's Poirot*. It relies upon a straightforward acceptance of a family curse that is rather difficult to swallow. The next story is the problematic and dull 'The Lost Mine', a tale of suspicious business transactions and Limehouse opium dens.

'The Plymouth Express' is a clever and cynical short story about the murder of a woman on the eponymous train that also formed the basis of the later (considerably weaker) novel *The Mystery of the Blue Train*, but manages to show how clever the central premise is.[34] The second story to tell us something more about Poirot then follows, with 'The Chocolate Box'.[35] Here, Poirot takes Hastings and the reader back to his days on the Belgian police force in a story in which, in the original typescript, he explains 'I was made a fool of – and by a woman...' Not only do we learn something of Poirot's early detection methods, and the pitfalls he has to avoid in this case of poisoning, but it's probably the short story that makes the most explicit reference to his Catholicism. The original version of the story included an additional section in which Poirot mentions an otherwise unheard-of sibling, which was removed for the book:

My vacation had just begun, and I was thinking of a little trip to Spa. I was reading an account of the various sources, and the maladies that were benefitted thereby when I was informed that a young lady was demanding me. Thinking that it was perhaps my little sister Yvonne, I prayed my landlady to make her mount. To my astonishment, the lady who entered the room was a total stranger to me.[36]

'The Submarine Plans' is the original version of the story 'The Incredible Theft', which was included in *Murder in the Mews*, and the tale of missing plans vital to the government is not particularly exciting in either version, but at least it's a nice contrast to murder. Christie seems to have liked 'The Third Floor Flat' as she contemplated expanding it for *The Adventure of the Christmas Pudding* in 1960, and the accidental discovery of a dead body in Poirot's apartment block by a group of jolly young people is as fun as murder can be, with a good range of characters. In 'Double Sin' the reader is forced to second-guess themselves as they try to work out where their sympathies should lie when some expensive miniature portraits go missing on a coach trip in a cleverly plotted case. 'The Market Basing Mystery' is another story that found its way into *Murder in the Mews* in some form, this time in its title story, but this wasn't a simple expansion – instead, they're actually quite different cases that hinge on the same explanation for the unusual events surrounding a death. 'Murder in the Mews' is stronger, but this original variant is still a very good companion piece.

'Wasps' Nest' is an understated character piece that also features a fair mystery, in which Poirot may be able to prevent a crime for once, rather than being present only in order to pick up the pieces and come up with a solution. 'The Veiled Lady' sees the detective coming to the aid of a distressed woman who wants the return of an indiscreet letter from a blackmailer. This story has thematic similarities with 'The Double Clue' as it has something to say about Poirot's relationship with women, which sometimes includes a remarkable ability to identify both their stockings and, in this case, shoes. The penultimate mystery is 'Problem at Sea', in which a woman is murdered on board a tourist ship while it's in dock. This case is full of excellent misdirection and is highly entertaining. This version of the story is slightly different

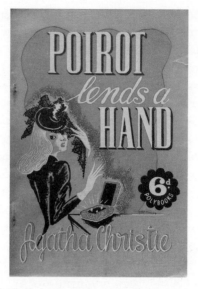

'The Veiled Lady' had previously appeared in *Poirot Lends a Hand*, a rare short story collection published by Polybooks in 1946. It also contained the short stories 'Problem at Pollensa Bay' and 'The Regatta Mystery'.

to the one that had been published by *The Strand* as 'Poirot and the Crime in Cabin 66' in 1936, which featured some small additional moments of characterisation. The collection then concludes with 'How Does Your Garden Grow?', which sees Poirot being asked to help an elderly lady who dies before he can meet with her, leading to his investigation of her murder. It boasts a great solution, but unusually for a Christie short story the mystery is perhaps a little over-egged with red herrings, although this is made up for with an excellent reveal of evidence at the end.

Collins created a photographic cover for the first edition of the book, published in September 1974. The picture shows the bottom of Poirot's trousered legs and his case, in what is actually a cropped version of the original photo due to

Christie's dissatisfaction with it. Billy Collins felt that the original was suitable as it didn't show Poirot's upper half, and Rosalind conceded that 'I think it is quite a good idea, at any rate much better than having his face! I do not feel that the general stance, the bag or the label looks as if they belonged to Poirot but I think it will be all right. I think you should send it to my mother for her approval and I cannot honestly say whether she will like it or not.' Christie's secretary had already told Rosalind that her mother was still not happy with the book, leading to a request that Rosalind should have final word on the proofs rather than her mother, but Cork refused to cut Christie out of the loop. 'I think this book is a very good idea and I enjoyed reading the stories myself,' Rosalind wrote. 'I am sorry my mother has been difficult about them and I really cannot see any reason for it except that they aren't her favourite stories.'[37] Christie was certainly not happy, as she wrote to Collins:

> I'm afraid I don't like the cover design – it is so dark which makes it very unattractive. These were early 'cases' of Poirot – he was a little man and unusually proud of his enormous moustache. His smartly dressed lower half seems entirely unlike him and represents him as six feet high at least. I never imagined him as prone to carry a little bag. Do you think you could send me one or two alternative suggestions to see if they could be one I liked better? Why should my poor Hercule [be] apparently going to a funeral and dressed accordingly.[38]

Collins was somewhat exasperated, although it's perhaps surprising that the photo wasn't sent to Christie earlier, or even explained at the design stage, given her unhappiness with so many of her covers. 'We all think the finished wrapper looks very attractive and has quite lost the funereal atmosphere of the photograph,' he argued. 'Surely with fore-shortened legs Poirot could now be quite dumpy as I imagine he always was. Surely too if he was travelling he would have had a little bag ... If you don't like it we will go ahead with a plain lettering jacket.'[39] A still unhappy Christie allowed the cover to be used, and it must be agreed that despite it seeming superficially unobjectionable the stance and bag don't feel particularly like the detective.

The Observer's review of the book was not particularly positive, but claimed that all the stories 'communicate that unique Christien [sic] euphoria,' which would surely be quite enough for most readers.[40] The Guardian reviewer offered more detail and objection, and legitimately wondered why some of the stories weren't tweaked for this book publication, given that they reflected attitudes and clichés from half a century earlier, but concluded: 'Hercule Poirot, the little Belgian detective, remains an enduring creation. He is the comic foreigner a xenophobic Britain took seriously and to its heart.'[41]

Britain certainly had taken Poirot to its heart, something that only became clearer when shortly after the book's publication the character finally headlined a major film that satisfied his creator.

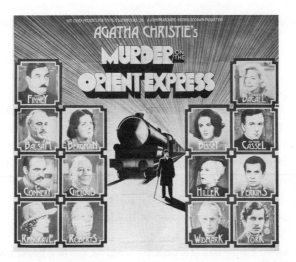

Murder on the Orient Express
(Film, 1974)

The 1974 film of *Murder on the Orient Express* brought with it two surprises – first, that it became such a phenomenal success, as only twice before had Agatha Christie films had any particular value attached to them by both critics and the general public.[42] But to any observer of Christie's own feelings, the second surprise was even greater – the fact that it existed at all. Its origins lay with Nat Cohen of EMI Films, who suggested the project as a possibility to film producer John Brabourne. Brabourne had a strong pedigree, both personally and professionally. He was formally known as The Right Honourable The Lord Brabourne, due to his inheritance of a barony, while he had also married the daughter

ABOVE: The theatrical poster for *Murder on the Orient Express* showed off its all-star cast.

of Lord Mountbatten, making them a heavily titled couple. These links with high society were no doubt impressive, even to a Dame, but his professional career had also been a prestigious one, including Franco Zeffirelli's *Romeo and Juliet* (1968), while *Tales of Beatrix Potter* (1971) was later viewed by Christie and her family as a good reason to trust in the quality of his work. Asked how Brabourne managed to convince an elderly Christie to grant him the rights, given her complete lack of interest in bringing Poirot to the screen, her grandson Mathew Prichard recalls a story that he assures us 'sounds apocryphal but it's not', which began with the producer making contact with Christie's agent:

Edmund Cork said 'I think it would be quite a good idea if you made an Agatha Christie film, but you can't really expect, first out of the traps, to pick up *Orient Express*, to do the best story'; 'I want to do *Orient Express*', [Brabourne] said, and Edmund Cork said 'Well, I don't think that has a cat's chance in hell of being accepted by Agatha Christie herself or anything, so just go away and think of another book and we'll do our best for you'. So John Brabourne went away in a sulk. About a week later my grandmother was at Wallingford, where she spent most of the year, and the phone rang, and it was John Brabourne. He said, 'Oh, is that Lady Mallowan?', she said yes, and he said, 'My name's John Brabourne and I want to make a film of *Orient Express*.' I think her agent had told her that someone had been sniffing around. She said, 'Why do you want to make a film of *Orient Express*?' 'Oh,' he said, 'your agent didn't ask me that, but I'll tell you – because I like trains!' She said, 'Well, I think we'd better have a little chat about it then.' He said, 'I'd like that very much, when would be convenient?' She said, well, we live forty miles from London... we could have lunch one day. He said, 'Well, what about now?' She said, 'but we're forty miles from London, and you're in London'; 'No I'm not,' he said, 'I'm in the telephone box at the bottom of your garden!'[43]

Slowly but surely an agreement was reached regarding the possibility of a new film, with partial motivation for the project being Christie's desire to expunge the memory of previous screen adaptations, most particularly the MGM films, including 1965's *The Alphabet Murders*. 'We would be delighted if a good film could be made – also one that my mother could give her blessing to,' Rosalind assured Cork in early 1973. One suggestion of Hicks's also explains why the eventual film cast so many high-profile actors, as she argued that Poirot need not be central to the whole of the film, mindful as she was of the difficulty in casting the character. She was also practical about the arrangements, writing that 'while I fully understand that Lord Brabourne would want full control of a script, casting, etc, he does seem to have given both my mother and Mathew the idea that he might make a good job of it'.[44] Agatha Christie Ltd's overall approach was both optimistic and practical, as it also gambled on an increased cut of profits in return for a smaller initial payment for the rights, and it was right to do so. However, unlike MGM this time the contract was gone over with a fine-toothed comb, to ensure that no rights beyond this one film were granted – this included an emphatic banning of any merchandising.

As pre-production continued apace, so the cast and crew for the film began to be finalised. Paul Dehn, who was probably best known for the screenplay of *Goldfinger* (1964), wrote the script, which adhered very closely to the

In the UK, Fontana released a tie-in paperback featuring Albert Finney as Poirot on the front (1974).

original novel, while Sidney Lumet went against his agent's advice by joining the film as director.[45] The tricky business of casting so many roles that were important, and yet had to share the screen with more than a dozen other actors playing characters of the same significance, meant that some delicate negotiation was needed. Securing Sean Connery first, in the role of Arbuthnot, was crucial to negotiations with other film stars, and perhaps justified the actor being given a superior payment package to the other suspects. Alongside Anthony Perkins as McQueen, Connery's name was used as an explanation to prospective actors that while the billing would be shared, all actors would get their chance to be in the spotlight, and the overall impression would be of a star-studded picture. A few casting suggestions reached dead ends – Katharine Hepburn was offered her choice of Mrs Hubbard or the Princess Dragomiroff, but in the end didn't appear – but the final quality of the cast was exceptional with names including Lauren Bacall (Mrs Hubbard), Ingrid Bergman (Greta), John Gielgud (Beddoes), Wendy Hiller (Princess Dragomiroff), Vanessa Redgrave (Mary Debenham), Jacqueline Bisset (Countess Andrenyi) and Michael York (Count Andrenyi). 'I am much interested to know that this film will at least contain a very distinguished cast,' Christie wrote to Cork when she saw the final list of actors in early 1974.[46]

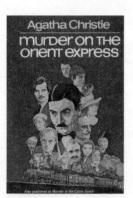

Dodd, Mead's US hardcover tie-in with art by Allan Mardon (1974).

Most of the production took place in Elstree Studios, but the departure and delay of the train itself was filmed in France (with a location near Paris doubling for Istanbul). The cast got on well, although took a while to warm up in the workshop environment of initial rehearsals, while a close eye was kept on events with visits to the set from Rosalind and Mathew. The key piece of casting for the film, that of Poirot himself, had in the end been rather uneventful. A shortlist of three was drawn up – Paul Scofield, Alec Guinness and Albert Finney. Finney's age put him as third choice (he was only 38) but when Scofield and Guinness proved to be unavailable he was cast despite the requirement for make-up in order to age him.[47] Christie was surprisingly nonchalant about her new Poirot. A short while before the film's release she was asked what would happen if she didn't like the actor cast in the role – 'You argue, and I think the publisher usually wins!' she replied.[48]

The film was cited in several press and trade reports as a great hope for the flagging British cinema industry, with the gamble of considerable all-British investment in the picture. This perhaps explains some high-profile visitors to the set in the shape of Princes Charles, Andrew and Edward – Charles even brought King Constantine of Greece along.[49] There was considerable pressure on the film to do well, but the industry generally seemed optimistic about its prospects, as evidenced by the rush to Christie's agents to discover availability for any other novel that might incite as much interest. Columbia Pictures enquired about the availability of *The Mystery of the Blue Train* for the screen (presumably reasoning that all that was needed for success was Poirot and a train), while there were several enquiries about other titles (including the entirety of *Poirot's Early Cases*) from just about every major studio. All were dismissed.

By the time production was finished all seemed to be going well, although it was impossible to know for sure until the film was edited. 'I hope I shall like it, but anyway I have certainly got to go and see it as soon as I have the oppor-tunity even if my feelings should not be as favourable as I would like them to be,' Christie wrote. 'But after all, nothing could be worse than Metro-Goldwyn-Mayer, could it?'[50] In 2017 producer Richard Goodwin remembered that 'I only met Agatha Christie briefly [and she was] using a wheel-chair. She was very much an observer, watching everything. We showed her the film and she liked it.'[51] She wasn't the only one, with Rosalind writing to Cork 'We both enjoyed the film of *Murder on the Orient Express* very much. I think they really have made a good job of it,' although she sounded one or two notes of caution – 'Sean Connery as Arbuthnot was bad and I didn't like the end but I hope it is a success.'[52]

A success is precisely what it was destined to be, as the film was soon showcased as a lavish and high-class affair that tapped into a sense of nostalgia surrounding both the pre-war period and the world of Agatha Christie, whose own life crossed borders and cultures just as the titular train did. Few of those watching the film could have experienced the same sort of experiences that Christie was drawing on for her original book, and as it happened such a variety of characters and the exotic setting made the story a perfect candidate for the big-screen treatment, even before considering the exceptionally strong puzzle that sits at the core of the story. Sidney Lumet imbues *Murder on the Orient Express* with a sense of utmost seriousness, with only Albert Finney's Poirot allowed to exist as a creation who it is difficult to imagine exists in the 'real world' – a fitting shorthand way of expressing how the character is not like the rest of us. The use of long takes in lengthy scenes, especially as suspects and witnesses are interviewed, gives the all-star cast the opportunity to play out small moments and subtle emotions that the audience is able to focus on when projected at large scale. Small but telling slips from key characters ('All my ladies have said so…') can then pass by without bombast, but their innate subtlety is amplified in a theatrical setting. The whole of the film has a heightened style, with subdued lighting and oppressive (if beautiful) wooden and brass interiors creating a sense of claustrophobia, as the mystery slowly works out its parameters and the film moves towards its inevitable and incredible conclusion. The opening sequence immediately establishes that this is not some quick attempt to bring a good mystery to cinemas. It uses excellent editing techniques and musical stings alongside brief live-action sequences and newspaper headlines in order to quickly and stylishly establish a backstory to murder that shows much but reveals little. The extent to which the film follows the source material reveals that Christie's best works were now being treated as high quality pieces of fiction, just as the output of Dickens or Austen would be, and she was not seen as a mere writer of disposable detective stories.

The film was the subject of a royal premiere, with Queen Elizabeth and Princess Anne among those in attendance on 21 November 1974. Pictures show a beaming Christie curtsying to both, having insisted on leaving her wheelchair. The screening was a success, although the British critics were hardly ecstatic about the film overall. Perhaps Russell Davies

Queen Elizabeth II and Dame Agatha Christie at Royal première in November 1974. Albert Finney is in the background.

of *The Observer* had fallen out with an Agatha Christie fan, as he seemed determined to make some sort of bad-tempered point with his complaint that 'Of course, one can't raise doubts about Dame Agatha Christie's work without at the same time raising the eyebrows, the hackles, and finally the temperatures of true Christie-an believers all over the country. But it has to be said that she doesn't transfer well to the screen. Some will say she doesn't even transfer well to the imagination.' As for the star of the show, Davies judged that Finney played Poirot as 'a rheumatic chimp'.[53]

The *Daily Mirror*'s reviewer was almost as grumpy, annoyed that Christie's solution had beaten him: 'Anyone buying a ticket for this particular express should lay in a store of chocs and settle back for a fairly uneventful trip. And as for the final revelations ... yes, I DID feel as if I had been taken for a ride.'[54] *The Guardian* felt that 'It's a stylish, confidently competent production the sum of whose parts don't add up to a really satisfying whole ... It's all just too well-organised, too neatly achieved to catch fire.'[55] The *Daily Express* was keener, headlining its review 'First Class to Murder'. In April the newspaper had asked 'Could this be the epic to pull the ailing British film industry out of the doldrums?', and by November it had its answer.[56] 'If at times you feel unable to keep up with the red herrings that swim in shoals through the plot, don't worry,' it said. 'You will, I'm sure, enjoy the brilliant performances of all concerned ... Costing about £2 million, the film is one of the most expensive to be backed entirely by British finance. We should be proud of it.'[57]

Pocket Books' tie-in was based on Richard Amsel's theatrical poster (1975).

Perhaps the most thoughtful review came from David Robinson in *The Times*, who reflected on the film as an artefact alongside Christie's original novel. 'It stays precisely at the level of Agatha Christie, demands the same adjustments, the same precarious suspension of disbelief,' he argued. 'Lumet accepts her on her own terms, doesn't question the unlikelihood, makes no attempt to apologise for Poirot's expository denouement ... No more nor less than the book itself, it is a perfectly pleasant entertainment, a couple of hours of nostalgic escape, if you're prepared to go easily with it.'[58] In later years there would be something of a collective amnesia from the press regarding their initial response to the film, as it became repeatedly

Collins also released a hardback tie-in.

cited as an obvious classic, and one that later pictures could not to compete with. This about-turn was no doubt fuelled by the film's extraordinary success across the Atlantic in particular, as in America it was the eleventh highest-grossing film of the year, while it was nominated for six Academy Awards, winning one (Ingrid Bergman for Best Supporting Actress). The gamble had paid off, and *Murder on the Orient Express* was only the beginning of a string of lavish adaptations that continue to this day.

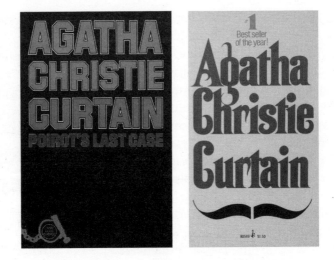

Curtain: Poirot's Last Case
(Novel, 1975)

In late 1974, just as preparations were underway for the premiere of *Murder on the Orient Express*, Rosalind Hicks made a somewhat surprising decision. 'I have been thinking again about Poirot's last book *Curtain*,' she wrote to Edmund Cork, 'my idea is that if there is no new Christie for Christmas next year we should publish this. I have not of course mentioned this to my mother as yet but would have to consult her ... it might be a good idea after *Hercule Poirot's Early Cases* to have *Hercule Poirot's Last Case*.'[59] The novel had its origins in 1940, when Christie had written the book with the expectation that it would be published posthumously – in part this

ABOVE LEFT: The first edition jacket for *Curtain* in the UK was black (1975). ABOVE RIGHT: In the US, the moustache was used as a defining symbol for Poirot on both the hardcover and this Pocket Books paperback shortly afterwards (1976).

was in order to provide an income for Rosalind, to whom she assigned the rights, which was particularly important prior to the formation of Agatha Christie Ltd in 1955. However, the plan was also to ensure that Poirot's story was not continued indefinitely by other authors (Christie later cited the post-Ian Fleming James Bond continuation novels as examples of the type of book she didn't want to happen), as his creator ensured that Poirot did not survive the events of this final case.

There was widespread advertising for the release of this final Poirot title.

More than three decades earlier, in March 1941, Cork had distributed a copy of the new typescript to his American colleagues at Dodd, Mead, with strict instructions regarding its contents. 'My cable asking you not to offer *Curtain* [for publication] must have seemed rather strange but you would understand it when you received the manuscript,' Cork wrote. 'Obviously this book can only be published as the last of the Poirot books. I need hardly say that *Curtain* should be regarded as strictly secret and confidential.'[60] Christie's American agents were confused – not helped by the fact that the first version they received had pages in the wrong order, meaning that it made little sense. It also didn't help that some letters seem to have gone astray, leading Harold Ober of Dodd, Mead to ask if Christie was quite sure that she wished to make Poirot's exit so final, as the story saw the death of the detective. This resulted in urgent clarification that the manuscript was not to be published for some time yet. 'I think Mrs Mallowan must have been in a rather despondent state when she decided to kill off Poirot,' Ober reasoned.[61] After reassuring his colleague that once read in the correct order and given a polish the book would be somewhat better (Ober suggested ways in which it could be reworked to ensure that Poirot survived after all),

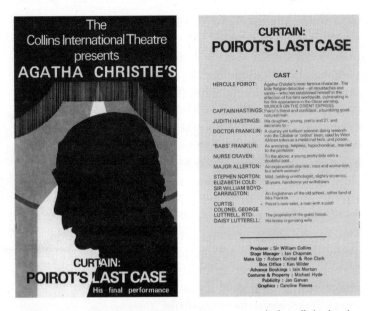

Collins produced a dummy theatre programme to help sell the book, complete with cover and cast list.

Cork insisted that 'It is a story that Mrs Mallowan has had in mind for a long time, although she appreciates that it cannot be published until after her death, as it must be the last Poirot novel.'[62] A corrected copy was finally distributed in September 1941, and it's this version that sat untouched for more than three decades, despite the initial plan being that it would be updated from time to time in order to keep it feeling current, having been written in a way that didn't specifically situate it in a particular time.[63]

Thirty-three years later, the conversation was picked up again. Rosalind sent Cork the typescript in November 1974, who in turn informed Dodd, Mead that 'Agatha has decided she will not write another Poirot book, and has agreed that *Curtain* should be released for publication for Christmas 1975'.[64] Unlike the novel that Christie left to her husband

Max Mallowan for posthumous publication (*Sleeping Murder*, featuring Miss Marple, published in 1976), there were no tax concerns when it came to *Curtain*. The biggest issue was working out its value as Rosalind was to sell it to Agatha Christie Ltd, as it was one of the properties that the company did not own. After a lengthy discussion of its value a figure was finally agreed upon in March 1975, and it was sold. 'I hope all goes well with it,' Rosalind wrote. 'I'm sure it is the right thing to do this year – I do not want nor do I see any necessity for there to be any publicity that this book was once given to me ... My mother and Max are coming down for Easter and staying till the end of April – they seem much the same, sometimes quite well and sometimes rather low. I hope we get some fine weather soon to cheer them up!'[65]

By May 1975 newspapers had heard about the plans for a final Poirot novel, with some reports that it would see Poirot's death, something that had been kept a secret from most. By the time more details were made officially available in the summer of 1975 the success of *Murder on the Orient Express* created more interest than ever, which may explain why an obituary of the detective was famously placed on the front page of the *New York Times* in August, where news of his demise shared space with steel price rises and Malaysian terrorists. Inevitably, the interest in the book as well as the success of the most recent Poirot film meant that movie studios were falling over themselves to try and get hold of the rights of this still as-yet unpublished novel. Edmund Cork reported to Rosalind that all of the major film companies had expressed an interest, while also commiserating that of course the finality of the novel meant that any film would make things very difficult for any

Hercule Poirot's obituary in the *New York Times*.

subsequent Poirot picture (although he pondered on the possibility of selling the rights in a way that would allow John Brabourne to make the film as a final part of a Poirot trilogy). Excitement in the publishing world was just as high, with exceptional deals struck – Pocket Books won a frenzied bidding war for the American paperback rights, paying an extraordinary $925,000.[66]

All of this excitement surrounded the book long before its eventual publication in September 1975, with the full title *Curtain: Poirot's Last Case*, and so it's fortunate that not only is the novel itself far from a disappointment, it also ranks in the top tier of Agatha Christie mysteries. It concerns an elderly Poirot, who's convalescing at Styles, the location of his first published case, which has now become a guest house. For one last time he is joined by his old friend Captain Hastings, in whom he confides a suspicion regarding a series of deaths that he believes may be linked to one of the residents. In order to solve this case Poirot will need to not only make the best use of his psychological analysis of suspects and victims, but also rely on Hastings picking up on some cleverly laid clues, allowing the detective's 'imbecile' friend to prove himself at last. *Curtain* is a superb final innings for both Poirot and Hastings, imbued with an unusually prominent set of complex emotions that affect not only our old friends but also the cast of characters who we meet for the first time, including Hastings' grown-up daughter. The ingenuity of the crime is breath-taking, and while the way in which the murderer operates may sometimes rely on good fortune the basic premise of their actions is chilling and believable. For once, Poirot may have bitten off more than he can chew.

An auspicious page about the author from the Collins sales material.

In *The Times Literary Supplement*, Christie fan (and interviewer) Francis Wyndham praised the author, writing that the book showed her 'Skilfully anticipating nostalgia' but that 'More than this no fair-minded reviewer could bring himself to say – except that the solution, when it is finally sprung, turns out to be as outrageously satisfying as *The Murder of Roger Ackroyd, [And Then There Were None], Murder on the Orient Express* and *Crooked House*. As she presumably intended, in this one Agatha Christie has brought off the bluff to end them all.'[67] *The Guardian* judged that 'For the egotistic Poirot, hero of some forty books, pursuer of evil-doers on Orient Express, Blue Train and Nile, it is a dazzlingly theatrical finish. "Goodbye, cher ami," runs his final message to the hapless Hastings. "They were good days." For

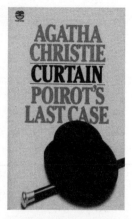

Fontana released three versions of the same cover design with typography in red, green and blue (1976).

addicts, everywhere, they were among the best.'[68] At the end of the year, the newspaper's reviewer judged that 'No crime story of 1975 has given me more undiluted pleasure. As a critic I welcome it, as a reminder that sheer ingenuity can still amaze. What Dame Agatha demonstrates, against the odds, is that there is life in the often despised puzzle story still.'[69] In *The Times*, H.R.F. Keating wrote an article bidding Poirot farewell, in which he calculated Poirot's age upon his death to be a mere 117 years old.[70]

As for Poirot's final words, in one version of the typescript Christie had hand-written an additional final theatrical flourish. 'Yes, they have been good days,' were his final published words, but she toyed with the addition: 'And now – bring down this curtain.'

On 12 January 1976, four months after the book's publication, an eighty-five-year-old Agatha Christie died at her home in Wallingford, Oxfordshire.

Death on the Nile
(Film, 1978)

Despite the fact that Agatha Christie Ltd had gone to great lengths to ensure that the contract for the film adaptation of *Murder on the Orient Express* was to be considered strictly a one-off, almost as soon as the movie premiered there was rampant speculation about a follow-up. Three titles were considered for the second picture, all of which were perfect for a sunny contrast to the snowed-in location of the previous picture – *Evil Under the Sun*, *Death on the Nile* and *Appointment with Death*. Early on it was decided that *Appointment with Death* would be put on the back burner for perhaps the third Poirot picture, while the producers and EMI Films had a strong preference for *Death on the Nile*. However, at the time this novel was one of the author's own

ABOVE: The theatrical movie poster for *Death on the Nile*.

'reserved' titles, which meant that it wasn't advantageous for the author or company to grant the rights to it. As a result, most early press reports cited *Evil Under the Sun* as the next Poirot novel to be filmed, with some claiming that Albert Finney had already signed on to reprise the role, while others stated that he was less sure.[71] In July 1975 Christie had written to Edmund Cork to ask about the newspaper articles that appeared to know more than she did, and her agent reassured her that the reports were 'jumping the gun' and that Brabourne only had an option to purchase the film rights from Agatha Christie Ltd – no deal had been finalised yet.

There were initial expectations that filming for the next picture would commence very soon, but upon Christie's death in January 1976 there was a hiatus in negotiations, no doubt because this change of circumstances suddenly meant that *Death on the Nile* would be available after all. In the end, it took until May 1977 for the picture to move into production. 'The new Poirot' announced *Screen International*, with a front-page splash accompanied by a photograph of a bearded Peter Ustinov, the actor and raconteur who would bring a new interpretation of the role. The short article informed its readers that Finney would not return 'because of stage commitments'.[72] Typically, the *Daily Mail* was more suspicious as it hoped for scandal. 'What has happened to Finney? Has he fallen foul of a plot as intriguing as one of Miss Christie's novels?' it asked. 'Last night EMI Films ruled out foul play. "The script makes Mr Ustinov ideal for the role," a spokesman said. "I was not aware that the policy was to have the same actor playing Poirot in each film."'[73] When quizzed about the part and his decision to sign on for the film by a

A hardback tie-in for the UK book clubs (1978).

newspaper reporter, Ustinov was honest about the fact that he was approaching the character afresh. 'I didn't know anything about Poirot before I took on the part,' he said:

> When I signed to do the role I read all Agatha Christie's books that featured him, and I think I got to know the fellow as well as anyone ... My approach has nothing whatever to do with Finney's portrayal. I didn't see it. I feel Poirot was something of a keyhole peeper! He had to be – how else could he be so omniscient and know everything about anybody.[74]

Filming on *Death on the Nile* commenced in Egypt on 12 September 1977. John Guillermin directed the $10 million picture, following his work on epics of a different kind with *The Towering Inferno* (1974) and the 1976 remake of *King Kong*, working from a script by renowned playwright Anthony Shaffer, whose previous screen work included the cult classic *The Wicker Man* (1973) and an adaptation of his own stage play *Sleuth* (1972). The casting recipe of *Murder on the Orient Express* was retained, with a host of high-profile actors, including Mia Farrow (Jacqueline de Bellefort), Bette Davis (Mrs Van Schuyler), Maggie Smith (Miss Bowers), David Niven (Colonel Race), Lois Chiles (Linnet Ridgeway), Angela Lansbury (Salome Otterbourne), Jane Birkin (Louise Bourget), Olivia Hussey (Rosalie Otterbourne) and rising star Simon MacCorkindale (Simon Doyle). Several newspaper reporters were invited to witness some of the location filming, which not only afforded the picture valuable publicity, but also allowed for some sympathy towards the conditions in which the cast and crew were

The Fontana paperback tie-in (1978).

Peter Ustinov as Poirot, with David Niven as Colonel Race.

working, despite the apparently luxurious surroundings.
As the *Sunday Express* reported:

> But it is not easy working here. For one thing, there is no
> telephone communication. Everything has to be done by
> Telex, which breaks down regularly about twice a week
> ... Bags get lost in transit through Cairo – which is why
> Maggie Smith is walking around in Mia Farrow's shoes.
> And the level of the Nile – regulated by the High Dam –
> has dropped in recent weeks, resulting in the riverboat
> on which they are filming getting stuck on a sandbank.
> Despite all this, morale remains high. Indeed, I would put
> the score at: Egypt – 1; *Death on the Nile* unit – 3.[75]

Despite the potential for a clash of egos the cast got on well
and managed to enjoy the sights on their time off, perhaps
in a bid to avoid the cramped conditions of their lodgings.

Angela Lansbury even enjoyed a trip to the aforementioned High Dam – a worthwhile experience if one finds dams interesting, she told her colleagues. Many of the actors knew each other only by reputation, which resulted in some unnecessary nerves, especially regarding the formidable Bette Davis. 'Miss Davis did nothing to put the cast or film crew at their ease,' reported the *Sunday Mirror*:

> Her first words to the producer were: 'I'm not used to being brought to Egypt. Egypt is usually brought to me.' On the eve of their first scene with her, Ustinov and David Niven decided to retire early and mug up on their lines in private. 'We thought it best to be word perfect next day because she is renowned to be a stickler on that score,' said Ustinov. 'In the morning, however, David and I were astonished when Bette couldn't remember her lines. "It's no good," she sighed. "I'm dead tired. I've been up half the night learning my lines because I was worried that I would get it wrong in front of you guys."'[76]

The finished film may be a little too long, at 140 minutes, but it's also a lot of fun. The casting allows the complex themes of betrayal and jealousy to be played out realistically and even sympathetically, while a host of formidable actors provide a lot of entertainment at the sidelines, even if few of the extraneous characters make for convincing suspects. While Finney's Poirot only threatened to move into camp in an entirely unwitting manner, due to the utmost seriousness with which his unusual mannerisms and speech were played, here Ustinov's attempts to lighten the mood with a bit of comedy are more overt. Angela Lansbury's Salome Otterbourne lights up the screen whenever she stumbles across it with a drink in her hand, while the quiet exasperation from both Maggie Smith and David Niven allows for

Poirot and Salome Otterbourne, played by Angela Lansbury, who would go on to play Miss Marple in *The Mirror Crack'd*.

some waspish comedy. *Death on the Nile* is certainly a more entertaining picture than *Orient Express*, partly because Ustinov's more amiable Poirot is a character that an audience is more likely to enjoy spending time with, even if the actor's idiosyncrasies sometimes dominate that of the character. The length of the film also has one advantage beyond the fact that it affords plenty of time for beautiful shots of the Egyptian landscape, as it means that some important character touches established in the first reel are safely put to the back of the audience's mind by the time the murder takes place, allowing the duplicitous nature of one character in particular to be established but under-emphasised.

Death on the Nile received its own royal premiere on 23 October 1978, which was so popular that it was played on two screens simultaneously, with the Queen in one and Prince Philip in the other. The film had actually already been released in the United States a month earlier, so as to coincide with a touring exhibition of Ancient Egyptian arte-facts. Several reviews complained about the film's length, while praising the cast and the cinematography. Trade paper *Screen International* expected the film to perform very well, especially among the middle classes, helped by the way in which 'the elegance and the eccentricities of the period are reflected in the costumes, and everything is given an extra shimmer of unreal perfection by Jack Cardiff's luminous photography'. Regarding Ustinov, the review argued that he was a 'screen actor of infinite subtlety'.[77]

Monthly Film Bulletin was less keen, feeling that 'one might have hoped for a sequel that was a little less slavish than this carbon copy, directed by John Guillermin with his customary eye for scale but with considerably less style than Lumet'. The review claimed that the story had 'a highly guessable denouement', while even the performances were criticised as 'peremptory at best'. Ustinov was considered to be a 'more central shortcoming', bringing to the film 'a com-

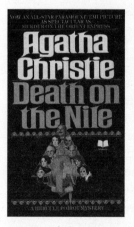

petent characterisation but one which (in con-trast to Albert Finney's thoughtfully controlled eccentricity in *Orient Express*) never escapes from the over-practised persona of Ustinov himself'.[78] *Variety* disagreed with that review almost entirely, including the likelihood that the audience could guess the solution, arguing that Ustinov was a highlight of a film that was 'clever, witty, well-plotted, beautifully produced and splendidly acted'.[79] Among the cast it was Angela Lansbury who was most often praised – she 'knows how to slice ham with delicious skill', stated one review.[80]

Death on the Nile proved to be a commer-cial success, albeit one that couldn't reach the heights of *Murder on the Orient Express*. 'Success

Pocket Books' tie-in was based on one of the movie's theatrical posters (1975).

on the Nile' was *Screen International*'s headline in December 1979, after the picture won Best Film, Peter Ustinov was awarded Best Actor, and Simon MacCorkindale designated 'Most Promising Newcomer' at the *Evening News* British Film Awards.[81] Ustinov also won the award for the best film actor of the year in February 1979 at the Variety Club of Great Britain awards, a further indication that his portrayal could happily be considered to be a winning one.

With *Death on the Nile* finally completed, EMI Films moved on to thoughts of the next Christie picture. In 1979 it was announced that Angela Lansbury would play Miss Marple in a new movie, and that it was planned to alternate between her and Poirot for future Christie films.[82] The next Poirot picture was announced as *Evil Under the Sun*, initially expected to commence production in 1978, with *Appointment with Death* following later. However, plans were thrown into disarray when Lord Mountbatten was killed in an IRA attack on his boat – also on board was John Brabourne and his family; Brabourne's mother and one of his sons were killed, alongside a local boy who was working on the boat. Inevitably, production was delayed.

The 1970s had seen the final chapter of Hercule Poirot as Christie had written him. However, this was not the end of his story. The 1980s would not only see Ustinov continuing in the role, but also have Poirot finding a new home, this time on television, where David Suchet's depiction would become the definitive vision of the Belgian detective for many. However, there were many issues to overcome before the vision of a prestige series of adaptations could become a reality.

CHAPTER SEVEN:

THE

1980s and 1990s

Any literary creation of note should be expected to survive the death of their creator, and certainly a character of Hercule Poirot's fame and reputation wasn't going to disappear quietly into the night just because there were no new Agatha Christie mysteries for him to solve. However, Christie's death in 1976 meant that the company set up in her name had to carefully consider Poirot's position. Although Christie had played only a small role in negotiations and discussions regarding the exploitation of her work since the mid-1960s, when her daughter and son-in-law Rosalind and Anthony Hicks largely took charge, she still wielded the power of veto and had influence on any developments of any note, such as new films. While Arthur Conan Doyle had famously told actor

OPPOSITE: David Suchet in the role that he would inhabit for the next 25 years.

and writer William Gillette that, regarding his creation Sherlock Holmes, Gillette 'may marry him, or murder or do what you like with him', Christie's feelings towards her own detective couldn't have been more different, as she held his reins tightly. Upon her death the company's Directors had to consider the author's writings as a complete set of stories for the first time, and were obliged to balance the preservation of a legacy with potential commercial ventures and a desire to ensure that Christie's works remained visible and widely read.

The 1980s and 1990s showed how Agatha Christie Ltd's board (comprising both family members and other professionals) tried to make commercial decisions in the interests of both legacy and visibility. This was complicated by the feelings of Rosalind in particular, and to a lesser extent her son Mathew Prichard, that as a basic principle the merchandising of Christie properties should be avoided. This was particularly the case with anything that might be construed as a continuation of Christie's mystery writings, and although Christie had made it quite clear that she didn't wish to have any more Poirot stories written by other authors, the extent to which these desires were adhered to was perhaps counterproductive in retrospect. For example, suggestions of Agatha Christie games were usually resisted (with this sort of merchandise often explicitly disallowed in contracts relating to other adaptations), and the closest that Poirot had come to such an adventure was his appearance as a character card in the Crime Club Card Game, first issued in 1935.[1]

Hercule Poirot featured in the Crime Club Card Game, devised by Peter Cheyney (1935).

At a few points in the 1980s there was much discussion about various proposed games based on Agatha Christie properties, and yet even potential projects from established companies were debated endlessly, usually until the proposers simply gave up. When approaches to make an Agatha Christie computer game in the media's fledgling year of 1984 were initially declined, mostly on the grounds that a decision was required too quickly, Mathew quite reasonably pointed out to his mother and stepfather that:

> I won't be losing sleep that we have said no; what I do feel is that the only way we are going to make up our minds whether these things are acceptable to us or not is to let someone do one ... Also, I do not think we ought to dictate to companies what stories they do. Nobody among us, including Brian [Stone, who had succeeded Edmund Cork as Agatha Christie's agent at Hughes Massie Limited] has the detailed knowledge of this new science to know what is likely to be suitable, and I think all we can and should do is to avoid them choosing sensitive titles which are likely to be suitable for other kinds of treatment.[2]

In the end the software developers could not count Christie among the authors whose works formed the basis of computer games (those who did consent included Michael Crichton, Ray Bradbury and Arthur C. Clarke), although *The Big Four* and *Cards on the Table* had been suggested by the board as possible titles. Whatever the outcome, there was certainly an awareness that there would be new challenges when it came to maintaining Agatha Christie's presence in the 1980s and beyond.[3]

Evil Under the Sun
(Film, 1982)

What an unmitigated joy the 1982 film of *Evil Under the Sun* is - although, in truth, much of the fun comes from the choices of the director, screenwriter and cast rather than Christie's original 1941 novel. A camp extravaganza, the film was the fourth Christie movie to be produced by John Brabourne and Richard Goodwin, following 1974's *Murder on the Orient Express*, 1978's *Death on the Nile* and 1980's *The Mirror Crack'd*, which starred Angela Lansbury as Miss Marple. *Evil Under the Sun* also saw Peter Ustinov appearing as Hercule Poirot for the second time, following the overall success of his first appearance, which had gone down well

ABOVE: The theatrical poster for *Evil Under the Sun* included a plot summary: 'While vacationing in the Greek Isles, famous detective Hercule Poirot spotted a beautiful woman on the beach. Realizing that she was dead, he did not ask her to dinner.'

with general audiences and most critics even if some afi-cionados felt that that he wasn't depicting Poirot as Christie had written him. Ustinov only pulls further away from the Poirot of the printed page in this story of a murder among holidaymakers, transplanted from the book's Devon to the even sunnier climes of the Mediterranean, filmed during May 1981 in Majorca – perhaps not coincidentally an island where director Guy Hamilton had a home. Ustinov's Poirot has several moments of comedy that set him apart from the rather more precise detective of the stories, although he's never less than entertaining. For the most part he's also a convincing detective who's attuned to the subtleties of rela-tionships as the glamorous Arlena Marshall (Diana Rigg) is found murdered on a secluded beach, following a dalliance with Patrick Redfern (Nicholas Clay), much to the annoy-ance of her husband Kenneth (Denis Quilley), her step daughter Linda (Emily Hone) and Patrick's wife Christine (Jane Birkin).

There had been a fair amount of debate regarding the order of adaptations to be filmed following *Murder on the Orient Express*, and pre-production work had been undertaken on *Evil Under the Sun* only a few months after the release of the first film, with *Variety* reporting on it in July 1975. Shortly after this the rights situation regarding *Death on the Nile* then changed following Christie's 1976 death, which made that preferred title available for filming. According to contem-porary reports, Paul Dehn (who had adapted *Orient Express*) had begun work on a script for *Evil Under the Sun* prior to his death in 1976, while Anthony Shaffer also worked on a script that was apparently completed while Christie was still alive. As a result, the title was an obvious choice for the next Poirot picture, although *Appointment with Death* was frequently mentioned as another possibility.[4] Shaffer's final *Evil Under the Sun* script as filmed is a sensibly condensed and somewhat arch presentation of Christie's mystery. The structure of the main plot, including the intricacies of the murder, is well presented and provides a clever and satisfying solution for the audience while less important red herrings are happily disposed of. More than this, however, the film itself is pure entertainment, with a host of famous faces alongside the aforementioned cast members having a great time, including Maggie Smith as hotel proprietor Daphne, Roddy McDowall as gossip writer Rex Brewster, and James Mason as theatrical producer Odell Gardener. It's the sparring relationship between old rivals Arlena and Daphne that provides the most delight however, with the latter recalling that in their youth Arlena could 'always throw her legs higher than any of us – and wider...', with the bitchiness deliciously delivered by both Rigg and Smith.

Although it's understandable to think of this as the third Poirot film of a franchise, given the fact that it was the same producers operating along what superficially seems to be the same star-studded template, it's really a very different beast to *Murder on the Orient Express*. In part this can be explained by the casting of Peter Ustinov, whose Poirot is undoubtedly a lighter one who's more prone to comedy moments, quite unlike the blustering, serious, and almost unnerving Finney portrayal. However, there's more to it than just the casting. The entire tone and perspective of the films has changed by this point, with a cast of characters now designed to be amusing entertainments (almost everyone gets a couple of decent moments of comedy) rather than psychologically significant in the roll call of suspects. In *Murder on the Orient Express*, the film opened with a stark depiction of a shocking crime, with the later murder on

The Fontana tie-in paperback featured photos of the cast (1982).

Peter Ustinov and an all-star cast during filming in 1981.

the train then treated with the utmost seriousness. In order to uncover the truth the case is approached methodically, just as in the book, with solemn interviews taking place in isolation. There's no opportunity for light-hearted moments to be the emphasis – instead, the film is concerned with the methodical uncovering of truth. By the time of *Death on the Nile* this has already started to change, with the Egyptian locations coming to the fore, and much more opportunity to spend time elaborating on the backstory before the murder itself, which occurs fairly late in the proceedings (just as in the book). As a result, the emphasis on characters and their relationships was strengthened, and this is continued with *Evil Under the Sun*, which is undoubtedly a picture that's designed to entertain more than puzzle, although it does both exceedingly well. The mystery is still important, but the ramifications are little considered, and by this stage the films have moved further towards a lighter take on the grisly reality of murder.

An Italian tie-in edition from 1982.

Pocket Books' 1982 movie paperback for the US.

From a production perspective, *Evil Under the Sun* was granted a (slightly) larger budget than the rather low-key Miss Marple movie *The Mirror Crack'd* had received two years previously. A trade press report on the production claimed that there was a palpable sense of relief to be moving back to Poirot and the glamorous 1930s, perhaps because of the disappointing – but not disastrous – box office reception of the previous Miss Marple film. Although four films had been made in eight years, the producers resisted claims that Christie adaptations were being 'churned out', as they argued, not entirely convincingly, that '"Churning" rather more applies to TV. We can make these glamorous and big. This one is very much in the mould of *Murder on the Orient Express* and *Death on the Nile*. With *The Mirror Crack'd*, we tried to make it a smaller film and it did not have the essential glamour the Poirot ones always have. This one has wonderful locations, Anthony Powell's costumes and a smashing cast.'[5]

Evil Under the Sun had its world premiere in Australia in February 1982, where it did well, before moving to a wider international release the next month. The film was greeted with yet another London royal film premiere, with Queen Elizabeth II in attendance once more, while the reviews were largely good. The *Monthly Film Bulletin* said that the film opened 'surprisingly and promisingly' with the discovery of a body on a misty moor, before complimenting Rigg and Smith as an 'inspired pairing', although the rest of the cast made less of an impression on the critic. Nevertheless, Ustinov was praised as 'the definitive Poirot' in an 'escapist enterprise'.[6] *Variety* criticised what they called Christie's 'deeply silly logic' but then embraced it as 'part of the fun'. Regarding Poirot, the review claimed that 'It is said that Ustinov, after *Death on the Nile*, was approached by a Christie heir who criticised his rebuilding of Poirot saying Poirot was never that way. To which Ustinov replied, "He is now." He certainly is,' while the film was expected to 'make for solid if not spectacular boxoffice everywhere'.[7] In the end, the picture certainly made money in the long run, but continued the decline seen in *The Mirror Crack'd* rather than reversing it. Not long after *Evil Under the Sun* was made, EMI was joined by esteemed producer Verity Lambert in order to formulate plans for the company's future, and she stated that she felt that they had 'done enough' of the Christie adaptations and that, as of January 1983, 'there's just no life there at the moment'.[8] However, Ustinov's Poirot refused to quietly shuffle off screen – he would soon be back.

Thirteen at Dinner
(Television movie, 1985)

By the early 1980s Agatha Christie Ltd was more accepting of both the inevitability and value of bringing the author's works to the small screen, even if it didn't sit easily with Christie's daughter Rosalind Hicks in particular, who remained suspicious of the medium. One demonstration of Rosalind's innate bias against television came in 1985, when she was consulted about a proposed documentary for the medium – Rosalind resisted the idea, wondering why it couldn't be made for radio instead. Nevertheless, both Rosalind and Mathew had been pleased with a recent selection of non-Poirot Christie adaptations on ITV in the UK, starting with *Why Didn't They Ask Evans?* in 1980, and then delighted with

ABOVE: Peter Ustinov and Faye Dunaway, with David Suchet as Inspector Japp, in *Thirteen at Dinner* (1985).

the BBC's lavish and faithful *Miss Marple* series starring Joan Hickson, which started in 1984. However, they needed to be provided with a strong rationale to authorise television productions, and sometimes these reasons were commercial rather than creative.

There had long been interest from various production companies in the United States regarding Agatha Christie on television, not only resulting from the ongoing interest in the author's works, but also the popularity of the televising of *Murder on the Orient Express* and subsequent cinema films that showed her to be a valuable property for producers. It was producer Alan Shayne who would eventually be granted permission to helm an initial run of five adaptations for Warner Bros, to be broadcast on CBS in the United States and sold internationally. The five titles in question were the matter of some discussion, but in the end it was standalone mystery *Murder is Easy* that was made and shown first, in 1982. The same year saw Mathew and Rosalind considering the future of Poirot on television following interest from Shayne in producing some 'well made' two-hour films, which tied in with the family's gradual decision that television had been somewhat overlooked when it came to bringing Agatha Christie to the public, and that it was time for this to change. In 1978 even Rosalind had championed the idea of television adaptations being taken more seriously, while Mathew later argued that the absence of Poirot and Miss Marple from television screens was becoming conspicuous. On American television, Shayne's further non-Poirot adaptations included *Sparkling Cyanide* and two Miss Marple stories, *A Caribbean Mystery* and *Murder with Mirrors* (a.k.a. *They Do It With Mirrors*), and so it seemed

The standard UK cover in 1985.

inevitable that the Belgian detective would soon make a small-screen appearance. By 1985 Warner Bros was just one of several companies approaching Agatha Christie Ltd with Poirot proposals, including Cinema Arts of Los Angeles, which wanted to make an in-period television film of either *The Mysterious Affair at Styles* or *Murder on the Links*. The Poirot-less *The Man in the Brown Suit* was its second choice, which it hoped would star Melissa Gilbert who had just finished a ten-year run on *Little House on the Prairie*. Gunnar Hellstrom was proposed as the director for either of the Poirot stories, with Mark Rydell as potential director for *The Man in the Brown Suit*, but Agatha Christie Ltd demurred. Instead, for the fifth picture in the five-title deal with Warner Bros the board agreed to allow Peter Ustinov to return as Poirot.

Rosalind hadn't liked any of the Warner Bros television movies, although the first of them, *Murder is Easy*, was viewed as the best of the bunch. All of the Warner Bros productions

Peter Ustinov in *Thirteen at Dinner*.

had incorporated an American cast, although there was also a strong British presence both among the actors and usually the locations, which meant that they were less 'Americanised' than they might have been, and perhaps demonstrated that their British origins were seen as a key part of their appeal. The basic structures of the stories were also largely left unaltered although inevitably simplified, and often groaning under the addition of a superfluous action sequence or two. Rosalind and Mathew had gone a little cold on Ustinov's depiction of Poirot, but recognised the popularity of both his portrayal and the movies themselves, which had performed quite well in the United States and very well indeed in international sales. Production on the chosen Poirot adaptation, *Thirteen at Dinner* (the American title for *Lord Edgware Dies*) began in London in February 1985, which lends the film a rather dull and worn appearance that robs it of any visual vibrancy, as the city disappears under the limited gamut of greys and browns visible under the British winter weather. The location was chosen not only because of the story's setting, but also because the exchange rate and British film-making facilities allowed the $2m budget to stretch even further than it would in America, although the schedule was tight at only four weeks, when at least eight would be the norm for a film of its scale if made for cinema.

During production Neil Hartley, one of the film's producers, pointed out the general value of bringing Christie stories to television, as he argued that the American viewers were 'not the kind of people who would necessarily go out to the theatre to see a show, but would love to see it in their own homes.'[9] Director Lou Antonio was keen to emphasis the fact that the star power went beyond Christie, however: 'Thank God we have Peter Ustinov,' he said. 'He's delightful. He's got the free-associating imagination of Robin Williams and Jonathan Winters, combined.'[10] Joining Ustinov for the production was the Oscar-winning Faye Dunaway in the dual role of impressionist Carlotta Adams and Jane Wilkinson, while the cast was also joined by future Poirot David Suchet as Inspector Japp, who in recent years has been more dismissive of his cockney turn than the entertainingly prickly performance deserves. Other familiar faces on set included Jonathan Cecil as a slightly redundant Hastings, Bill Nighy as Ronald Marsh, and Lesley Dunlop as Alice Bennett. After production had finished, but before the results had been seen, Rosalind expressed her reservations about the project to her son. Mathew replied that:

> Although I do not always agree with you, I can see the force of your arguments about Warner Bros, and certainly have a great deal of sympathy with your nervousness. But I really feel you must accept that a large percentage of the population of America just do not go out to bookshops and buy books. They have to be got at in some other way. When we are offered the chance to approach these people, I think we ought to accept it.[11]

In the end, *Thirteen at Dinner* is perfectly competent as an adaptation, if a little dull and workmanlike as a production, although it has the advantage that it's generally quite well paced across the course of its ninety minutes. It sets out its stall as a tale of Poirot in modern times early on, as the detective joins David Frost on a television chat show (the sort of environment where Ustinov was very much at home), where we are told that Poirot is making his 'television debut' – which, for much of the audience, he was. However, this rather surprising intrusion of modernity makes sense as it introduces us (and other characters) to the charms of impressionist Carlotta Adams, who will become an important part of the story. We also see Poirot being harangued to star in a television mini-series, while an array of action sequences are at least given some narrative plausibility because of a film being produced that concerns several characters, seemingly introduced only so that explosions can be deployed while stuntmen run around alongside the banks of the Thames. Although the British setting harks back to the original novel, the drabness of London is not a pleasant contrast with the glamour of Poirot's more exotic recent adventures.

A cover by Nina Tara for an unpublished comic book edition (2013).

Following the production's first broadcast on CBS in October 1985, critics seemed to feel that they understood what made Christie work a little better than the producers. 'Somewhere the spirit of Agatha Christie has been dumped; *Thirteen at Dinner* turns out to be a characterless puzzle,' stated *Variety*, which called the script 'pedestrian at best'. Although Dunaway's performance was commended the critic argued that 'someone has overlooked the important point: Christie mysteries are built on the interaction of credible characters, as well as on the puzzle itself, and these folks don't pull that much attention. They have been, horror of horrors, popularized.'[12] However, the film did reasonably well commercially (despite disappointing ratings in the United States) and was felt to be very important to maintaining Christie's presence in the crowded American book market. No one involved with Agatha Christie Ltd was particularly excited about the actual films produced by Warner Bros, but they were mostly seen as unobjectionable and a means to assist Christie's appearance in book shops across North America. Perhaps more notably, when shown in the UK in June 1986, the 9.75m viewers demonstrated an appetite for more Poirot on the small screen.

Dead Man's Folly and Murder in Three Acts
(Television movies, 1986)

Thirteen at Dinner and the earlier Warner Bros television movies had demonstrated to Rosalind and Mathew that, although they weren't to their own taste, they didn't seem to do any harm to the reputation of Christie herself, while they undoubtedly increased her visibility. In fact, plans were in motion to approve further television movies even before *Thirteen at Dinner* had completed post-production, as by this stage the style and tone of the film was eminently foreseeable. During March and April 1985 producer Alan Shayne had several conversations with Mathew Prichard in which they discussed further plans, now that the five-picture deal had been concluded. Initially Shayne had proposed a 22-episode

ABOVE: Peter Ustinov with Jonathan Cecil as Captain Hastings in *Dead Man's Folly*.

Poirot series to follow on from *Thirteen at Dinner*, and the family considered the possibility of allowing American producers to adapt the later Poirot stories, with earlier ones reserved for the British market. However, the conversation soon changed to Shayne's desire to license two further Poirot novels for the 1985-86 television season, which would result in three Poirot movies on screen during the year. Mathew felt that this would 'give them (and us) a chance to evaluate Poirot as a character for further exploitation,' indicating the possibility of more regular appearances of the character on American television.[13]

However, the stories on offer needed some discussion, as the Christie board usually considered pre-1945 novels to be the 'premium' titles but were generally more flexible when it came to the later mysteries. Resultantly, Shayne was asked to pick from a selection of later Poirots, and those under consideration included *Third Girl*, *Cat Among the Pigeons* and *Dead Man's Folly*. Shayne had already read *Sad Cypress* and *Three Act Tragedy*, which both hailed from the 'premium' period, and although attempts were made to persuade him against these titles he was eventually granted permission to film the latter alongside *Dead Man's Folly*, which would go in front of the cameras first when filming began in September 1985. Although no one in Christie's family had seen *Thirteen at Dinner* at the time the deal for further films was struck, Mathew reasoned that 'I really do not think that matters before entering into a commitment of this kind. We have seen Peter Ustinov as Poirot and we have seen Warner's films – the combination is I think fairly predictable though I freely admit they will be more popular in America than at Greenway.'[14] The Agatha Christie Ltd board also considered

Collins' 1980 Crime Club reprint.

this new deal in a holistic sense, as they were mindful of the presence of a more faithful series of period Miss Marple adaptations on the BBC, which they felt offered a useful counterpoint to the modernised Poirot productions.

Dead Man's Folly opens with a pleasant tourist-eye view of London, with the Houses of Parliament, Harrods and red buses, before moving to the country house environs of Sir George Stubbs' estate. Stubbs is played by Tim Piggott-Smith, fresh from the highly successful Granada production of *The Jewel in the Crown* in 1984. Stubbs' houseguest, Ustinov's Poirot, is much the same as ever, although he's even more genial in these television appearances, bumbling along and enjoying the views of both characters and locations as he manages to conjure up a solution to the mysteries he encounters. He's accompanied once again by Jonathan Cecil as Hastings, who didn't appear in the novel and is inevitably forced to the background here. More interesting is Jean Stapleton as Ariadne Oliver, who had initially been approached for the

Dead Man's Folly's cast included Jean Stapleton as Ariadne Oliver.

role of Jessica Fletcher in the CBS series *Murder, She Wrote* and, with Ustinov, helps to increase the energy of the cast and production.

Dead Man's Folly isn't the most subtle of adaptations, as clues are laid with unusual obviousness early in proceedings, while some crucial duplicity is also rather transparent. Later star of *Desperate Housewives* Nicollette Sheridan gives an odd performance as Lady Stubbs that is somewhat distracting, especially because most of her lines have been rather obviously dubbed later. Once more it's a shame that the weather doesn't seem to have been kind during filming, as the story is crying out for bright exuberance

The Fontana cover from 1986.

and a dash of summer spectacle, but the production does its best to showcase the more interesting exteriors by staging as much outside as possible. The locations are generally attractive regardless of the weather, which adds charm, as does the easy-going nature of many of the performances, including Poirot's ongoing attempts to avoid reading Ariadne Oliver's novel.

Broadcast in January 1986, only three months after the previous Poirot movie, critics were starting to tire of the formula and production methods seen in the Warner Bros productions, especially when compared to not only the big-screen films but also the BBC's *Miss Marple* series, which was now screening on PBS in America. Reflecting on Warner Bros's adaptations, the *New York Times* argued that 'The results so far have been spotty, and no more so than in this evening's labored romp,' before drawing some comparisons:

> As it happens, there are neatly contrasting examples available of how Miss Christie is treated by American and British producers. The Americans are addicted to the

theory that stars are essential to the success of any television enterprise. That is why, surrounded by a supporting cast of familiar names and faces, Mr. Ustinov must play Poirot and, also in television films, Helen Hayes must play Miss Marple. The British, on the other hand, trusting more to the script, are willing to employ little-known but very accomplished character actors. Witness the current Miss Marple adaptations being shown on public TV's *Mystery!* series with the key detective role being filled to perfection by the 80-year-old Joan Hickson. The British method is almost invariably a better deal for Miss Christie.

In summary, the reviewer felt that the film 'leaves little or no time for any significant character development. The actors are shunted on and off camera, barely able to recite their lines, take their paychecks and run.'[15] *Variety* was uninterested rather than hostile in its own take on the film, arguing that 'The solution doesn't matter,' as 'the diversion is beyond far-fetched and credible. But getting there – watching Peter Ustinov's Hercule Poirot trot up and down hillocks, for example – makes the puzzle entertaining.'[16]

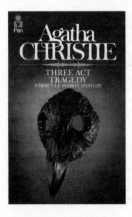

Pan's 'Double-dagger series' cover (1983).

The third of Ustinov's television Poirot adventures was *Murder in Three Acts*, the American title for *Three Act Tragedy*, which co-stars Tony Curtis as flamboyant actor Charles Cartwright and would be the last of Ustinov's small-screen films in the role.[17] The movie wasn't broadcast until 30 September 1986, and by this time interest was seriously waning. The producers did attempt to find a new way to bring fresh visual interest to the story by relocating many of the events to Acapulco, which is a perfectly good idea as it doesn't affect the bare bones of the mystery and does make the film more distinctive than the rather visually bland predecessors, even if the weather wasn't at its best once more. Hastings also returns, principally to perform some unsubtle comedy and, at one point, seemingly in order to slow down the solving of the case by Poirot so we don't reach the solution too early in the ninety minutes. Nevertheless, the distinctive visuals, pacey opening and strong performance from Curtis (who is clearly having a great time, perhaps trying to do the impossible and out-showman Ustinov) elevates the movie above most of those made by Warner Bros for television.

At this point the writers were trying to find things for Poirot to do in order to give Ustinov some interesting business to focus on away from the mystery, and here the detective is shown at a computer while trying to write his autobiography, which keeps him from some key events. This version of Poirot isn't particularly methodical, and has drifted even further towards Ustinov playing himself rather

Peter Ustinov with Tony Curtis and Emma Samms in *Murder in Three Acts*.

than the character, something that the reviewer in the *New York Times* also noticed, stating that with this adaptation:

> ... Peter Ustinov will have played the Belgian detective Hercule Poirot five times on film. With each succeeding impersonation, however, Mr. Ustinov seems to have become more superficial, relying on assorted tics and mannerisms designed, it seems, to amuse himself as much as the audience. In this latest Poirot caper, Mr. Ustinov's performance is one unrelieved 'shtick' from beginning to end.[18]

Ustinov and Poirot had now merged in the eyes of much of the audience, and it would soon be the case that they would have to be untangled – but not before one final outing towards the end of the decade.

Murder by the Book
(Television drama, 1986)

Although many of the proposals that were submitted to
Agatha Christie Ltd during the 1980s were straightforward
adaptations of Christie stories, there were some projects that
were a little more unusual, and the reactions of Rosalind,
Mathew and the company's board were not always easy to
predict. In December 1983 there had been a 'secret' try out
of a revised revival of the play *Peril at End House*, which had
been adapted from Christie's novel by Arnold Ridley in 1940,
and now played out at Windsor's Theatre Royal with George
Little in the role of Poirot. This would seem to be a straightforward project for approval, and Ridley himself approved
of the revisions, but while Rosalind did not see the production she was unhappy to see mention of humour in reviews,

ABOVE: Ian Holm as Poirot and Dame Peggy Ashcroft as his creator.

The US paperback edition of Agatha Christie's posthumously published *An Autobiography* depicted both Poirot and Miss Marple.

and along with a fear of overexposing Poirot she declined to allow a touring production that had been hoped for by the play's producers. Less surprisingly, the decision by producer and writer Peter Reichelt to turn up uninvited at Greenway (where Rosalind now lived) in order to discuss a proposed German television serial for ZDF did not go down well. The series would have dramatised portions of Agatha Christie's life along with key Poirot and Miss Marple incidents. A stern letter from Mathew to the producers reinforced the proper procedure and fiercely protected copyright status of Christie's works, and plans don't seem to have gone any further.[19]

One title that attracted a lot of interest during the 1980s was Christie's novel *The Hollow*, as well as her stage version of the story that removed Poirot. In January 1985 Trevor (T.R.) Bowen, who had just adapted two Miss Marple novels for the BBC, proposed a film version of the story, as he admired the novel as one of Christie's best and most psychologically convincing. The Christie board had greatly liked Bowen's work on the Miss Marple stories, but this was bad timing for a new Poirot screen project, although Bowen would later contribute a script for the David Suchet series that began in 1989.[20] However, a film version of the story was successfully made in Japan in 1985 as *Dangerous Women*, which didn't include Poirot and was met with bemusement and amusement by the Agatha Christie Ltd board.

One of the more interesting projects was a proposal from theatre director and writer Simone Benmussa, who wished to create a new play to star Poirot and be performed in Paris. Benmussa's original plan, submitted in April 1986, had been to combine the narratives of *Evil Under the Sun* and

The Hollow because they both relied on questions of appearances and the creation of illusions. Rosalind immediately objected, not least because her mother had already dramatised The Hollow herself. It was testament to the esteem in which Benmussa was held, as well as her tenacity, that Rosalind and Mathew eventually approved of a second idea. This used Christie's script for The Hollow as the play's basis, but included Poirot, despite the fact that Christie had excised him, and added passages from the book that Benmussa felt should be included (while removing sections that she felt were unnecessary – otherwise it would have been a very long night at the theatre).[21] Benmussa was interested in depicting Poirot as an observer of other people's lives and relationships, with the play set by the swimming pool where the murder took place. It eventually opened for previews as Le Vallon at Rond Point Theater on 28 January 1988, with Alain Ollivier starring as Poirot.

Ian Holm as Hercule Poirot in Murder by the Book.

Before the French stage production of *The Hollow* there had been another indication that both Rosalind and particularly Mathew were attuned to the worth of projects that had genuine artistic or scholarly value, with their approval of *Murder by the Book*. In this fifty-minute television film, written by Nick Evans, Agatha Christie is confronted by her own creation, Hercule Poirot, as both move towards the end of their lives. Evans had been inspired by Janet Morgan's 1984 biography of Christie and sent a treatment for the film, at this stage called *Murder by Writing*, to the Christie company's agent, Brian Stone, in July the same year. Evans had already approached Melvyn Bragg of ITV's *South Bank Show* who had indicated interest in funding the project, following Evans' earlier project for the arts strand which had studied David Lean during the making of *A Passage to India*. Morgan had also seen the extended synopsis for this proposed television production, which she approved of, while Evans acknowledged that the script inevitably used some artistic licence but would overall be sensitive and sympathetic.[22] Having disapproved of the 1979 film *Agatha*, which presented a fictionalised account of her 1926 disappearance, it says something of the regard with which Rosalind and Mathew held Evans' ideas, as well as the *South Bank Show*, that they even considered allowing the production to go ahead.[23] Mathew was particularly keen, albeit with some reasonable reservations, but even Rosalind liked the idea and also liked Evans himself, although she initially wanted it to be a shorter film, which Evans resisted in order for it to be presented as a serious piece of quality drama.[24] In response, Rosalind wrote to Evans that:

> It is true that after some thought I said I was prepared in principle for you to go ahead and prepare a script – I think it <u>is</u> a clever idea and handled in the right way could make

Murder by the Book was released commercially on Laserdisc in the USA.

an entertaining and serious piece of drama. I still feel that 30 minutes would be the best length and have no doubt about this but if you have 50 minutes at your disposal on *The South Bank Show* I can see you want to use it! It will of course depend on the quality of the script. I will of course be very interested to see this and when it is available I do hope you will come down here and we can discuss it – I am sure Janet Morgan could be a help too. I think this is a sensitive matter for me as I do not really wish to see my mother and stepfather portrayed on the television … I am not even sure that I wish to see Hercule Poirot as over the years we do not seem to have found anyone remotely like him! However in this perhaps I shall be agreeably surprised. I really think I might be able to help you in some way so please let me know how things are progressing.'[25]

Mathew also supervised the project closely, writing to Evans in November 1984 that 'I am happy to accept your assurances concerning the quality of production … but nevertheless you will appreciate that a story containing these particular characters does make us all extremely nervous!'.[26]

Ian Holm drawn in the classic *Sketch* pose for publicity material.

Plans now started to solidify, and Evans even visited Rosalind at Greenway where discussion turned to casting ideas, and both of them had come up with the same name for Poirot – David Suchet.[27] However, Suchet would need to wait in the wings for a few more years before his time as Poirot would come.

By April 1985 both Rosalind and Mathew had received a full draft of the script, and they were particularly concerned by a single close-up ('the infamous shot 92') which depicted Christie carefully spooning out cyanide from a bottle, as neither liked to see Christie depicted as a (possible) actual poisoner. They also reinforced the fact that Edmund Cork, Christie's agent who was depicted in the script, was still alive and would need to be consulted. Mathew also pointed out that a gratuitous reference to Peter Ustinov being 'awful' should be removed as his grandmother never saw him in the role, and 'Anyway, I don't happen to agree with you'.[28] In summary, Mathew felt that 'some of the dialogue is excellent and the idea comes through very well', while the depiction of Christie's dog was also commended – 'I congratulate you on an extremely accurate portrayal of Bingo's character!'.[29] Writing to his mother, Mathew stated that 'Actually I thought it was rather good. *The South Bank Show* is quite high class viewing and, if you don't find it offensive, I think they could be relied upon to consult us properly and produce something decent. I don't think anyone envisages much, if any, money changing hands, and it is simply a question of whether we want to engage in what is, in effect, some high class and elaborate good-natured publicity'.[30]

Evans responded to the comments by agreeing to delete the poisoning shot and address other issues as well as he could. Upon receipt of a revised version of the script Agatha Christie Ltd granted written permission for Benbow Productions and ITV franchise TVS to use the name and character of Hercule Poirot for the token sum of £1. Rosalind continued to be interested in the project, and had tea with Dame Peggy Ashcroft when she was approached to portray her mother in the production. Ashcroft had, in fact, met Christie at least once herself, at Dame Sybil Thorndike's eightieth birthday party in 1962.

Filming with Ashcroft as Christie and Ian Holm as Hercule Poirot took place in October and November 1985, with the programme finally broadcast on 28 August 1986 in most ITV regions. The final film is a delightful, sympathetic and fascinating character portrayal, with both Holm and Ashcroft embodying their characters in a completely convincing manner. *The Times* highly commended the film, citing its 'total success in reanimating Christie and Poirot'.[31] Christie fan Nancy Banks-Smith of *The Guardian* was less keen on some elements, including the Poirot dialogue, but overall felt that it 'rang right and looked lovely'.[32] Most viewers in the United States had to wait until 1990 to see the film, when it was broadcast to tie in with the celebrations marking a century since Christie's birth. *Variety* referred to it as a 'nifty production' that 'flirts with preciousness but misses it thanks to ingenuity', with the reviewer commending Ashcroft and director Lawrence Gordon Clark.[33] Archival issues have meant that *Murder by the Book* has been little seen in the last few decades, but it's a good demonstration of the overall attempts during this period to ensure that the trajectory of Christie projects was towards the quality end of the spectrum, even if this wasn't always the case in practice.

Appointment with Death
(Film, 1988)

Although Peter Ustinov's Poirot was making himself comfortable on American television in the mid-1980s, Rosalind in particular felt that there was no need to offer any more titles featuring the sleuth to Warner Bros. Instead, it had to make do with the likes of Christie's standalone global thriller *The Man in the Brown Suit*. Elsewhere there were plans for Poirot films that would return the detective to his proper period and, perhaps, be a little more faithful in tone than his more recent outings. One such title considered for adaptation was *Murder in Mesopotamia*, which was suggested as early as 1985, with a 1986 script written by Julian Bond. This project was created by the Australian animation studio Burbank Films, which had adapted several well-known

ABOVE: Peter Ustinov in his final outing as Hercule Poirot.

titles in this way, including Sherlock Holmes mysteries and Charles Dickens stories. In this case the studio was looking to expand into live action, which might explain why the early travelogue sections were removed at an early stage as their cost was likely to have been prohibitive.

On the whole the script conformed closely to the novel, although one draft portrayed both Agatha Christie and Max Mallowan at the beginning, setting the stage for the fictional story by giving some sense of the context of the writing of the story. The physical description of Poirot as 'a small, slight man' showed that he was expected to be different from recent portrayals (and now called 'Hercules' Poirot), and the detective was scripted to make a dramatic arrival on a small aeroplane, looking 'like the ageless but very dapper maitre d'hotel of some extremely expensive five-star restaurant. The famous moustaches have gone limp in the heat, with regrettably comic results, but he makes a point of brushing off his suit'. An initial suggestion for the part of Poirot was Ben Kingsley, although the production company soon backtracked on this (perhaps mindful of how unlikely it was that they would secure his services), while a later suggestion of Anthony Hopkins was dismissed by Rosalind. Eventually, the production company had to concede that various financial backers would only come on board if Ustinov returned. In April 1987 Mathew Prichard wrote to producer John Erichsen with two points to make – firstly, that the board had approved the casting of Ustinov in the film. Secondly, and more significantly for the development of Poirot, Mathew also warned that Ustinov's casting wasn't necessarily the best way to go, although he was aware that another film project from the company Cannon was also likely to cast Ustinov, which meant that he remained the de facto Poirot in many people's eyes. The bulk of the letter bears reproduction, indicating as it does the keenness of Agatha Christie Ltd to unshackle Poirot from Ustinov:

> However, we would like you to remember that in our view the success of recent Agatha Christie productions on film and television has not usually been the result of employing an internationally famous actor or actress in the "title" role; *Murder on the Orient Express*, a brilliant critical and financial success, was the result of a happy collaboration between Paul Dehn as scriptwriter, Sidney Lumet as director and a team of actors, actresses, producers (led by John Brabourne) etc; *Death on the Nile* was produced by the same team, fed on the success of the previous film but did not suffer by using a different actor for Poirot (or did it?). Later Brabourne productions were less successful and were not rescued by sticking slavishly to the same Poirot.
>
> In the television field (which I know has important differences) a real breakthrough was achieved by the BBC casting a relatively unknown but talented character actress as Miss Marple and by surrounding her with a more famous cast and excellent production – the ghost of Margaret Rutherford is well and truly laid! We feel you have a wonderful script, attractive locations and in short the best chance to make an independently successful Agatha Christie film that anyone has had for some years. It is to us a pity that your associates have felt it necessary to remind the public of previous, less successful, films both on cinema and television, by casting Ustinov as Poirot who was the symbol of those films. We recognise that the Cannon situation made it even more difficult for you, and that there are gut reactions amongst those who finance films which, whatever the feelings of the public, are difficult to ignore.
>
> I write this solely so that you (and any of your colleagues to whom you wish to show this letter) should be aware of

our feelings, in case we should ever be in the same position again; and I want you to know that all of us, unreservedly, have tremendous admiration for the way you have prepared this project and wish you every success in bringing it to fruition.

See you in Turkey, if not before![34]

A last-ditch attempt was made to find another Poirot, with French actor Michel Blanc being suggested, but the project was running into insurmountable funding difficulties. While the unconvincing final revelations in *Murder in Mesopotamia* mean that it isn't one of the better candidates for screen treatment, the Christie board were much more keen on this project, which did not make it into production, than the other Poirot movie that they seemed to be tied to, *Appointment with Death*.

The 1988 film of *Appointment with Death* had two important points of origin – the first was the original run of heritage films that began with 1974's *Murder on the Orient Express*. Producers John Brabourne and Richard Goodwin had contemplated *Appointment with Death* for one of their productions, and it's possible that Anthony Shaffer wrote a version of the script in the late 1970s. Initially, Brabourne and Goodwin were announced in the trade press as producers, but instead ended up working on an adaptation of Charles Dickens' *Little Dorrit* for the same production company, Cannon. It's Cannon that was the second important point of origin for the film, as the company brought with it quite the reputation. More broadly, Cannon was well known for cashing in on recognisable properties with cheaply made films that were most at home on the video rental market. More

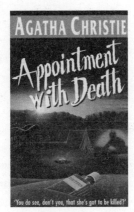

A Collins edition for children (1996).

Fontana's new look (1988).

specifically for Christie, it had been behind the 1984 film adaptation of her novel *Ordeal by Innocence*, which starred Donald Sutherland and been troubled by an array of production difficulties and a breakdown of trust between the Christie board and the production company. However, it seemed that the deal to make a film of *Appointment with Death* couldn't be cancelled, and so they had to endure the production of the film, despite being unhappy with it. By the time a draft of the script was received in early 1987 two other names were added to Shaffer's as the writers of the screenplay, Peter Buckman and Michael Winner, the latter of whom was now on board to direct. Rosalind noted that the script made no mention of her mother, and then went on to detail a range of issues that she had with it. These included: the character of Jefferson Cope being made into a crooked lawyer; various inaccuracies in the ways that relatives referred to each other; the type of camera used by Lady Westholme; perceived Americanisms ('English doctors don't say "Are you taking medication?"'); issues with what a newly qualified doctor would or would not have in their possession or be trained in, and questions of period accuracy, including the amount of money discussed and the status of the King. Rosalind acknowledged that more 'action' was needed in the transfer of the book to the screen but argued that these elements, including a coronation ball and an extra murder, were not well integrated. 'It is very important that a plot like this should be as plausible as possible in all ways,' she wrote.[35] However, very few changes were made in line with her comments. In March 1987 Mathew raised his concerns with the film more generally with casting director Dyson Lovell. 'He assured me there was no intention of filling it with sex or undue violence and was sympathetic about the gratuitous murder,' he later wrote to his mother:

> I remonstrated strongly with him about the *Ordeal by Innocence* situation and pointed out that Cannon's failure to abide by any of the normal business practices usually associated with a relationship between producer and copyright owner was itself enough to prevent the ACL board considering Cannon for any future films. It was then that he told me that he was leaving Cannon and that his sole job for them remained the casting of *Appointment with Death*.
>
> The whole situation will have to be very carefully watched.[36]

So it was that when filming began in Israel (replacing the book's Petra, Jordan) in April 1987 most of those involved with the movie had already given up on it being much of a success, artistically or commercially. In July a report from the set from Andrew Duncan in *The Times* revealed a deeply unhappy crew and cast. The movie had managed to attract an excellent array of known actors to accompany Peter Ustinov, including Lauren Bacall, Piper Laurie, Carrie Fisher, Sir John Gielgud, David Soul (replacing Michael Sarrazin after he was involved in a car crash) and Hayley Mills, but most seemed to regret their involvement. 'Winner is a charming dinner companion, but his aggressive attitude to filmmaking is not always popular with his stars,' Duncan wrote, rather underplaying the situation.[37] Gielgud rather wistfully told the journalist that 'I love to work, and it's nice to have the money', stating that he enjoyed working in an ensemble and had taken the part of local official

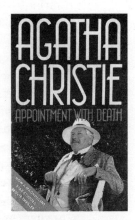

Peter Ustinov featured on a photo cover produced by Fontana for the film.

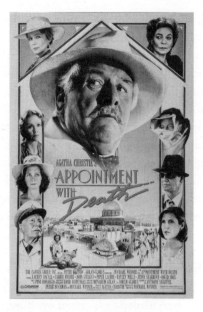

Appointment with Death movie poster (1988).

Colonel Carbury because both Bacall and Ustinov asked him to, even if the character was 'one of the least rewarding I have ever played'. Bacall, returning to film after many years working on stage, reflected that 'We all have to pay the rent' and that Winner didn't 'do anything for actors, except make you nervous'.

The film starts with an outlandish but entertaining cliché with the reading of a will during a thunder storm, while Piper Laurie's pantomime villain take on eventual victim Mrs Boynton sets the tone of the film as embracing excess and melodrama, with little attempt at realism for either setting or characters. Had the film continued along these lines then it might have been good fun, albeit out of keeping with the psychological drama of the original novel. Instead, it soon descends into a rather dull film that fails to be either an exciting mystery nor an enjoyable period piece. The review in *The Guardian* pondered that the film had not been able to solve 'the problem of how to convert this sort of dated who-dunnit to anything resembling valid cinematic currency'.[38] Tabloid newspaper *Today* called it an 'appointment with abject boredom', while the *Evening Standard* concurred with most reviewers by blaming the director first and foremost: 'Winner switches locations more competently than he shuffles suspects and serves the needs of Israeli tourism better than the interests of justice.'[39] In summary, *The Times* felt that the film 'cannot be counted even a moderate success'.[40] The film performed poorly at the box office success, but did achieve one important (albeit unwanted) distinction when Mathew Prichard declared it to be 'quite the worst Agatha Christie film I have ever seen'.[41]

It seemed to all involved that Peter Ustinov's take on Poirot had reached the end of his successful screen life. 'It's not my ambition to spend my life playing Poirot, but I'd be a little annoyed if anyone else did him now,' he told Andrew Duncan on set.[42] However, with Miss Marple finding her way to television with a series of prestige productions made by the BBC, the Christie board was keen to reinvent Poirot along similar lines, and they were fortunate that such an idea had also occurred to television producer Brian Eastman. Together, they would create what would become for many the definitive screen portrayal of Christie's Belgian sleuth.

Agatha Christie's Poirot
(Television series 1–6, 1989–1997)

Television was calling Hercule Poirot in the 1980s, but his guardians were not always responding. In 1982 Golden Eagle Films, which would later make the series *Dempsey and Makepeace*, pitched *The Mysteries of Hercule Poirot*, which would have drawn on the short stories featuring the detective and been produced by Tony Wharmby. However, this wasn't the right time for Agatha Christie Ltd to approve the proposed run of thirteen episodes, which incorporated a range of mysteries with the alternating categories of 'Murder', 'Kidnap', 'Jewel Theft' and 'Disappearance'. Nevertheless, by late 1984 Rosalind in particular was starting to soften when it came to the idea of a Poirot series, as

ABOVE: David Suchet. enjoying 'Hercule Poirot's Christmas' (1994).

she mentioned to the producer of the new BBC *Miss Marple* series, Guy Slater, that 'someone has put a feeler out for a Poirot series,' and that 'it could be well done too in a different way'.[43] This was something of a breakthrough when it came to Rosalind's feelings regarding Poirot on television, but although the BBC had been desperate for such a series just a few years earlier, Slater wasn't as keen. He wrote to his superior that 'I haven't read [the Poirot stories] since I was at school but my impression is he's too cold a fish as a character to sustain a series.'[44]

One place where Poirot was always welcome at the BBC was on the radio, and on 29 December 1985 Maurice Denham starred as the detective in the first of a six-episode dramatisation of *The Mystery of the Blue Train* on Radio Four. This polished and faithful adaptation was followed the next year by *Hercule Poirot's Christmas*, this time with Peter Sallis playing the lead in a ninety-minute production on Christmas Eve 1986. In 1987 a third Poirot was cast for the Christmas Christie adaptation, John Moffatt, who would appear in the famously difficult-to-adapt *The Murder of Roger Ackroyd* on Christmas Eve 1987, with John Woodvine as the narrator Dr Sheppard. Moffatt then stayed in the role until 2007, joined by Jeremy Clyde and Simon Williams as Captain Hastings, and Stephanie Cole and Julia McKenzie as Ariadne Oliver. Chief Inspector Japp was portrayed by Norman Jones and Bryan Pringle, as well as Philip Jackson who continued the role that he was also playing in the ITV series.[45]

For many fans, this BBC radio series would become some of the strongest Poirot adaptations, and it isn't difficult to see why. The productions follow the original stories closely, and benefit from high quality cast members working

John Moffatt, BBC radio's Poirot for 20 years.

MYSTERY! PRESENTS AGATHA CHRISTIE'S

POIROT
SERIES IV

A DETECTIVE
OF DISTINCTION
STARRING
DAVID SUCHET
HOST: DIANA RIGG

An Eight-Part Series
Begins Sunday
November 22, 8 PM

KOCE 50
TELEVISION

Mobil

PBS secured Diana Rigg to host the Poirot series in the *Mystery!* slot when it launched on American television in January 1990, continuing for several series.

from excellent scripts by Michael Bakewell. The written word is also inherently easier to bring to the radio than the screen or stage, as it doesn't require the additional flourishes and practicalities that need to be addressed when making a story more visual. This may also explain why it is the favourite form of many, who enjoy its close relationship to the original text while still being brought alive in another dimension. Perhaps a little of Agatha Christie's subtlety is lost in the mix, but there will always need to be a trade-off when transferring stories from the page.

In terms of television, 1985 saw a new pitch for a lavish series, which this time would have adapted the linked short story collection *The Labours of Hercules* in an ambitious production that would have been filmed across Europe. Producer Brian Eastman was approached by Terri Winders, who had worked at the BBC as a floor manager but was now working independently, and with actor Mario Adorf sought assistance to help turn their idea into a reality through his company Picture Partnership Productions. Eastman agreed, and Winders contacted agent Brian Stone in order to arrange a meeting to discuss the plans. The pitch document for the series stated that it would be an Anglo-European production, with Adorf to play Poirot. The pitch also suggested that this Poirot should be younger and more vibrant than had been seen on screen previously, and that European audiences would appreciate the classical connotations of this selection of mysteries, while British audiences would apparently find pleasure in their superiority over Poirot's foreign eccentricities. 'It would have been incredibly difficult to do,' Brian Eastman now concedes. 'To make an hour out of each of those stories would have been very, very difficult.'[46] Nevertheless, a meeting then took place between Eastman, Winders, Adorf and both Rosalind and her husband Anthony Hicks, which would establish Poirot's small-screen future in an unexpected way. After Adorf and Winders left the meeting Rosalind revealed to Eastman that she wasn't keen on this particular plan, but that perhaps she could discuss a different approach with him. So was born *Agatha Christie's Poirot*, the series that would debut in 1989 and become for many the definitive portrayal of the detective on screen. Although Brian Eastman met with the BBC's Michael Grade in late 1985 to discuss the potential of working with them on the new series (with Grade suggesting Richard Dreyfuss as the lead), plans progressed no further, and in the end the programme looked towards the commercial broadcaster ITV instead.[47]

Many of the subsequent discussions about the series in this very early stage of development concerned the fidelity of the series, and in particular what changes Agatha Christie Ltd would allow. While Mathew Prichard had scoped out the likelihood of interest for a variety of scenarios, Rosalind was adamant that only close adaptations would be acceptable. In November 1985 Rosalind wrote to another member of the company's board that:

I did not know that Mathew had discussed with publishers in the UK, US and France what their reaction would be to a series with genuine Christie material or with *made-up* stories using Agatha Christie characters. I am horrified at the suggestion even – it seems to give people ideas that such a situation might arise when you might consider such an idea. I seem to remember there was general agreement at a previous meeting that Agatha Christie should *not* be treated in this way. I'm sure Anthony [also a member of the board] can and will answer for himself – I am equally sure he would never agree to anyone using Agatha Christie's characters in any way.[48]

In the end, there was no serious consideration that the series would feature entirely new stories. However, other issues concerning the series' fidelity were more concerning for those involved, especially in a programme that would be expanding some very slight stories to an hour of television. As Eastman points out, 'some of the stories are so insubstantial' and that while they are 'fine as a read' a producer needs to be aware of the difference between an entertaining short story and what's needed for the television audience.[49] This required some essential consideration of how the stories would be expanded, and both Eastman and Agatha Christie Ltd spent several months grappling with what would and what would not be permitted. Other issues concerned finances and the number of episodes, as well as the interpretation of Poirot. Mathew pointed out that some actors would be unacceptable – Peter Ustinov, for example, whose portrayal had 'outlived his use', or a comedy turn from, say ('and I really have plucked this from thin air!') Frankie Howerd. 'On the other hand, we must not use our veto lightly,' he went on to say, although all involved would be mindful of the fact that one particular name was already in mind – David Suchet. Rosalind had considered the actor when meeting with Nick Evans about *Murder by the Book* in 1984, and the idea was further cemented in her meeting with Brian Eastman, as Eastman had produced the series *Blott on the Landscape* in which Suchet had starred in 1985. However, Mathew also wondered if the various issues made it impossible to continue, and drew attention to the board's priorities:

It is unquestionably the most important item on the agenda for ACL at the moment to find a successor to the BBC *Marple* of equal stature and quality. I believe that this will be exceedingly difficult to find, and in order to do so we shall have to be guided by our nose far more than by our lawyer. We shall do our best not to be constricted by too many self-made rules, and to be guided far more by our collective judgement of whether a particular man or company is likely to produce, with discreet assistance, the genuine article.

In the midst of the contractual wrangling and a seeming sudden loss in confidence in the project, Mathew asked 'Guy Slater, where are you?', referring to the producer of the BBC *Miss Marple* series who had already signalled his lack of interest in Poirot adaptations.[50] In the end both parties gradually made compromises, although the introduction of regular characters (such as Captain Hastings) to stories in which they didn't originally appear was a recurrent sticking point, to the frustration of Eastman. As an experienced producer he knew that these regulars would be essential to bring many of the short stories to the screen, while the copyright holders still felt burned by events of two decades earlier when such clauses had been exploited by MGM to the horror of Christie herself, as well as Rosalind.

In December 1985 Rosalind and Anthony Hicks sat down to consider which titles would be best for the first run of ten stories, following an initial list of suggestions from Brian Eastman. Their choices weren't entirely guided by the stories they felt would make the best drama – instead, a strong aspect of their initial rationale

Poirot Investigates in a Granada paperback that evoked the *Early Cases* edition (1983).

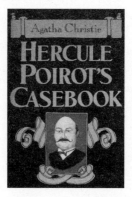

Dodd, Mead collected all 50 Poirot stories in one book for the first time in 1984.

was that the mysteries in the first run should not be taken from the 1923 *Poirot Investigates* collection, but instead from later collections, with *Poirot Investigates* held in reserve. Their first idea was that all stories should come from *Poirot's Early Cases* and *Murder in the Mews*, which could then be reissued in the UK to accompany the series, while a special collection could be published in the United States. Additionally, at this point Rosalind was still keen that characters should only appear in stories where they originally featured, and they didn't want Captain Hastings or Inspector Japp to appear in more than five of the first series' ten episodes. They didn't like Eastman's suggestion of 'The Kidnapped Prime Minister', not only because it hailed from *Poirot Investigates*, but also because they judged it to be 'far-fetched'. They also felt that 'The Dream' was 'weak' and had the problem of not featuring Hastings in the original story, while they were also not keen on 'The Third Floor Flat', which was felt to be 'poor', lacking in Poirot and 'out of tune' with the others (in the end both stories would be filmed for the first series). The Hicks' own initial list included a couple of titles that would not be adapted until later series, including 'Double Sin' and 'The Double Clue', while the 'finalised' list featured 'Dead Man's Mirror' and 'The Affair at the Victory Ball', neither of which ended up being in this first run, but both of which they were keen on. They liked the first because it would have meant all four stories from the *Murder in the Mews* collection would have been included in this first series, and the latter because it was judged to be a good story. In the end, 'Dead Man's Mirror' became one of the very last short stories to be filmed for the programme, while 'The Affair at the Victory Ball' appeared in the third series. More surprising was the fact that 'The Lemesurier Inheritance' was cited as a possible alternative for 'The Third Floor Flat', as 'The Lemesurier Inheritance' was not adapted for the programme – by the time of the second season it no longer featured on the shortlist of possible titles, although it would be considered again later in the run. Once the series moved into production two stories from *The Adventure of the Christmas Pudding* had been added, 'The Dream' and 'Four and Twenty Blackbirds'. Brian Eastman had been keen to ensure that there was a mix of Poirot mystery types (as not all involved a murder) for not just this first run, but also any subsequent ones, and so he sketched out an idea of how each subsequent series could offer a good variety.

The first script to be written was one of the mysteries without a murder, 'The Adventure of Johnnie Waverly', which involves the kidnapping of the titular child. Although the rather stronger 'The Adventure of the Clapham Cook' was the first episode shown, 'The Adventure of Johnnie Waverly' is a good example of the challenges that had to be overcome in making the series – namely the fact that Christie's original short mysteries are often very slight (in this case, running to only thirteen pages in *Poirot's Early Cases*) and require considerable embellishment. Eastman's first thought had been to approach Anthony Shaffer, given his successful screenplays for Ustinov's Poirot, but the writer declined the offer. His discussions with screenwriter Clive Exton were more promising, however, as Exton was a fan of Agatha Christie who also had a strong vision for how the scripts could work. Exton's previous work had included the likes of 10 *Rillington Place* (1971) and *Dick Barton: Special Agent* (1979), while he would later write all twenty-three episodes of *Jeeves and Wooster* (1990–93), once again for Brian Eastman. Although he didn't write every episode of *Poirot*, Exton became the touchstone for the scripting side of the series, later joined by Anthony Horowitz. Exton was particularly skilled at tying different strands of the story together for an hour of television, including an adeptness for the closing coda (which often humorously resolves a character's subplot), which he sometimes wrote for other people's scripts when they realised how difficult it actually was to resolve everything in a light-hearted manner. The 'Johnnie Waverly' script was used in order to pitch the series to various broadcasters, and it was Nick Elliott at London Weekend Television who agreed to go into a partnership with Eastman's Picture Partnership Productions (later Carnival Films) and Agatha Christie Ltd to make the series.

One area that required surprisingly little effort was that of casting Poirot himself, as David Suchet was the only name seriously considered by both Rosalind Hicks and Brian Eastman. Nevertheless, Rosalind needed to be completely sure, as her son Mathew later recalled:

> David will tell you, even to this day, how he was summoned to Greenway to be interviewed, and even in those days he was not accustomed to that. David convinced my mother that if he was going to do this he was going to do it in a properly authentic way, read all the Poirot books, read how he walked and talked etc., and constantly be there to protect the original image of Poirot on screen.[51]

This wasn't Suchet's first brush with Poirot, as he'd played Japp in the Peter Ustinov television movie *Thirteen at Dinner* a few years earlier, but it was immediately obvious that the Belgian detective was a rather better fit for the actor. Suchet took some time to consider if taking on the part was the right move for him, especially following warnings from his older brother John, but as he wrote later, 'the more I thought about the man in Dame Agatha's books, the more convinced I became that I could bring the true Poirot to life on the screen, a man no audience had seen before.'[52] After the casting was announced in March 1988 Suchet undertook a series of screen tests, to assess his styling (including the important moustache), voice and preferred walk amongst other factors – Rosalind was delighted with the results. On set, Suchet would take the part so seriously that he didn't like to slip out of character between takes, while he also retained a list of Poirot's characteristics that he had written down during his reading of the stories.

By this point Eastman had also won the battle over the supporting characters, who he felt were essential to the series. While initially there were thoughts that Poirot could have been accompanied by his valet George as well as Hastings and Japp, concerns that this would veer too far into *Jeeves and Wooster* territory meant that occasional secretary Miss Lemon became a more regular presence in the series instead

The 'gang of four' – Philip Jackson, David Suchet, Hugh Fraser and Pauline Moran filming *Peril at End House*.

Hercule Poirot's Casebook collected together the stories from the first series (1990).

(with George arriving much later), despite her few appearances alongside Poirot in print. For Brian Eastman, this cast of supporting characters 'became a very important element of the show, and the interaction between the team was really what the audience was relating to,' he explains. 'That was not felt by [Agatha Christie Ltd], they felt that we went too far with that, but I thought our success was very largely based on audiences coming back each week to see the team's interaction.'[53] As the series went on, so trust in Eastman developed, and there was a slightly more relaxed approach to new (or previously absent) characters appearing in the adaptations. For many, the gently sparring but warm relationship between David Suchet's Poirot, Hugh Fraser's Hastings, Philip Jackson's Japp and Pauline Moran's Miss Lemon were indeed a large part of the attraction of the show, and certainly enabled it to feel like a more welcoming world for Sunday evening viewing.

Filming for the series began in July 1988, initially under the title *Hercule Poirot's Casebook*, which it retained in several pieces of pre-transmission publicity, and even some early reviews, as well as a tie-in story collection. A decision was made to situate the series in 1936 for the most part, with a 1930s modern look. 'If you concentrate on one year it gives the show a real identity,' Brian Eastman points out, especially considering that the 1930s spans everything from the financial crash to the outbreak of the Second World War.[54] While some have wondered why the series stuck to one year for so long, Mathew Prichard explains that 'You can't expect the audience to move at will. If my mother had had her way I think we would have tried to do the books in the period as written, but you can't really. How do you keep the public up with you? The public don't care a damn when the books were written.'[55] The visual appeal of the series was an important factor in its production, and the healthy budget of £5m for the ten episodes was a big part of LWT's heavily signalled investment in drama in the late 1980s. This was a crunch time for British broadcasting as new regulations to assist independent production companies came into place, just as regional franchises for the ITV network were being put out to tender. The partnership between Eastman's company and LWT meant that there were still some surprises for the producer, who did not have full control over the budget. He particularly recalls a strikingly ambitious scene in 'The Adventure of the Clapham Cook' which featured many vintage cars and pedestrians in period dress crossing a London bridge:

Hercule Poirot's Casebook was redesigned then reissued as Agatha Christie's Poirot Book One (1991).

> When I went down that afternoon to see them shooting it I thought, this is ridiculous! That's the difference with it being an in-house production, I didn't have full control of the budget and the art department were prone to doing things of their own accord. To my eye that just looks silly, too much traffic and too many pedestrians on one London bridge, and it distracts from the story.[56]

Such excesses were curtailed as the series moved on, but it remained lavishly produced. After an early viewing of this episode Mathew Prichard was effusive in his praise, writing to Eastman that 'Of special significance, I felt, was the atmosphere created ... If this episode is a fair foretaste of the rest of the series then no wonder LWT are keen!'[57] Mathew also remembered the project that had first brought Eastman to

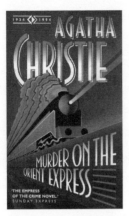

the family, as he expressed his hope that *The Labours of Hercules* would be attempted at some point, even if it required an unusual broadcasting pattern. Unfortunately, in the end this selection of short stories wouldn't be given the chance to shine, as it was eventually reduced to a single film long after Eastman left the programme.

The high quality extended to the award-winning title sequence, made at a cost of £50,000, as well as the evocative saxophone-led score by Christopher Gunning. Even Poirot's block of flats, Whitehaven Mansions, became a well-known piece of iconography for the programme.

The title sequence inspired the look of HarperCollins' 60th Anniversary paperback of *Murder on the Orient Express* in 1994.

However, the filming of most of the establishing shots for the whole series took place in one forty-eight-hour period, during which lighting, curtains, pedestrians and cars were all adjusted to provide a selection of footage that would be drawn on for years to come, as renovations at the block meant that any future footage of it would need to be carefully shot.

The series debuted on the ITV network on 8 January 1989, accompanied by a wave of publicity, which included several interviews with the cast (in which Suchet confessed that he had watched other portrayals of Poirot, so that he could adequately differentiate himself from them) and an ongoing discussion of the lengths the production went to in order to get period details correct.[58] After transmission, the critical and popular reaction was exceptionally positive. The first series didn't stray from ITV's top twenty programmes of the week, often taking a spot in the top ten, while even the sniffiest reviewers found themselves swept away by the quality of the production. *The Daily Star* headlined its preview 'The Case of the Perfect Poirot', while the *Daily Express*'s reviewer joyfully opened with her feeling that 'It is very exciting when you finally see the definitive portrayal of a well-loved character ... Poirot now lives.'[59] Alan Coren in *The Mail on Sunday* called the programme 'A triumph', and insisted that not only had Suchet improved on the likes of Peter Ustinov in the role, but that Clive Exton had improved on Agatha Christie's dialogue.[60] In *The Guardian* Nancy Banks-Smith ruminated on an old mystery highlighted by the series:

> The subject we have to address today is one of crime's strangest unsolved mysteries. What kind of moustache did Hercule Poirot wear? Was it a dizzying succession of interlocking circles like an exploding watch? Did it leap out left and right like wild horses trying to tear him apart? Did it stay aloft by its own built-in bounce or was it artificially assisted? Or was it the laughably small moustache affected by David Suchet in *Hercule Poirot's Casebook*?[61]

Despite her reservations about his facial hair, Banks-Smith considered Suchet's performance to be 'magnificent'. Positive interest in the series also came from abroad, including approaches from both Russia and America to have Suchet star as Poirot in local productions (a television series and feature film, respectively).

Certainly the first series of *Agatha Christie's Poirot* makes an uncommonly good job of immediately establishing itself as a high quality, hugely entertaining and lavish television series. It shows fidelity to Christie's original stories where it matters while suitably embellishing them in order to make the mysteries suitable for an hour of television. The selection of stories is brave but sensible – some excellent puzzles are presented, with a good selection that belies the

Anne Hart's lively fictionalised biography of Poirot was published by Pavilion in 1990.

fact that there was already a hope that the series would have a long run, and so didn't need to frontload the most obviously appealing mysteries. As a result, murders feature alongside a theft and kidnapping, while the series skilfully navigates the line between the comforting nature of the lead characters (whose relationships are not all quite as warm as they'll become) and a willingness to preserve the brutality of the reality of murder. Despite moments of comedy, this isn't a series that's dismissive of the real distress caused by crime, whatever its type. While Poirot understandably plays the most active part in the investigations, his companions in detection each get their own chance to shine in a series that makes good use of its ensemble characters, but never forgets who the star is. This is an approach that extends to the guest cast, almost exclusively made up of strong character actors who were nevertheless not household names, even if their faces may be familiar – a deliberate decision in order to not distract from the mysteries and Poirot himself.

Dropping the Casebook title, *Agatha Christie's Poirot Book Two* tied in with the second series.

Following the positive reaction LWT could breathe a sigh of relief, because plans were already afoot for more *Poirot* episodes. For this second run, which debuted in January 1990, producer Brian Eastman decided to make the launch a more eye-catching event by opening with the first feature-length episode (a decision supported by Agatha Christie Ltd). Although *The Murder on the Links* was considered as a 1989 Christmas special, the first novel to be adapted was *Peril at End House*, a strong choice for a season opener. [62] This summery story (partially filmed in Salcombe, Devon) has a surprising and cold-hearted villain at its core and was an excellent choice to open the second run, with the subsequent eight episodes drawing on stories from both *Poirot's Early Cases* and, at last, *Poirot Investigates*.[63] The series also featured the three regulars in support of Poirot on a more permanent basis, with Japp, Hastings and Miss Lemon appearing in every episode, unlike in the first series.[64] However, these supporting characters were to be an ongoing bone of contention, especially from Rosalind Hicks. In response to the script for *Peril at End House* she wrote to Eastman that 'I consider as a general comment that Hastings is getting much sillier which is a pity. I consider Miss Lemon should sit in the office and not dabble in yoga or go to St Loo looking "very chic" in a travelling suit, or be made to hold a séance.'[65] The family's objections to the frequent presence of Miss Lemon would be a recurring complaint over the coming years, but for television the appearances of Poirot's companions allowed the series to function as a single entity more effectively. They also helped to paper over the cracks between a series of stories that are inevitably inconsistent in every sense, including the quality of story, tone, characters and the types of mystery on display. While it's understandable that Rosalind would wish to protect her mother's works from changes that she deemed to be unnecessary or excessive, while also ensuring that Poirot remained the star of his own series, there is also much to be said for the reassuring comfort of reacquainting ourselves with old friends.

1990 was a bumper year for Poirot, and Agatha Christie more generally, as it marked a hundred years since the author's birth and many of the celebrations took place in Torquay, Devon, where she was born and lived for many years. The centrepiece of the centenary events was the Orient Express arriving from London, carrying the main cast of *Poirot*, which culminated with David Suchet stepping off the train in character in order to meet Joan Hickson's Miss Marple. On television, Brian Eastman convinced ITV to commission a special episode to mark to occasion, as the series turned back the clock in order to dramatise Poirot's first case, *The Mysterious Affair at Styles*, in an accomplished production that was shown almost precisely one hundred years after Christie's birth.[66] With the assistance of the make-up and wardrobe department a younger Poirot and Hastings meet each other in a production that immediately feels different due to the change of period to 1917, with newsreel footage sitting alongside newly shot material that shows troops and vintage vehicles a stone's throw from St Paul's Cathedral. These establishing shots give a sense of scale and importance to a story that subsequently becomes much more focused as a country house mystery. We are reminded of the traumas and devastation that united our amiable Captain with the Belgian detective prior to their first case, which gives the viewers a greater understanding of the men. This is an important piece of context for the audience when watching the lighter escapades that followed two decades later and form the bulk of the series, as it is made clear that our lead characters haven't led completely sheltered lives.

The third series continued the successful pattern of the earlier adaptations, with its ten one-hour episodes beginning transmission in January 1991. The programme continued to present a polished selection of mysteries for the screen in its confident take on Christie's stories.[67] Discussions with Rosalind Hicks continued, and there were frequent cordial but strongly worded differences of opinion regarding both minor points of dialogue and description, as well as more significant ones of characterisations and tone. A recurring complaint of Rosalind's was a general objection to elements that she considered to be silly (an exception being the similarity between Poirot and the 'Lucky Len' of a newspaper in the fifth series' 'Jewel Robbery at the Grand Metropolitan', which she enjoyed). Rosalind was quite candid with Eastman about stories that she considered that were weaker and so not as good candidates for adaptation, including 'The Cornish Mystery', 'How Does Your Garden Grow?', 'Double Sin' and 'The Mystery of Hunter's Lodge'. For the latter, she wrote that 'I have never thought this was a good story but I didn't realise that it could become quite such an impossible tale', clearly believing that changes made to it had not been for the better.[68] More positive comments were made about 'The Adventure of the Egyptian Tomb', 'Wasps' Nest' and 'The Theft of the Royal Ruby', which Rosalind felt were particularly strong candidates for screen adaptation. As an experienced producer who knew what worked well for television, Brian Eastman did not always agree with these comments, but always respected them. There had never been any doubt that compromises would need to be made in order to bring Poirot to television on a weekly basis, simply because what works well on screen isn't necessarily what works well on the page. Short stories normally required expansion and the addition of newly scripted subterfuge to keep the mystery interesting while never threatening a resolution too early. Often, new subplots would be introduced to create a marriage between entertaining Sunday night viewing for a general audience and the core puzzle and key characters depicted by Christie. Sometimes this is where Hastings, Japp or Miss Lemon would be given the chance to make new acquaintances – some of whom are inevitably destined for the gallows before the end credits roll. The discussions between producer and Agatha Christie Ltd were usually about the nature of these compromises, and there is no single approach taken by every adaptation.

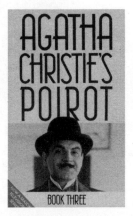

Agatha Christie's Poirot Book Three continued to attract new readers to the stories.

The presence of 'The Plymouth Express' in the third series

might indicate that there wasn't the expectation that the programme would complete the entire run of Poirot stories as this story was expanded into the novel *The Mystery of the Blue Train*, and generally the programme picked expanded versions of mysteries to adapt if more than one existed. However, the following fourth series showed that the programme was also happy to try something new, as instead of ten episodes, three feature-length mysteries were made for 1992. This came about for various reasons, including the availability of David Suchet, who hadn't been placed under option and decided to commit to stage work, while Brian Eastman was also busy on a variety of film and television projects. ITV also had a say on such matters, and discovered that high quality productions in a two-hour slot were particularly appealing for advertisers, who felt that the viewers of such programmes were more attentive. The first of the three was *The ABC Murders*, which may be considered to be one of the very best Poirot adaptations. The production is a taut thriller as well as an intriguing mystery, which emphasises the best elements of Christie's original story while ensuring that the pace was not dented by the necessary episodic nature of the story. This was followed by *Death in the Clouds*, a novel that is a good candidate for a visual retelling with its emphasis on the location of characters and objects, the script of which sensibly expands and reduces events as necessary to maintain the attention. The final episode, *One, Two, Buckle My Shoe*, fares a little less well by comparison, at least in part due to not being a particularly strong tale for the screen, lacking a strong visual hook (beyond the torturing of Poirot in the dentist's chair). These three productions exposed the benefits and risks of adapting full novels that require different pacing and structure to the short stories, which only had to sustain the attention for an hour, and so could sprinkle character moments and subplots that were designed to entertain only briefly alongside the central mystery. For two hours of television (between 90 and 100 minutes without adverts), a different structure and approach was needed. The novels usually boasted a large cast of characters that generally needed to be reduced in order for the story to be properly portrayed as a television production, while the plotting needed to have a series of peaks in order to maintain the interest and quicken the pace. This is where a second murder could so often come in handy, and explains why *The ABC Murders* works so well on screen, with new locations and new murders sweeping the story along.

The fifth series in 1993 saw a return to the hour-long adaptations of short stories, which almost completed the set. Those involved in the series must have been grateful for Brian Eastman's foresight when it came to the choice of stories, as it meant that a good selection of mysteries could be filmed.[69] By this point nine eligible short stories remained, and while initially this was supposed to be a series of six episodes, LWT then increased the commission to eight, which meant that one story would be left unadapted. Although 'The Lemesurier Inheritance' had featured on the shortlist of stories for the programme's first and second series, as well as the list of titles to be offered to LWT for the fifth run, in the end it lost out. By November 1991 an agreement had been reached about six titles, which meant that Brian Eastman was left with three further 'possible' stories, of which he needed to adapt two. Mathew Prichard was pragmatic about the development, even if it meant agreeing to titles that had previously been declined: 'My own feelings are that we have to have very good reasons to say no and that 8 stories does make a better series than 6,' he wrote to his mother and stepfather. He also pointed out that, although Anthony had apparently objected to the use of 'Yellow Iris' because elements were later reworked as the non-Poirot novel *Sparkling Cyanide*, a British television adaptation of the story might expunge the memory of the American television movie of the novel from 1983.[70] 'Yellow Iris' had also experienced a new lease of life when it was included in the 1991 Christie collection *Problem at Pollensa Bay*, and so its inclusion in the series would make sense. The result of these discussions was that 'Jewel Robbery at the Grand Metropolitan' and 'Yellow Iris' became the final two mysteries for this fifth run and – because it was considered to be a 'poor' story – 'The Lemesurier Inheritance' lost out on its chance to be a part of the series.

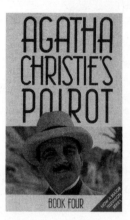

Book Four tied in with the fifth series, and finished the run of short story tie-ins.

There's no avoiding the fact that Christie reused themes and ideas throughout her career, and by this time the types of stories seen would have felt very familiar to the casual viewer, no matter how they were arranged, with the exception of 'The Chocolate Box', which had Poirot recall a case from his younger days. The series had always been a visually stylish one, and taking Poirot back to Belgium in his younger days is one way that the series could maintain its freshness, as did other forays abroad (such as southern Spain standing in for Egypt in the series opener, 'The Adventure of the Egyptian Tomb'). Nevertheless, perhaps it was for the best that more heavyweight material in the form of the novels would need to be drawn on in the future. However, the series' adaptation of the very brief story 'The Case of the Missing Will' initiated a lengthy correspondence with Brian Eastman. There were not only objections to elements of the mostly newly created plot that Rosalind felt was 'a very bad story, a pure fabrication', but most of all a horrified reaction to the original plans to have Poirot share a stage with Oswald Mosley as part of a debate (in which Poirot would have spoken against the fascist).[71] Even the downgrading of Poirot to an observer wasn't enough to satisfy Rosalind and Mathew, who disliked seeing Poirot mix with real-life politics, especially of Mosley's type. In the end Eastman had to concede the strength of their feelings and removed the character entirely. Mosley had been included in order to make the series seem fresh and interesting to casual viewers, and when the fifth series concluded with 'Jewel Robbery at the Grand Metropolitan' in March 1993 it was clear that there would have to be something of a change in direction for a programme that had principally been presented as an ongoing series at this point. Not only were some of the creatives involved getting a little restless, but ITV was also scrutinising its accounts more closely than ever.

The sixth series consisted of more feature-length adaptations, and it was initially difficult to work out which they should be as at this point Rosalind and Anthony Hicks wanted to offer only titles from the 1920s to 1940s, and were still opposed to having Hastings inserted into novels that he did not originally feature in (while also understanding that Eastman considered him to be an important element of the programme). As a result, *Dumb Witness*, *Murder on the Links* and *The Big Four* were proposed as three novels that fitted the bill.[72] The first two were duly adapted at this point, but *The Big Four* was swapped out for the more traditional mysteries *Hercule Poirot's Christmas* and *Hickory Dickory Dock*. Neither featured Hastings in either the novel or on screen, although Japp appears in both adaptations, as does Miss Lemon in the latter.[73] Probably chosen in the spirit of compromise, *Hickory Dickory Dock* therefore became the first of the post-Second World War Poirot novels to be adapted for the series, having been originally published in 1955. However, Eastman argued that a decision on moving the series beyond the 1930s should be postponed for the time being.[74]

Filming on the four titles began in March 1994, and the first, *Hercule Poirot's Christmas*, was shown on New Year's Day 1995. Up against strong competition, and perhaps hit by festive fatigue at this point in the seasonal schedules, it underperformed in the ratings, which panicked ITV.[75] Provisional plans for the following week had placed the next *Poirot* in the same slot, but it was quickly replaced by another crime drama, *A Touch of Frost*. At this point ITV was struggling to work out its priorities as a company that had undergone major changes since *Poirot* had begun in 1989., This included LWT losing some of its distinctive identity as ITV became a rather more monolithic company, rather than one made up of regional broadcasters. One accounting strategy would be to *Poirot's* particular detriment, as the cost of productions did not need to be registered until the programme was shown – and so if ITV wished to save some money, then it was an easy decision to push the relatively expensive *Poirot* into the next financial year. Although *Hickory Dickory Dock* was delayed only a month to February 1995, this loophole partially explains why twelve months then passed before the third of the new episodes (*Murder on the Links*) was shown, with *Dumb Witness* finally appearing in March 1997, almost three years after it was filmed. By this point the press was openly claiming that ITV had cancelled the programme, with the network only giving vague non-committal statements. Even the show's producers and Agatha Christie Ltd were unsure of the position, despite earlier attempts to sketch out a road map to the completion of the Poirot stories. To most observers it seemed like the end of the road for *Poirot*.

The Centenary Celebrations
(1990)

1990 marked a hundred years since Agatha Christie's birth, and while the events that marked the occasion are fondly remembered, the celebrations were perhaps more significant in the way that they marked a more concerted effort to maintain Christie's place in book shops and on bookshelves. This may have had its genesis a few years earlier, when Agatha Christie Ltd began negotiations with the author's first publisher, The Bodley Head, to buy back the publishing rights to the first six Christie titles. This would then allow a complete run of her stories to be licensed together and make such publishing deals rather more straightforward. The Bodley Head was in the midst of financial difficulties, and

ABOVE: Joan Hickson and David Suchet at Agatha Christie's 100th birthday celebrations in Torquay on 15 September 1990.

Agatha Christie: A Celebration marked 100 years with a selection of articles and a short story (1990).

the sale of the titles was only reluctantly agreed to after personal intervention by Mathew. This indicated an increasingly pragmatic approach to the exploitation of Christie's work, which was important as there was a feeling in some quarters that the Christie catalogue of books was not being handled as well as it could be. There was dissatisfaction with some covers and the fact that titles were being allowed to slip out of print for the first time since the Second World War.

The centenary helped to unleash a new lease of life for Agatha Christie books, spearheaded by the publication of a long-forgotten story, 'Trap for the Unwary', in a souvenir paperback for the celebrations. There were still a few Agatha Christie short stories that hadn't appeared in a major UK collection, although several of them had already been published in American books. Many of the uncollected stories were not mysteries, and nor did they tend to be among the author's best work, but their diversity said a lot about Christie's wide-ranging talents when it came to telling an entertaining tale. Eight of these stories were collected into 1991's *Problem at Pollensa Bay*. Poirot features twice in the book, first in 'The Second Gong', which had first been published in a 1932 edition of *Ladies' Home Journal*, before being expanded into the story 'Dead Man's Mirror' for Christie's 1937 collection *Murder in the Mews*.[76] The other story, 'Yellow Iris', had originally been written in 1937 alongside the radio play of the same name, and elements of it were reused for the non-Poirot novel *Sparkling Cyanide*.[77] Although the short story had appeared in the American collection *The Regatta Mystery* in 1939, this was its first appearance in a book in Christie's home country.

The specially created official logo for the centenary.

In 1987 permission was sought to publish the Poirot story 'Christmas Adventure' in an anthology called *Crime at Christmas*. This was an unexpected request because the story had been pretty much forgotten about, as it was better known in an expanded form as 'The Adventure of the Christmas Pudding', published in the book of the same name in 1960.[78] The original, shorter, version of the story was originally published in *The Sketch* in 1923, and in 1997 it finally appeared in another new UK collection, *While the Light Lasts*, as 'Christmas Adventure'.[79] Here it was published alongside 'The Mystery of the Baghdad Chest', the original shorter version of 'The Mystery of the Spanish Chest', the longer version of which had also appeared in *The Adventure of the Christmas Pudding*. (It would be another twenty-three years before 'Christmas Adventure' appeared in a US edition, in the seasonal collection *Midwinter Murder*.)

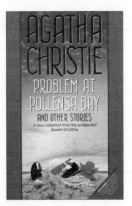

HarperCollins' *Problem at Pollensa Bay* featured two Poirot stories hitherto unpublished in a UK book (1991).

Several of Agatha Christie's lesser-known works were starting to have their time in the sun, and this included her Poirot play *Black Coffee*, which had slipped into relative obscurity. In part this was reversed by an adaptation of the script into a novel by Charles Osborne, published in 1998, which allowed her publishers to sell a 'new' Poirot book that had been constructed by Christie herself. Given Rosalind's dislike of others controlling her mother's creations, it's no surprise that the novel itself (which Osborne submitted unsolicited) is a straightforward retelling of the story for readers, and it even reproduced an only slightly amended version of the staging plan. However, the well of available stories was starting to run dry, and in the twenty-first century more difficult decisions would need to be made in order to maintain interest in Poirot and other Agatha Christie creations.

CHAPTER EIGHT:

2000 and
BEYOND

While Hercule Poirot has always been a popular literary character, the consistent appearance of David Suchet's performance on television screens across the world elevated his status even higher, reaching audiences far beyond those who would consider picking up an Agatha Christie book. However, the turn of the twenty-first century was also a time that required consideration of what the world of Poirot needed to be beyond the Suchet series, which itself was in a state of flux and reinvention. The character of Poirot is bigger than one man, perhaps even bigger than his creator, and new media afforded almost endless opportunities for him to maintain his status as the world's greatest detective.

OPPOSITE: Sir Kenneth Branagh brought Hercule Poirot back to the big screen for the first time in nearly 30 years with the ambitious box office success *Murder on the Orient Express* (2017).

Agatha Christie's Poirot
(Television series 7-8, 2000-2002)

The *Agatha Christie's Poirot* television series endured an enforced hiatus in the late 1990s, largely due to the whims of ITV. 'We never really understood why sometimes there were big gaps and why sometimes not,' Mathew Prichard admits. 'There was quite a bit of coming and going, ill-feeling even, between us and [series producer] Brian Eastman.'[1] Eastman had kept himself busy on other ventures while awaiting a new commission for the series, but was also working hard to find a solution to the impasse with the programme's broadcaster. He recalls that ITV 'never said to me "we don't want it" but they kept on saying "we haven't decided yet"':

ABOVE: The series regulars on location at Burgh Island for the filming of *Evil Under the Sun* (2001).

Eventually I got a bit fed up with that, and thought what can we do to push them into wanting it. I thought the way to do that was to bring more money to the table, so what had happened in America was that [public service broadcaster] PBS had bought the rights for all the early *Poirot* episodes. I must have gone to PBS and said if you want more, will you pay more for them, and will you tell me now so I can go to ITV and say PBS will pay more than they used to pay. PBS were not in a position to do that. But at that time their rival A&E had started to move into acquiring British programming, and they said if you bring it to us we will give you more money than PBS and we'll pay it up front. And they paid considerably more, so I went to ITV, and that did the trick.[2]

When the series returned to ITV in January 2000 it first tackled the novel that has often been called Christie's masterpiece, *The Murder of Roger Ackroyd*, a story that is famously difficult to translate to the screen or stage. The series had always needed to take a flexible approach to adaptation; for example, visual tricks and clues do not always work when staged rather than written, while literary devices designed to conceal and misdirect can be nearly impossible to transplant wholesale to the screen. In terms of Poirot himself the adaptations had always planned to neatly sidestep questions of his own age, even if the details of how this would be achieved were initially unclear. Nevertheless, it was agreed that no one was expecting to see Poirot investigate *Elephants Can Remember* in an adaptation set in the 1970s, when it was written and published.

The press greeted the return of Poirot to

The return of the series was heralded by two tie-in paperback covers in December 1999.

television warmly, even though this seventh run only consisted of two episodes. Over the years some fans have expressed their dissatisfaction with this particular adaptation, as have both David Suchet and Mathew Prichard. Certainly this version of *The Murder of Roger Ackroyd* struggles with the personal nature of the murderer and the way their relationship with various characters is expressed, but Brian Eastman felt that the adaptation worked around this innate difficulty as well as it could. Eastman points out that elements of the story are well known to much of the audience:

> So when Clive [Exton] wrote it first of all we had Selina Cadell [playing Caroline] as the narrator. She recorded the narration, which she did very well, and we put it all together and it just didn't work. So we were then faced with the choice, do we take out all of the narration? We came up with the idea that the diaries were in a vault somewhere, and Poirot discovered them ... I thought that was a big success and David did it very well. I don't think I'd do it differently now.[3]

Accompanying press articles did not allude to any drop in quality, and critics were pleased to see the next film in the series, *Lord Edgware Dies*, the following month. By this time reviewers were claiming to enjoy the perceived predictable nature of the adaptations ('The dialogue rings with the usual clichés', said *The Times* in its positive write-up), and saw the series as an old friend to be welcomed back into the home.[4] *Poirot* then returned with another two episodes for the eighth series, with *Evil Under the Sun* in 2001 (partially filmed at Burgh Island in Devon, one of the influences on the original book) and *Murder in Mesopotamia* the following year. *Evil Under the Sun*, which was actually filmed after *Mesopotamia*, would prove to be not only the last hurrah of

Hastings, Japp and Miss Lemon as regulars, but also Brian Eastman as producer, although he didn't know it at the time. Eastman had resolved the finance issues but Poirot would soon be in new hands.

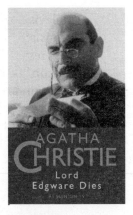

In 1998 the media group Chorion had purchased a 64% stake in Agatha Christie Ltd, which brought with it new priorities for the company. Chorion brought in a new Director of TV & Films, Phil Clymer, who felt strongly that the screen output needed to be modernised.⁵ To this end various projects were sketched out, including a Tommy and Tuppence venture that didn't make it into production, and a modernised American television movie of *Murder on the Orient Express*, which did. There had been some friction between the company and Eastman due to a perception from some at Agatha Christie Ltd that the programme was not receiving the attention it needed, although Eastman had also worked to ensure that *Poirot* could have a safe future with both A&E and ITV. There were even suggestions that perhaps Agatha Christie Ltd didn't need the services of an independent production company in order to bring *Poirot* to the screen with its partner broadcasters. In the end, the relationship with Eastman broke down, as he couldn't see a way to make the series as he wanted to in a way that made financial sense for him, while Agatha Christie Ltd was happy to start afresh. There had already been discussions about how the series could complete the Poirot stories (including, in some versions of the outline, the play *Black Coffee*), with Eastman sketching out a full seven-year plan. This would have moved Poirot beyond the Second World War, mixing up the better-known mysteries with those new to most of the audience, while also starting to gradually adapt the books featuring

Lord Edgware Dies for the millennium.

Ariadne Oliver in a way that wouldn't allow her to overshadow the character of Poirot. However, these plans would not be executed by Brian Eastman, who moved on from the series. Although this wasn't a happy ending to his work, years later Eastman was invited to attend the wrap party following the filming of the very last episode of *Agatha Christie's Poirot*, which allowed him to conclude his relationship with Agatha Christie on happier terms. However, at the time the situation left David Suchet in an awkward position, as he felt loyal to Eastman, but he was persuaded to stay as ITV brought in new producers for what would effectively be a new programme, albeit with Suchet still present in the title role. The next battle concerned the question of what would be meant by a 'modern' Poirot.

Murder on the Orient Express
(Television movie, 2001)

Perhaps the most enduring legacy of the 2001 television movie of *Murder on the Orient Express* is as a cautionary tale for those looking to find a new way to modernise Agatha Christie. Just as thoughts swirled about reworking the long-running David Suchet series, plans solidified to produce a new version of *Murder on the Orient Express* for a network television audience in America. Such opportunities were not to be sniffed at, as whatever the quality of the production it was bound to draw attention to Christie in a crowded market. This film combined television network desires for programming aimed at younger audiences with the then-recent decision to modernise Agatha Christie screen productions, as the setting for the story was changed to the present day. The

ABOVE: Alfred Molina as a twenty-first century Hercule Poirot.

International appeal: the very first paperback of *Murder on the Orient Express* was published in 1934 by the Albatross Crime Club.

casting of the esteemed Alfred Molina as Poirot was the first, and perhaps only, positive sign in the film's development.

The film opens with Poirot investigating the murder of a belly dancer in Istanbul, drawing on palindromes to solve the case. Once the murderer's identity is revealed Poirot flirts with a beautiful young Vera Rossakoff (a character not present in the novel); here, she's now a singer following her retirement as a jewel thief, and she longs for a life with Poirot. We soon meet the vile soon-to-be murder victim, Ratchett, who astutely understands the not-exactly-implicit meaning behind an anonymous telephone call which informs him that 'You're about to be a very dead man' ('Are you threatening me?' he asks, redundantly). After boarding the Orient Express, Ratchett recognises Poirot from the television show *Sleuth Supreme* (the format of which remains tantalisingly unexplained) before the train is forced to stop, although the novel's snowdrift appears to have been beyond the limits of the budget. Following Ratchett's murder Poirot insists on testing 'the limits of technology' when pushing a VHS tape into a portable TV combi unit. He then uses the internet to search for clues in a way that even a casual web user would have recognised as bearing no relation to reality, even in 2001. Poirot's explanation of the case (played out in front of ten suspects, rather than the book's twelve) is probably the best part of the film, with a nicely thought-out 'flashback' sequence that depicts the detective's alternative solution for the murder.

Some viewers will note that the opening caption reads 'From Agatha Christie', rather than 'By Agatha Christie', and this is a key indicator of their likely enjoyment of the production if they're looking for a close adaptation of the book. In its defence, the production makes no claims that it's faithful – indeed its *raison d'être* was to be an attempt to rework the basic narrative of an Agatha Christie story for an audience that relates more to the modern world than period trappings. However, the implementation of this is its greatest downfall. Rather than a contemporary retelling that presents a changing world in order to make it more applicable to an audience in the twenty-first century, instead we have heavy-handed attention paid to the likes of VHS tapes, handheld computers, home movies, and a laptop with a satellite internet connection. When a handheld

The unused HarperCollins tie-in book cover design from 2001.

computer stylus is presented as a clue and given portentous emphasis, the audience is more likely to be amused by such clunky attempts at modernity than impressed.

The film has been widely disparaged since its transmission, and although it contained hints that we might follow Molina's Poirot on another adventure, none were forthcoming on television. However, in 2021 Molina reprised the role in an audio adaptation of *The Murder on the Links* for L.A. Theatre Works. Joined by Simon Helberg as Captain Hastings, this time the production was well received, with *AudioFile* magazine claiming that of all the Poirot portrayals there had been 'none better than Alfred Molina here. His Poirot is still punctilious and obsessive, but also warm and funny'. After twenty years, Molina was finally able to give his definitive portrayal of the detective.

Agatha Christie's Poirot
(Television series 9-13, 2003-2013)

Having been placed very firmly in the background of ITV's priorities in the second half of the 1990s, there was an abrupt about-turn in *Poirot*'s fortunes in the early twenty-first century. In 2002 one of the broadcaster's major regional franchises, Granada, was soon to become one of the two dominant partners in a newly merged ITV that discarded most of the regional approach that had been the basic tenet of the network since its 1955 inception. The broadcaster's more explicit commercialism was partly motivated by the collapse of the digital subscription service OnDigital (later ITV Digital), which left a hole in its finances, and led to a rethinking of its business and transmission strategy. With

ABOVE: David Suchet with Toby Jones as Samuel Ratchett aboard the Orient Express (2010).

the David Suchet series generating £20m in revenue, *The Times* reported that 'Ailing Granada calls in Poirot', as the broadcaster announced four new adaptations featuring the detective to help its cause.[6]

A *Death on the Nile* tie-in featuring David Suchet on the cover (unpublished).

When Poirot returned in December 2003 in *Five Little Pigs* it was immediately apparent that new producers Michele Buck and Damien Timmer had overseen a change in strategy for the series. 'We thought, in the late 90s, they'd got rather tired and formulaic,' Mathew Prichard explains.[7] As a result the programme not only lost Miss Lemon, Hastings and Japp as regular sidekicks, but it was also imbued with more directorial flourishes than had been the case in earlier episodes, while the darker side of stories were often brought to the fore. This first adaptation under the new regime is one of this later era's best, with its powerful knitting together of themes, style and story. The changes didn't go unnoticed by critics, including *The Guardian*'s Gareth McLean, who outlined the traditional *Poirot* elements that the adaptation included, before writing:

> But wait. There's a twist in the plot, a swing in the tale. The camerawork was jittery, the direction terribly modern, the palette washed out. There was no moustache-waxing, no tie-straightening, no comedy-fastidiousness. There wasn't a hint of Captain Hastings or a whiff of Miss Lemon. Instead of picture-postcard vistas, we had painful, lingering close-ups. Jaunty out. Gritty in. *Poirot* has gone *NYPD Blue*. Christie's come over all *Cops*. It was all the better for it.[8]

It seemed that *Poirot* had managed to embrace the modern style in a way that echoed the most fashionable of contemporary television series. To an extent the direction of *Poirot* from this point on was dictated by the nature of the remaining stories to adapt, most of which were from after 1939 and tended to have a darker edge. The series needed to find a way to bring together a range of disparate novels in a programme that required at least some consistency of style. How can the same series create adaptations of the likes of action-adventure drama *The Big Four* (encompassing its own selection of shorter tales), swinging sixties concerns of *Third Girl*, and classic whodunnit *Death on the Nile*? There's then the added problem that some of the later mysteries require embellishing in order to make a feature-length adapta-

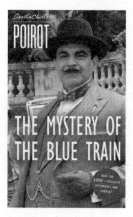

The tenth series began in 2006 with *The Mystery of the Blue Train*.

tion. There needed to be some uniformity of approach, and this often meant further exploration of characters with inevitably differing results of effectiveness, but generally an emphasis on hidden secrets and trauma. This was a darker, more vicious, but perhaps more stylish *Poirot*.

The next adaptation, *Sad Cypress*, certainly emphasised psychology in a thoughtful and well-structured film, which like its predecessor drew on a range of actors who would be familiar to the audience (such as Paul McGann and Rupert Penry-Jones), unlike the previous era of the show where well-known faces were actively avoided. In the increasingly cynical world of commercial television Poirot needed to remain fresh for audiences, and commercially appealing for broadcasters and advertisers. *Poirot* was expected to earn its keep, and even this close to the end it wasn't guaranteed that all the novels would be adapted. *Sad Cypress* was followed by *Death on the Nile*, which also broke another self-imposed rule of the earlier era – to generally avoid the 'big hitters' that already had a satisfactory film adaptation. Priorities had changed, and both the growing possibility that all Poirot novels would be filmed at some point, plus ITV's desire to exploit Poirot as much as possible, meant that one of the most famous Poirot novels was an obvious candidate. This take on the story was not afraid to highlight the sexual undertone to many of the characters and framed the ending in a way reminiscent of a Shakespearean tragedy. An accomplished take on *The Hollow* was then the final film in this run, completing an excellent choice of novels for this revived series, which successfully showcased the strengths of both Poirot and Christie.

New Year's Day 2006 saw the tenth series of *Poirot* begin with an adaptation of *The Mystery of the Blue Train* in a production that particularly emphasises directorial flourishes and a somewhat non-real-ist style. This adaptation had a longer genesis than most, as it had originally been written in the 1990s with the hope that it would be made as a cinema film. Brian Eastman even flew out to New York to see Sidney Lumet, director of the 1974 film of *Murder on the Orient Express*, to see if he would consider taking on the mantle again for this new film, although Lumet declined. Following this, *Cards on the Table* then saw a further reinvigoration of the series in the form of Zoë Wanamaker's performance of Ariadne Oliver, whose no-nonsense attitude and various

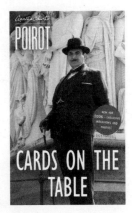

The *Cards on the Table* tie-in cover from HarperCollins (2006).

foibles enliven the adaptation of a novel that doesn't easily lend itself to the screen. The adaptation is also a prominent example of sexual proclivities being altered and emphasised for the series. *After the Funeral* then followed, a polished and nuanced take on one of Agatha Christie's most satisfying Poirot mysteries, while *Taken at the Flood* is forced to make alterations in order to fit the story into the pre-war setting but benefits from a strong cast. This adaptation also saw the series debut of Poirot's valet George, played by David Yelland, who then appears in a further six of the thirteen remaining films. By this point the production team had become used to finding ways to depict visual trickery (such as disguises) in a way that worked well on screen, often achieved through clever plotting as well as make-up and prosthetics; if one character is another person in disguise, then generally quite some time will elapse between seeing one and then the other.

More than two years passed before the eleventh series debuted in September 2008 with *Mrs McGinty's Dead*, which contrasts the brutal and serious criminal act at its core with lightness and commentary from Poirot on the world of the working classes that he usually avoided. This was followed by *Cat Among the Pigeons*, which successfully integrates Poirot earlier in proceedings than the novel had it, thanks to a script from Mark Gatiss that also allows for a more visual and striking method of murder for one unfortunate victim. *Third Girl* had often been cited as an example of a book so rooted in its period (in this case the 1960s) that many fans

David Suchet dons the famous moustache for his 2004 journey in *Death on the Nile*.

could not see how it could be effectively brought to the series' pre-war setting. However, Christie's mysteries rarely required specific settings in order to work, although the story undoubtedly loses some of its original charm by being moved three decades earlier. Such slight disappointments are nothing in comparison to *Appointment with Death*, an extraordinarily ill-conceived adaptation that overlooks the strongest elements of the novel in favour of unsophisticated embellishments, including the addition of a slave-trading nun. It's no surprise that it sat on the shelf at ITV for well over a year, even being released on DVD before the broadcaster finally showed it at the end of 2009.

By this point the range of Poirot books still to be filmed had been reduced to just nine titles, and those announced for the twelfth series made fans wonder if some would be too awkward for adaptation – unless they were being left until last. The four adaptations announced for this series were the 'Golden Age' classic *Three Act Tragedy*, followed by the macabre *Hallowe'en Party* from 1969, with its often sinister tone and ghoulish imagery benefiting any adaptation. ITV held its big title in reserve for the all-important Christmas schedules, as David Suchet's Poirot finally solved *Murder on the Orient Express* in a downbeat film that emphasises Poirot's character above all else. Adapting the more well-known titles was certainly a double-edged sword, as (along with *Death on the Nile* and *Evil under the Sun*) the most famous previous screen version is not only beloved and frequently seen, but could also boast a budget far above that available for even the most prestigious television productions. A different emphasis was needed, and for these three stories in particular the adaptations take a different approach to the earlier films that some fans may like less, but ensures that the series can't be accused of treading over old ground. A year then passed before *The Clocks* was shown, another 1960s novel that required a substantial reworking of contextual motivations due to the different political climate of the 1930s.

Poirot fans then collectively held their breath waiting for news of the remaining five Poirot books. These included one traditional Poirot mystery, *Dead Man's Folly*, as well as *Curtain: Poirot's Last Case*, which had to be left until the end for obvious reasons. The other three books each had their own issues – *Elephants Can Remember* was the final Poirot novel written by Christie, and it suffers from repetition and a dearth of plot. More problematic would be *The Big Four*, a collection of stories very loosely woven into an overarching narrative about international masterminds that is out of keeping with the stories and style that the rest of the series had featured. Meanwhile, *The Labours of Hercules* is a short story collection that has only a linking theme, not an overall story, and so would seem to be impossible to properly adapt in one film for two hours of television. When it was then announced that all of these final five books would indeed be produced for the last series of *Agatha Christie's Poirot*, no one was quite sure what to expect. Those who had advocated the inclusion of the play *Black Coffee*, a bona fide original Christie story starring Poirot, were pleased when David Suchet took part in a special event in order to attempt to have performed in all the major Poirot stories. Suchet appeared as Poirot in a reading of the play in Chichester, with David Yelland swapping his role of George in the series for Hastings on stage on 15 July 2012, supported by the Agatha Christie Theatre Company.

The first of the films to be shown, *Elephants Can Remember* in June 2013, proved to be a pleasant surprise to those who had assumed that any adaptation of such a weak novel would be a low point for the series. It sensibly introduces a new parallel plot with an additional murder, and is a rare example of an adaptation that improves on Christie's original work.

However, the transplanting of the story from the early 1970s to the 1930s makes a nonsense of musings on chemotherapy as an explanation for a character's wigs. The next film, *The Big Four*, then proves to be a last hurrah for the original Poirot ensemble, who appear together for the first time in over a decade. Miss Lemon, Captain Hastings, and Japp, now promoted to Assistant Commissioner, return in an adaptation that does all it can to try to bring the sprawling collection of stories into a logical single film that retains the spirit of the less outlandish sections of the novel. It's no surprise that Poirot's rather unbelievable 'twin', Achille, fails to make an appearance. Following this in transmission order was *Dead Man's Folly*, which was the final adaptation to be filmed. The original novel was set in a version of Christie's own house in Devon, Greenway, which by this point had been restored and opened to the public by the National Trust, and the production used the house and its surrounding locations for much of the filming. However, High Canons House in Hertfordshire was its double for many scenes as Greenway's steep lawn made it unsuitable for hosting a fête – and by a remarkable coincidence was the same house that had appeared as the Armstrong residence in the 1974 film of *Murder on the Orient Express*.

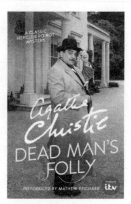

Dead Man's Folly, filmed at Greenway House, was one of two tie-in editions for the last series (2013).

It's an unfortunate irony that a programme that had started with a speculative idea about *The Labours of Hercules* as a series should wait until the penultimate film almost thirty years later for it to be brought to the screen. Inevitably, the condensation and consolidation of stories can't satisfy those who had so enjoyed the original short story collection. 'I think it was an absolute tragedy that Brian never did *The Labours of Hercules*,' Mathew Prichard says:

I did try but perhaps I should have tried harder. What I wanted them to do was to do them properly, perhaps you'd do ten over Christmas, and maybe you could have done it as a special. I think ITV wouldn't buy that, but then you couldn't persuade them what a jewel this was. You could only persuade them in terms of television scheduling. And when they finally did *Labours* it was a travesty, actually – it wasn't a bad film but it didn't even have a flavour of what the original was.[9]

All that was left, then, was the long-awaited finale for the series, some quarter of a century since production had started on the programme's first episode. Kevin Elyot adapted the novel, following his success with *Five Little Pigs* and *Death on the Nile* nearly a decade earlier, and it remained a largely faithful and atmospheric production that was a fitting final case for the detective. Because of the emotional nature of the final story Suchet had requested that it was not filmed last. In fact it was the first of the final batch of stories to go in front of the cameras, with a cast of well-known

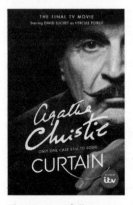

The *Curtain* falls – a final TV tie-in paperback in 2013.

actors, including Anne Reid, Helen Baxendale and Philip Glenister, as well as Alice Orr-Ewing playing Hastings' daughter (with Hugh Fraser returning as the Captain). Although the fact that the case features Poirot's death had never been kept as a surprise, contemporary reaction showed that many viewers were shocked to see his fate, most memorably shown in an episode of Channel Four's *Gogglebox*. The run up to the transmission meant that there was a spate of tie-in articles and programmes, all designed to celebrate and commemorate the life and passing of Agatha Christie's great detective, this time as played out on screen rather than in the

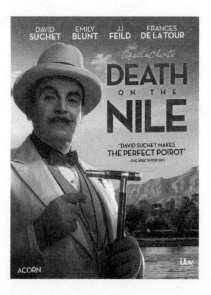

The timeless series continues to be popular with fans and distributors – repackaged *Death on the Nile* DVD (2020).

pages of a book. After *Curtain* was shown, Caroline Frost of *Huffington Post* wrote that:

> The real finale for his millions of fans had come half an hour before the credits, as Poirot faded away, pills ignored, crucifix in hand, moustache intact – impeccably and movingly acted by both Suchet, and Hugh Fraser as his 'cher ami'. As in life, so in fiction and, if it remains loyal, TV adaptation. The slow decline of a once-great man didn't make it any easier to bid adieu, only to admire one last time David Suchet's committed, comedic and compassionate take on Agatha Christie's most singular character, complete with pince-nez, egg-shaped head and, to the very end, those tireless little grey cells. Salut, cher ami![10]

When the final series made its American television debut in 2014 the *New York Times* looked back to the programme's origins and claimed that it 'delivers pretty much the same cozy-mystery package as the first, back in 1989. But why be unkind? If you're part of the *Poirot* audience, you can soak unashamed in the pleasures of these episodes, carefully calibrated to usher out the detective and the man who has played him for 25 years, David Suchet, with the proper mix of sentiment and reserve.'[11] Certainly, the completion of the series was an incredible feat, and both audiences and reviewers alike were sad to see it go, with the *Telegraph* calling it 'one of the great TV achievements – and great TV performances – of the past 30 years.'[12]

Reinventing Poirot

The character of Hercule Poirot has always been ripe for parody. As early as 1936 he featured in *A Case for Three Detectives* by Leo Bruce, where he was (slightly) reinvented as Amer Picon, who joins Lord Plimsoll (a take on Lord Peter Wimsey) and Monsignor Smith (Father Brown) in order to solve a bizarre locked room murder mystery. In 1937 a version of him featured in *Gory Knight*, a novel concerning a country house mystery that is investigated by a host of resident fictional detectives.[13] These sleuths include a take on Poirot, who's presented as Frenchman M. Hippolyte Pommeau, and is instantly recognisable. 'Hélas, *m'sieu*, it is the misfortune of the famous nevair to escape recognition,' Pommeau says

ABOVE: The twenty-first century brought interactive Poirot games, including (inevitably) *Murder on the Orient Express* and *Death on the Nile*.

with the typical pleasure exhibited by Poirot when his fame and skills were properly acknowledged. 'What hope have I to disguise these features, so universally known? Do I remove my trifle of a moustache?' In this novel Poirot's contemporaries include Lord Robert Mooney and his manservant Bunyan, takes on Dorothy L Sayers' Lord Peter Wimsey and his manservant Bunter – and it was Sayers who had further provided the inspiration for the title, which spoofs her original mystery *Gaudy Night* from 1935.[14] In 1955 a parody Poirot was once more placed alongside his fictional contemporaries, this time to solve a murder on sea in Marion Mainwaring's novel *Murder in Pastiche*. Here, Atlas Poireau retains all the recognisable tics of his original near-namesake, including his approval of careful, regular arrangements of furnishings and instant annoyance when his fame is not recognised. The book demonstrates the author's careful study of the detective characters, although the story leads to a solution that seems designed to amuse more than thrill.

Towards the end of the twentieth century Hercule Poirot had become such a firmly established figure in popular culture that he regularly made further appearances beyond the officially licensed adaptations and performances. Versions of the detective appeared in the likes of BBC television comedy *The Two Ronnies*, in which he was played by Ronnie Barker who had also performed as a 'straight' version of the detective in Oxford Playhouse productions of *Black Coffee*, *Peril at End House* and *Alibi* in 1952 and 1953. In 1997, Hugh Laurie adorned himself with a moustache for a special Poirot appearance with the Spice Girls in the classic comedy caper *Spice World*, in which he is misled by the innocent charms of guilty party Emma 'Baby Spice' Bunton. Even

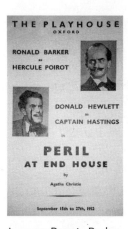

A young Ronnie Barker appeared as Poirot in *Peril at End House*.

David Suchet slipped out of the official world of Poirot when he swapped broadcasters for a spoof appearance on 2009's BBC Children in Need appeal, in which Poirot investigates the apparent kidnap of charity mascot Pudsey the bear, with the detective imploring viewers to pay a 'ransom' to the charity to ensure his release. Meanwhile, Poirot's distinctive moustache has made an appearance on an anthropomorphic vegetable for younger viewers, as Peppa Pig's family enjoy watching a mystery series starring the 'world famous' Detective Potato, while *Paddington 2*'s villain, the actor Phoenix Buchanan (Hugh Grant), even has a costumed mannequin of Poirot in his attic, with whom he converses in a Belgian accent.

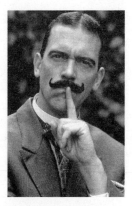
Hugh Laurie in *Spice World* (1997).

Elsewhere, Poirot's unofficial appearances have sometimes been a little less charitable, such as in 'unofficial' Soviet screen adaptations, which have included 'The Augean Stables' in 1968 and *Peril at End House* in 1969, 1981 and 1990. The 1969 version of the story was a parody of Christie's perceived shortcomings, but the 1982 version is a more serious videotaped production starring Vidas Petkevicius as Poirot. The 1990 film is rather more stylish, with Anatoliy Ravikovich playing Poirot in a captivating production that makes great use of music and lighting to emphasise key moments such as the murder at a firework display, with strong performances resulting in an emotional and powerful denouement.[15] In 2002 Russian television produced a five-part serial of *The Murder of Roger Ackroyd* (renamed *Poirot's Failure*), an impressive production that sticks extremely closely to the original text, to the extent that the novel can be read alongside it to guide non-Russian speakers. Many other countries have unofficially reworked

The French language series *Les Petits Meurtres d'Agatha Christie* proved popular enough to sell in English markets with subtitles.

Poirot novels for films expected to have only local distribution, with recent examples including India's *Grandmaster* (2012, which draws on ideas present in *The ABC Murders*, and eventually made it to Netflix in the United States) and *Chorabali* (*Quicksand*, 2016, a reworking of *Cards on the Table*).

The reworking of Poirot stories for local audiences has also occurred in France since 2006, when mini-series *Petits Meurtres en Famille* (*The Little Family Murders*) aired, based on *Hercule Poirot's Christmas*, but removing the titular detective. The success led to Agatha Christie Ltd allowing the production of the popular and ongoing series *Les Petits Meurtres d'Agatha Christie*, which began airing in 2009. The series reworks elements of Christie mysteries while removing the original detectives and replacing them with the series' own sleuths – the more grizzled and senior Commissaire Larosière (Antoine Duléry), and Inspector Lampion (Marius Colucci), a naïve and gay young man. Their sometimes awkward professional relationship provides much entertainment for the 1930s-set series, which was a great success, and offered mysteries based (sometimes very loosely indeed) on Christie's stories, including several written for Poirot.[16] In 2013 Duléry and Colucci left the programme and were replaced by new investigators Commissaire Laurence (Samuel Labarthe) and newspaper reporter Alice Avril (Blandine Bellavoir). The programme remained a particularly good example of a local market embracing elements of Agatha Christie and reworking them in a way that doesn't pretend to be faithful, but instead a new product using key ideas from Christie's mysteries.[17]

Recent years have seen an explosion of interest in Agatha

Christie around the world, particularly in Asia, and in the twenty-first century there have been several appearances of Poirot in Japan. For example, 2004 saw the launch of *Agatha Christie's Great Detectives Poirot and Marple*, in which the writer's two lead sleuths share top billing in a charming television anime series. Twenty-five of the thirty-nine episodes adapted Poirot stories, sometimes in multiple parts.[18] Superficially it might be assumed that an animated series that has as its lead protagonist a young girl called Maybelle and her pet duck, Oliver, would be a radical departure from the source – but, in fact, these are some of the most faithful adaptations even seen on screen. Maybelle is presented as a niece of Miss Marple, and an assistant to Poirot (the two detectives do not meet, but know of each other's existence), and functions as a narrator for the most part, only occasionally being an important and active part of the investigations. These well-written stories retain the best of Agatha Christie's original mysteries, including their period setting.

In late 2005 the Japanese television network NHK produced live-action adaptations of two Poirot mysteries, *The*

Poirot anime-style, from Japan's 2004 series *Agatha Christie's Great Detectives Poirot and Marple.*

ABC Murders and *Murder on the Links*, which were broadcast under the banner name *Great Detective Akafuji Takashi*, with this Poirot replacement played by Shiro Ito. These serious productions boast a Film Noir-ish style, albeit a little diluted by the videotaped look of the two films, which embrace the added visual interest presented by being set in pre-Second World War Tokyo. Unlike the anime series, these two adaptations make a point of showcasing the Japanese locale as the two films transplant the basic stories into their own country in adaptations that effectively emphasise character and emotions, sometimes in a disarmingly understated manner. [19]

Much fanfare was made for the Japanese adaptation of *Murder on the Orient Express* in 2015, as this prestigious production formed part of Fuji Television's fifty-fifth birthday celebrations. This adaptation transplanted the action to Japan in 1933, and although the detective is not named as Poirot, his replacement Suguro Takeru (played by Nomura Mansai) clearly shares many characteristics, including an eye-catching moustache. Takeru is eccentric, with heavy leanings towards quite broad comedy in his physicality and mannerisms, but this means he's also an endearing figure. The lavish production is particularly notable for the fact that the second of its two parts is a lengthy dramatisation of events unseen in Christie's original book, in which we are shown the events that led to the decision to commit murder, as well as how the mechanics of this crime were worked out. The second part acts as a character drama rather than a mystery, and is a commendably fresh take on a story that is likely to be familiar to much of the audience. In 2018 Mansai returned in the role of 'Superb Detective' Suguro Takeru in another adaptation

Nomura Mansai as Suguro Takero in Fuji TV's *Murder on the Orient Express* (2015).

of a Poirot classic, *The Murder of Roger Ackroyd*. Once more the production sticks closely to the essence of the plot, and even features a Japanese take on the detective's famous meeting with the narrator of both the novel and this film, his neighbour, the local doctor (Dr Shiba Heisuke here, replacing Dr Sheppard). Much comedy is also preserved in the role of the doctor's sister, who just like the novel's Caroline provides an entertaining sideline of gossip, and in this production she's particularly unabashed in her attempts to find out more information about her neighbours, including chasing them down the road.

2009's portable Poirot - *The ABC Murders* on Nintendo DS.

Whatever the country, Poirot has continued to be a strong media presence away from television, including in media that only came to mainstream prominence after Agatha Christie's death. The Belgian detective finally dipped his toe into the world of computer games in 2006, more than twenty years after the first proposal. The first of these was *Murder on the Orient Express* in 2006, a PC game that allowed the player to control a number of characters in an inter-active investigation that resulted in a different ending to Christie's original. Undoubtedly a good choice in principle, unfortunately the gameplay and graphics infuriated many purchasers. *Evil Under the Sun* followed the next year, to a slightly warmer reception, with *The ABC Murders* eventually following in 2016 for the PC, XBox and PS4, after another version had been produced in 2009 for the Nintendo DS only. 2021 then saw new adventures for the detective, with the release of *Hercule Poirot: The First Cases* for multiple plat-forms, and a *Death on the Nile* themed collaboration with the puzzle app *Mystery Match Village*. Arguably better for both the customer base and mystery format is the more straight-forward 'hidden object' type of game – *Death on the Nile* had

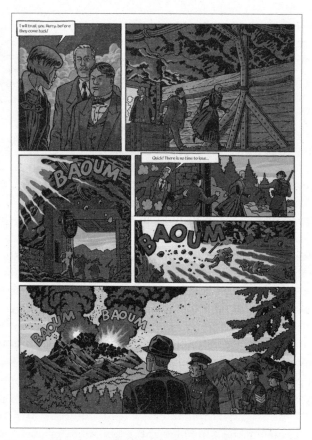

The Big Four comic book, illustrated by Allain Paillou.

been released in such a format for the PC in 2007, followed by *Peril at End House* in 2008 and *Dead Man's Folly* in 2009. Perhaps the most suitable game for the genre was an interactive DVD of *After the Funeral*, which could be enjoyed on standard DVD players and featured special links from David Suchet as Poirot. The detective helped the player to solve the mystery guided by clips from the television adaptation and mini puzzles, in a package that would entertain any fan of the series looking for an interactive experience. Fans who wanted even more interactivity might have purchased a Murder Mystery Dinner Party pack from Paul Lamond Games. There was a choice of either 'A First Class Murder' (based on 'The Plymouth Express') or 'The Mystery of the Pyramids of Giza' ('The Adventure of the Egyptian Tomb'). Specially shot Poirot scenes appeared on the included DVD (in which he was played by Sean Rees), supplemented with some footage taken from the ITV series. A more traditional form of entertainment arrived in 2019, when Poirot joined Miss Marple and Ariadne Oliver as characters in the card game *Death on the Cards*.

The Poirot card in the 2019 game *Death on the Cards*.

Another striking series of visual adaptations of Poirot stories began in 2007 with graphic novel versions of fourteen Poirot novels, translated from French originals dating back to the 1990s. These vibrant and lively graphic novels boasted a small but distinctive array of artists, who all imbued Christie's stories with different atmospheres, but always approached the stories, the murder and the suspects with the utmost seriousness – they did not allow bright colours to disguise dark truths. *The Big Four* particularly benefits from the comic book treatment, as Poirot's antics with a poison dart disguised as a cigarette now seems tense and thrilling rather than incongruous, as does the long-awaited visualisation of the exploding mountain at the story's conclusion. Elsewhere, attention to detail is made clear by the welcome use of identifiable elements of Greenway in the adaptation of *Dead Man's Folly*. Such reworkings of Christie, from anime to graphic novels, demonstrate that faithful depictions of Poirot can exist even in forms that Christie herself would never have had the opportunity to encounter.

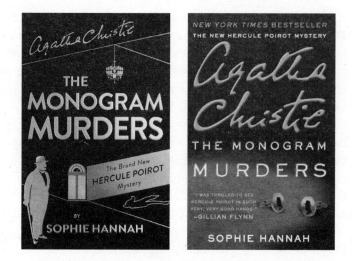

The Monogram Murders
(Continuation novel, 2014)

For Agatha Christie's original Poirot stories, the cupboard has now become bare when it comes to unearthing and reprinting long forgotten mysteries. In 2008 the volume *Hercule Poirot: The Complete Short Stories* reproduced a version of 'The Regatta Mystery' featuring the Belgian detective. This version of Christie's Parker Pyne story had previously been seen in American newspapers in 1936, in *The Strand Magazine* and in a single story pamphlet *Poirot and the Regatta Mystery*, published by Vallancey Press in 1946. The differences between the Poirot and Parker Pyne versions of the story are minimal, with the change in character made presumably for commercial reasons at the time.

ABOVE: Following the tradition of Agatha Christie's own books, *The Monogram Murders* had very different covers in the UK and USA in 2014.

Two more Poirot stories emerged in 2009, on this occasion for the very first time, as John Curran's *Agatha Christie's Secret Notebooks* included two short mysteries that Christie had elected to rewrite or rework. The first, 'The Capture of Cerberus', was likely written at the beginning of the Second World War and was originally intended to form part of *The Labours of Hercules*. It was not published in the initial serialisation, probably because of the way it drew on contemporary politics, with a character clearly based on Hitler. The second story, 'The Incident of the Dog's Ball', is an early version of the mystery that was expanded for the novel *Dumb Witness*, with it seeming likely that almost as soon as Christie finished writing it (probably in 1933) she realised that it would stand up to a more profitable expansion as a novel.[20]

Another early version of a well-known Poirot novel was published in 2014, this time as the standalone volume *Hercule Poirot and the Greenshore Folly*, with a new cover painting by prolific Agatha Christie cover artist Tom Adams. Originally written in 1954 to raise money for Christie's local church in Churston Ferrers, the story failed to sell to magazines because of its awkward novella length. The mystery was then rewritten in a fuller form as *Dead Man's Folly*, published as a novel in 1956, while a new Miss Marple mystery was written under a similar title ('Greenshaw's Folly') for the benefit of the church.

With no more known Poirot stories that could be dusted off for republication, there was one possibility that had been scarcely considered since Agatha Christie's death in 1976. In April 2014 an unexpected announcement was made – Hercule Poirot would return in a new continuation novel, to be written by bestselling thriller and mystery author Sophie Hannah. Predictably, Christie fans on social media gave strong reactions, both positive and negative. Some contributors to the Agatha Christie Facebook page simply dismissed

The original appearance in book form of the Pyneless *Poirot and the Regatta Mystery* in 1946.

the project outright ('No no no no no no no'), while others professed outrage or presumed that the new mystery would resurrect the deceased detective: 'Preposterous to imitate Agatha Christie. Is Poirot to be one of the "Walking Dead"?' Drowned out, but definitely present, were more enthusiastic fans. 'I like the idea of a new Poirot!' said one, 'I love Christie and having read all her books (many times) long for a new one'. Another expressed that they 'can't wait to read this author's story of Poirot ... love Sophie Hannah's books and I think she is so brave to take on this project'.

Sophie Hannah had certainly been brave, but could feel reassured by the fact that Christie's family had decided to consider a continuation Agatha Christie novel even before Hannah's agent had raised the possibility. Agatha Christie Ltd had long resisted the possibility of a continuation novel featuring any of her characters, but there were commercial realities to consider – most significantly, the difficulties of convincing booksellers to give any prominence to an author who died four decades ago, even if she is the best-selling novelist of all time. Other literary estates were demonstrating that resurrecting characters using new authors could have a positive outcome in attracting new readers to an established canon of work, and HarperCollins was keen to follow suit. In 2010 the company had acquired the book rights in North America and after eighty-four years had finally become Agatha Christie's exclusive English language publisher worldwide. Now everyone was keen to prove that, at a time when licensing activity in new media and on stage and screen seemed to be accelerating, Christie was still very much a brand leader in her heartland of book publishing. To achieve it, however,

HarperCollins needed a new book, and when Sophie Hannah's agent serendipitously put her forward (initially without her knowledge), a meeting was arranged for her to outline her approach.

It was never Sophie Hannah's intention to impersonate Agatha Christie herself, and in order to reinforce this point she decided to create her own narrator, the Scotland Yard detective Edward Catchpool, so that she could create a new voice through which we can hear Poirot's deductions. In terms of period, there was no desire to create a prequel to *The Mysterious Affair at Styles*, nor to revisit the detective at the end of his life. With a story in mind that would be best suited to the 'Golden Age' period of the late 1920s/early '30s, Hannah identified a gap between 1928's *The Mystery of the Blue Train* and 1932's *Peril at End House* and settled on her

Tom Adams came out of retirement to paint the cover for *Hercule Poirot and the Greenshore Folly* in 2014.

new Poirot novel, *The Monogram Murders*, being set in 1929. In this adventure, an extremely well characterised Poirot is approached by a young woman who confides that 'I'm a dead woman, or I shall be soon', before imploring the detective not to track down her murderer. Soon, the mystery deepens when three guests at a London hotel have been murdered, and each has had a monogrammed cufflink placed in their mouths. Sophie Hannah explained her thinking behind such an intriguing premise in an interview with *The Guardian*, in which she pointed out that:

> Agatha Christie never wrote books that just started with a dead body, and a 'let's find out who the murderer is', which is kind of mysterious but not that mysterious. She always started with, 'how can this thing be happening, isn't it strange?' And I realised that I've always been doing that ... trying to think in an impossible scenario sort of way. So I feel as though it's kind of in my literary DNA ... So many people say, 'Oh yes, Agatha Christie, she's good at plot but her writing's not that good, her characters are a bit thin.' Certainly I didn't find that to be true when I reread them. I found there was a huge amount of psychological perceptiveness and insight. The books are wise, witty and brilliantly written. She set the pattern in my mind for what crime novels should do.[21]

The critical reaction to the book was mostly positive, with author and Christie aficionado Andrew Wilson writing in *The Independent* that 'Christie fans need not have feared. Within the first few pages of *The Monogram Murders* it is obvious that we are in safe hands,' and that 'The novel – which has a rich skein of black humour running through it – is immensely satisfying on many levels, including its ingenious ending ... Hannah is a gifted artist indeed.'[22] Christie

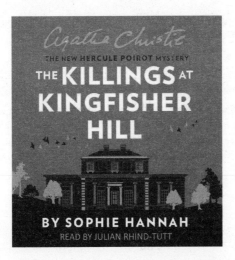

The audiobook cover for *The Killings at Kingfisher Hill* (2020).

biographer Laura Thompson was a little more reserved in her praise, but pointed out that it was clearly not easy for any writer to 'act as a medium' in the way demanded of Hannah, but that 'The twisted journey that Sophie Hannah takes us on is an enjoyable diversion in its own right. It is best read as such'.[23] Elsewhere, *The Spectator* reviewer argued that 'I doubt if anyone could have done a better job of resurrecting Poirot than Sophie Hannah,' while the four-star review in the *Daily Telegraph* felt that the book 'is infused with such love and energy that if [HarperCollins] hadn't commissioned this book – the first Poirot novel since Christie's death in 1976 – I am quite convinced Hannah would have written the whole thing gratis for a fan fiction site.'[24,25]

The first Sophie Hannah Poirot book was a success, and so it was almost inevitable that another would follow. *Closed Casket*, published in 2016, took Poirot to Ireland in order to solve a country house mystery, while in 2018's *The Mystery of Three Quarters* Poirot has to work out why someone seems to have been sending letters in his name accusing others of murdering someone named Barnabas Pandy, a man he has never heard of. Poirot's centenary year then saw Hannah's *The Killings at Kingfisher Hill*, in which Poirot's travels by luxury passenger coach take a curious turn, which eventually leads to murder. A fifth book is already under contract.

Murder on the Orient Express
(Film, 2017)

Murder on the Orient Express has always held a certain allure for those looking for new projects in all types of media, no doubt not only due to the story's strong plotting and sensational denouement, but also its evocative title and iconography. Although the novel's title alludes to grand foreign landscapes, in reality the story is a small-scale one, and so it's no surprise that Christie herself felt that it had potential to be a play one day, although she never got around to actually writing it. In 2015 the story was adapted for the stage by American playwright Ken Ludwig, winner of two Tony and two Olivier awards, in a script that reduces the cast of suspects to eight. Set in the novel's publication year of 1934, the

ABOVE: Kenneth Branagh as Poirot aboard one of the full-sized replica carriages of the Orient Express train.

The teaser poster formed the basis of the first tie-in edition of the book (2017).

story itself is largely presented as per Christie's original mystery, but adds a new opening in which a kidnapping of a young girl is heard (but not seen). Poirot speaks directly to the audience at the beginning of the case: 'The story you are about to witness is one of romance and tragedy, primal murder and the urge for revenge,' he tells his onlookers. 'What better way to spend a pleasant summer evening?' For the play's German performances in 2021, Poirot was played by Katharina Thalbach, the first woman to play the part in a major production.

However, while this stage version's script was being written, potentially even grander plans were being formulated for the story. November 2015 saw the official announcement that Sir Kenneth Branagh had signed on to a new film adaptation for Twentieth Century Fox, which he would both direct and star in, but these plans had a lengthy genesis that long predated Branagh's involvement. Discussions with director Sir Ridley Scott, who would eventually have a producer role, had been ongoing for some time. *Murder on the Orient Express* was originally envisaged as a film with a younger man in the role of Poirot, with options for a further two titles if the first outing were deemed a success. Michael Green, a screenwriter familiar with the Agatha Christie canon, was brought on board to adapt the novel for Branagh's film, while a host of stars were lined up in a way that was clearly an echo of the 1974 movie. However, some rumoured actors would fall by the wayside before production started, such as Angelina Jolie and Charlize Theron.

Filming began in November 2016, and despite the shoot taking four months the entire cast were only together for approximately twelve days. Branagh's outstanding choice of actors includes Penélope Cruz, Willem Dafoe, Dame Judi Dench, Johnny Depp, Josh Gad, Sir Derek Jacobi, Leslie Odom Jr., Michelle Pfeiffer and Daisy Ridley. The film boasts so many stars that Olivia Colman, who would win a Best Actress Oscar only two years later, was not even featured on the two main posters and had only a very small role as Hildegarde Schmidt, companion and assistant to Dench's Princess Dragomiroff. Unlike the 1974 film, on set the cast were thrown straight into the deep end and were generally expected to perform their extensive interrogation scenes first, an approach that some of the cast embraced, but others were less keen on.

Branagh decided to shoot on high quality 65mm film, just as he had for his prestigious *Hamlet* (1996), while some scenes of the moving train were staged on a mile-and-a-half of track at Longcross Studios in Surrey, England. The interior of the Orient Express wasn't an exact replica of the rather cramped original, but a reworking more in line with what the audience might expect the original carriages to have looked like. 'We were able to make contact with the original

The cinematic scope of *Murder on the Orient Express* was expanded with scenes set outside the snowbound train.

Orient Express company, and they were very generous and provided us with original construction drawings of the compartments and carriages, kitchen and locomotive,' explained production designer Jim Clay. 'And we took from those what we needed, and obviously you adapt for movies, but it was accurate in pretty much in every respect. The exteriors were a perfect reproduction.'[26] Clay, Branagh and screenwriter Green even joined the genuine Orient Express for a small portion of its journey, in order to get a sense of the real thing.

In May 2017 *Entertainment Weekly* broke a big exclusive about the film – not just a selection of cast photographs, one of which adorned the magazine's cover, but more significantly the first sighting of the moustache sported by Branagh's Poirot. The reaction to the elaborate, huge, grey facial apparatus was certainly one of surprise. Branagh himself recalled that when fellow cast member Daisy Ridley first saw the moustache she simply called it 'bold'. Branagh and his team had not made the decision lightly, however. He recalled meeting with the team at Agatha Christie Ltd: 'The first thing they asked in their creative meeting was, "What are you doing about the moustache?" There was no twinkle in the eye, I knew it was critical. This moustache is serious business.' The finished design took an hour each day, and the Chairman and CEO of Agatha Christie Ltd (and Christie's great grandson) James Prichard declared that 'I think Ken has got the greatest moustache of all England.' Branagh reflected that 'This moustache is like Poirot's superpower, his calling card. It's what people see before they see him.'[27]

This version of *Murder on the Orient Express* ensures that Poirot is clearly established from the very beginning, and certainly gives him star status – perhaps one that even eclipses the rest of the story at times. Alternative openings for the film were considered, one of which featured the Armstrong family's home movies, which Branagh felt would have emphasised the script's 'emotion and depth and the sense that the centre of the story was the death of the innocent,' but was ultimately felt unnecessary.[28] Another opening established the family through newsreel footage, which Branagh acknowledged was an homage to the 1974 Sidney Lumet film, but the final cut of the film instead begins with scenes set in Jerusalem, 1934 (but filmed in Malta).[29] Here we see Poirot as a character who demands precision – including equal sized eggs for his breakfast – and is happy to rail against the de facto system of justice, as he uncovers a corrupt British Chief Inspector. He lays out his thinking with élan and even has a moment of action when he uses his cane to help to trap the perpetrator. All this is depicted as high-spirited fun, with Poirot shown as a charming and conscientious person, friendly with local children but also spoken to with respect. This Poirot has a more casual demeanour and body language than usually seen (such casualness rather than formality is made even more plain when, later in the film, he keenly shares a dessert during a nonchalant conversation with a man he hardly knows), and the whole sequence allows for a sunny and upbeat opening to contrast with the darkness that is to come. The early scenes show Poirot to be effortlessly in charge of the situations he finds himself in, but those who know the story will be aware that the detective's declaration that 'There is right, there is wrong, there is nothing in between' will come back to haunt him. Later in this film Poirot becomes more clinical when there is serious work to be done, and angry when he knows that he is being deliberately deceived by some of those on board. In the final film, he occasionally consults a photograph of a woman called Katherine, but Branagh has explained that 'for a while we had this picture

The all-star cast on another tie-in, based on the theatrical poster.

contain images of former military companions.' Green felt that both photos emphasised an important part of the character, indicating that this version of Poirot has seen active service: 'there were two aspects of his past that were very much of interest to us, that military beginning that showed he had seen some darkness in his youth both as a policeman and in World War One... and also romance, if he'd ever had his toes in those dangerous waters.'[30] Green saw both of these elements as potentially troubling for Poirot: 'For a man who is quite literally obsessed with order and finding balance in things war and romance would be anathema.'[31] In the end, according to Branagh, 'We landed on Katherine and I believe were we lucky enough to pursue the adventures of Poirot in Egypt we think that there is gold in them thar hills,' with Green confirming 'we know the story we want to tell'.[32]

Other characters are similarly quickly established, with Judi Dench's Princess Dragomiroff boarding the Orient Express with her dogs (and assistant) in tow, dismissing the

Poirot with M. Bouc (Tom Bateman) and Gerhard Hardman (Willem Dafoe).

initial selection of cabins before she finds one to her liking. With such a large cast of well-known names it might surprise viewers that some are left out of the spotlight for so long that they might wonder why they are there at all – this is particularly true of Rudolph and Elena Adrenyi (Sergei Polunin and Lucy Boynton), although of course the presence of each character is properly explained by the end. There is a surprising emphasis on Josh Gad's Hector MacQueen, who gets extra scenes that aren't in the book; Daisy Ridley's Mary Debenham provides one of the most human and naturalistic elements of the film, while Penélope Cruz's Pilar Estravados (a name borrowed from *Hercule Poirot's Christmas*, to replace Greta Ohlsson) offers an understated emotional performance. Derek Jacobi's performance as valet Masterman, assisting Depp's Ratchett, is something of a thankless role but the actor projects subtlety and believability on to the character's actions, while Michelle Pfeiffer's Mrs Hubbard is the standout among even such a distinguished cast, as she offers nuances to the character.

Just as with Sherlock Holmes's *The Hound of the Baskervilles*, so it is that Hercule Poirot's most famous case isn't necessarily the one that lends itself best to a screen adaptation, even if it's difficult to resist. The mystery is necessarily talky, with backstories to be established among a large cast of characters that cannot be reduced without dispensing with one of the cruxes of the book. This explains the film's attempts to play around with the necessary scenes of interrogation and exposition by setting them in a variety of locations, as Poirot moves outside in the snow for tea and contemplates events from every conceivable area of the train – inside and out. Green and Branagh have explained the difficulties of compressing a lengthy denouement on page to something more manageable on screen, which means that at the end of the film Poirot spends less time giving his final conclusions

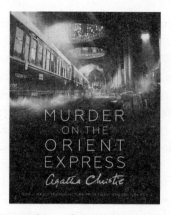

A rare commemorative edition of the novel illustrated with film photos.

than some might expect from previous Poirot adaptations. One consequence of this is that even close observers may need to work out the meaning of some clues by inference only during the powerful denouement, which is played out visually as a re-enactment of The Last Supper.[33]

Murder on the Orient Express had its world premiere at the Royal Albert Hall on 2 November 2017, with the film released in the United Kingdom the following day. The critical response was unusually mixed, just as had been the case for the 1974 film, and seemed to depend on what individual critics were looking for in the film. The best indication of the variety of responses is that *The Observer* offered a four-star review from Simran Hans, in which she wrote:

> The whole thing works especially well if you don't remember the book's original ending (or Sidney Lumet's 1974 film), though it's not exactly spoiled if you do. Written by *Blade Runner: 2049* scribe Michael Green, it doesn't try (and so can't fail) to reinvent Christie, though it does update her slightly, keeping the opulent colonial trappings but having characters call out the period's racism.[34]

Meanwhile, Peter Bradshaw in *The Observer*'s sister paper *The Guardian* described the film as a 'dusty, old fashioned dud' in his two-star review.[35] A middle ground was found in the *Daily Telegraph*, which called the film 'star studded but frustratingly pedestrian' in its three-star write-up, while Dan Murrell of *Screen Junkies* wondered if the film 'may be too slick for people who are Agatha Christie purists, but may be too old-fashioned for people who have a more modern sensibility'.[36]

In the end, with such a high-calibre cast and the twin attractions of both Christie and her famous mystery, audiences interested in this particular selection of names were unlikely to be too worried about what critics felt about it. Instead, they could assume that with such high-quality actors on board, an evening spent watching the aftermath of a murder on the Orient Express was unlikely to leave them feeling disappointed. The cast performed their publicity duties on an array of chat shows, and while there was not exactly 'Poirot mania' there was increased and sustained interest in the works of Agatha Christie, which included an illustrated tie-in book and a timely but separate Audible audio dramatisation starring Tom Conti as Poirot. Twentieth Century Fox had hoped that the likely slightly older demographic would sustain the box office for the film, as such audiences have proven to be strong patrons of recent hits outside of the blockbuster mould. Fox was right to be hopeful, and the film grossed over $100m at the US box office, and an impressive quarter of a billion dollars internationally, resulting in a worldwide total of over $350m. It's little wonder that plans for a second film were soon accelerated, and only weeks after the film's release the trade press reported that *Death on the Nile* was expected to be confirmed soon.

The ABC Murders
(Television series, 2018)

In 2014 the BBC announced its first major Agatha Christie adaptation for many years, with a three-part production of *And Then There Were None*, scripted by Sarah Phelps. Phelps is a respected screenwriter whose previous work includes a television adaptation of J.K. Rowling's *The Casual Vacancy*, but to this point was probably best known for her work on soap opera *EastEnders*, for which she wrote many acclaimed episodes. Following the success of *And Then There Were None*, shown at Christmas 2015, the BBC quickly commissioned an adaptation of the 'The Witness for the Prosecution' short story for 2016, and with Agatha Christie Ltd then announced plans for seven more Christie adaptations, which began

ABOVE: John Malkovich in Sarah Phelps' reimagining of Poirot for the BBC, with Rupert Grint as Inspector Crome.

with *Ordeal by Innocence* at Easter 2018. After such a selection there was some anticipation when *The ABC Murders* was announced as the next production, given its high reputation and the presence of Hercule Poirot in the mystery, who on this occasion would be played by celebrated Hollywood actor John Malkovich.

If the BBC's adaptation of *The ABC Murders* for Christmas 2018 was intended to make an impact, then those in charge of the production could be satisfied that they achieved their aim. Whatever the outcome and reception, this extensive reworking of the Agatha Christie book wasn't designed to please die-hard fans, but rather to excite a modern television audience used to more hard-edged dramas. While the three-part miniseries proclaims itself to be *Agatha Christie's The ABC Murders*, it doesn't take long for it to become clear that its world is really one created by screenwriter Sarah Phelps. This realisation shouldn't be read as an inherently negative one – after the superb and faithful adaptation of the novel for the David Suchet *Poirot* series, there was only so much that could have been done with any new version of the tale if the intention had been to stay similarly close to the original story. Production company Mammoth Screen certainly seemed keen to ensure that their adaptations stood out from the crowd, and a deal with Amazon for international distribution indicated that the appetite for these stories was expected to go far beyond the traditional murder mystery viewers. This was designed to be a drama in its own right.

Nevertheless, the audience's enjoyment of this particular adaptation will rely heavily on how they respond to its approach to characters and the wider scenarios that Phelps felt lay beneath the surface of the original mystery and then chose to embellish. The mini-series embraces the grim reality of life in the disaffected classes during the 1930s, as well as what Phelps seems to see as a repressed underbelly that she is keen to shine a light on. This is a deliberately provocative, dark and difficult world that doesn't make for comfortable viewing. Many reviewers and observers were swift to point out that the world then was not a cosy one, but few conceded that nor was the one in Agatha Christie's books.

There had been some surprise following the news that a Poirot novel was next to be adapted, as the memory of David Suchet's depiction was still fresh, while Branagh's own take on the character had been a success just the previous year. However, the decision to make a standalone adaptation meant that Poirot could be seen as more than just one incumbent actor, while it also meant that a 'star name' could be cast who would have no interest in an ongoing part. Reportedly, John Malkovich's real interest in the part came as a result of Poirot's new backstory, invented by Phelps and directly at odds with what we know of Christie's character. Phelps had been open about the fact that she had not read any other Poirot novels, and as a result this version of *The ABC Murders* functions only as a standalone production, existing outside of the rest of the world of Agatha Christie. This is something that James Prichard readily conceded, saying that Phelps 'has pared it back to exactly the one described in *The ABC Murders*, and that is very different from probably anything that has gone before'.[37] This adaptation takes the themes and some of the mystery mechanics present in the original novel, and conjures a brand new drama out of them.

The adaptation focuses closely on Poirot, who struggles against a cynical and disbelieving police force, headed by Inspector Crome (Rupert Grint), and embedded issues surrounding the rise of fascism and racism in the 1930s. There are clear comparisons between the hostile anti-immigrant feelings expressed in a country that Poirot was forced to move to as a refugee, and more contemporary issues for the modern viewer in a world divided by politics. The programme depicts an unhappy Britain, not least for Poirot after the death of Inspector Japp (Kevin McNally), his only real link with the country's society. Poirot then feels lost, and when the murderer seems to be directly taunting him the story only becomes more personal. Once the murderer is apprehended (this adaptation gets as far as an 'E' murder, one more than Christie had written), they even go to great pains to align their motivation with Poirot's character. As a result Malkovich's Poirot is a sad figure, portrayed as somewhat pathetic when others laugh at his dyed beard. This version of Poirot is often subdued, and certainly is miles away from the rather caricatured portrayals often seen on screen, and the audience can believe that this is a real man, stripped of his dignity.

In another break with tradition, Malkovich's Poirot sported a goatee beard.

The production embraces a train motif, including in the titles and an action sequence in the final episode played out on the railway tracks. This railway chase sequence is an example of how the serial offers action-focused peaks of energy alongside sections dealing more with atmosphere and dialogue, which demonstrates its focus on character and emotion over murders and mystery. Overall, this is an Agatha Christie story filleted for ideas and reworked, which benefits from another excellent cast and moody direction, and may be indicative of how Christie can be reworked in the twenty-first century for new audiences.

Although several newspaper articles focused on the angry reaction on social media from the many Christie fans wanting productions more in keeping with the original stories, their own reviews of *The ABC Murders* were more positive on the whole. The *Daily Telegraph* gave four stars to the first instalment, which it called 'Slow-moving but

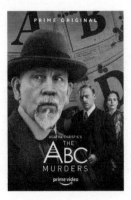

US distribution of the BBC series was on Amazon Prime.

intense,' with Malkovich's Poirot described as one 'we've never seen before'.[38] Lucy Mangan in *The Guardian* opened by outlining her dislike of the Suchet series, arguing that this new production was 'for those who like their Christie underbelly-up and a nail raked down its pale, fetid flesh. It is Christmas, after all.'[39] However, The *New York Times* was one publication that was not happy with the results, with reviewer Mike Hale writing of Phelps that 'Her method is extreme makeover, redoing Christie's plots and reshaping her sensibility in a lurid and ominous fashion that, combined with top-flight casts, produced entertaining results with *And Then There Were None* and *Ordeal by Innocence*. The *ABC Murders* is Phelps's most thorough teardown yet, and this time she's so suffocatingly revisionist that what's left isn't really Christie at all. The insistence on making everything grimmer and grosser is almost comically complete.'[40] This version of *The ABC Murders* certainly got audiences and critics talking and asking questions of the nature of adaptation in the modern landscape of film and television - something that Poirot needs to continue to be a part of.

Death on the Nile
(Film, 2022)

It had always been the hope that *Murder on the Orient Express* would not be Kenneth Branagh's only foray into the world of Hercule Poirot, and while the commercial success of the film cemented plans for a follow-up, ideas had already been discussed during its production. The potential for cinematic spectacle in *Death on the Nile*'s period trip through Egypt was surely one factor to be considered in the story's favour, but for the returning team of actor and director Kenneth Branagh and screenwriter Michael Green it was the novel's themes that most appealed. Speaking to *Empire* magazine's Alex Godfrey, Branagh said that he was attracted to a story that in which Christie 'discovered something different

ABOVE: Kenneth Branagh returns as Poirot, here on the exotic Abu Simbel set.

through exploring the corrosive power of lust', and that 'sex and death are absolutely the centre of it'.[41]

While not inviting a direct comparison with the 1978 film of *Death on the Nile* that had followed the 1974 *Murder on the Orient Express*, Branagh's further statement that 'we stayed away from a milder, more reserved, more superficially sophisticated cocktail language and music of Cole Porter and Irving Berlin, and took it to a seamier and more soulful setting' indicates his intentions for his film would offer an approach that contrasts with the earlier adaptation, emphasising different elements of the story. In particular, Branagh cited filmic influences that included *Dial M for Murder* (1954), *Double Indemnity* (1944), and *Fatal Attraction* (1987) – stories with passion and betrayal at their core.

Production on the film took place at Longcross Studios and on location in Egypt, and when the beginning of filming was announced Branagh keenly established that the film would be emphasising characterisation and relationships alongside the central murder mystery. 'Crimes of passion are dangerously sexy,' he said. 'Agatha Christie has written a riveting story of emotional chaos and violent criminality

Hercule Poirot asserts his authority in this latest big-screen interpretation of Agatha Christie's work.

Armie Hammer and Gal Gadot lead an all-star cast in the glamorous new movie.

and Michael Green has once again written a screenplay to match.'[42] Once more, the announced cast was a star-studded affair, with familiar big names and some surprising famous faces. Armie Hammer was cast as Simon Doyle, with Emma Mackey as Jacqueline de Bellefort and Gal Gadot as Linnet Ridgeway. For some of the filming Gadot wore a recreation of the yellow 128 carat Tiffany Diamond, the original of which was previously worn by Audrey Hepburn and was unearthed in South Africa in 1877. 'The Tiffany Diamond is a priceless symbol of the highest standards of virtuosity and craftsmanship at Tiffany, and rarely makes an appearance beyond its vault,' said Reed Krakoff, chief artistic officer at Tiffany. 'A central role in the adaptation of Agatha Christie's classic novel is deserving of our priceless diamond.'[43]

Other well-known cast members include Annette Bening, Russell Brand, Rose Leslie, Ali Fazal, Jennifer Saunders, and Dawn French, while Sophie Okonedo plays Salome Otterbourne, who is now a singer rather than a writer.

Otterbourne is accompanied by her daughter, Rosalie (Letitia Wright), with whom Bouc (Tom Bateman) gets involved, as he returns to assist Poirot after his adventure with the detective on the Orient Express. Prior to the film's release Bateman spoke about his character's relationship with Poirot, and alluded to wider questions that the film would be asking of its lead character: 'Poirot and Bouc love each other very much. And the film takes Poirot's backstory further. What is the cost of being this great detective, who's outside of the world?'.[44] As part of this exploration of Poirot's character, Branagh was de-aged in order to show a 22-year-old Poirot as a soldier. 'We get a chance to see not only what forged Poirot in the roughty-toughty world that people might not imagine him to have engaged with, that is action,

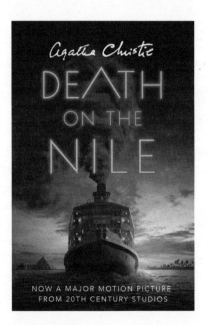

The official tie-in book cover for the movie (2020).

Kenneth Branagh strikes a commanding pose, reminiscent of many of the early Poirot illustrations.

and guns, and fighting and all of that, but also in the affairs of the heart,' said Branagh.[45]

Although *Death on the Nile*'s release was repeatedly delayed due to Covid-19, interest in Poirot remains as high as ever. With different aspects of the Belgian detective still able to be explored after more than a hundred years, these new adventures show that the character can thrive even as the world around him changes, and there is every chance that this is not the last we have seen of Kenneth Branagh's Poirot.

EPILOGUE

2020 marked a hundred years since the first publication of Poirot's debut, *The Mysterious Affair at Styles*, and there's no sign of flagging interest in either the character or Agatha Christie's mysteries more generally. However, there's no way of knowing how the character will transform in the coming decades, or even centuries. One thing we can be sure of is that things will not, and cannot, stay the same. Might it be that Poirot and the mysteries that Agatha Christie wrote for him will not be so inseparable in the future – could the character find a home in an original series on a modern streaming service featuring in brand new stories? Certainly France's television series *Les Petits Meurtres d'Agatha Christie* has already shown that Poirot mysteries can be reworked with new detectives or scenarios for a fresh take on the author's genius. This sort of scenario may be anathema to die-hard fans, but keeping the world's greatest detective fresh and visible for new generations is an unenviable task, and no one with an interest in Agatha Christie properties could wish to see him forgotten and neglected. The idea that there is only one Poirot is an increasingly untenable one and it seems likely that, as with Sherlock Holmes, the original Poirot will eventually stand alongside reinventions and reworkings. We

OPPOSITE: Hercule Poirot by Bill Bragg. 'Probably the greatest detective in the world.'

have already had the surprise appearance of Poirot in tights in a twenty-first century ballet adaptation of *Murder on the Orient Express*, staged in Memphis and New York. Might we now see an exciting series of *Young Poirot*? Maybe a *Sherlock*-style Poirot series for film or television that places him in the present day? Perhaps a genteel *The Romantic Adventures of Hercule Poirot*? Or even the sci-fi adventures of *Poirot in Space*? Probably not soon, but perhaps one day. Whatever emerges, it will be up to individuals to pick and choose the Poirot incarnations that take their interest. One thing we can be sure of is that whichever Poirot adventures one chooses to engage with the original stories will remain available, ready to be enjoyed by new generations. Agatha Christie's Hercule Poirot, (probably) the greatest detective in the world, will outlive us all.

KEY NAMES

Dame Agatha Christie – born Agatha Miller in 1890, died in 1976. Married Archibald Christie in 1914; separated in 1926, divorced in 1928. Married Max Mallowan in 1930; they remained married until her death. Also known as Lady Mallowan (from 1968); awarded a DBE in 1971. Alongside the sixty-six detective novels that made her famous, Christie was author of more than two dozen plays, over 150 short stories and many poems. She also wrote six novels under the name Mary Westmacott (these focused on relationships between characters rather than crime), and two books under the name Agatha Christie Mallowan (one non-fiction, one a collection for children). Christie had one child, Rosalind Hicks, born 1919.

Archibald ('Archie') Christie – Agatha Christie's first husband, and father of Rosalind. Born 1889, died 1962.

Sir Max Mallowan – Agatha Christie's second husband. Born in 1904, died in 1978. A notable archaeologist, knighted in 1968. Married Barbara Parker in 1977.

Rosalind Hicks – Agatha Christie's only child, born in 1919. Married **Hubert Prichard** in 1940, who was killed in active service in 1944. With Hubert she had her only child, Mathew Prichard, who was born in 1943. Rosalind married **Anthony Hicks** in 1949; they remained married until her death in 2004.

Mathew Prichard CBE – born in 1943, son of Hubert Prichard and Rosalind Hicks, and Agatha Christie's only grandchild. Retired Chairman of Agatha Christie Ltd, succeeded by his son James Prichard in 2015.

James Prichard – Chairman and CEO of Agatha Christie Ltd since 2015. Agatha Christie's great grandson.

Edmund Cork – Agatha Christie's agent from 1926 to 1978.

Harold Ober – Agatha Christie's American agent for much of her career (died 1959).

Dorothy Olding – Agatha Christie's American agent from 1959.

Brian Stone – Agatha Christie Limited's agent following Edmund Cork's retirement in 1978.

SELECTED BIBLIOGRAPHY

The list below is by no means an exhaustive selection of worthwhile books about Agatha Christie and Poirot, but are titles that readers may find interesting, and often expand on areas only touched upon in this book.

Aldridge, Mark, *Agatha Christie on Screen* (Palgrave Macmillan, 2016)

Barnard, Robert, *A Talent to Deceive* (Dodd, Mead & Company, 1980)

Bayard, Pierre, *Who Killed Roger Ackroyd?* (Editions de Minuit, 1998)

Bernthal, J.C., *Queering Agatha Christie* (Palgrave Macmillan, 2016)

Curran, John, *Agatha Christie's Complete Secret Notebooks* (HarperCollins, 2016)

Edwards, Martin, *The Golden Age of Murder* (HarperCollins, 2015)

Goddard, John, *Agatha Christie's Golden Age* (Stylish Eye Press, 2018)

Green, Julius, *Agatha Christie: A Life in Theatre* (HarperCollins, 2018 [revised ed.])

Gregg, Hubert, *Agatha Christie and All That Mousetrap* (William Kimber & Co., 1980)

Haining, Peter, *Agatha Christie: Murder in Four Acts* (Virgin Books, 1990)

Haining, Peter, *Agatha Christie's Poirot: A Celebration of the Great Detective* (Boxtree, 1995)

Hart, Anne, *The Life and Times of Hercule Poirot* (HarperCollins, 2019 [revised ed.])

Harkup, Kathryn, *A is for Arsenic: The Poisons of Agatha Christie* (Bloomsbury, 2015)

Keating, H.R.F., *Agatha Christie: First Lady of Crime* (Weidenfeld and Nicolson, 1977)

Morgan, Janet, *Agatha Christie: A Biography* (Collins, 1984)

Osborne, Charles, *The Life and Crimes of Agatha Christie*
  (HarperCollins, 1999 [revised ed.]
Palmer, Scott, *The Films of Agatha Christie* (B.T. Batsford, 1993)
Prichard, Mathew (ed.), *Agatha Christie: The Grand Tour*
  (HarperCollins, 2012)
Saunders, Peter, *The Mousetrap Man* (Collins, 1972)
Suchet, David, and Geoffrey Wansell, *Poirot and Me* (Headline, 2013)
Thompson, Laura, *Agatha Christie: An English Mystery* (Headline,
  2007)

PICTURE CREDITS

The editor and publishers would like to thank Agatha Christie Limited, Alamy Stock Photos, AP, Associated Newspapers, A&E, Cannon, CBS TV, the Christie Archive Trust, the Everett Collection Inc., Getty Images, Yoni Hamenachem, ITV, Kobal, MGM, Neville Mariner, Moviestore Collection, Shutterstock, Trinity Mirror/Mirrorpix, 20th Century Studios, United Archives Gmbh, Warner Bros Television, and the many publishers for their cooperation in enabling us to share 100 years of Poirot visuals in this book.

Every effort has been made to trace all owners of copyright. We apologise for any errors or omissions and would be grateful if notified of any corrections.

ENDNOTES

The following archives are referenced in the notes:

ACA   Agatha Christie Archive, Christie Archive Trust, Wales
BOD   The Bodley Head Archive, University of Reading
HC   HarperCollins Archive, Glasgow
HMA   Hughes Massie Archive, University of Exeter

INTRODUCTION

1   1920 saw the story's serialisation in *The Times*'s 'Colonial Edition', and it was published as a book in the United States this year, before its 1921 publication as a novel in Britain.

2   A brief note on dates and titles – unless otherwise noted, I cite the years in which stories were published in book form in Great Britain, and I have used the British titles. Alternative titles from the United States are noted as 'a.k.a.' The structure of this book conforms to the stories' first book publication in Britain. Most Poirot stories were initially published in magazines or newspapers, months or even years in advance of their appearance as (or in) a book. Similarly, Christie's books were often published in the United States before her home country, and short story collections frequently differed between countries. I have highlighted the main discrepancies when relevant, but I have stuck to the British publications unless otherwise noted.

3   Although as J.C. Bernthal has pointed out, Poirot did feature in a book originally published in Italy in 1989, in which he

joined several fellow detectives to solve the mystery of Charles Dickens' unfinished novel *The Mystery of Edwin Drood*. Called *The D Case, or the Truth About the Mystery of Edwin Drood*, it was co-written by Carlo Fruttero and Franco Lucentini (alongside Dickens) and authorised by Agatha Christie Ltd.

4 Interview with Marcelle Bernstein for *Observer* magazine, 14 December 1969. Subsequently referred to as Bernstein interview, 1969.

5 Interview with Francis Wyndham in *The Sunday Times*, 27 February 1966. Subsequently referred to as Wyndham interview, 1966.

6 *An Autobiography*, p.193. Eventually this story was reworked and published as the short story 'The House of Dreams' in 1926. The play may be *The Lie*, which was not performed until 2018.

7 It is, in fact, a quotation attributed to Omar Khayyam in Edward Fitzgerald's *Rubaiyat of Omar Khayyam*, an 1859 collection of poetry attributed to the eleventh-century Iranian man of science, although its veracity is doubted. In this case, the poem reads: 'The Worldly Hope men set their Hearts upon / Turns Ashes, or it prospers, and anon / Like Snow upon the Desert's dusty face / Lighting a little hour or two, is gone.'

8 The couple were then occasionally revisited for the rest of Christie's career, including in the final book she wrote, *Postern of Fate*, published more than six decades later, in 1973.

9 Bernstein interview, 1969.

CHAPTER ONE: THE 1920s

1 *An Autobiography*, unpublished material [ACA].

2 This may be an exaggeration, but there is little doubt that it was some considerable time. One of the reader reports from the publisher is dated October 1919, and Christie started to send the story out to publishers upon its completion in 1916.

3 The original ending was painstakingly transcribed by John Curran from Christie's original notebooks for *Agatha Christie's Murder in the Making*.

4 Although as John Curran has pointed out, the Hastings of *Styles* is referred to as Mr, not Captain – the military title comes into repeated use later.

5 Draft version of Christie's introduction to an *Appointment with Death* serialisation in the *Daily Mail* [ACA].

6 Wyndham interview, 1966.

7 *An Autobiography*, p.256.

8 *Appointment with Death* serialisation intro draft [ACA].

9 *Appointment with Death* serialisation intro draft [ACA].

10 Some have suggested a subconscious memory of a character by novelist Marie Belloc Lowndes called Hercule Popeau.

11 AC to Willett, 19 Oct 1920 [BOD].

12 *An Autobiography*, p.283.

13 AC to Willett, 24 Oct 1920 [BOD]

14 *The Church Times*, 15 April 1921. *The Church Times* would prove to be one of the best reviewers of Christie's works, in terms of attention paid to her.

15 *Times Literary Supplement*, 3 Feb 1921.

16 Wyndham interview, 1966.

17 *An Autobiography*, p.282.

18 John Curran also makes this point in his introduction to The Detective Club edition of *The Mystery of the Yellow Room*.

19 Wyndham interview, 1966.

20 *An Autobiography*, unpublished material [ACA].

21 *An Autobiography*, p.282.

22 Wyndham interview, 1966.

23 Michael Gilbert introduction, 1969 Hodder & Stoughton edition

24 *An Autobiography*, p.282.

25 AC to Willett, 15 Jan 1923 [BOD].

26 *An Autobiography*, p.282.

27 *Times Literary Supplement*, 7 June 1923.

28 *The Observer*, 10 June 1923.

29 *Daily Express*, 18 May 1923.

30 AC to Willett, 15 Jan 1923 [BOD]. In this letter, she declines to send the short stories 'back' to her publisher as she had sent them on to an agent instead, implying that they had not found any immediate use for them.

31 Although the idea of thought transference had briefly been mentioned in her second published novel, *The Secret Adversary*.

32 The publisher stated that their decision not to publish was due to concerns that this old manuscript was too dissimilar to Christie's other books, leading to possible confusion of her readership.

33 By some accounts, *Vision* was not even a full-length novel.

34 AC to Willett, 4 Nov 1923 [BOD].

35 The American edition of this book features three more stories, 'The Chocolate Box', 'The Veiled Lady', and 'The Lost Mine'. These are all included in the 1974 collection *Poirot's Early Cases*, and discussed there.

36 *The Sydney Morning Herald*, 3 November 1936.

37 AC to Willett, 17 Jan 1924 [BOD].

38 'Why not a round dozen?' asked the review in *The Observer*.

39 Robert Barnard is among those who have made this argument. Several of the stories in this later collection had been seen elsewhere in the meantime, and all had been published within book collections in some form in the United States by the time of the 1974 collection.

40 Drawn by W. Smithson Broadhead.

41 *The Observer*, 30 March 1924.

42 *An Autobiography*, p.319.

43 *An Autobiography*, p.433.

44 Initially printed in *The Royal Magazine* before becoming part of the short story collection *The Thirteen Problems* in 1932.

45 It had been serialised in the *London Evening News* between July and September 1925, under the title *Who Killed Ackroyd?*

46 Wyndham interview, 1966.

47 Interview with Valerie Knox in *The Times*, 1 December 1967.

48 *The Mysterious Dame Agatha*, BBC Radio, 1975.

49 Bernstein interview, 1969.

50 Bernstein interview, 1969.

51 She did give a version of the events in an interview with the *Daily Mail* on 16 February 1928, in response to a mention of the disappearance in an unrelated libel case. There is no explicit mention of it in her lengthy autobiography.

52 AC to EC, 10 Jan 1970 [HMA].

53 Largely unseen since the 1920s, the original short stories were republished by HarperCollins in 2017 within their Detective Club series, with an introduction by Karl Pike.

54 *Daily Express*, 27 Jan 1927, and *The Observer*, 13 February 1927.

55 *The Manchester Guardian*, 28 April 1927.

56 Wyndham interview, 1966.

57 *An Autobiography*, unpublished material [ACA].

58 Later collected as simply 'The Plymouth Express'.

59 Green's book is called *Agatha Christie: A Life in Theatre*, and is published by HarperCollins. It has been an invaluable resource for this book when discussing the stage plays.

60 *An Autobiography*, unpublished material [ACA].
61 *An Autobiography*, p.434.
62 *TV Times*, 31 August 1956.
63 *Daily Express*, 16 May 1928.
64 *The Church Times*, 25 May 1928.
65 *Daily Express*, 16 May 1928.
66 *The Manchester Guardian*, 11 Dec 1928.
67 Some productions in the United States used a further different title, *The Ackroyd Mystery*.

CHAPTER TWO: THE 1930s

1   Allen Lane would soon create the Penguin Books imprint with his brothers, John and Richard Lane..
2   Bernstein interview, 1969.
3   Specifically, in John Curran's 'Agatha Christie's Black Coffee: A Mystery within a Mystery', *CADS: Crime and Detective Stories*, 67 (2014).
4   AC to MM, 11 Dec 1930 [ACA].
5   *Agatha Christie in Close Up*, BBC Radio, 1955.
6   AC to MM, 11 Dec 1930 [ACA].
7   *Daily Express*, 10 April 1931; *The Manchester Guardian*, 10 April 1931.
8   *The Observer*, 14 December 1930.
9   AC to Clara Miller, 9 May 1922 [ACA].
10 A contemporary novelisation of the film has been republished as part of HarperCollins' Detective Club collection.
11 *Variety*, 20 March 1930.
12 *The Bioscope*, 6 May 1931.
13 *Picturegoer Weekly*, 19 September 1931.
14 AC to Lord Mountbatten, 15 November 1972 [ACA].
15 *Variety*, 1 September 1931.
16 *Picturegoer Weekly*, 12 December 1931.
17 *Variety*, 2 August 1932.
18 *Monthly Film Bulletin*, August 1934.
19 *Picturegoer Weekly*, 2 February 1935.
20 *Variety*, 3 April 1935.
21 Wyndham interview, 1966.
22 *Curtain* was almost certainly written in 1940. More of which later...
23 Wyndham interview, 1966 and Bernstein interview, 1969.

24 Although he was beaten by Miss Marple in this regard, as 1930's *The Murder at the Vicarage* was Christie's first title to form part of the range.

25 *Times Literary Supplement*, 14 April 1932.

26 *The Observer*, 20 March 1932.

27 *The Church Times*, 8 April 1932.

28 *The Observer*, 8 May 1938.

29 *The Manchester Guardian*, 4 May 1940.

30 *The Observer*, 5 May 1940.

31 AC to MM, 13 Oct 1931 [ACA].

32 AC to MM, 16 Oct 1931 [ACA].

33 *The Church Times*, 13 October 1933.

34 *The Observer*, 3 September 1933.

35 *Times Literary Supplement*, 21 September 1931.

36 *Yorkshire Post*, 27 September 1933.

37 *An Autobiography*, p.363.

38 *An Autobiography*, p.361.

39 *An Autobiography*, p.422.

40 Bernstein interview, 1969.

41 As outlined in EC to HO, 8 October 1948 [HMA].

42 A minor exception was a short adaptation for West German television in 1955.

43 *Times Literary Supplement*, 11 January 1934.

44 *The Manchester Guardian*, 12 January 1934.

45 Satterthwaite would later make a brief appearance in the Poirot story 'Dead Man's Mirror', collected in 1937's *Murder in the Mews*.

46 Wyndham interview, 1966.

47 *The Manchester Guardian*, 29 January 1935.

48 *Times Literary Supplement*, 31 January 1935.

49 *The Daily Mirror*, 14 January 1935.

50 *The Observer*, 30 June 1935.

51 Bernstein interview, 1969.

52 *The Observer*, 30 June 1935.

53 Wyndham interview, 1966.

54 Previous addresses for Poirot included Farraway Street in *The Big Four*. Oddly, the fact that the first letter of the victims' forenames *and* surnames is also the same (ie, Alice Ascher of Andover) goes unremarked when the detective's sleuthing team try to find and protect the potential fourth victim – even though this narrows the pool of names considerably.

55 Churston's name is probably influenced by Churston Ferrers, a village close to Christie's Greenway holiday home in south Devon.

56 *The Yorkshire Post*, 5 February 1936.

57 HO to EC, 3 March 1936 [ACA].

58 Inflation calculated at the United States Department of Labor website: https://www.bls.gov/data/inflation_calculator.htm

59 According to the Bank of England calculator at https://www.bankofengland.co.uk/monetary-policy/inflation/inflation-calculator

60 *The Manchester Guardian*, 6 February 1936.

61 *The Yorkshire Post*, 5 February 1936.

62 *Times Literary Supplement*, 11 January 1936.

63 It was also proposed that *Peril at End House, Three Act Tragedy* and *The Mysterious Affair at Styles* should be licensed for a slightly lesser amount of $6250 because the studio perceived them to be 'much poorer' stories.

64 *Variety*, 28 March 1936.

65 EC to AC, 20 Feb 1936 [ACA].

66 *Times Literary Supplement*, 18 July 1936.

67 *Action*, 30 July 1936.

68 *The Yorkshire Post*, 8 July 1936.

69 *The Observer*, 12 July 1936.

70 Wyndham interview, 1966.

71 Wyndham interview, 1966.

72 EC to AC, 13 November 1936 [ACA].

73 EC to AC, 24 November 1936 [ACA].

74 Hughes Massie NY office to Fisher, 25 May 1936 [ACA].

75 *The Manchester Guardian*, 20 November 1936.

76 *Times Literary Supplement*, 14 November 1936.

77 *The Observer*, 15 November 1936.

78 'The Market Basing Mystery' was eventually included in 1974's *Poirot's Early Cases*, as well as the earlier teen-orientated volume of Christie short stories *13 for Luck!* (1966).

79 'The Submarine Plans' was eventually included in 1974's *Poirot's Early Cases*.

80 *The Observer*, 18 April 1937.

81 Hughes Massie to Fisher, 23 October 1936 [ACA].

82 In the end, it would take more than seventy years for the Poirot version of 'The Regatta Mystery' to be published as part of a collection in the UK – see Chapter Seven for more details.

83 *The Observer*, 18 April 1937.

84 *Times Literary Supplement*, 27 March 1937.

85 See Julius Green's *Agatha Christie: A Life in Theatre* for more details.

86 *The Observer*, 20 June 1937.

87 *The Observer*, 7 November 1937.

88 *The Manchester Guardian*, 3 November 1937.

89 *The Manchester Guardian*, 13 July 1937.

90 *An Autobiography*, p.342.

91 Allegedly some editions of the novel use this title, although none have been uncovered during the research for this book.

92 In the end the *Saturday Evening Post* paid $16,000 for the rights, which was seen as lower than they might have offered considering the extra work. In the UK, the £700 from Amalgamated Press for the serialisation in *Woman's Journal* was £100 more than they had previously paid.

93 *Times Literary Supplement*, 10 July 1937.

94 *The Observer*, 18 July 1937.

95 Bernstein interview, 1969.

96 Otterbourne also refers to one of her books, the title of which has a familiar ring to it – *Snow on the Desert's Face*, which may well show how little Christie thought of her own unpublished first novel *Snow Upon the Desert* at this point.

97 Taken from Christie's foreword.

98 EC to AC, 21 August 1936 [ACA].

99 *The Observer*, 14 November 1937.

100 *Times Literary Supplement*, 20 November 1937.

101 *The Manchester Guardian*, 10 December 1937.

102 *The Yorkshire Post*, 10 November 1937.

103 AC to MM, 27 October 1942 [ACA].

104 Bernstein interview, 1969.

105 *Times Literary Supplement*, 7 May 1938.

106 *The Manchester Guardian*, 27 May 1938.

107 *The Observer*, 1 May 1938.

108 [Spoiler for the play] In the play, Mrs Boynton is revealed to have committed suicide and deliberately staged events to cast suspicion on her family.

109 Bernstein interview, 1969.

110 Some reprints rename the story further, to *A Holiday for Murder*.

111 *Times Literary Supplement*, 17 December 1938.

112 *The Church Times*, 6 January 1939.

113 *The Observer*, 18 December 1938.

114 *The Manchester Guardian*, 13 January 1939.

CHAPTER THREE: THE 1940s

1 Peter Lord's name is surely a play on Dorothy L. Sayers' detective Lord Peter Wimsey.

2 [Spoiler] 'I don't drink tea.' John Curran has also pointed out that certain other circumstances relating to the murderer's plan also rely on chance and good fortune, but the issue with the tea is probably the most obvious. A line of dialogue was added for the *Agatha Christie's Poirot* adaptation to make the solution more believable.

3 Poirot's entrance at the beginning of Part II references 'The Dream', a short story written not long before *Sad Cypress* and first published in 1938, in another example of the detective being renowned for his past cases.

4 Wyndham interview, 1966.

5 EC to AC, 5 August 1938 [ACA].

6 AC to EC, 6 January 1940 [HMA].

7 As discussed by John Curran in *The Complete Secret Notebooks*, p.314.

8 AC to EC, 12 Jan 1940 [HMA].

9 EC to AC 19 January 1940 [HMA].

10 *Times Literary Supplement*, 9 March 1940.

11 *The Manchester Guardian*, 2 April 1940.

12 *The Observer*, 10 March 1940.

13 AC to WC, 15 September 1940 [HC]. Billy Collins was the fifth William Collins to assume a leading role in the running of Collins publishers – the first had established the company in 1819.

14 Not only was Greenway acquisitioned, but another of Christie's properties, Sheffield Terrace in London, was hit by a bomb and heavily damaged.

15 You can see the frieze and more details at https://www.nationaltrust.org.uk/greenway/features/greenway-library-frieze

16 AC to EC, 18 April 1940 [HMA].

17 EC to AC, 14 June 1940 [HMA] – Cork does say that changes

Christie had made to the character of Alistair Blunt should not be retained for the novel.

18 EC to AC, 2 January 1940 [HMA].

19 Some later paperbacks used the schlocky title *An Overdose of Death*.

20 AC to WC, 25 June 1940 [HC].

21 AC to WC, 15 July 1940 [HC].

22 *Times Literary Supplement*, 9 November 1940.

23 *The Manchester Guardian*, 13 December 1940.

24 *The Observer*, 10 November 1940.

25 AC to Mr Horler, 16 November 1940 [HMA].

26 The other is the opening of the BBC adaptation of *Nemesis*, a Miss Marple novel, in 1987. In the novel of *Evil Under the Sun*, the island is simply referred to as 'the island off Leathercombe Bay' – in the real world, it's situated by Bigbury-on-sea.

27 AC to WC, 8 April 1941 [HC].

28 *Times Literary Supplement*, 14 June 1941.

29 *The Observer*, 8 June 1941.

30 *The Yorkshire Post*, 3 October 1941.

31 *The Manchester Guardian*, 26 August 1941.

32 HO to EC, 25 September 1941 [HMA].

33 WC to AC, 9 July 1942 [HC].

34 AC to WC, 25 Feb 1943 [HC].

35 *The Observer*, 10 January 1943.

36 *Times Literary Supplement*, 16 January 1943.

37 *The Manchester Guardian*, 20 January 1943

38 From surviving correspondence we know that a rather mangled typescript was sent to Harold Ober at some point prior to 10 March 1941.

39 EC to AC, 11 November 1940 [HMA].

40 I am indebted to the work of Victor A. Berch, Karl Schadow and Steve Lewis at the Mystery File website, whose hard work in piecing together so much research about this show was invaluable. You can find much more information at their website, http://www.mysteryfile.com/M_Clinic.html

41 The story is also referred to as 'The Tragedy *of* Marsdon Manor' during the production.

42 The short story was not made available in a British collection of stories until 1991's *Problem at Pollensa Bay and Other Stories*. The BBC play uses the definite article in its title, *The Yellow Iris*.

43 The paperwork disagrees a little on the date of this Canadian

broadcast, which seems to have been on either 1 October or 1 November. Either way, Christie received a $200 fee for it.

44 HO to EC, 10 March 1944 [HMA]. In the end she earned £65 an episode, which translated to around $250 at 1945 exchange rates.

45 *The Billboard*, 25 March 1944.

46 According to the announcer, atmospheric conditions precluded a planned live introduction from Poirot's creator, although this may have been a bit of added drama for the listener considering the existence of a perfectly satisfactory recording played in its place.

47 The substitution is not even referred to within the broadcast – we only know the actor's name because of a passing mention in *Variety* on 11 April 1945.

48 The best resource for episode titles was http://www. digitaldeliftp.com, which sadly is not available at the time of writing. However their research has proven to be invaluable.

49 *Variety*, 21 November 1945.

50 *Variety*, 21 August 1946.

51 *Billboard*, 26 January 1946.

52 AC to EC, 27 January 1947 [HMA].

53 Other Australian radio adaptations included 'The Incredible Theft' in 1938, and *Peril at End House* in 1946

54 Wyndham interview, 1966.

55 Bernstein interview, 1969.

56 EC to HO, 15 June 1945 [HMA].

57 Kenneth Littaeur, Executive Editor at Collier's, 14 November 1945 [HMA].

58 WC to AC, 3 April 1947 [HC].

59 *The Church Times*, 29 November 1946.

60 *Daily Worker*, 28 November 1946.

61 It also has a strong band of advocates – in *Agatha Christie's Complete Secret Notebooks* John Curran describes the book as 'one of the greatest collections in the entire crime fiction genre. It is brilliant in concept, design and execution.'

62 Although why *The Labours of Hercules*, rather than *The Labours of Hercule*, which would have been a better play on words?

63 [Possible spoiler] *After the Funeral* (1953).

64 This is also the first time that we see the secretary Miss Lemon in a British book collection with Poirot, although she had previously worked for Poirot in an earlier magazine short

story 'How Does Your Garden Grow?', first published in 1935 and collected in 1974's *Poirot's Early Cases*. This story was also collected in the American book *The Regatta Mystery and Other Stories* in 1939.

65 A novel that was an expansion of the superior short story 'The Mystery of the Plymouth Express'.

66 AC to EC, 6 January 1940 [HMA].

67 AC to EC, 16 November 1940 [HMA].

68 The original version was published in *Agatha Christie's Secret Notebooks*.

69 In 'The Double Clue' (later collected in *Poirot's Early Cases*) and *The Big Four*.

70 AC to WC, 9 April 1947 [HC].

71 *The Church Times*, 12 September 1947.

72 *The Observer*, 5 October 1947.

73 Wyndham interview, 1966.

74 AC to WC, 27 December 1947 [HC].

75 The American edition was also published several months prior to the British publication in November 1948.

76 AC to EC, 12 June 1950 [HMA].

77 Reader's report, 9 Dec 1947 [HC].

78 *The Church Times*, 19 November 1948.

79 *The Daily Worker*, 18 November 1948 and *The Observer*, 21 November 1948.

80 HO to EC, 3 October 1947 [HMA].

81 AC to EC, 7 December 1947 [HMA].

82 Although Christie rarely wrote during summer, preferring to do so over winter.

CHAPTER FOUR: THE 1950s

1 AC to EC, 12 February 1955 [HMA].

2 AC to EC, 12 February 1955 [HMA].

3 AC to EC, 12 February 1955 [HMA].

4 Anthony Hicks died in 2005.

5 AC to EC, 6 September 1951 [HMA].

6 Such a calculation requires the inclusion of different short story editions in both the United States and Britain.

7 *Daily Mirror*, 9 June 1950.

8 EC, 4 September 1951 [HMA].

9 Specifically, the Rendells.

10 AC to EC, 6 September 1951 [HMA].

11 *The Observer*, 23 March 1952.

12 AC to 'Anthony Gilbert', 19 April 1952 [HMA].

13 Internal letter, 17 April 1953 [HC].

14 AC to WC, 5 August 1953 [HC].

15 Bernstein interview, 1969.

16 Bernstein interview, 1969.

17 As covered in the next chapter.

18 *The Observer*, 17 May 1953. A spoiler has been removed from the quote.

19 Mr Smith to WC, 4 November 1953 [HC].

20 Bernstein interview, 1969.

21 There had not been a Christie novel in 1947, but the gap between the publication of *The Hollow* in 1946 and *Taken at the Flood* in 1948 was only around sixteen months.

22 Mr Smith to WC, 4 November 1953 [HC].

23 For readability, I have dropped the usual '…and other Stories' from the end of the title of many of these collections.

24 Memo 28 July 1954 [HC].

25 AC to EC, 21 March 1956 [HMA].

26 EC to HO, 29 April 1954 [HMA].

27 WC to AC, 21 March 1955 [HC].

28 *Times Literary Supplement*, 23 December 1955.

29 *The Observer*, 30 October 1955.

30 Morgan, p.332. According to Morgan, Peter Sellers was set to star as Poirot, although as Poirot does not feature in the final script (he is replaced by Inspector Sharpe) perhaps Sellers was considered for another role, or his name was part of very early discussions before the character was removed.

31 AC to EC, 24 [month indecipherable] 1954 [HMA].

32 *The Church Times*, 11 March 1955.

33 AC to EC, 19 March 1953 [HMA].

34 In fact, the appearances of Maurice Denham as Parker Pyne and Angela Easterling as Miss Lemon in two episodes of *The Agatha Christie Hour* are the first occasions where the same actors played the same Christie characters on television more than once.

35 *Personal Call* TX 31 May 1954; 'The Third Floor Flat' TX 21 April 1954.

36 Drama Script Reader's Report, 14 May 1954, Agatha Christie RCONT1 1937-62 (BBC WAC).

37 *The Observer*, 11 March 1956.
38 AC to EC, 27 February 1956 [HMA]. In the end the Miss Marple story was first published in the *Daily Mail* in December 1956. More details about the original Poirot story can be found in John Curran's afterword essay in the 2014 publication of the story from HarperCollins.
39 *Times Literary Supplement*, 21 December 1956.
40 *The Observer*, 18 November 1956.
41 *The Manchester Guardian*, 7 December 1957. Francis Iles was one of the pen-names used by crime writer Anthony Berkeley Cox, who often used the name Anthony Berkeley, and was also a journalist.
42 *The Times*, 15 November 1956.
43 *Daily Express*, 13 November 1956.
44 *Daily Express*, 19 December 1957.
45 Reader's report for *The Innocent*, 1 May 1958 [HC].
46 Reader's report, 16 June 1959 [HC].
47 *Times Literary Supplement*, 18 December 1959.
48 *Daily Express*, 4 November 1959.

CHAPTER FIVE: THE 1960s

1 Wyndham interview, 1966.
2 Michael Hoare to WC, 27 Jan 1960 [HC].
3 Memo, 22 March 1960 [HMA]. 'Three Blind Mice' had first been a radio play, which was then adapted as a print story, before making it to the stage as *The Mousetrap*.
4 EC to AC, 11 April 1960 [HMA].
5 AC to EC, 12 April 1960 [HMA].
6 I have mentioned the known first publication of stories even when in America here, drawing on Karl Pike's excellent research, published in the 2008 collection *Hercule Poirot: The Complete Short Stories*. '[The Case of] The Perfect Maid' is a Miss Marple story, the others are Poirot.
7 AC to EC, 12 April 1960 [HMA].
8 EC to AC, 14 April 1960 [HMA].
9 AC to EC, 12 April 1960 [HMA].
10 DO to EC, 6 July 1960 [HMA].
11 Michael Hoare to Mr House, 4 May 1960 [HC].
12 Although it took until 1997 for the 'The Mystery of the Spanish Chest' to appear in America, in *The Harlequin Tea Set*

(the original 'Baghdad Chest' story had featured in the 1939 American collection *The Regatta Mystery*).

13 *Times Literary Supplement*, 18 November 1960.
14 AC to EC, 20 January 1960 [HMA].
15 *News Chronicle*, 12 May 1960.
16 *News Chronicle*, 12 May 1960.
17 Field Roscoe & Co to EC, 4 May 1960 [HMA] and EC to AC, 11 April 1960 [HMA].
18 EC to RH, 17 March 1960 [HMA].
19 EC to AC, 11 April 1960 [HMA].
20 Lyndon had written the scripts for several Hollywood films, including the 1953 adaptation of *The War of the Worlds*. His name was a pseudonym for Alfred Edgar.
21 John Curran, *Agatha Christie's Complete Secret Notebooks*, pp.603-4.
22 Wyndham interview, 1966.
23 AC to EC, 20 January 1963 [HMA].
24 Wyndham interview, 1966.
25 *Times Literary Supplement*, 21 November 1963.
26 *The Observer*, 10 November 1963.
27 Memo of 26 November 1963 meeting [HC].
28 Draft *New York Daily News* interview c.1970 [ACA].
29 AC to Raymond J. Fullager, c.20 April 1963 [HMA].
30 AC to EC, 24 May 1963 [HMA].
31 Lawrence Bachmann to AC, 30 July 1963 [HMA].
32 AC to EC, 20 August 1963 [HMA].
33 RH to EC, 25 March 1964 [HMA].
34 Albeit with uncredited similarities to *They Do It With Mirrors*.
35 RH to EC, 6 April 1964 [HMA].
36 *The Financial Times*, 21 April 1964.
37 LB to AC, 7 April 1964 [HMA].
38 Wyndham interview, 1966.
39 EC to AH, 4 May 1964 [HMA].
40 AH to EC, 7 May 1964 [HMA].
41 RH to EC, 14 May 1964 [HMA].
42 Harbottle & Lewis to J.C. Medley, 2 July 1964 [HMA].
43 Harbottle & Lewis to J.C. Medley, 6 July 1964 [HMA].
44 *Film and Filming*. April 1965.
45 *Eastern Evening News*, 30 January 1965.
46 AC to EC, 6 Dec 1964 [HMA].
47 *Daily Mirror*, 20 January 1965.

48 *Monthly Film Bulletin*, 1 January 1966.
49 *Variety*, 16 March 1966.
50 *Daily Mirror*, 30 March 1964.
51 Although some elements of the story were reworked for 'Murder in the Mews', which had appeared in the eponymous 1937 volume.
52 AC to EC, 31 December 1966 [HMA].
53 This type of living situation had been briefly mentioned in *The Clocks*.
54 Interview with Valerie Knox in *The Times*, 1 December 1967.
55 Wyndham interview, 1966.
56 Interview with Valerie Knox in *The Times*, 1 December 1967.
57 Responses to a questionnaire sent to Christie by the Italian imprint Il Giallo Mondadori.
58 Reader's notes, c.August 1966 [HC].
59 Reader's notes, c.August 1966 [HC].
60 AC to EC, 14 February 1967 [HMA].
61 *Times Literary Supplement*, 8 December 1966.
62 *The Observer*, 13 November 1966.
63 *Daily Express*, 17 November 1966.
64 Bernstein interview, 1969.
65 Interview with Valerie Knox in *The Times*, 1 December 1967.
66 *The Observer*, 9 November 1969.
67 Wyndham interview, 1966.

CHAPTER SIX: THE 1970s

1 AC to Nora Blackborow, c.1972 (undated) [HMA].
2 Although she played no great part in it, some of the publicity managed to annoy Christie, especially when Collins confused the date of her birthday (15 September) with that of her grandson, Mathew, which is six days later.
3 Christie detailed her follow up discussion with her surgeon in a letter on 20 December 1971, AC to EC [HMA].
4 AC to Miss Michelle C. Cliff, 10 Jan 1972 [HMA].
5 AC to EC, 10 January 1972 [HMA].
6 *The Guardian*, 3 April 2009: https://www.theguardian.com/books/2009/apr/03/agatha-christie-alzheimers-research
7 Another late stage change was the replacement of references to India with Malaya, to reflect the fact that India had not been under British rule for twenty-five years.

8   *Daily Express*, 9 November 1972.
9   *The Observer*, 5 November 1972.
10 *The Guardian*, 30 November 1972.
11 *Daily Mirror*, 29 August 1970.
12 AC to EC, 8 April 1974 [HMA].
13 AC to EC, c.Sept 1970 [HMA].
14 Broadcast on 27 December 1974, 6 June 1975 and 9 June 1975 respectively. Other readings include *Death on the Nile* (Anna Massey, twelve parts from 8 March 1976) and *Taken at the Flood* (Cyril Shaps, twelve parts from 2 August 1976).
15 Renamed from Sir Claud Amory in Christie's original play.
16 In this writer's opinion, Bollmann gives the best performance of Poirot on screen until Ian Holm in 1987's *Murder by the Book*.
17 An ITV company.
18 Wolfgang Löhde of Zweites Deutsches Fernsehen to Hughes Massie, 22 March 1973 [HMA].
19 Allen Roberts to AC, 22 June 1973 [HMA].
20 Michael J. Cooper to AC, 9 August 1973 [HMA].
21 Reply written on original letter from EC to AC, 14 August 1973 [HMA] and AC to EC, 24 August 1973 [HMA].
22 RH to WC, 29 Oct 1973 [HC].
23 RH to WC, 15 Nov 1973 [HC].
24 WC to EH, 16 Nov 1973 [HC].
25 AC to EC, 13 Jan 1974 [HMA].
26 EC to AC, 21 Jan 1974 [HMA].
27 AC to WC, 28 Jan 1974 [HMA].
28 AC to WC, 25 March 1974 [HC]. Christie's suggested titles were 'The Red Signal'; 'The Lamp'; 'The Gypsy'; 'The Dressmaker's Doll'; 'The Call of Wings'; 'The Last Séance'; 'Sanctuary'; 'S.O.S.'; 'The Mystery of the Blue Jar'; 'The Case of Sir Andrew Carmichael'; 'The Love Detectives'; 'Swan Song'; *Death Comes as the End*; 'In a Glass Darkly'; 'Death by Drowning' and *Dumb Witness*, while she also mentions *The Mystery of the Blue Train*, the origin of which she seems to confuse with *The Big Four*.
29 AC to WC, 2 April 1974 [HC].
30 All stories originally appeared in *The Sketch* during 1923, with these exceptions: 'The Lemesurier Inheritance' first appeared in *The Magpie*, December 1923; 'The Third Floor Flat' first appeared in *Hutchinson's Story Magazine* in January

1929; 'Double Sin' first appeared as 'By Road or By Rail' in the 23 September 1928 edition of *Sunday Dispatch*; 'Wasps' Nest' was first published as 'The Wasps' Nest' in the *Daily Mail*, 20 November 1928; 'Problem at Sea' first appeared in *This Week* on 12 January 1936, and as 'Poirot and the Crime in Cabin 66' in *The Strand* the following month; 'How Does Your Garden Grow?' was first published in *Ladies' Home Journal* in June 1935, and *The Strand* two months later.

31 *The Sketch* also uses different opening to both the typescript and book version of the story in order to introduce Poirot: 'Formerly Chief of the Belgian Force, my friend Hercule Poirot came to England as a refugee in the early days of the war. Pure chance led him to be connected with the case which I have already chronicled elsewhere under the title of *The Mysterious Affair at Styles*.'

32 The mark was inserted just before the reader is told 'The following Tuesday was fixed upon by Poirot...'. This is the only surviving typescript that is known to have included this device.

33 Originally published as 'The Adventure of the King of Clubs'.

34 Originally published as 'The Mystery of the Plymouth Express'.

35 Originally published as 'The Case of the Chocolate Box'.

36 This section features in both the original typescript and the version of the story published in *The Sketch*.

37 RH to WC, 26 May 1974 (HC).

38 AC to WC, 4 June 1974 (HC).

39 WC to AC, 11 June 1974.

40 *The Observer*, 22 September 1974.

41 *The Guardian*, 3 October 1974.

42 *And Then There Were None* from 1945, and 1957's *Witness for the Prosecution*. The Margaret Rutherford Miss Marple films had been reasonable commercial successes and were mostly received with indifference by critics.

43 Interview with the author, August 2013.

44 RH to EC, 5 Feb 1973 [HMA].

45 Lumet had made his name with 1957's *12 Angry Men*.

46 AC to EC, 25 Jan 1974 [HMA].

47 The tradition of Poirot being a new bright young thing of the acting world seems to have carried on from Charles

Laughton's casting for the play *Alibi* in 1928, when he was only twenty-eight.

48 Discussion with Lord Snowdon, 1974 [ACA].
49 *Evening Standard*, 5 August 1974.
50 AC to EC, 20 June 1974 [HMA].
51 *The Guardian*, 13 November 2017: https://www.theguardian.com/culture/2017/nov/13/how-we-made-the-original-murder-on-the-orient-express
52 RH to EC, 20 Oct 1974 [HMA].
53 *The Observer*, 24 November 1974.
54 *Daily Mirror*, 20 November 1974.
55 *The Guardian*, 21 November 1974.
56 *Daily Mirror*, 3 April 1974.
57 *Daily Express*, 20 November 1974.
58 *The Times*, 22 November 1974.
59 RH to EC, 20 October 1974 [HMA].
60 EC to Harold Ober, 10 March 1941 [HMA].
61 HO to EC, 24 April 1941 [HMA].
62 EC to Ober, 14 May 1940 [HMA].
63 EC to RH, 3 March 1950 [HMA].
64 EC to Dorothy Olding at Dodd, Mead, 26 Nov 1974 [HMA].
65 RH to WC, 14 March 1975 [HC].
66 'PW' at Dodd, Mead to Patricia Cork, 14 March 1975 [HMA].
67 *Times Literary Supplement*, 26 September 1975.
68 *The Guardian*, 8 October 1975.
69 *The Guardian*, 11 December 1975.
70 *The Times*, 20 September 1975.
71 Some did mention *Death on the Nile* as the likely next picture, but generally with the sense that they were reporting the wishful thinking of producers.
72 *Screen Intl*, 28 May 1977.
73 *Daily Mail*, 24 May 1977.
74 *Evening News*, 23 October 1976.
75 *Sunday Express*, 30 October 1977.
76 *Sunday Mirror*, 29 October 1977.
77 *Screen Intl*, 4 November 1978.
78 *Monthly Film Bulletin*, October 1978.
79 *Variety*, 27 September 1978.
80 *The Independent Film Journal*, October 1978.
81 *Screen Intl*, 1–8 December 1979.
82 *Screen Intl*, 5 May 1979.

CHAPTER SEVEN: THE 1980s and 1990s

1 Superintendent Battle was the only other Christie character to make an appearance. For more about the game, visit https://www.collectingchristie.com/post/crime-club-game. Also, there were non-Agatha Christie games based on the idea of a murder on the Orient Express, most notably in the 1960s (called 'Murder on the Orient Express', featuring both Sherlock Holmes and Dr Watson with the mystery credited to Conan Doyle) and 1980s (simply called 'Orient Express'), as well as a 1968 Agatha Christie game based on *And Then There Were None*.

2 MP to RH & AH, 7 September 1984 [ACA].

3 One of the developers interested in making a computer game in the 1980s, Spinnaker Software, did release VHS games based on the stories 'The Scoop' and 'Behind the Screen', which Christie had co-written with fellow Detection Club authors in 1930-1. Despite the fact that Christie wrote only part of the stories hers was the name prominently featured on the packaging.

4 As the eventual 1988 film of *Appointment with Death* also credits Shaffer as a co-writer it's possible that this screenplay followed the tradition of *Evil Under the Sun* and was a reworked version of a script that the writer initially drafted years earlier before being replaced by another film.

5 *Screen Intl*, 15 August 1981.

6 *Monthly Film Bulletin*, March 1982.

7 *Variety*, 27 January 1982.

8 *Variety*, 23 January 1983.

9 *Screen International*, 27 April 1985.

10 *Women's Wear Daily*, 17 October 1985.

11 MP to RH & AH, 6 August 1985 [ACA].

12 *Variety*, 23 October 1985.

13 MP to RH and AH, 2 April 1985 [ACA].

14 MP to RH and AH, 2 April 1985 [ACA].

15 *New York Times*, 8 January 1986.

16 *Variety*, 15 January 1986.

17 The production also follows the American version of the book, which differs from the British one in terms of the murderer's motivation, among other things.

18 *New York Times*, 30 September 1986.

19 MP to Peter Reichelt, 22 October 1986 [ACA].

20 'The Mystery of Hunter's Lodge' in 1991.

21 Brian Stone to RH, 22 April 1986 [ACA].

22 Nick Evans to BS, 9 July 1984 [ACA].

23 ACL also co-operated with the *South Bank Show* documentary about Christie that was shown in November 1986.

24 Nick Evans to RH, 30 July 1984 [ACA].

25 RH to Nick Evans, 9 September 1984 [ACA].

26 MP to Nick Evans, 23 November 1984 [ACA].

27 Nick Evans to RH, 7 November 1984 [ACA].

28 MP to Nick Evans, 18 April 1985 [ACA].

29 MP to Nick Evans, 18 April 1985 [ACA].

30 MP to RH, Undated c. April 1985 [ACA].

31 *The Times*, 28 August 1986.

32 *The Guardian*, 29 August 1986.

33 *Variety*, 13 June 1990.

34 MP to John Erichsen, 2 April 1987 [ACA].

35 RH notes on script, dated 26 Feb 1987.

36 MP to ACL board, Brian Stone and Keith Allison, 5 March 1987 [ACA].

37 *The Times*, 20 July 1987.

38 *The Guardian*, 26 May 1988.

39 *Today*, 27 May 1988 and *Evening Standard*, 26 May 1988.

40 *The Times*, 26 May 1988.

41 MP to Brian Stone, 17 June 1988 [ACA].

42 *The Times*, 20 July 1987.

43 RH to Guy Slater, 10 November 1984 (BBC WAC: *A Pocketful of Rye* production file). As previously reproduced in *Agatha Christie on Screen* by this author (2016).

44 Guy Slater to Jonathan Powell, 16 November 1984 (BBC WAC: *A Pocketful of Rye* production file). As previously reproduced in *Agatha Christie on Screen* by this author (2016).

45 Although his appearances on the television series were about to become very infrequent by the time of his radio debut in the role in April 2000's *The ABC Murders*.

46 Interview with the author, April 2019.

47 However, even by April 1987 both the BBC and Granada were still showing interest in producing the series.

48 RH to 'John', 14 November 1985 [ACA].

49 Interview with the author, April 2019.

50 MP to ACL Directors, 24 June 1986 [ACA].

51 Interview with the author, August 2015.
52 Suchet and Wansell, p.19.
53 Interview with the author, April 2019.
54 Interview with the author, April 2019.
55 Interview with the author, August 2015.
56 Interview with the author, April 2019.
57 MP to BE, 1 September 1988 [ACA].
58 The first series adapted the stories 'The Adventure of the Clapham Cook', 'Murder in the Mews', 'The Adventure of Johnnie Waverly', 'Four and Twenty Blackbirds', 'The Third Floor Flat', 'Triangle at Rhodes', 'Problem at Sea', 'The Incredible Theft', 'The King of Clubs', and 'The Dream'. 'Murder in the Mews' reuses elements from the shorter story 'The Market Basing Mystery', and consequently the latter was not adapted for the programme. Similarly, 'The Incredible Theft' reworks and expands 'The Submarine Plans', which consequently is not adapted.
59 *Daily Star*, 19 December 1988; *Daily Express*, 9 January 1989.
60 *The Mail on Sunday*, 15 January 1989.
61 *The Guardian*, 16 January 1989.
62 Many overseas and repeat broadcasts split *Peril at End House* into two parts, with a new recap scene at the beginning of the second part. It took until the sixth season for *The Murder on the Links* to be adapted.
63 The other episodes are 'The Veiled Lady', 'The Lost Mine', 'The Cornish Mystery', 'The Disappearance of Mr Davenheim', 'Double Sin', 'The Adventure of the Cheap Flat', 'The Kidnapped Prime Minister', and 'The Adventure of the Western Star'.
64 Hastings appeared in nine of the first series' ten episodes, Japp was in eight, and Miss Lemon in seven.
65 RH to BE, 3 April 1989 [ACA].
66 The episode was shown on 16 September 1990; Christie was born on 15 September 1890.
67 The third series adapted 'How Does Your Garden Grow?', 'The Million Dollar Bond Robbery', 'The Plymouth Express', 'Wasps' Nest', 'The Tragedy at Marsdon Manor', 'The Double Clue', 'The Mystery of the Spanish Chest', 'The Theft of the Royal Ruby', 'The Affair at the Victory Ball', and 'The Mystery of Hunter's Lodge'. 'The Mystery of the Spanish Chest' is an expanded version of 'The Mystery of the Baghdad Chest', while

'The Theft of the Royal Ruby' is an alternative name for 'The Adventure of the Christmas Pudding' – although, curiously, this episode was shown in late February. Repeat runs have given it more festive scheduling.

68 RH to BE, 18 November 1990 [ACA].

69 As well as 'The Lemesurier Inheritance', some stories that featured alternative versions of the same basic mystery were excluded, as well as some stories that were not published until after Christie's death. There is also 'The Regatta Mystery', which was originally written as a Parker Pyne story, but altered to feature Poirot as the detective on its first publication in *Chicago Tribune* and *Hartford Courant*. It was the Parker Pyne variant that was subsequently published in short story collections, until 2008's 'Hercule Poirot: The Complete Short Stories'. The fifth series episodes are 'The Adventure of the Egyptian Tomb', 'The Underdog' [sic], 'The Yellow Iris', 'The Case of the Missing Will', 'The Adventure of the Italian Nobleman', 'The Chocolate Box', 'Dead Man's Mirror', and 'Jewel Robbery at the Grand Metropolitan'. 'Dead Man's Mirror' is a reworked and expanded version of the story 'The Second Gong', which consequently is not adapted for the series.

70 MP to RH and AH, 27 November 1991 [ACA].

71 RH to BS, 27 May 1992 [ACA].

72 Brian Stone to MP, 7 February 1991 [ACA].

73 Japp is not in either novel, but then Christie was never very precious about which police inspector should be called into service to assist the main detective. *Taken at the Flood* was another suggested title for this season, which was replaced by *Hercule Poirot's Christmas*.

74 BE to RH, 9 October 1992 [ACA].

75 7.98m viewers tuned in to *Poirot*, but 16.34m were watching *One Foot in the Grave* on BBC One.

76 'The Second Gong' had previously featured in the American collection *The Witness for the Prosecution* in 1948.

77 In its original play form (and in the *Poirot* series) it was called 'The Yellow Iris'.

78 The story had also featured in inexpensive short publications, *Problem at Pollensa Bay and Christmas Adventure* in 1943, and *Poirot Knows the Murderer* in 1946.

79 Confusingly, the short version of the story was also called 'The Adventure of the Christmas Pudding' when first published in

The Sketch, before being called 'Christmas Adventure' for other publications.

CHAPTER EIGHT: 2000 and BEYOND

1 Interview with the author, August 2015.
2 Interview with the author, April 2019.
3 Interview with the author, April 2019.
4 *The Times*, 19 Feb 2000.
5 This 64% stake is now owned by RLJ Entertainment.
6 *The Times*, 24 July 2002.
7 Interview with the author, August 2013.
8 *The Guardian*, 15 December 2003.
9 Interview with the author, August 2015.
10 *Huffington Post*, 13 November 2013 https://www.huffingtonpost. co.uk/2013/11/13/poirot-review-curtain-final-case-david-suchet_n_4269653.html
11 *New York Times*, 25 July 2014 https://www.nytimes. com/2014/07/26/arts/television/agatha-christies-poirot-comes-to-an-end.html
12 *The Telegraph*, 13 November 2013 https://www.telegraph.co.uk/ culture/tvandradio/tv-and-radio-reviews/10447645/Poirots-Last-Case-ITV-review.html
13 The same year Poirot also made a tongue-in-cheek appearance in *Murders at Turbot Towers* by S. John Peskett.
14 Martin Edwards has written an excellent article on this book, which includes his untangling of the true identity of the authors, credited as Margaret Rivers Larminie and Jane Langslow: http://www.martinedwardsbooks.com/goryknight. htm
15 I am indebted to Alexander Orlov who made me aware of the 1960s productions, and sent me a helpful newspaper cutting.
16 Specifically *The ABC Murders, Peril at End House, Cat Among the Pigeons, Sad Cypress, Five Little Pigs, Taken at the Flood*, and *Lord Edgware Dies*.
17 The Poirot stories investigated by this new team included *Dumb Witness, Hallowe'en Party, Cards on the Table, Murder on the Links, Hickory Dickory Dock, Mrs McGinty's Dead, 'The Adventure of Johnnie Waverly', The Mysterious Affair at Styles, Third Girl, Three Act Tragedy, Hercule Poirot's Christmas* (again), *Evil Under the Sun*, and *Appointment with Death*.

18 Namely 'The Jewel Robbery at the Grand Metropolitan', 'The Adventure of the Cheap Flat', *The ABC Murders*, 'The Kidnapped Prime Minster', 'The Adventure of the Egyptian Tomb', *Peril at End House*, 'The Adventure of the Christmas Pudding', 'The Plymouth Express', 'The Adventure of the Clapham Cook', 'Four-and-Twenty Blackbirds' (renamed 'Twenty-Four Japanese Thrushes'), 'The Disappearance of Mr Davenheim', and *Death in the Clouds*.

19 Many thanks for Haruhiko Imatake, who helped me gain access to several Japanese adaptations.

20 John Curran, *Agatha Christie's Complete Secret Notebooks*, p.254

21 *The Guardian*, 19 September 2019: https://www.theguardian.com/books/2014/sep/19/sophie-hannah-agatha-christie-poirot-interview

22 *The Independent*, 11 September 2014: https://www.independent.co.uk/arts-entertainment/books/reviews/the-monogram-murders-by-sophie-hannah-book-review-fans-are-in-safe-hands-in-modern-day-recreation-of-9726440.html

23 *The Guardian*, 9 September 2014: https://www.theguardian.com/books/2014/sep/09/monogram-murders-sophie-hannah-hercule-poirot-agatha-christie-novel-review

24 *The Telegraph*, 8 September 2014: https://www.telegraph.co.uk/culture/books/bookreviews/11081517/Sophie-Hannahs-new-Poirot-review-recalls-the-best-of-Agatha-Christie.html

25 *The Spectator*, 11 October 2014: https://www.spectator.co.uk/2014/10/the-monogram-murders-by-sophie-hannah-review/

26 *Hollywood Reporter*, 10 November 2017: https://www.hollywoodreporter.com/behind-screen/how-orient-express-was-rebuilt-at-a-uk-studio-1054400

27 *USA Today*, 10 November 2017: https://eu.usatoday.com/story/life/movies/2017/11/10/kenneth-branaghs-epic-mustache-poirots-superpower-murder-orient-express/843140001/

28 Branagh and Green commentary track for the DVD and Blu-ray release.

29 Branagh and Green commentary track for the DVD and Blu-ray release.

30 Branagh and Green commentary track for the DVD and Blu-ray release.

31 Branagh and Green commentary track for the DVD and Blu-ray release.

32   Branagh and Green commentary track for the DVD and
     Blu-ray release.

33   Branagh and Green commentary track for the DVD and
     Blu-ray release.

34   *The Observer.* 5 November 2017: https://
     www.theguardian.com/film/2017/nov/05/
     murder-on-the-orient-express-review-kenneth-branagh

35   *The Guardian,* 2 November 2017: https://www.theguardian.
     com/film/2017/nov/02/on-the-orient-express-review-kenneth-
     branagh-judi-dench-johnny-depp-agatha-christie

36   *Fandom Entertainment,* 8 November 2017: https://www.youtube.
     com/watch?v=E2bupPJy_5E&feature=youtu.be

37   *The Telegraph,* 29 December 2018: https://www.telegraph.co.uk/
     news/2018/12/29/bbc-rewrites-poirots-history-finale-divisive-
     adaptation-reveals/

38   *The Telegraph,* 26 December 2018: https://
     www.telegraph.co.uk/tv/2018/12/26/
     abc-murders-episode-one-review-intriguing-new-take-poirot/

39   *The Guardian,* 26 December 2018: https://www.
     theguardian.com/tv-and-radio/2018/dec/26/
     abc-murders-review-john-malkovich-poirot-magnificent

40   *The New York Times,* 1 February 2019: https://www.nytimes.
     com/2019/02/01/arts/television/abc-murders-review-john-
     malkovich-poirot.html

41   *Empire,* October 2020.

42   'Production begins on Twentieth Century Fox's *Death on the
     Nile*'; https://www.agathachristie.com/news/2019/production-
     begins-on-twentieth-century-foxs-death-on-the-nile

43   'Famed Tiffany Diamond dazzles in new Hollywood murder
     mystery'; https://www.tatler.com/article/death-on-the-nile-
     2020-film-tiffany-diamond-gal-gadot-audrey-hepburn-lady-
     gaga

44   *Empire,* October 2020.

45   *Empire,* October 2020.

INDEX